Celeste,

THE BOOK OF ADAM - HYPNOTIC

Gems & Gents Book 6

Printed in the United States of America

ISBN- 978-0-9913426-7-9

Library of Congress Control Number: 2016903514

This is a work of fiction. Names, characters, places and incidents are with the product of the author's imagination or are used fictitiously, and any resemblance to actual persons, living or dead, business establishments, events, locales is entirely coincidental.

Siri Austin Entertainment, LLC
RICHMOND, VIRGINIA
www.siriaustin.com

Chapter One

Scientist Cyrus McCoy had just completed his review of the specifications for the J.M.A.L.T.S. device invented by Adam Lassiter, a young recruit for the Federal Bureau of Investigations, better known as the FBI. Cyrus felt the FBI was a waste of the young man's talents. A man with his knowledge and skill set should be in the field of science where he would be free to explore more possibilities with micro devices. He sat back in his chair and patted the top of the book containing the specs and his notes. He would begin the process of duplicating the device while Lassiter played at Quantico for the next five months. He smiled, thinking it was an honor to be given the task. His experience over the last seven years as a scientist with the Department of Defense was laudable, but even he had to admit his mind did not match that of Lassiter's. Just reading over the notes and reviewing the detailed written instructions on the assembly of the device, had him in awe. Cyrus and his selected team of scientists had been preparing for months for this project. Now that the time had come, the thought of getting started put him on a natural high. No longer able to control his excitement, Cyrus picked up the telephone and dialed, then activated the speakerphone.

"Dr. Lassiter," he said into the phone. "One last conversation before we begin production of J.M.A.L.T.S."

Adam replied, "Not 'Dr'. yet."

"Just a technicality, young man. A simple technicality." He stood and walked over to the model of J.M.A.L.T.S. "I have to tell you I'm excited about being a part of this project, Adam. I thank you for approving my participation. The thought of having a device with the capability to help reduce the number of lives lost in hostage situations, in addition to its surveillance component, is amazing." He picked up the small clear box and examined it. "The model is complete and I must say," he laughed, "If I did not know what to look for, I would not see it. I hope you have a chance to stop by to see it."

"Give me a minute." A few seconds later, Adam spoke again. "Okay, Doc. Step aside."

Cyrus looked to his side to see Adam standing next to him. The sight of the man caused Cyrus to jump.

"It's a hologram, Doc," Adam laughed. "I locked into your GPS coordinates to join you." He looked at the device. "Who worked on the model?"

Cyrus shook his head in awe as he responded, "Reyes Sugden, Jack Dalton and myself." He raised an eyebrow as he put his hand through the hologram. "Is it stable?"

"Quite. I haven't figured out how to make it last more than a few minutes," he replied as if it was still a puzzle to him, then shrugged it off. "It will come eventually."

Cyrus crossed his arms over his chest. "You have a wonderful mind, Dr. Lassiter. Continue to explore. Inventions are only limited to what your mind can conceive. Remember that when people tell you things are impossible."

Adam gave a shy smile. "You sound like my father. He has always said anything you dream about can become a reality. Just don't let other people's limited minds deter yours."

"Sounds like a wise man. I am certain he is very proud of all you have accomplished." Cyrus smiled then leaned back against the table where the model sat in a glass case.

"Yes, he is." Adam blushed, then changed the topic back to J.M.A.L.T.S. "He is also a little concerned. Was the weaponry aspect included in the model?"

"No. While I trust my staff completely, the weaponry aspect is kept in my binder. This device could cause havoc in the wrong hands."

"I agree." Adam nodded. "Has Director Davenport been advised we are ready to begin?"

"Yes. Will you have time to drop in during your training?"

"I'm not certain of my schedule or assignments until I get to Quantico. But have no doubts, I will find a way to drop in. Is security in place?"

"Yes. In fact, the director has assigned me personal protection starting Monday morning."

Adam nodded. "Good. There were only two concessions. One, you head up the production and two, security is provided to the team."

Cyrus nodded. "I thank you for your faith in me. Each time I open the pages of the manual, I imagine this device placed in a room of our country's enemies as they plan attacks against us. This device will allow us to avert those attacks and save lives."

"That is my vision." Adam frowned. "I'm losing my connection." He looked up at Cyrus. "I look forward to meeting you in person, Dr. McCoy."

"Same here, Adam. Enjoy your graduation."

The hologram faded. Cyrus shook his head as he smiled. "The mind of youth and unlimited possibilities."

Cyrus stood, put his jacket on then glanced around the room. Nodding his head, he believed he had taken care of everything that he needed to begin the task of recreating J.M.A.L.T.S. on Monday morning. He picked up the manual, opened the door, glanced one last time around the room, then stepped into the hallway.

As he walked down the corridor, his mind drifted to the music that was waiting in his vehicle for him. Yes, he was a rock-n-roll kind of guy. Not the soft stuff. No, on a day like this, hard rock was the only way to go. He pushed the button to the elevator and stepped inside as he played the air guitar with the manual under his left arm and his hands strumming the strings on his imaginary guitar. He reached over and pushed the button to take him to the garage and to the rock-n-roll music waiting in his car. His head was bobbing from side to side as the elevator descended with the long screeches of the string guitar echoing in his mind. He felt a sting similar to a mosquito bite and using his right hand slapped the side of his neck. He glanced at his hand wondering why a mosquito would be inside of an elevator.

Upon reaching the ground floor the elevator doors swooshed open. Cyrus McCoy lay on the floor of the elevator, eyes wide open, mind shutting down, and breathing shallow. A pair of black leather shoes in plastic shoe covers stepped inside the elevator. A man stood there looking down over his body. He bent over, picked up the manual, hit the seventh floor button with his gloved finger then stepped out of the elevator. The elevator traveled back to the fifth floor nonstop. The doors to the elevator opened to an empty hallway.

Inside, on the floor, was the now dead Dr. Cyrus McCoy.

CHAPTER TWO

"This is murder."

"Are you certain? How do you know?" Agent Brent Pierce of the Federal Bureau of Investigations asked.

"Yes, he was poisoned," Dr. Amber Nicolas stated as she bent over the body of Dr. McCoy. "You see this red area here?" She pointed to the right side of the deceased's neck. "It's raw."

The agent looked at where she was pointing. "Looks like a mosquito bite."

Amber stood and looked around. "In an elevator? Inside a five story building? With no open windows?" She shook her head. "Not likely. There's no standing water or anything to draw a mosquito to this area. A mosquito bite would leave a little swelling, or irritation to the skin. This looks more like a needle insertion." She shook her head then looked up at him. "No, as much as you want this to be a simple death, I can't rule it as such."

"Thank you, Amber."

"You are welcome." She began removing her gloves. "It wasn't an inconvenience. I was in the building. But you already knew that." She raised an eyebrow. "What made you suspicious?"

"Surveillance recording from the elevator." Agent Pierce grinned at being caught tracking her. They stepped out of the elevator.

"Seal the area," he said to the police officers standing nearby then turned and continued walking with Amber. "From what we could see, moments before he collapsed he hit the side of his neck as if he had been bitten by something."

"If you suspected foul play, why call me and not the coroner?"

Brent smiled. "It was a way to get to see your beautiful face." When he received no response, he looked away. Slowly turning to her, he spoke softly. "The man you just examined is working...was working on a sensitive project. Before I alert anyone to this situation, I needed to know what I was dealing with."

"Well, Agent Pierce, with your teasing blue eyes, I can definitely tell you this was murder. He was injected with something that caused his heart to stop beating. I don't know how or what, but when the coroner examines him, I'm willing to bet the farm he will find some type of poison."

"If this is what I think it is, you will probably be receiving the body. That means the deceased Dr. McCoy will have the pleasure of your hands on his body."

"There are hundreds of scientists at the FBI Labs. This case can be assigned to any one of them."

"Why do you ignore me when I say nice things to you?"

Amber stopped at the door to the stairway, then looked up at him. "Because you are a flirt, Agent Pierce. I know it and so do you. And while I enjoy your smooth words, I have enough will power not to succumb to your charm." She opened the door. "I suggest your next call should be to the Director."

"Your father is going to assign this case to you."

"My father isn't my boss, technically."

"He's the Deputy Secretary of Defense. He is boss to all of us."

"Then I suggest you put this case through the process as protocol dictates and allow it to fall into the proper hands."

"Do you always have to go with protocol?"

"Of course." She shrugged. "It's the only way to keep things under control. Policy and procedures are the best protection against chaos and bedlam. Enjoy your investigation." Amber flashed her pearly whites at him then walked out the door.

Brent watched Amber walk down the stairs. "Bedlam?" he said, smiling at the backside of Amber Nicolas and shaking his head. He turned to find his partner, Kalli Hayes, standing behind him grinning. "Bedlam, uproar, confusion. Exactly what you are going to get if you keep going after the Deputy Secretary's daughter."

"What are you talking about?" Brent quickly masked his expression.

"Don't get testy with me 'cause the doctor isn't falling for the sweet talk." Kalli shrugged her shoulders. "Smart lady, if you ask me." She tilted her head to the side. "Are you calling your 'daddy-in-law to be' or should I?"

Brent pushed a button on his phone. "We follow protocol, Hayes. The first call goes to the Director." Brent stepped away before speaking. "Secretary Nicolas, please."

Kalli shook her head. "The Director is going to be pissed."

CHAPTER THREE

Amber Nicolas had the kind of looks that would make any man stop in his tracks and women frown from jealousy. She had curly shoulder length hair that bounced with every step and smooth olive toned skin, which she inherited from her mother. Her height of five feet six inches, she received from her father. Most men viewed the feisty pep in her step with hips swaying as a natural turn-on to the male species, but for her it was the speed walking required to get her quickly from patient to patient when doing her residency in the emergency room. The funny thing was, she never recognized the reaction she got from people when she walked by. Her mind was always on exploring the human body.

As a military brat, she traveled from base to base following orders her parents had received. Stability did not come to her until she attended college. Her father, Phillip Nicolas, a military man from the age of eighteen, became Deputy Secretary of Defense under the Harrison administration and her mother became the Human Resource Director for the Federal Bureau of Investigation. Amber always thought they made the career change just to be close to her since she was at John Hopkins University and then subsequently the hospital.

The support her parents always gave her was the reason she graduated from medical school at the age of twenty-one, completed her residency by twenty-four and was considered one of the leading plastic surgeons for burn victims in the United States at the age of twenty-six. Now, at twenty-eight, she was one of the most sought after forensic scientists for the FBI.

Being the smartest person in the class never fazed her. It was just a norm in her life. However, being referred to as beautiful, was a different can of worms.

Brent Pierce was good looking, tall, well built and a smooth talker. He had been pursuing Amber since the first time they met at her mother's office two years ago. She paid him no attention then, and even less now. Especially when he came at her with his really bad come on lines, which she had come to expect whenever they ran into each other, like this morning. Amber had no doubt that her mother, Jill Nicolas, called Brent the moment they finished breakfast and left the cafe. Her mother could push all she wanted, but Amber had dreams and she had no time for a man like Brent to slow her down.

Amber shook her head as she walked towards her car thinking of her mother's schemes. She stopped to cross the street just as her telephone buzzed. She glanced at the caller ID and smiled.

"Hello, Mother. Yes, I ran into Brent. Yes, he still has dreamy eyes, and no, I am still not romantically interested in him."

"Now, Amber, you are getting older." Her mother laughed into the phone at the whirlwind of a response from her only child.

"I'm twenty-eight years old, Mother. That is not considered old."

"I know how old you are, and some of my friends' daughters are married and they have at least one child.

All I'm saying is you've worked hard to accomplish professional success. It's time to pay a little attention to personal accomplishments, like a husband and a family." She continued before Amber could speak. "Now, you know your father and I would have had more children if I was able. I don't want you to wait until it's too late to have the family you want."

Amber knew all too well the pain her mother suffered to have her. During her eighth month of pregnancy, her parents were flying back to the United States for her birth. The plane was shot down by an enemy aircraft. Emergency surgery had to be performed. With the best medical assistance, they were able to save the child. Unfortunately, her mother's injuries were so substantial, they could not repair the internal damage, leaving her unable to carry another child. Rendering Amber an only child. They would tell her the story often, adding how grateful they were to have her.

"Mother, I know how fragile life can be and I know people tend to take each day for granted. I can assure you I am not one of those folks. No one has sparked my interest in a romantic way and until they do, I will not settle."

"Honey, how can you say that? Brent is crazy about you. Why, it's all over that boy's face every time he sees you."

"Mom, Brent is in lust. I want what you and Dad have, something you were both willing to fight for. I want that kind of love that I can feel deep inside my soul. You know, the toe curling love. That man who makes you sweat every time he says your name. Has your body shivering whenever he looks your way."

"You're not asking for much, are you?" her mother laughed, making her smile.

"No, not much," she laughed along. "Just someone who will keep me laughing just like Dad does with you."

She heard her mother sigh. "I guess I can't blame you for that. After thirty-one years, your father still makes my heart sing every time he walks into a room."

"So, tell me, why would you ask me to settle for less?"

"Are you sure you would be settling with Brent?"

Amber sighed as she looked around at the traffic. "Brent is nice. And Lord knows he is easy on the eyes. But I don't feel that jolt when I see him."

"He makes you laugh."

"That he does," Amber agreed as she walked across the street with her curls bouncing.

"At least that's something," her mother said. "I have to go. Talk to you soon. Love you, my Redbird."

"Love you back, Mother."

The moment she disconnected the call, her phone buzzed again.

She glanced at the number and was pleased when it wasn't the lab calling on her day off.

"Hi, Dad." She paused once she reached the corner. "Are you calling to cancel lunch?"

"No. I was wondering if you were free to meet me at my office."

Amber was surprised by her father's request. Since September 11, 2001 her father had forbidden her from coming to the building. "You want me to come to the Pentagon? You stated you never wanted me to enter that building. Too much testosterone, if I remember correctly."

She heard her father's soft laughter. "I still feel that way. However, you seem to have stumbled onto something we need to keep a lid on."

Amber thought for a moment. "That was fast. I take it you are referring to the poison victim."

"As I said, Redbird. I need you in my office, stat."

Redbird was the nickname he gave her when she had the measles as a child and her face was covered with red bumps. Whenever he called her Redbird instead of My Redbird, she knew he was attempting to soften a blow.

"All right, Dad," she agreed, her mood suddenly solemn. "I'll be there as soon as I can."

CHAPTER FOUR

Thirty minutes later while standing in the reception area of the E Ring of The Pentagon, her flirty black and grey sweater dress with her slouchy strap boots lost the carefree effect she was going for today. Everyone around her walking through the corridors had on sharply pressed uniforms all neatly tucked in, with crisp seams and speaking that military language of 'yes, ma'am', 'no, ma'am'. One or two of the men held their glance at her a little longer than need be, making her feel a little self-conscious. It had only taken her fifteen minutes to reach the city unto itself, known as The Pentagon. It now seemed it was taking forever for her father to appear. According to the officer, this was expedited service.

"We are not used to having someone dressed like you around here," the officer stated as he noticed the men staring. "You are wearing that dress very well." He blushed then resumed his rigid stance. "Deputy Secretary Nicolas has been notified of your arrival, ma'am."

"Is he coming in from China?" she asked as she stepped towards the only human like person in the building. "It was my day off. I wanted to wear something flirty and fun instead of a lab coat," she explained while looking around self-consciously.

"I'd say you accomplished that." The officer smiled. "There's the Deputy Secretary now."

Amber turned to see the tall, slim, suited body of her father. "Is this a new recruit, Sergeant?"

"No, sir." The officer winked. "We are not that fortunate."

Phillip Nicolas, a dead ringer for Richard Roundtree, looked up at the officer and frowned. "Keep your eyes off my daughter."

The Sergeant looked surprised. "Your daughter, sir?" He then looked at Amber. "It's an honor, ma'am."

"That's right. It is. Now drop and give me fifty pushups for disgracing my daughter with your eyes."

The Sergeant dropped to his hands and toes.

"Dad," Amber chastised him.

Phillip smiled at his daughter. "Oh all right. At ease, Sergeant."

The Sergeant jumped up as he and Phillip had a good laugh over the expression on Amber's face.

"Ha ha. Very funny."

Phillip put his arm around her waist and steered her toward the elevator. "Don't be mad at me. I had to ease the tension I saw in your face."

"The tension you put there when you summoned me to your office."

He waited until the elevator closed before replying to her. "You were supposed to be having breakfast with your mother. How did you get involved with the McCoy situation?"

"Agent Pierce called and asked if I would take a look at something. I didn't know what until I reached the floor."

Phillip inhaled. "I wish he hadn't done that."

"Why? What's going on, Dad?" Amber asked as they walked into his office.

"Hello, Amber."

She turned to see Secretary of Homeland Security Royce Davenport standing near the window. "Hello, Mr. Secretary." Amber walked over to give Royce a kiss on the cheek. "How is Shelly?"

The mention of his wife always made Royce smile. "Beautiful as ever."

Amber smiled. She glanced at her father and the smile faded. "One of you please tell me what's wrong," she hissed.

The two men looked at each other.

"Have a seat, Redbird."

Now the Secretary was calling her by her nickname, Amber thought, as she took a seat in the black leather chair. "Okay."

"You saw the body of Dr. Cyrus McCoy this morning. You told Special Agent Pierce you believed the man was poisoned."

"Yes, I did. Why?"

"Tell me why you think he was poisoned."

Amber sat back in the chair. "Special Agent Pierce pointed to an area on the man's neck where I observed a puncture mark. There was no swelling around the entry. That eliminated the Agent's assumption of a mosquito bite. Contraction of his pupils, along with drooling around his mouth were all signs. Now, I can't swear by it, but as I told the Agent, once the coroner examines the body I'm fairly certain he will find the man was poisoned."

Another look passed between the two men.

"Did Special Agent Pierce mention why he directed you to the man's neck?"

Amber nodded as she replied to her father. "He mentioned watching surveillance tape from the elevator."

Her father tensed.

"Do you have any cases scheduled for the next few days?" Royce asked.

Hesitantly, Amber answered, "No. I'm just reviewing a few cases."

"Good," Royce replied as he stood. "Phillip, I will see you at the meeting." He kissed Amber on the forehead. "See you tomorrow morning." He then quickly walked out of the office.

Amber took pause at his quick departure, then looked at her father. "Tomorrow morning?"

He frowned at his friend's back as he rushed from the room. "Your godfather is a chicken." He sighed. "Looks like you will be assisting your dad with a case for the Bureau for the next few days. We have a meeting tomorrow at 5 am."

"Meeting? What meeting? Why do I have to be there? And why does it have to be at 5 am?"

"The meeting will be at Quantico. Why you? Because Special Agent Pierce brought you in. Why 5 am.? Our main component is there and it's the only time he can meet. "

"Quantico?"

"Yes. That is the training facility for the Bureau. The place where you work."

"Daddy." She stood with a huff. "I know where I work. What I don't understand is why I need to be in a meeting at five o'clock in the morning. I work in the lab for goodness sake."

"This morning you became an analyst on this case."

A blank look appeared on her face. "All of this is because I saw the man's body?"

"Not just any man, Redbird. You examined Dr. Cyrus McCoy. A man who has been assigned to work on a top-secret device. You also stated that the man was poisoned, declaring this a murder. We need to determine if you are right and who is potentially behind an act of treason."

"Daddy, I can examine the body in my lab and pass on my findings. Being an analyst is way out of my league. Not only do I have little interest in being a part of anyone's investigation, I have no knowledge or skill set to be of any use."

"Did you declare Dr. McCoy was murdered?"

Amber sighed as she dropped her head. "Daddy...." she whined.

Phillip had to smile. She was all grown up, beautiful like her mother, and quite successful in her own right yet, here she was in his office whining.

"Look." He walked over, pulled her into his arms and kissed her forehead. "You are more than capable of handling a number of things. I have no doubt you will be very helpful to the team."

"Now there's a team." She looked up at him. "You know I don't play well with others. Men get testy when they find out I'm more than I appear to be. And women, well they get testy when they find out I'm more than I appear to be too. I like working according to my schedule, in my lab, one-on-one with me and the corpse."

"I know no such thing." He stepped back. "I hate to do this, but... Your President is asking you to serve. You do not have the option of saying no."

"And why not?"

"Because you are the daughter of the Deputy Secretary of Defense and the Human Resource Director for the Federal Bureau of Investigation. Our family doesn't say no to this country and certainly not to this President."

As much as she loved her daddy, this was one time she was happy to get away from him. Sitting inside her vehicle she closed her eyes and exhaled. There was never a time when the dreams of her life included working for the government. Working for the FBI gave her a sense of independence while not straying too far from her parents. The way the government controlled her parents' lives was not something she wanted to experience. Move here. Stay there for x number of years. Yes, she understood their dedication to the country. And yes, she was a patriot. But she was just beginning to live her life on her own terms, not by government standards.

Besides, no matter how many times she denied it to her mother, she was ready to meet that man who would prove worthy of her unconditional love. Meeting him was right around the corner. Amber knew it. She could feel it in the air. The love of her life was on his way.

"Why now?" she yelled. "Just when I was ready to let my guard down."

She pushed the button to start the car, then drove out of the parking lot. She wasn't asking for a lot, Amber thought. All she needed was some time to find someone to love her the way she would love him. The truth was she did not have a lot to offer a man. She wasn't the kind of woman to shut down her intelligence to stroke a man's ego. Or the type to be seen and not heard. But she was sure there was a man out there who would accept her as is. She laughed, "Not in this day and time." She shrugged. "Maybe tomorrow." She started singing *Maybe Tomorrow* by The Jackson Five. "Yeah right." She laughed at herself. She had been singing that song for years. Since her one and only love during her sophomore year of college, Amber hadn't really allowed anyone to get close. Now she wanted the intimacy. The knowing looks with laughter long into the night. She wanted that feeling of contentment when she was lying in a man's arms. Knowing he was the yin to her yang. The king to her queen. The Clyde to her Bonnie. Maybe tomorrow.

The exit for I-95 appeared. She took the exit and headed back to her home in Georgetown, asking God to bring the love of her life to her soon. Her telephone chimed. She hit the telephone decline icon on the dashboard. It was Brent calling. She looked towards the heavens. "Is this your idea of a joke? If it is, it is not funny, Lord. Not funny at all."

CHAPTER FIVE

The president of the university stood at the podium, then lowered his head. "This is indeed a historic day. For the first time in our university's history we present to you the most unlikely candidate as your valedictorian. There were times, many times, I encountered this young man on campus, when I wondered, if the children are our future, will the earth still be standing when we release him into the world."

The crowd of proud graduates dressed in their caps and gowns with their family and friends looking on, laughed at the statement, for they well understood where the president was coming from. Most of them wondered, with all the lab explosions, the discoloration of skin on certain fraternity members, and the earthquake, or something like it that had occurred in the last few years at the hands of Adam Lassiter, whether they would live to see this day.

"I prayed for this day to come with the University intact. There were times when I did not believe my prayer would be answered; however, here we stand and surprisingly so does the University." The crowd laughed. "With a Masters in Biometric Engineering, a Masters in Nuclear Engineering and a Ph.D in Chemical Engineering, I proudly give to you the next secret weapon of the United States of America..." The students laughed as murmurs travelled throughout the audience. President Holland paused as he chuckled and looked down at the students. "Graduates, most of you are too young to remember a character named Dennis the Menace. You see, Dennis was the nicest kid on the block and always meant well, but everything he did always seemed to go wrong. Usually, causing harm to his neighbors. Well, it seems we have our own version of Dennis. It is an honor to present to you, the valedictorian of your class, the one, and thank GOD only, Dr. Adam Fitzgerald Lassiter."

The student body gave the six-two, one hundred ninety-five pounds, strikingly handsome Adam Lassiter, who was now strutting to the podium in his cap and gown, a standing ovation. He thanked the president with his own version of a handshake that resembled a secret code then stood at the podium. Adam waited as the crowd settled down for the speech they believed would give them a clear picture of what to expect from the world they were about to enter. Better yet, it would give them the confidence that they were ready to take on the challenges of this new world. The truth of the matter was, they weren't ready. With all his degrees and hours of learning, he was certain he was not ready. With a country so full of hatred towards one another and a world of enemies near and far, he had an idea of what was coming their way. However, rather than sending them out with what he believed to be the true picture of the world, he decided to send them out with the joy of their accomplishments.

Adam looked over the now silent crowd. He displayed the most ridiculous wide grin he could muster. The crowd laughed as they had all come to recognize that look from him as a warning that something unexpected was about to happen.

"It seems we have come to that moment that our parents, friends, colleagues, and faculty have prayed for. We will now release the purse strings, leave the shoulders we've cried on for years, and stop looking at the clerks in the financial aid office with long glares and move forward. We now enter into a world of uncertainty, wars and an unprecedented amount of open racism among ourselves. 'No Justice-No Peace' and 'Black Lives Matter' have become a daily chant amongst us. Police officers who are supposed to protect us are killing people. While some of us are killing police officers, who we were raised to respect. It almost makes you want to stay in the comfort of college life. In the embrace of our parents' love. And on the protected campus with our trusted faculty and friends. That would be the comfortable thing to do. However, we are a class of champions. We don't settle for comfort. Comfort is dull, boring, and complacent. We seek more. We are here to develop new vaccines, build new cities, and create new government policies. To explore the possibilities of travel throughout the universe and beyond. Nutrition that will heal common illnesses. Medicines that will cure what we have deemed incurable. Then share all of our knowledge with the world. We, all of us, are here to discover the new meaning of the expansion of life from one solar system to the next and to defeat the enemies who threaten our way of life. We did not spend the last few years getting to this point, to turn back and cower into the warm embrace of our parents' loving arms. NO." He shook his head. "We've come to this point to conquer, to change life as we know it. We are the new innovators of this world. It is incumbent upon us, the ones blessed with knowledge and courage, to take steps to heal Alzheimer's, to develop infrastructures for our cities' transportation systems and for some, to find a solution for those who cannot tolerate differences in our races. It is our duty and honor to go out and make this world a better place for those who dare to follow. Make your steps into this new journey so deep that our followers will have to climb higher to walk in our footsteps." The crowd stood, applauding the encouraging words, and the seemingly undaunted faith Adam had in his classmates. They settled down as Adam remained at the podium indicating there was more to come.

"It would be unkind of me to leave you without sharing one last invention." The president of the university and several faculty members groaned loudly behind him. Adam laughed.

"President Holland used this song too many times to count. Let us take his words literally." Adam pushed a button in his pocket. An explosion rocked the stage. When the smoke cleared a hologram of singers McFadden and Whitehead appeared performing their song, *Ain't No Stopping Us Now.*

The crowd stood in wonder as the graduating class began dancing. President Holland, along with other stage members stood, putting their hands through the mirage. One stage guest stepped through and then back just to ensure the two men singing were not actually there.

"It's only going to last for a few minutes. I suggest you enjoy the moment." Adam laughed. Several professors took his advice and began dancing to the music. Adam took a seat and laughed at the reaction of President Holland. Once the song ended, the crowd settled and the graduates retook their seats.

President Holland stood at the podium grinning at Adam. "There Ain't No Stopping Us Now," he excitedly yelled into the microphone. "I can see only wondrous things in line for Dr. Lassiter and this class. We often hear about the negative escapades of our youth. Very seldom do we hear or experience the positive. I am proud to say, Dr. Adam Lassiter and all of you are ours. Graduates, please rise." The graduates on the stage and on the floor stood. The excitement of the moment filled the air. "By the powers vested in me, I now pronounce you graduates." Adam turned his tassel from left to right along with his classmates.

Proud parents Joe and Sally Lassiter, along with Samuel, their oldest son and his wife, Cynthia, Joshua and his wife, Rochelle, Mathew, Timothy, Luke, their oldest daughter Ruby, Diamond and her husband, Zackary, Pearl and her husband, Theodore, Jade, Opal and their baby daughter Sapphire, sat in the stands watching the baby boy in the family accept awards, and accolades. His twin sister Jade had graduated the year before with a Masters, while Adam opted to receive his doctorate before leaving. Sally prayed Adam would become a medical doctor, that way she would have her baby boy safe from harm, but this prayer went unanswered. Adam was following in the footsteps of her older sons, Samuel, who was once a Navy Seal and now worked on the private protection detail for the President of The United States, and Joshua who was a CIA operative. While she understood her sons' desire to serve their country, Sally did not understand why it had to be in a life threatening capacity. However, as she watched her youngest son walk across the stage her heart was bursting with pride. She would let the fear settle in when he took the oath at the FBI Academy.

"Show off." Joshua grinned as the explosion from the hologram Adam created played.

"You created that monster," Samuel laughed. "He will surpass you and your antics."

"Lord help us all when he is released into society." Joe smiled at his wife.

Seated in the stands with parents, friends and supporters of the graduates, two men whispered, "He is as impressive as we were told."

"Indeed," the man sitting next to him stated. "The Bureau would smother his mind. Determine why he chose them over us. Then change his mind."

"By any means necessary?"

The man nodded. "Only a country as arrogant as the United States would put a weapon of mass destruction in the hands of a child. Do we have someone on him?"

"Yes."

The man looked to the person at his left. "Make contact. I want a day by day report from the moment he steps foot in the Academy."

CHAPTER SIX

"You know Sally is not happy with your decision to join the FBI." Jade adjusted her twin brother Adam's tie as they prepared for a private ceremony at the White House. The ceremony was being given for his invention J.M.A.L.T.S, a surveillance device that can be dispersed through an item about the size of a small straw and sent airborne.

Adam was the baby boy to Joseph and Sally Lassiter, number eleven of the twelve children. He was considered the shy one who had his parents concerned for years over his inability to socialize. Now, he was the one they all feared would blow up the world. After years of threats of being expelled from school for his inquisitive nature, and for literally blowing up a few labs, he had several inventions under his belt. COR, Children Obesity Resolution; PYA, Protect Your Assets, a suit of body armor designed to absorb the impact of explosives or firearms, that was tested by his own brother, and the most lucrative invention, Genevieve, a human like computer system installed in covert action vehicles that can detect life threatening situations then administer evasive action. While all of the aforementioned inventions were credited to the university, thereby foregoing any financial debt on his parents' part for the destruction of buildings. Adam's last invention was commandeered by the Department of Defense at its first testing. The completion of the J.M.A.L.T.S. was financed completely by the government. Not only was the University compensated, it also received national acclaim. In fact, his creation of an anti-obesity program for children was revered as one of the best in the United States. The Center for Disease Control thought he would join them after graduation to continue his work in that area. However, it seemed after working on a case with his friend Xavier Davenport and the President's Chief of Staff, James Brooks, his attention went in another direction. Adam found he liked investigative work and he decided to join the FBI instead of going into the medical field.

"What are you talking about? Mom is excited about this decision." He looked over his sister's shoulder into the mirror as she worked on the thin tie.

"She is excited about all you have accomplished. But Sally is not happy that you will be dodging bullets as an Agent." Jade pulled the knot of the tie tight. "Her fear is that you are going to become another Joshua and vanish in and out of our lives for the next ten years."

"Joshua is a CIA Operative. I will be an FBI Agent. Two totally different fields. Besides, Joshua has been a home body since he married Roc." Adam smiled at his reflection in the mirror. "Damn I look good."

Jade hit him on the back of his head. "Don't get cocky. You will still be in the line of fire, just like Joshua and Sammy."

"Sammy is on personal protection detail for the President of the United States. He has more security around him than the Pope."

"Yeah, like the President isn't shot at...regularly." Jade stepped back and looked at her brother. "You are another one of her babies stepping into the line of duty."

"I have to do this." Adam strolled out of the hotel bathroom into the sitting area. "Joshua is bigger than life; Sammy exceeds him. Look at Pearl, she's the Press Secretary to the President. I need my own identity."

"Listen," his brother Luke said from the sofa, with his eyes still on his phone as he sent text messages. "You can't go around trying to live up to Samuel and Joshua. You are doing the right thing in establishing your own path, like I did."

Adam picked up his wallet from the dresser as he looked from Luke to the other set of twins in the family, Opal and Timothy. They both shrugged their shoulders as he shook his head.

"This coming from the top running back in the National Football League. Another over achiever." Adam straightened his suit jacket, smiled at the younger set of Lassiter children and asked, "How do I look?"

Timothy picked up his trench coat, put it around his little brother's shoulders. Luke took his black fedora and placed it on Adam's head. Opal put the black sunshades on his face and Jade put the gold cross and chain around his neck. The four stood back and looked at the now poised Adam and nodded.

Adam, with his devilish grin, turned 360 degrees giving them a full view. "How you like me now?"

"Sexy," Jade stated.

"Mysterious," Opal added.

"Smooth." Timothy nodded his approval.

"Dangerous," Luke said as he stood.

The door opened. Their baby sister Sapphire, whom they all called Phire, walked in. "Where do you think you are going looking like a dark Humphrey Bogart from Casablanca?"

The older siblings laughed at the ever so blunt Phire.

"Leave it to her to mess up your groove." Opal laughed.

"Groove or no groove, I know you better take off those shades before Sally sees you." Phire laughed. "You're going to see the President, after all."

"You don't like the man," Adam replied. "What do you care how I look?"

"I care because you are a Lassiter," Phire said as she held the door open. "We represent at all times."

Luke nodded his head as he walked out the door still texting on his phone. "She does have a point there."

"Okay." Opal looked Adam over. "For the ceremony get rid of the hat."

"And the shades," Timothy added as he followed Opal out the door.

"I feel stripped." Adam frowned.

"Close the door behind you," Jade said to Phire. "We'll be out in a minute."

"You better hurry up. You don't want to keep the President or Sally waiting." She closed the door as she left.

Jade turned back to Adam and smiled. "I'm proud of the fact that you are doing your own thing. You are not following Samuel, Joshua, Matt, Luke or Timothy." She pushed a finger into his chest. "You are being you. With that said, I'm proud of you." She smiled up at him. "The shy Adam has emerged to be a formidable man that any woman would be proud to have."

"You forgot handsome," Adam added with his chin held high.

"You have been a cocky little something since you started getting some from that Rosa woman." Jade grinned.

"You should try getting some yourself." Adam laughed as he turned towards the door.

"Excuse me. I get mine. And you need to stay out of my business." She rolled her eyes then walked towards the door. She opened it then stared at him. "Shall we go?"

He took one last look in the mirror then walked towards the door. He stopped when he reached her. "Touchy, touchy. You can lecture me on my sex life, but the moment I question you it's none of my business."

Jade sighed. "Sorry, I just worry about you when it comes to women. Especially one as experienced as Rosa."

Adam blushed and turned away. "I knew I should not have told you about her past."

She pulled him back. "There's nothing wrong with testing the waters, so to speak. But, know that she is a test...right?"

Adam turned Jade towards the door, placed his arm around her shoulders and began walking. "Your concern touches me. However, allow me to ease your mind. I am simply fascinated by her lovemaking skills. I am not in love or otherwise infatuated with the ever so fine specimen by the name of Rosa. Besides, I'm saving myself for the woman who can match my intellect, my considerable charm and unyielding stamina. You know, the yin to my yang." He opened the door.

Jade rolled her eyes. "Not another Joshua. Why couldn't you have taken after Samuel or Timothy?"

Adam laughed. "No worries, sister of my zygote. I'm looking for that woman who will challenge me, touch something in my soul, and give me a reason to cast my mother aside as the number one woman in my life. Until I meet that woman, you don't have to worry." He kissed her temple. "Once this ceremony is complete, my concentration is solely on the Bureau and nothing else." The door closed behind them. "Well, maybe after she teaches me that leg lift number she does. That move can make a brother scream like a woman."

"Adam!" Jade gasped as they erupted into laughter.

CHAPTER SEVEN

The customary location for White House ceremonies is the Rose Garden. President Jeffrey "JD" Harrison and his wife Tracy love entertaining in the garden. However, due to the National Security nature of this presentation it was being held in the Oval Office with only a few cabinet members and the family of recipient Adam Lassiter present.

The President's newly appointed Chief of Staff, James Brooks and the ex-chief of staff, now the newly appointed Attorney General of the United States, Calvin Johnson were standing outside the Oval Office chatting as they waited for the honoree and his family to arrive. James picked up a utensil, took a cookie from the cookie jar sitting on the corner of the desk, then replaced the top.

Calvin reached for the top and Mrs. Langston, the President's secretary, smacked his hand. He snatched his hand back.

"What was that for?"

"You are no longer a member of the West Wing," she replied. "Your customary cookies now go to Chief of Staff Brooks."

"See what happens when you move to a new building." James grinned at Calvin as he bit into a homemade oatmeal-raisin cookie.

They turned to see Director of Homeland Security Royce Davenport walk into the outer office.

"Good afternoon. How is everyone?" he asked as he took a cookie from the jar and bit into it.

"He doesn't work in the West Wing." Calvin glared at Royce eating the cookie.

"He's a frequent visitor," Mrs. Langston stated as she stood to put a folder away. "This is the first time I've seen you all week." She sat back down.

"I have different responsibilities now, Mrs. Langston. In fact, I need the sugar break more now than I did before."

A Secret Service Agent walked in the back door of the office followed by President Harrison, Tracy, the First Lady and the Lassiter family. The outer office was suddenly filled to capacity.

"Mr. President," everyone spoke.

"Mr. President," Calvin complained, "Mrs. Langston will not allow me to have any cookies. Can you believe that?"

JD glanced at his secretary with a grin, then glared at Calvin. "You shouldn't have left the West Wing, Mr. Attorney General." He winked at Mrs. Langston then turned to his press secretary Pearl Lassiter-Prentiss. "Will you show your family into the office?"

"All Lassiters this way, please." Pearl smiled as she held out her hand. The family followed her into the office. Samuel and Cynthia walked by the men standing at the desk and spoke.

Joshua stopped at the desk. Took a cookie from the jar, grinned, then bit it in front of Calvin. "Hmmm, that's a good cookie." He then turned to Mrs. Langston. "How are you on this beautiful day, Mrs. Langston?"

"I'm well, Joshua. How is Rochelle?"

"Nice and fat. Off her feet for a while. Doctor's orders."

"It's about that time." She reached into the desk, pulled out a container and gave it to him. "Give these to her for me."

Joshua took the container. "I'll do just that." He grinned as he walked by Calvin.

Calvin looked at JD in disbelief, then glared at Mrs. Langston. "We worked together for years and this is the way you treat me?"

"You left us."

He pointed to JD. "He asked me to."

"You didn't have to go."

James and Royce laughed as JD looked around. "Where is Adam?"

Everyone looked around. "He was right behind us as we walked from the residence," Tracy said as she took a cookie from the jar, placed it on a napkin then put it in her pocket.

JD nodded to the Secret Service Agent at the door. "Would you locate Mr. Lassiter before he blows something up?" He then smiled at Mrs. Langston, who reached into the desk and gave him a container of cookies. "Thank you," JD said as he bit into a cookie then grinned at Calvin as he walked into the office. "These are good, man."

"That's cold, man."

The agent found Adam a few steps down the walkway leading from the residence. He had been pulled from the family by General Gerald Ashton, Vice-Chairmen of the Joint Chiefs of Staff as they walked towards the Oval Office.

"Mr. Lassiter, a moment of your time."

Adam stopped to see General Ashton standing in the doorway leading to another section of the West Wing.

"Yes, sir," Adam said then turned to his sister Jade. "I'll catch up." He stepped away. "What can I do for you, sir?"

"You are due to report to Quantico on Monday, aren't you?"

"Yes, sir," the proud Adam replied.

"Congratulations on your acceptance to the academy. I must say I was a little disappointed you did not choose the Central Intelligence Agency. I thought I gave a rather convincing argument for your consideration."

"You did, sir. The decision came down to the opportunity to establish my own identity."

"Did not want to be in your brother Joshua's shadow?"

"Exactly."

"Understandable." He looked towards the crowd walking inside the building. "What's the occasion today?"

The question caused Adam to pause before answering. The private ceremony was on a need to know basis and for whatever reason General Ashton apparently was not included on that list.

"The President and my older brothers have been friends for years and of course my sister Pearl is the press secretary. The President and First Lady had us over for dinner to celebrate another Lassiter joining the ranks of service to our country."

"Who all's in there?"

"My family, The President and the First Lady."

"Mr. Lassiter," the Secret Service Agent called out. "The President is waiting."

Adam nodded to the agent then turned back to the General. "Is there anything else, sir?"

"No, son. You go ahead. Enjoy your celebration."

"Thank you, sir." Adam began walking away then turned back to the General. "Sir, how did you know I was here?"

"I keep up with those important to my mission," the General replied with a smirk.

Adam nodded, then followed the agent, noting that the General referred to a mission. What mission?

Entering the outer office, Adam noticed the men standing around the desk laughing.

"Ah ha, the man of the hour." JD reached out, placing an arm around Adam's shoulders.

As they walked by the desk, Adam smiled at Mrs. Langston. "Are those oatmeal raisin cookies?"

"Yes, they are." Mrs. Langston smiled as she reached for the jar. "And we also have macadamia nut. Would you care to have one?"

"Yes, thank you." Adam reached in and helped himself then followed JD, James and Royce into the office.

Calvin shook his head. "That's just cold, Mrs. Langston, just cold." As Calvin walked through the door of the Oval Office, Tracy gave the napkin from her pocket to him.

Mrs. Langston stood in the doorway. "I saw that, ma'am. No more cookies for you." Then she closed the door.

Inside as his family and friends stood around, Adam's pride was clear as he accepted the Presidential Medal of Freedom, the highest civilian award of the United States. It recognized his contribution to the security interests of the United States. Having JD pin him was indeed an honor. However, the real honor came with the picture of the President of the United States, his parents Joe and Sally, with his oldest brother Samuel on one side and his brother Joshua on the other. That was the picture he would frame and treasure always.

The celebration had now moved to the Mural Room as everyone chatted, took pictures and teased. As things began to mellow, Royce Davenport and James pulled Adam aside.

"How you doing, son?" James asked.

Alarms went off in Adam's brain. Whenever a person older than you asked that question, they were about to tell you something you probably didn't want to hear.

"Seemed like a pretty good day until you asked that question. Am I being thrown out of the academy before I arrive? I swear I haven't blown up anything. What's going on?"

The two men shared a glance between each other. "We are all aware of the possibility of J.M.A.L.T.S.," Royce began. "We know our purpose is to use your invention as a surveillance device for situations such as kidnappings, or hostage negotiations."

Nodding his head in agreement, Adam took a drink. "However, we all know it can be altered."

Adam nodded as he took another drink. "True, it can be altered to use as a weapon to carry any substance. Some not so nice."

Royce nodded. "We thought we were years away from that discovery."

Adam raised an eyebrow. "Something's happened?"

"We are not certain." James placed his glass on the tray as a waitress walked by. "We have a meeting scheduled with the Secretary of Defense, tomorrow morning at 5 am."

"We will meet in one of the offices at Quantico. We don't want to delay your training," Royce added.

Adam pointed from one to the other. "Duck and Dodge. That was good." He grinned. "What happened?"

The two men glanced at each other. "The manual for J.M.A.L.T.S. is missing."

"Missing?" Adam raised an eyebrow.

"Cyrus McCoy was found dead in the elevator at the lab this morning by one of the lab technicians," James explained. "It seems the manual was taken."

Adam was stunned at the statement. "I just spoke with him regarding J.M.A.L.T.S. He had the manual with him when he left for the day. Was his home office checked?" Adam asked.

Royce nodded. "Yes. Another tech indicated McCoy was working on the manual when he left last night. He indicated to the tech that they were ready to begin manufacturing the device Monday morning."

Adam nodded his head in agreement. "That is what he mentioned to me. We were looking forward to working together on the project." He sat the glass down. "How did this happen?" He took in the information as his brother Joshua glared at him. He knew Joshua sensed something was awry.

"The investigation is on-going," Royce stated. "The concern is whose hand that manual could be in."

"There's good news and good news," Adam stated. "I have another manual with Dr. McCoy's notes. At least the ones he made through yesterday. He sent me an electronic version last night. Because I tend to think more in-depth than the average man I installed a failsafe that was not revealed to Dr. McCoy's team. The installation included a GPS type signal that will lead us to it once it's launched."

"You did not mention this to the DOD when you sold the device?"

"No."

"Why the hell not?" Royce asked, infuriated.

A few heads turned their way. Adam smiled and waved at his family. However, he knew that did not appease Joshua. He glared at Royce.

"You asked why not in the same breath you tell me the manual is in the hands of an unknown. You should be thanking me for having the foresight to put a failsafe mechanism in place."

"Thanking you for perpetrating a fraud on the United States...."

"Interesting conversation?" Joshua asked as he stood next to his brother.

"Very," James replied as he looked over his shoulder to curious eyes. "So much so, I believe it's time to wrap up the ceremony and this conversation."

"Secretary Davenport, there was no fraudulent intent when I sold J.M.A.L.T.S. to the government and I mean you no disrespect. But it would have been treasonous for any scientist who has inventions that can be altered into weapons of mass destruction not to put a failsafe in place."

"That information should have been shared with the administration," Royce admonished.

"Lower your voice," James ordered.

"Is there a problem, gentlemen?" Sally Lassiter stood behind the men smiling as they all turned.

Sally, mother of twelve, was someone you did not lie to or try to deceive in any way. For one, she was the mother of Joshua Lassiter, who was the CIA operative the United States depended on for many overseas operations. Two, she was also the mother of Pearl Lassiter-Prentiss, the press secretary for the President. Three the mother of Samuel Lassiter, one of the personal bodyguards for that same president. Not to mention the person they were at odds with, at the moment, Adam, who happened to be her brilliant youngest son.

"No," James stated smoothly. "We are simply having a difference of opinion on how best to protect the country."

"That was good." Adam pointed to James. "That was smooth."

"Mind your manners, Adam," Sally stated. "Respect your authorities."

"Respect goes two ways," Adam said as he glared at Royce.

Joe walked up and stood next to Adam. The physical presence of the man was intimidating to even the most secure men. At six-eleven and a solid two hundred thirty pounds, he wasn't one to take lightly. However, the gentle manner in which he spoke caused people to immediately become at ease. "If there is a misunderstanding, gentlemen, I am certain Adam is willing to clear any issue with disclosure. I don't believe this celebration is the place or time." He looked at Adam. "I suggest it would be best to table this conversation for another time."

"I couldn't agree more," JD said from the other side of the room. JD sensed there was tension between the men; however, he learned early in his first term as President not to question his Chief of Staff. He was certain James would advise him of the situation when needed. For now, he wanted to celebrate the invention and the man behind it.

"Everyone in this room has the best interest of the country in the forefront of their minds. Every invention has pros and cons. Our job is to find the most efficient way to use the devices our scientists provide." He raised his glass as he looked at Adam. "Will everyone please raise your glass?" He watched as glasses were in the air then nodded. "Adam Lassiter. Your brothers have preceded you in their individual careers with the government. Your sister has served this administration with continuous grace. You bring another aspect to the table with your intelligence and creativity that most of us can only imagine. I am grateful you are on our side. May your extraordinary mind continue to be the pride of your family, your friends and your country. To Adam Lassiter. May God bless you and the United States of America."

"Hear-hear," voices rang out, as people in the room saluted.

"Is that it?" Phire glared at the President.

A few groans were heard in the room as Sally sent her youngest opinionated child a very subtle glance as a warning.

"My brother just gave your administration a device that will revolutionize the intelligence community and all you have in return is a pat on the back. Come on, Mr. P, you can do better than that."

JD smiled at the young woman's feistiness. "You are going to run some young man crazy one day."

"I know." Phire smirked. "And the lucky man will have a gem of a lady."

"I am going to have a gem of a time on that behind if you don't tame your mouth," Joe stated.

"Daddy!"

Sally glanced at her husband Joe then gave Phire a look. "Apologize to the President, right now."

"I apologize for speaking in a disrespectful manner, however, you disrespected my family first."

"How so?" Tracy asked.

"When you interfered in Joshua's life causing him to leave us, you generated an unforgivable loss to our family. We will never be able to get that time back."

JD nodded in understanding. "You've been upset with me that long?"

"I have and I no longer find you sexy."

"Phire!" every member of her family in hearing distance yelled out.

"What?"

JD glanced at Tracy. "I'm not sexy anymore, babe."

"You are to me." Tracy smiled.

JD sat his cup down then held his hand out to Phire. "Let's take a walk."

"Mr. President..." Sally started to speak.

"We'll be fine, Mrs. Lassiter." JD put his hand on the small of Phire's back, then stepped outside with her. Pearl looked on as the two walked down the hallway with their backs to them. "I wonder who will learn more?"

"My odds are with JD." Tracy laughed.

Sally turned to Samuel and Joshua with a very pertinent glare. "I don't know what's happening between Secretary Davenport and your brother, but I expect both of you to look out for him."

"Mom, I'm good," Adam replied.

Sally gave Adam a stern look, then did the same with Samuel and Joshua.

"Message received." Samuel nodded.

"Loud and clear," Joshua replied as he turned to Adam. "Don't make me regret this."

This was the one thing Adam had been trying to avoid. Having Sammy and Joshua looking over his shoulder.

CHAPTER EIGHT

The door closed with a thump behind Adam as he walked inside. It felt as if his freedom had suddenly been taken away. Inside there were several men of power within the government, dressed in suits and uniforms. Some he recognized, others he did not. The one thing each of the men had in common was they all appeared to be seriously pissed at him. To make him feel a bit more insecure, he was dressed in his FBI issued uniform with his toy gun and all. He was certain the weapons on the men in the room were the real thing.

"You are late, NAT," Deputy Secretary Philip Nicolas stated.

Yes, he recognized the man who held his career in his hand. He did not want to antagonize the man, but Adam glanced at his watch. It was now one second past 5 am. He grinned, but was cut off before he could speak.

"When a meeting is scheduled for 5 am that is the time we begin, not the time we arrive."

The look on the Deputy Secretary's face indicated he was not in the mood to hear that most humans are asleep at five in the morning, so Adam kept that response to himself. "It will not happen again, sir,"

Adam assured him as he pulled out a chair to take a seat.

"You are conducting this meeting, Lassiter," Director Davenport stated as he nodded to the head of the table. "You can start by telling us all the capabilities of this J.M.A.L.T.S."

Adam was half way in the seat when the statement was made. "I'm conducting the meeting?"

"You are. Front and center." Chief of Staff Brooks pointed.

Pushing the chair back under the table, Adam took the walk to the front of the room and could feel all eyes on him. He took a moment to scan the participants' table. There were three men he recognized. Sitting on the far side of the table were the President's Chief of Staff, the Director of Homeland Security, and at the near side of the table sat Deputy Secretary Phillip Nicholas. Next to him was a young woman with reddish brown curly hair, adorable blushing cheeks, kissable thick lips and eyes any man could drown in. He had seen those eyes somewhere before but couldn't quite place them at this time. Next to her, giving him the territorial look, was a blond gentleman who looked to be an Agent and there was a nerdy looking man with long hair, hiding his face, wearing a V-neck sweater with an open collar shirt and jeans. His eyes traveled back to the woman and he must have stared at the woman longer than he should have for he finally heard Chief of Staff Brooks clear his throat.

"Mr. Lassiter, please."

"Of course. Good morning, gentlemen and lady," he started. "J.M.A.L.T.S. was developed as a surveillance device to assist government and law enforcement in hostile situations to have surveillance of the enemy. It's size is our greatest asset. It can be launched through a small tube, which sends it airborne. The tubing can fit through a keyhole or under a door, the crack of a window - the possibilities are endless. J.M.A.L.T.S. is capable of retrieving up to 4 TB of data. It is also capable of distributing live audio and video feed to a remote site."

"It apparently can also be converted into a weapon of mass destruction," the FBI looking man stated with a tinge of accusation.

"Any item can be converted to a MD weapon if you know what you are doing," the nerdy looking guy stated.

"True." Adam raised an eyebrow. "Take the button on your dull everyday JC Penny white shirt. Add a drop of nitroglycerin, a little heat and you will have a weapon strong enough to blow up this room and all its occupants. If there is more than one, you have a MD weapon."

"That is not what I meant and I think you know that, NAT."

"When around scientists you have to speak in factual, not literal terms," the nerdy guy replied.

Adam did not know who the man was, but he liked him.

"I believe Special Agent Pierce is speaking factually," the woman stated. "The device, J.M.A.L.T.S., when airborne can and was used as a weapon. If unleashed on the general public, it can kill innocent bystanders."

"That has yet to be proven," Chief of Staff Brooks stated.

"I'm not here to debate J.M.A.L.T.S.' capabilities," Adam stated. "I've conceded it can be converted to be used in a multitude of ways. Those uses could be deadly or destructive if in the wrong hands."

"What prompted you to make such a device?" Deputy Secretary Nicholas asked.

"Scientists don't need reasons," Adam replied. "We play around with pieces until we find a way to make them fit." He saw a smirk on the nerdy guy's face.

Special Agent Pierce reached for the center of the table and pushed a button. "Well this is the result of your playtime," he said sarcastically.

The image showed Cyrus McCoy stepping on the elevator, playing his air guitar, slapping the side of his neck then falling to the floor. They then all watched as the killer picked up the manual and walked away. Special Agent Pierce pushed the button and the image froze.

"What do you think of your toy now?"

Adam turned to face him. "It's not a toy. It's a viable invention that has fallen into the wrong hands." Adam took control of the panel on the table. He rewound the tape then stopped right before Dr. McCoy smacked his neck.

"Wow," the woman mumbled.

"You see it?" Adam asked, amazed.

"See what?" Royce asked.

"The device," the nerdy man replied.

Adam nodded, pleased at the fact that others in the room apparently also possessed a higher level of intelligence. "This is not J.M.A.L.T.S. If it was you would not be able to detect the device by normal eyesight."

"I don't see anything," Special Agent Pierce stated.

"Nor do I," Deputy Secretary Nicolas stated.

The woman leaned over. "Dad, look to the right of the hand then pan upwards."

Dad, Adam thought. Okay she is the Deputy Secretary's daughter. But why was she in this meeting?

"Dr. Lassiter, I've studied the specs of J.M.A.L.T.S. You've put together a unique combination of resources.

I welcome the opportunity to discuss it further," the nerdy guy exclaimed.

"We don't have time for a love fest," Special Agent Pierce stated. "We have a victim of this J.M.A.L.T.S. device."

"No," Adam corrected, "you have a victim of a person who has attempted to duplicate J.M.A.L.T.S. Since you brought it up, who determined Dr. McCoy was poisoned?"

"I did." The lone woman in the room spoke.

The voice was low and sexy, yet confident. "And you are?"

Amber looked into those brown eyes that had haunted her for weeks when they first met. The intensity at that time damn near knocked her off her feet. The young man she met a few years ago was barely twenty, but the intelligence in his questions was evident. The harshness that was once there seemed to have softened. He was more relaxed, almost playful. "Dr. Amber Nicolas. We've met."

He stared at her until recognition hit him. "A few years ago when my sister was injured in a fire." He nodded. "The hair was flat ironed. Now you're naturally curly."

Amber held his gaze. "The device you refer to as J.M.A.L.T.S. was used as a weapon and you want to discuss my hair?"

"It seemed like an easy transition." Adam smiled.

"NAT, is this a joke to you?" Special Agent Pierce angrily sat forward.

"Everyone else in this room refers to me as Dr. Lassiter. Yet you want to show your dominance by referring to me as NAT. While I wear the title proudly, I think you should understand that there is no situation where I would not out think you. Does that fact intimidate you in some way, Special Agent Pierce?"

"Gentlemen," Royce cautioned. "Let's stay with the matter at hand."

"Your degrees don't impress me, Lassiter. To me you are a NAT - New Agent in Training. If it were up to me, I would advise the Secretary to terminate your training and send you packing. Your invention of this device alone shows your total disregard for humanity. In my opinion."

"Well, you know what they say about opinions." Adam held the man's glare. "Here's my opinion. Instead of attempting to dehumanize me, I believe you should be asking who had access to the information prior to the manual being taken off of Dr. McCoy. The components needed to construct J.M.A.L.T.S. are not easy to come by. Who had access to those components? Who put the poison in the device? What poison was used? Who had access to that poison? The most important question should be why would someone want to kill Dr. McCoy?"

"You believe Dr. McCoy was targeted?" Chief of Staff Brooks asked. "Why?"

"Why not?" Amber stated. "This was a test," she continued.

"I agree." Adam nodded.

"Someone wanted to see if they could make the concept of J.M.A.L.T.S. come to life," the nerdy man stated. "However, they are missing some components, aren't they, Dr. Lassiter?"

"Who are you?"

The nerdy man finally looked up. Without the sandy blonde hair hiding his face, Adam could see he wasn't as old as he first thought. "Dr. Edward O'Sullivan III. Your brother Joshua knows me as Ned." He stood, pointing. "What is said in this room is not to be shared." He stopped as he reached Adam at the front of the room. "Several of Dr. Lassiter's inventions have proven to be invaluable in the field of espionage. J.M.A.L.T.S. has the same capabilities. Someone has discovered that." He looked at the people in the room. "Spending time pointing fingers is counter-productive. Dr. Nicolas, you indicated poison was used yet there was no swelling or damage to the skin. How do you explain that?"

"Intravenous injection."

Ned nodded. "Directly into the vein. How did that occur, Dr. Lassiter? Is there a homing mechanism in J.M.A.L.T.S.' database?"

"Yes," Adam replied.

"You indicated you had a failsafe in place in the device," Royce added with a nod.

"That's correct."

"Yet it has not been tracked," Ned stated.

"The sequences of responses may have been altered when the mechanism used to insert the poison, was placed," Amber suggested.

"So you're not just curls and a pretty face."

"Dr. Lassiter, your concentration should be on the problem at hand," Pierce stated.

Adam stood. "That's just it, gentlemen. I'm not clear on what you need from me. Secretary Davenport, the manual along with Dr. McCoy's notes on J.M.A.L.T.S. was delivered to your office an hour after our conversation yesterday. As you know my training begins at 9:00 am. Exactly what do you want from me?"

"I would think you would have some interest in who altered your invention to kill a man," Amber stated.

"There is some." Adam glanced at her then turned back to Royce. "I'm not certain what role you think I can take at this point, Mr. Secretary."

"Secretary Davenport and Chief of Staff Brooks believe you are invaluable to this investigation." Deputy Secretary Nicolas spoke.

"There are certain insights you have regarding J.M.A.L.T.S. that we do not have," Ned added. "With the addition of poison to the mix, we need to locate and eliminate the threat of this weapon."

"Adam." James spoke. "We believe you are capable of locating this device and defusing it."

"Some of us do not believe that." Special Agent Pierce spoke.

James gave him a look. "The President is asking Deputy Secretary Nicolas to give you a little leeway in your training to assist with this investigation."

"I don't want to skimp on my training. I researched long and far for just the right agency to fit into. I want to fulfill my training requirements with my class."

"From what I'm told, NAT, not many in your class like you anyway."

"What is your problem?" Adam faced Brent, but Ned stood square between the two men. "The lady isn't paying enough attention to your hard on or what?"

"Excuse you?" Amber raised an eyebrow.

"His hand has been itching to touch your thigh from the moment I walked in the door. Every time you look my way, he squirms in his chair. Whenever you speak, his Adam's apple bobs from the sheer sound of your voice. Not that I blame him. You have a very pleasing voice."

Special Agent Brent stood. "You are out of line. Do you think for one minute the Bureau needs or wants someone who has no respect for authority or decorum?"

"Maybe they need a pencil head with a stick stuck up his ass like you to teach me."

"I think that's a good idea." Everyone froze at the Deputy Secretary's words.

"What's a good idea?" Brent asked.

"Which part?" Adam asked.

James, Royce, and Phillip stood, adjusting their jackets. "Pierce, you are going to mentor Lassiter during his training," Nicolas advised. "Lassiter in turn will assist you with this investigation and others as needed."

"Sir, that is not workable," Brent agued.

"Not a good first impression in the decision making category, sir," Adam countered.

"I believe the four of you will locate and eradicate this threat," James stated.

"Four? What four?" Amber asked.

Phillip looked at his daughter. "Why, you, Pierce, and Lassiter will be reporting directly to Dr. O'Sullivan until this threat is eliminated."

"Why me?"

"If this person is using poison to kill people we will need that identified immediately," Royce stated. "You have proven to be quite capable in that area."

"The three of you are our best chance at eliminating this threat," James Brooks added. "The President is asking you to serve your country. None of you are turning him down...right?"

"No, sir," Brent answered immediately.

"No," Amber replied hesitantly.

All eyes went to Adam. He looked from one to the other. "I'm thinking," he stated.

James stared at him with that you better give the right answer look that Adam was used to coming from his father. "I'm in, but training comes first."

"This investigation comes first." James nodded. "You will get your training in. Special Agent Pierce will see to it."

Royce looked at Ned. "This is our future." He pointed to the group. "Prepare them."

The men walked out of the room closing the door behind them. The four people remaining inside did not move. Then the laughter from the outside erupted.

"It seems we have an amused group of superiors expecting great things from us," Ned stated. "We can do one of two things. We can prove them right and fail miserably." He sat in the chair at the head of the table. "Or, we can surprise the hell out of them by bringing in the person responsible for Dr. McCoy's death and for threatening our way of life. So what is it going to be?"

Brent looked from Amber to Adam then to Ned. "It's my case. He follows what I tell him to do and curbs that damn mouth."

"I have every confidence in Brent. I've seen him at work and know he is thorough." Amber looked at Adam. "Your intelligence is evident, Dr. Lassiter. However, based on your statements today, I question your maturity level."

Adam smirked. "You question my maturity level and you've been around me all of," he looked at his watch, "thirty-five minutes." He shook his head. "We will find this person, eliminate the threat and retrieve the manual. Afterwards, I will resume my boring, immature life as an FBI Agent under the uncertain tutelage of the horny Agent Pierce." He looked at Ned. "It's apparent I'm the one getting the short end of the stick here."

Ned sat at the desk watching the three. He smiled to himself as he remembered the group of CIA Operatives he'd had the honor of handling. His orders were clear. Develop each participant in the room to the best of his ability. Special Agent Pierce with his background in Special Forces, computer technology and hand-to-hand combat put him on the short list to work in a different capacity for his country. Dr. Amber Nicolas, her connections and understanding of military operations and her medical expertise put her on the short list to work for her country as well. Last, but one of the most intriguing candidates he had seen in years, Adam Lassiter. The man's resume read like the who's who in scientific genius. His inventions alone should have this man in a fully funded lab doing nothing but using his mind to create. Yet he chose to join the FBI. He was certain there was a story there, one that would have to wait until another time to be told. For now he had to lead, develop and assess each one of them to determine which of them would become a new handler for the Central Intelligence Agency.

CHAPTER NINE

"The superstar of the Federal Bureau of Investigations class of 2015-10-10 has just entered the room," Flex Lander whispered to Karen Johnson who sat to his left in the theater style classroom at Quantico, Virginia.

She looked up to see Adam Lassiter walk into the room dressed in the same blue polo and khaki pants the same as the other class members. "Give the man a break. I'm certain he did not leap into his pants in a single bound this morning." Karen grinned at Flex then went back to writing on her tablet.

"You say that because you did not have to deal with the visit from the Lassiter clan last night."

"So the man has a supportive family."

"A supportive family is great. The problem comes in when the family includes the press secretary to the President of the United States, the top running back in the NFL, an ex Navy seal, and a brother who is a CIA operative."

She looked up at Flex, surprised. "They seem to be a family of overachievers."

"Yeah and I have to live with that for the next six months." Flex held out his hand as Adam walked down the row to take the seat next to him. "Hey, man, missed you this morning."

Adam shook his hand. "Sorry about that, I had a 5 am meeting." He took the seat next to Flex on the right. "Have I missed anything?"

"No, the professor hasn't appeared yet." He glanced at Johnson. "Did you get a notice about a 5 am meeting?"

Adam had picked up on the animosity from his roommate the night before. He chose to ignore it then and would continue to do so now. If Lander had insecurities about being accepted into the Bureau that was his problem to contend with. Adam glanced at the syllabus.

Flex continued. "The 5 am meeting. What was that all about?"

"Classified," Adam replied without thinking.

Flex stared at Adam for a moment then turned to Johnson. "The 5 am meeting was classified. We peons wouldn't have anything to contribute."

Adam wanted to get along with people and he was going to do his part, but damn if he was going to put up with stupid. "In this instance you are right. Let's stick to something you know about."

"Oh, something I know." Flex glanced at the syllabus. "Special Agent Vanderbilt is listed as the instructor for this course." He glared at Adam. "Do you know anything about him? Is he a long lost relative or something?"

Adam glanced over his roommate's shoulder to see the classmate sitting next to him shake her head and smirk at the question. He reached behind Flex to extend his hand. "Adam Lassiter."

She extended her hand. "Karen Johnson." She gave Flex the side eye.

"Nice to meet you," Adam replied then sat back as another member of the class walked down the aisle to the seat on his right.

"Good morning." He extended his hand to Adam as he took a seat. "Clive Mason."

Adam shook his hand. "Adam Lassiter." He then pointed. "Flex Lander, and Karen Johnson."

"Nice meeting you." Clive smiled then nodded towards the front. "Have I missed anything?"

"Yeah, a 5 am meeting this morning. But don't sweat it, most of us weren't invited." Flex shrugged his shoulder as he smirked Adam's way.

Clive glanced at Adam who closed his eyes in a sign of exasperation. "I made the 5 am meeting. Interesting stuff." He turned at the sound of the door closing.

Adam checked the man sitting next to him with the accent. "Good comeback. Mississippi?"

"Gulf Port, born and raised." He nodded, then sat back.

Adam sat back doing the same.

"Good morning. I am Special Agent Vanderbilt."

The man walking in the door placed his tablet on the table, then glanced around the theater seating room of exactly 47 men and 6 women.

"No, it is not Van for short. If anything you can call me Special Agent and pray you receive the honor to be addressed that way someday. Welcome to the world's premier law enforcement learning and research center. You've made it through months, and in some cases years, to get to this point. Look around, ladies and gentlemen. Not everyone you see today will be here five months from now. It takes intelligence, instinct, physical endurance and simple common sense to become an Agent with the Federal Bureau of Investigations."

Flex slapped Adam on the shoulder. "Lassiter here doesn't have to worry about any of that. He has connections."

Members of the class turned to see who had spoken. Flex pulled away laughing as Adam inhaled.

"It seems you are missing a major component." Special Agent Vanderbilt glanced at his tablet. "Lander."

"What is that, sir?"

"Common sense. You see, if Lassiter does have connections he would be the last person in the room I would want to antagonize. Yet, you do so openly."

"I have confidence in my abilities, sir."

Vanderbilt held both hands out to the side. "On a scale of connections you have ability in the left hand and stupidity in the right." He raised his right hand. "Ability loses every time." He held Flex's glare daring him to speak further. When he was certain the young man understood his meaning he continued. "First lesson, don't ruin your chances to become an Agent for a moment of attention. Let's move forward. Class 20151010, please rise to take your oath."

"Translation," Adam whispered as he stood, "don't be an ass."

Flex sat back, glared at Adam but said nothing more for the rest of the class.

After class, Clive caught up with Adam walking out the door. "What's with you and Lander?"

"No idea," Adam replied. "You heading to PT, Mississippi?"

"Yeah." He all but rolled his eyes.

Adam smiled. "It can't be that bad."

"Depends on how you look at it," Karen said as she walked up beside them.

Adam looked to his side and smiled at the tall statuesque sister. "You look to be in pretty good shape to me."

"Looking good in clothes and being in shape are two different things."

Adam turned to see Lander walking up behind them.

"That's true." Clive nodded. "I'll wager she will outdo all of us. What say you, Lassiter?"

Adam looked Karen up and down. "I wouldn't bet against her."

"She sure as hell will beat you out." Flex smirked.

Adam stopped to confront Flex. "What's your problem with me?"

"My problem with you is while the rest of us busted our asses to get in here, you came on family credentials."

"Did you fill out an application? So did I. Did you take a test? I did too. Did you have a background investigation conducted on you? I did too. Did you have to take a physical examination? I did too. In addition to all that's required by the Bureau, I have a Masters in Biometric Engineering, a Masters in Nuclear Engineering and a Ph.D. in Chemical Engineering. I speak four different languages fluently." He stepped in Flex's face. "I have skills I have yet to demonstrate." He stepped back. "I don't need family connections. I'm the United States of America's next secret weapon." He began walking, leaving the others standing watching him. Then he stopped. "Oh, I forgot to mention I'm cocky as hell."

"No," Karen sarcastically added. "I don't believe it."

"Hell as long as you can back it up, who cares?" Clive laughed.

Flex took a minute then reluctantly joined in. "There is a story behind you, Lassiter."

"There's a story behind all of us," Adam replied. "The story I want to know is what's up with the PT?"

"Physical Training." Clive waved his hand. "A breeze."

"NAT." They all turned to Agent Pierce.

"Couldn't wait to see me again, Special Agent Pierce?" Adam grinned.

Brent stepped into Adam's space. "Let's make something clear. I am your superior during this investigation. You have one time to piss me off and you will be out of this class before you land on your ass. Do I make myself clear?"

"It's been my experience that superior people do not have to announce to the world that they are indeed superior. It's detected by the way you carry yourself. Take me for example. I haven't said a thing and people around know I'm far more superior than you."

Brent reached out to grab Adam by the shirt, but each of his classmates dropped their backpacks and stepped in front of him.

"Special Agent whatever your name may be, that doesn't seem to be a good example from a mentor," Clive cautioned.

"Lassiter may be a smart-ass, but he's our smart-ass and you will have to go through us to get to him," Flex stated.

Brent stepped back to compose himself. He looked around discreetly, then glared at Adam. "Keep your distance from Amber." He held up his finger. "One warning." He held one long glare at Adam then walked away.

As the classmates picked up their gear, Karen glanced up at Adam. "You hitting on an Agent's woman?"

Adam continued to stare at Brent until he was out of the door. "I wasn't." He finally turned away, looking at Karen. "I will now." Adam then grinned at Flex. "You jumped in there like you were going to punch the man on my behalf."

"I was," Flex stated. "I figure if anyone is going to knock you on your ass it should be me." He walked side by side with Adam down the hallway. "What investigation was he talking about?"

"Classified."

Flex gave him a look that indicated he was not pleased by the response.

"No, seriously, I can't talk about it."

"How did you get on an investigation on your first day at the academy?" Karen asked.

"It's connected to something I worked on prior to coming here."

"Hence your 5 am meeting?" Clive nodded.

"Exactly," Adam replied as they reached their quarters.

"See you at PT." Karen and Clive went their separate ways as Adam and Flex entered their dorm room.

He didn't have to see him, but he knew someone was in his room.

"I see you have an enemy and it's just your first day. Do you want me to handle him?"

Adam looked to the window to find his brother Joshua leaning against his desk. He dropped his knapsack. "What are you doing here?"

"Just checking in on your first day." Joshua stood dressed in a black suit, black tie, black shirt and a midnight blue trench coat.

If Adam didn't know better, he would have thought his brother was on his way to a photo shoot for some high-class magazine. But this was the way Joshua dressed everyday. He never understood it, but he liked it.

"How did you get in?"

"There isn't a building on these grounds I cannot get into."

"It's the FBI academy, Joshua, you should know better."

Joshua picked up on Adam's frustration. "You want to fill me in on Pierce?"

"No."

"He threatened bodily harm to a Lassiter. You know what that means."

"I don't need you fighting my battles, Joshua," Adam retorted, the anger clear in his voice.

"Whoa." Joshua stood then walked over to stand in front of his little brother, who stood just as tall as him now. "Not fighting your battles, just protecting my family."

Adam sighed. "Joshua, all my life I've been trying to live up to my big brothers. Sammy and you were bad enough, but then there's Luke with the football and Timothy with the stocks. The only one I felt I could reach at some point was Mathew and it even looks like his coaching thing is about to really take off." He looked away then back. "I chose the FBI to establish my own identity. If you and Sammy jump in every time it looks like I'm about to fall on my face, then I will never learn to stand on my own. You feel me?"

Joshua nodded. "I do and yet I don't." Joshua took a seat on the edge of the desk. "You see yourself as the little brother. We see you as a man who will probably exceed all of us. Your decision to join the FBI is beneath you. I know it. Sammy knows it and deep down you know it too. However, I see a young man who needs to prove himself." He softened his tone. "We also see what the scientific community sees, a man who has the intelligence to change the world. In our line of work, Sammy and I are trained to protect minds like yours. Don't think for one moment we doubt your ability to do anything you choose to do. But understand, we know the world and how far some people in it will go to control a mind like yours. You are my little brother, and I will protect you with my life whether you want me to or not. The first reason is because I love you. The second is if anything happens to you, Sally will kill us."

Adam smiled as he nodded. "Yes, she would." He sighed. "Can I ask that you give me a little space? Let me battle with Pierce and whoever else may come along. If you see the big bad guys coming after me, then you step in."

"Fair enough." Joshua nodded. "Why is Pierce in your face?"

Adam grinned as he took a seat at the desk. "Do you remember when Diamond pulled Xavier's mother from the fire?"

"Yes."

"There was this doctor that was treating Mrs. Davenport. We had a meeting of the minds, so to speak, a few years back."

"This is about a woman?" Joshua asked confused.

"Not any woman," Adam replied grinning. "A gorgeous woman with big brown eyes, and lips that look sweet enough to taste."

Joshua laughed. "What's her name and what does Pierce have to do with her?"

"Her name is Amber and I'm not sure about Pierce's place in her life, but I'm going to find out."

Joshua stood. "Seems like you can handle Pierce. But you know" -he frowned- "you haven't had a lot of experience with women. You should play a little before you get serious."

"Why do you all think I can't handle women?"

"Because you haven't. Last I heard you were still a virgin."

Adam glanced nervously around the room divider. "Say it louder, why don't you?" he whispered loudly to Joshua.

"It's nothing to be ashamed of. It is what it is."

"I'm not a...virgin. I've been learning from a pro."

"You've been sleeping with a prostitute?" Joshua stood, appalled. "You're a Lassiter. You don't have to pay for a woman."

"No, she is not a prostitute and I'm not paying for anything." Adam tried to hush Joshua. "I am, however, enjoying every lesson she gives."

Adam looked up to see Flex walking towards them. "PT in five, Lassiter."

He nodded acknowledging his announcement. When he turned around Joshua was gone. Adam shook his head. He was used to his brother appearing, then vanishing. He only hoped that Joshua got the message. He wanted to do this on his own. The truth was, he understood his brother's concern for his safety. He knew people wanted to control him. That was one of the reasons he took a low profile position with the FBI. Besides his fascination with investigative work, it would give him an opportunity to determine how deep into the clandestine field he wanted to venture. Right now, the scientific world knew of his creative mind. Working for the FBI would give him cover for a moment. They would not be anticipating any further inventions from him while he was with the FBI. They would only assume he was just another under achieving brother with a brilliant mind. And for now, that was okay with him.

Adam changed quickly and caught up with Flex as he walked down the hallway.

"So," Flex began. "You're a virgin being taught by a prostitute, huh?"

Adam froze.

Flex grinned over his shoulder. "Don't worry. Your secret is safe with me."

They met the others in the lobby leading to the field for their daily run.

"Ready for PT, Lassiter?" Karen teased as she stretched.

"As ready as I can get."

Flex hit him on the shoulder as he spoke. "Don't worry. Lassiter has plenty of energy to spare." He took a step out the door and yelled, "Make way for the virgin Adam."

Clive looked over his shoulder at Adam. "Either you are going to kill him before we leave here, or I will on your behalf."

"Ignoring him is the worst consequence he can receive. He uses the tactic of belittling others to cover his own insecurities. In this case, it's fear of failure, not measuring up. When he sees I'm not a threat to his success he will cease."

"And you are okay with being his target?"

Adam shrugged. "For now. When the time is right I'll establish my dominance over him in a way that will not crush his spirit."

Clive gave Adam an incredulous look. "You're joking, right?"

Adam looked up at him in a serous manner. "No."

Karen ran out the door in front of Adam. "Virgin?" She looked him up and down as she ran backwards. "Let me know if you need some help with that."

Adam turned to Clive and grinned. "There's a benefit to Flex being stuck on stupid." He ran after Karen.

CHAPTER TEN

The moment Amber entered her laboratory she knew something was off. Uncertain what, she continued through her normal routine of placing her purse in the locker along with her keys. She took her cell phone and placed it on the desk next to the entrance. From her locker she pulled out her white lab coat, put it on, then put her phone in her pocket.

Walking through the double doors of the secured environment, she pulled her case files from the cabinet, then placed them on her desk next to her computer. Yes, files were kept electronically, but she also believed in having a backup hard copy of everything she worked on. On the back counter she opened the top drawer, withdrew a pair of latex gloves, then covered her hands. Her job was to work cases involving chemical warfare agents such as nerve, blood or blister agents that can be used as weapons. It was her habit to wear gloves whenever she worked in the lab to keep from contaminating any evidence she was working with. She took a set of keys from the desk to open the cabinet above her countertop. She took out a petri dish with specimens inside. It was her plan to review the results from another case while she waited on Brent to bring the results from McCoy's autopsy. She checked the microscope, then placed the dish beside it. She thought for a minute and on a small, very minute level, maybe her father was right to put her on this case. But it should be as an analyst, not as an investigative agent. To complicate matters more, she was assigned to a case with the one man who made her sweat at night, for weeks on end. *Where in the heck did that come from?* She thought as she struggled to push Adam Lassiter from her mind.

"Yet another reason I should not be on this project." She spoke out loud to the empty room. She shook her head as uneasiness seeped through her mind. Glancing around the room, everything seemed to be in place, but she couldn't shake the feeling that something was off. She ran her fingers through her curly hair and shook it off. This case was already getting to her. As soon as she spoke to her mother, she would make certain her father would take her off this case. "Yes, Mother will convince him." As soon as the thought cleared her mind, her cell phone buzzed.

"Mother, I was just about to call you."

"Hello, darling. I just spoke with your father. He told me you will be working on a case with Brent. That is marvelous. It will give you a chance to see him at his best."

"Mother, I..."

"It will also give you two a chance to spend more time together. You know, get to know each other in a different way."

"But Mother..."

"How exciting. I get chill bumps just thinking about it. Listen, my other line is ringing. I have to go. Love you, Redbird."

And with that, the call was disconnected.

"Mother?" Amber sighed at the realization that her mother was not going to be much help. She slumped down into her office chair and murmured a small curse.

She clicked on her computer and did a search on Adam Lassiter. The man who stirred her blood appeared on the screen. She sat up. "My goodness he has beautiful eyes."

Amber looked through pages and pages of information on Adam and his many accolades. He was indeed an impressive man, on paper. In person, he seemed to be a juvenile with no manners. A picture of him with the children he used in his obesity study appeared. It captured her attention - with the warm smile, the genuine look of happiness with the children around him. A smile appeared on her face as she read the article.

"Wow, the baby boy of twelve siblings. That explains a lot." She sat closer to examine the picture and decided, of all the pictures of him, she liked this one the best. He was in his natural environment doing something he apparently loved, working with children. "Why are you in the FBI academy, Lassiter number eleven?" She picked up where the article referred to him as the eleventh child to Joe and Sally Lassiter. The more she read, the more she liked the man and that was something she did not want. She did not want to like anything about Adam Lassiter.

Amber clicked the articles closed then sat back. She closed her eyes to clear her mind of the sexy, smart mouth doctor of science. Once her eyes closed and her mind cleared, other senses tuned in.

That was when she heard it. She had learned long ago how to clear her mind to allow other senses to dominate. It was her hearing that was taking precedence at the moment. There was a low humming sound in her office. The only device on was her computer. She isolated that sound, then concentrated more on the low, almost faint humming. In that moment, she knew what it was. The device that killed

Dr. McCoy was in her office. But how? The labs were sealed. Then she remembered what Adam said. It can fit through a keyhole, which they did not have. However, the door did open when she swiped her card and walked in. The device followed her into the lab. Now there was another question to be answered. Was the device here to observe or kill? Knowing that panicking would not get her anywhere, she remained calm. Let her mind free of everything else, then allowed her senses to locate where the device was in the room. She determined it was near her computer. The image from the video earlier that morning came to her. She knew not to look directly at it for whoever was on the other end would know she saw it.

Amber sighed then sat up. Opening her eyes as she turned her back to where she believed the device was located. She reached into the cabinet, removed an empty petri dish then pulled out her glass slide from the drawer. Taking a specimen from the petri dish, she placed under the microscope. She then took the top off the empty petri dish. Her hope was to make the person observing her think she was working on something in an effort to entice the device to come closer. After a few minutes, the device did not move. Amber turned to her computer. Sighed as if distracted, then keyed the word J.M.A.L.T.S. on to her computer. Almost immediately the device moved.

She could see it. It looked more like a mosquito than a fly. It landed on her keyboard. It was eerie the way it sat there as if monitoring what she put into the computer.

As if on cue, an email message came through with the subject line J.M.A.L.T.S. She could hear the mini motor kick in on the device, as if reading or securing the information from her screen. She took that moment to cover the device with the bottom half of the petri dish.

Amber jumped up, pushing her chair against the back counter. Her heart rate increased to a point where she was now panting. She immediately pulled out her cell phone to call Brent.

"Are you still on the grounds?" she asked as she pulled her magnifying glass from the drawer.

"Yes." Brent stopped walking. "Are you okay? You sound winded."

"You should come to my office. If Dr. Lassiter is anywhere nearby you should bring him too." She disconnected the call, then lowered the magnifying glass down to take a closer look at the device. She could see the device hitting against the glass dish in an attempt to escape.

"Wow," she whispered. "Look at you."

She reached up to turn the computer off, then pulled a flashlight from the drawer. Turning it on, she examined the device. "What are you doing here, little fella?"

With the flashlight and the magnifying glass she could clearly see it was indeed a micro-sized electronic device. The scientist in her took over, as her heart rate from the initial fear began to subside. She smiled. "You are a little wonder, that is what you are."

It was then that Brent tapped on the lab door. Amber reached under her desk, pushed a button releasing the lock and the doors slid open.

"You are not going to believe this," Amber laughed out.

Brent walked behind the desk to stand next to her. He looked around. "Believe what?"

She looked up at him in surprise. "You don't see it?"

"See what?"

Amber pointed to the petri glass on top of her keyboard. He reached to pick it up. "No," she yelled. Then looked at him with a frown. "It will escape if you move that."

Brent looked confused. "What will escape?"

"J.M.A.L.T.S." -she shrugged -"or the fake J.M.A.L.T.S."

"Where is it?" Brent glanced down at the container.

Amber frowned. "You really don't see it?"

"No. I don't see anything there, Amber."

Then she remembered, he did not see the device on the screen that morning. Amber sighed in frustration. "Close your eyes."

"Amber?"

She spoke softer. "Close your eyes." He did as she asked. "Now, relax your mind."

"Amber?"

"Brent, if you want to see it you will have to trust me."

Brent unbuttoned his suit jacket, closed his eyes, then tried to clear his mind. The image of Lassiter with that smug look on his face appeared. "This is not going to work."

"It won't if you do not give it a chance," Amber admonished. "Now relax your mind. Clear everything out." She could see him physically relaxing. His breathing was becoming shallower. "Okay, now slowly open your eyes and look at the keyboard."

Brent did as she asked only to shake his head. "I still don't see anything."

"Use this." Amber gave him the magnifying glass. "Now look down at the letter "t"."

He did as she asked. "Whoa." He looked at her then back to the device. "It looks like a mosquito."

Amber nodded.

"How did it get here?"

"I don't know," she replied as she looked back down at the device. "It's remarkable."

"It's dangerous," Brent declared with a little too much irritation in his voice.

"It's progress. Can you imagine how many ways this could be used?"

"I don't have to imagine. I already know it can be used to kill." Amber was in awe of the device and Brent did not like that one bit.

"That's because it got into the wrong hands. You have to think about the possibilities a device of this magnitude could be used for. Oh my goodness, the medical implications alone are staggering." Amber smiled. "A device this size, when altered, could do remarkable exploratory missions inside the body making the need for invasive surgery non-existent. Think about the wonder of being able to guide this minute of a device inside the human body to take pictures before cutting the person open. It could save millions of lives."

"It could also kill millions."

Amber sighed, then looked around. "Where is Dr. Lassiter?"

"I didn't call him."

"Why not? He needs to know we have this."

"No he doesn't. I sent Dr. Sullivan a message. He will know what to do."

"He is as new to this device as we are. He will have to call Dr. Lassiter."

"Lassiter is in training," Brent stated as he stepped away from the desk. "Dr. Sullivan will be here in a minute. He will know what to do with the device."

"You are being a jerk, Brent Pierce. You know Dr. Lassiter is the only person familiar with the device. Why not just call him?"

"Frankly, I've had my fill of Lassiter for the day. On top of that he is disrespectful and I don't like the way he looks at you."

Amber's eyes widened. "Really, Brent. We are looking for a possible traitor to this government and you are concerned with the way a man looks at me?" She shook her head. "I thought you were supposed to be the mature one."

Brent clenched his jaw. "So you did not pick up on Lassiter's signals? They were loud and clear to me."

"Could it be you were looking for them? I wasn't. I was interested in what he was saying about J.M.A.L.T.S. more than his childish antics. Maybe you should try paying attention to the case rather than the man."

Brent ran his hand down the back of his head. "Look, you know I have this thing for you. Any man in the room with you will catch my attention if he is trying to invade my territory."

"Your territory? When did I become your territory?"

"You know what I mean, Amber." He reached out to her, but she stepped away.

"Brent, you and I are teasing buddies, nothing more."

"You know I want more."

Amber held her head down. "But I don't, Brent." She looked back up at him. "Please don't make working on this case with you a problem."

Brent's nose flared. "You like him."

"Who?"

"The damn owl in the tree," he said sarcastically. "Lassiter. You mentioned you had met him before."

"I did, but I don't know the man well enough to say if I like him or not. From the small amount of contact we've had thus far, I will say I am impressed with his accomplishments, but not with his manners."

Ned knocked on the door. Amber reached under the desk to push the button. "I don't want to discuss this any further." She turned to Ned. "Dr. Sullivan, take a look at this."

Ned walked around the desk as Brent stood back staring at Amber. When Ned bent over he spoke. "Well, what do we have here?"

"You see it too?" Brent asked with a dumbstruck expression as he dropped the magnifying glass on the desk.

"Ah yes." Ned looked up, excited, at Amber. "It's one thing to read about it. Quite another to see it in person."

"Yes, it is." Amber's voice was filled with excitement.

"What did Dr. Lassiter say when he saw it? Did he have an opportunity to examine it? "

"We haven't called him yet," Amber replied. "I thought it would be best for you to see it first."

Brent looked over Ned's back as his eyes met Amber's. His shoulders slumped as he pulled out his cell phone then reluctantly dialed the number he had for Adam.

Within minutes Adam was buzzed into the lab.

"Hello, gorgeous." He smiled at Amber.

"Dr. Nicolas," she sternly replied.

"Oh. Okay. Hello, gorgeous Dr. Nicolas." He then saluted Brent. "Special Agent from hell." He grinned.

"Dr. Sullivan." Adam bent over the desk. "Looks like we have an imposter here." He reached into his pocket and pulled out a pair of tweezers. He slowly removed one side of the dish, reached in and gently picked up the device.

"Cap."

Amber picked up the cap from the back counter and gave it to him. Adam placed the device inside the petri dish then covered it.

"It seems to have shut down," Amber stated.

Adam nodded as the three scientists loomed over the device.

Brent stood back, leaning against the counter with his arms folded and legs crossed at the ankle. "I suppose you can see it too?"

Adam turned to him. "Yes. You don't?"

"Of course you do, and no, I don't see it."

"You know I could stand here and explain how to clear your mind to do a number of things, including seeing this device. But I won't embarrass you at this time."

"Is that a fact?"

Adam stood straight from bending over the microscope to glare at Brent. Sometimes you had to prove your abilities before people could truly respect them.

"Lassiter," Ned warned.

"No, don't call him off." Brent clenched his teeth. "Let's see what you got, Lassiter."

"Brent." Amber frowned. "Let's work on the case."

"Do I sense some animosity in the air?" Ned raised an eyebrow as he looked at the three people he was now charged with assessing.

"Not on my part," Adam stated, "but Captain America over here seems to be a bit distracted."

"You little..." Brent stood from his leaning position on the counter.

"Remember, you are supposed to be an example for me," Adam teased.

Ned looked between the two men and determined it was in the best interest of the case to let them establish their place now. He glanced at Amber whose face was marked with indignation.

"Pierce, stand down," Ned stated.

"I'll be happy to after I take a piece out of Lassiter's ass."

Adam held Brent's eyes. He never blinked, he simply stood there clearing his mind of everything and concentrating solely on Brent's eyes.

Brent stood there attempting to intimidate Adam with his glare. But as moments passed, Brent's anger slowly dissipated. His pupils began to dilate, his shoulders relaxed and his head tilted slowly to the side.

Amber watched in awe as the transformation came over Brent. Ned looked on, amazed, as Adam slowly took control of Brent's mind.

"Are you relaxed, Special Agent Pierce?"

Brent slowly nodded.

"What is our mission, Special Agent Pierce?"

"To locate and apprehend the person responsible for the death of Cyrus McCoy."

"Correct. You need me to accomplish that goal, agreed?"

"Agreed."

"I also need you, agreed?"

"Agreed."

"Together we will find who killed my friend, agreed?"

"Agreed."

Adam nodded. "When I count to five you will be calm. Thank you. Resume your position." Brent stepped back into the same position he was previously in.

Amber watched then turned on Adam. "What did you do to him?"

Adam shrugged his shoulder. "Just a slight power of persuasion. He'll be back in one, two, three, four, five." Adam bent down to the device. "Now, let's see if we can disengage and disassemble."

Amber looked from Adam to Brent, then up at Ned. "He'll be fine," he reassured her, then turned his attention to the device.

CHAPTER ELEVEN

Adam, Amber and Ned were bent over the device with tweezers when Brent's senses were fully restored. Adam had disengaged the device as Amber looked on.

"This should help in locating who is behind McCoy's death."

"What is it?" Brent strained to see the small device.

"It's a miniature transmitter," Amber replied in awe. "It's what the device uses to communicate with whoever is controlling it."

"Yes, it is." Adam put the item under the microscope. Then he motioned for her to look inside.

She looked up smiling. "There's a serial number."

"What is it?" Brent pulled out his cell and keyed in the numbers as she read them off. "We should be able to track the manufacturer."

Adam and Ned glanced at each other. "What's the problem?" Brent asked, causing Amber to look up from the scope.

Adam sighed. "That transmitter has not been released to the public."

"So...whoever we are looking for has government connections," Amber summarized.

Adam nodded.

"How did you get it?" Brent asked.

"I built it."

Brent stared at him. "You built that?"

"Yes. That was the easy part. Electronics 101."

"The key," Ned added, "is connecting the right components with the transmitter to create the surveillance device."

"There aren't many people who have the knowledge, skill set or patience to accomplish such a feat," Amber added, still looking into the microscope as she spoke. "This is remarkable." She finally looked up. "We have to salvage this project. The possible functions of this device are limitless."

"The medical implications alone could turn the world upside down." Adam spoke, excited that someone in the room was getting it.

"I totally concur," Amber stated. "I realize this is being used for surveillance, but I can't help visualizing its medical use."

"I used something similar to help with my study of obesity among children when I was with the CDC." Adam spoke with excitement in his voice. "We were able to see the inside of each child prior to the study."

"I read about that," Amber said as they turned to the microscope, drifting into their own world.

Ned stepped over to Brent. "There are a limited number of people who had access to anything connected with J.M.A.L.T.S. The question is which of them has access to this transmitter. The number should be minimal since it has not been released to the public."

"Only the members of the developmental team."

"That made the person who is doing this one of us."

Brent glanced at Amber and Adam seeing the conversation between them flow effortlessly. "Is it possible that someone in Lassiter's camp may be aware of this? It is feasible to me he may have shared this information with someone at his university."

"Not likely." Ned shook his head. "Scientists have a way of keeping things close to the vest, especially during the exploratory stages. I don't see Lassiter sharing this information with anyone other than his family."

"Then wouldn't that place family members on the possible suspect list?"

"I don't think you want to open that can of worms. The Lassiter family is a close bunch. That I can vouch for." Ned grinned. "They are not the ones you want to cross."

"Well, Dr. Sullivan, at this point I consider everyone a suspect until I can eliminate them." Brent witnessed as Adam removed a curl from Amber's face as they continued to dissect the device.

Ned picked up on his distraction. "When scientists get together it's as if no one else exists in the world." He hit Brent on the shoulder. "You'll get used to it."

Brent glanced at Ned. "It's not the scientist talk that concerns me." He glanced at the two talking again then walked towards them. "Amber," he called out. He stepped between the two as he spoke. "I'm going to run down this lead, if you need me for anything call."

"I'll be here with her. She's in good hands, Special Agent Pierce," Adam replied. "Let us know what you find."

"I'll be fine, Brent." She and Adam turned back to the device and just like that Brent had been dismissed.

Ned could not give Brent any words of encouragement as he slowly took a step back, turned then walked out of the room. The attraction between Adam and Amber was evident to him even if they did not recognize it themselves...yet. He did not bother to interrupt them as he stepped outside the door to make a call.

"What's your status on coverage?"

"I have Ashton in sight," CIA operative Monique Day replied. "What role do you think he's playing in all of this?"

"I don't have a clear answer on that, however, there have been indications of abnormal activity on his part when it comes to Lassiter."

"You know I don't question your hunches, but if this involves a member of Absolute's family don't you think we should bring him in on this?"

"Spicy," he referred to her using her operative name. "What do you think Absolute would do if he knew the General has had surveillance on his brother for the last two years?"

"Kill him and ask questions later."

"That's exactly what I think he would do too. Let's keep him out of this."

"Any intel on what Ashton wants from Lassiter?"

"Not clear at this time. However, I do know that Ashton is taking orders from someone else. The question is which invention captured their attention?"

"By process of elimination, you believe it's this J.M.A.L.T.S. device. Why?"

"It is the only one that can be weaponized."

"I'm sure I don't have to tell you how many ways this can actually go wrong by running an unauthorized surveillance on General Ashton."

"Are you having second thoughts about this mission?"

Monique thought for a moment. Joshua Lassiter had been her trainer. She'd watched him go through a very difficult time in his life. One that should have turned him against this government yet he remained true to his country. Not only did she like and respect him, she had recently become more attached to other members of his family. If any one of them were in danger, she wanted to be a part of the team that would take out the enemy. "No. I haven't had a good fight in a minute now. Besides, this one is hitting a little close to home." She thought for moment. "I knew the little brother was smart but according to you he is a borderline genius."

"No, he is not borderline. He is one of the biggest minds of this century. It is incumbent upon this country to keep this man protected. The last thing we need is for a mind like his to be corrupted."

Monique nodded. "I will keep my eye on Ashton. You will have a full report in twenty-four hours."

"Good enough." Ned glanced through the window at Adam and Amber still chatting away at the microscope. "Spicy, it's going to be interesting to see how this all plays out."

"Adam is the quiet Lassiter, but I have a feeling he has the potential to be the most dangerous."

Ned smirked. "I think that's an understatement. I just watched him hypnotize an FBI Agent in less than two minutes. We've got to get this guy on our team."

"I would not be your friend if I did not say this again. Absolute needs to be told. It is going to be hard to protect him without Joshua picking up on us."

"We have to find a way, Spicy." Ned sighed. "My orders are clear, no one is to know what we are working on."

Ned ended the call, then tapped on the window. Amber let him back into the room then erupted into laughter.

"I can't believe you did something like that. They actually allowed you to test it in the lab at the school?"

"Allow is such a speculative term. Have you ever heard of doing something then asking permission later?"

"No. I have always been told you ask permission first."

"You must live a very sheltered life." Adam smiled. "Where is the adventure? Living that way makes a person so predictable people know exactly what to expect before you even do it. I find that life is more interesting when people have no idea what you might do next."

"Living life that way puts your world in turmoil. There are no controls, no accountability, no limits."

"Why should there be limits? Each day God gives us a day to find our purpose for being on this earth. I say we should live it to the fullest. As the old adage says, tomorrow is not promised. Go for the gusto while you can."

"That is an immature way of looking at things." Amber sobered. "There has to be structure in a person's life. And while you say it's being predictable to live within one's limits, I find it being dependable. People know what to expect from you. It's clear that you can be counted on when needed."

"You're a military brat, aren't you?" Adam frowned.

Amber's defenses rose. "Yes, I am and very proud of it."

Adam suddenly came to attention, saluted her with his hand. "Yes, ma'am," he laughed. "I bet you have a daily regimen, don't you? Get up at six in the morning. Dressed and showered by 6:30, breakfast by 7:00, in the office precisely at 7:30. Am I right?"

For a moment, the routine Amber always looked at as a good quality suddenly felt dirty. She should get off the subject. "I get up at 5:30, dress, take a run and I am back home by six. I shower, get dressed for work and I

am out of the house and at my office no later than
7:30." She frowned. "You make it sound like being
dependable is a dirty or bad thing. I look at it as being
an adult. Allow me to correct that - a responsible
adult."

Adam leaned back against the counter top, folded
his arms then tilted his head to stare at her. "Where is
the time for your man to make love to you in the
morning so that you are full of energy and an
awareness of your sexuality each day?" He took a step
towards her. "What about lunch time when your man
has an unquenchable desire to hear you scream his
name in the middle of the day?" He took another step
towards her. "What about at night when dinner is on
the table, the candles are lit and the dessert your man
wants is between your legs rather than on the plate?
When does your way of living allow for a gentle kiss
that leads to hours upon hours of sexual satisfaction?
Do you have time in your schedule for that? Or does
that have to be timed and placed on a schedule as
well?" He stood a mere breath away from her. "Where
is the spontaneity, the building fire, the lingering
desire-you know the normal reactions between a man
and woman?"

Amber was visibly flustered by his words. Her
breathing increased, her eyes widened, beads of
perspiration formed right above her lips as if a flame
had just been struck under them. She stepped back
until her desk blocked her escape. Slowly her eyes rose
to meet his. They really were beautiful. Or can a man's
eyes be classified as beautiful, she thought. And his
lips, they were thick, smooth, suckable lips. And they
had the nerve to be calling out to her. As if on
command, her tongue involuntarily snaked out to coat
her lips.

Adam watched as her tongue glided slowly across her lips and smiled. "I think I know the answer." His eyes held hers. "You haven't met a man who would make you want to throw all your schedules and controls out a window just to have a taste of him." His lips brushed against hers with the lightest touch. It was the jolt he felt that forced him to pull back. The urge to cover her lips with his did not dissipate. The heat rising between them had increased to an unbearable temperature. He knew she felt it too. But this wasn't the time or place to act on what he was feeling. "One day soon, you will know that feeling." He stepped back and resumed his stance against the back counter.

"Dr. Sullivan. You have a concern?" Adam asked as he slowly moved his eyes from hers.

Amber swung around to see Dr. Sullivan standing in the back of the room. She had completely forgotten she had let the man in. How did she become so engrossed in Adam that she completely forgot where she was?

Ned wasn't surprised by Adam's question. He knew the moment Adam's mind picked up on his concerns. "A small worry. Special Agent Pierce is needed to complete this investigation. He is clearly infatuated with you, Dr. Nicolas. You in turn are obviously attracted to Dr. Lassiter."

"You are mistaken, Dr. Sullivan."

"No, dear, I don't think I am. At some point you too will realize the attraction."

Adam looked at her and smiled.

"Dr. Sullivan, I assure you nothing," she glanced at Adam, "is going to happen here. Dr. Lassiter will keep his hands and words to himself." She turned back to Ned. "However, I do see the need for expediency on this investigation. We will handle it in a professional manner with all sides respecting boundaries," she said with a huff.

"And you, Dr. Nicolas? Will your will power be able to withstand what is clearly an inevitable."

"Good question, Dr." Adam smiled. "What do you think, Amber?"

Even when he spoke her name, it was at a feverish pitch. "Stop that," she insisted. "There is nothing to withstand."

Adam smiled. "The flame has been lit, Amber, there is no stopping it." He unfolded his arms then looked at Ned. "It will be temporarily contained."

"Dr. Lassiter will be contained," Amber huffed. "That's for sure."

Ned looked at the two with doubt. "Astrolabe explosives." He shook his head.

Adam smiled. "I agree. She is ammonium nitrate."

"I take it you are anhydrous hydrazine?" Ned smirked.

"Twice as powerful as TNT."

Amber raised her eyebrow. "If you two are finished, I believe we have a device to track down."

"Speaking of which," Adam spoke. "How did this device get into your lab?"

Amber shrugged. "The lab is sealed when I leave each night. I can only conclude it followed me here and entered when I unlocked the door."

Adam and Ned glanced at each other. "It followed you?"

"I would think so. It has that capability, correct?"

Adam frowned. "Yes, but why would it follow you?"

"I have the feeling whoever is behind this wants to know what we know," Amber replied.

"You were at the scene of the crime," Ned suggested.

"You were also the person who immediately recognized Dr. McCoy had been poisoned."

"True."

Adam came to alert. "I don't like that."

Ned did the same as they both stared at Amber. "What?"

"You may be a target," Ned suggested as he pulled his phone from his pocket.

"There is no reason to assume that." Amber shook her head. "What are you doing, Dr. Sullivan?"

"Contacting your father."

"I don't think that's necessary, really."

"I think it is," Adam stated.

Ned had barely hung up the phone when her father appeared at the door of her lab. He placed his palm on the keypad and walked in. "How serious of a threat is this, Ned?"

"Serious enough for me not to want to take a chance. The device followed her here. It could have very easily taken her out."

"If that was the intent, I would be dead," Amber protested. "I was in here with it for a while before I captured it."

"Tell me step by step what occurred once you walked in the door," Adam asked as Royce walked in.

Amber's eyes rolled upwards. "Really, Daddy, you called Uncle Royce?"

"Yes, I did. This device has killed one person I don't want there to be another. Especially not my daughter."

"Your mother would kill him," Royce added.

"There is that." Phillip nodded in agreement.

"Amber," Adam demanded her attention. "Tell me what happened. How did you notice it?"

"I felt it first," she said as she sat behind her desk. "I felt like someone was watching me. So I closed my eyes. Cleared my mind of all mental chatter and just listened." She looked up at Adam. "That's when I heard it."

"Okay." He bent down in front of her to obtain eye to eye contact. His hands covered hers. "Then what did you do?"

"Once I was able to isolate where it was located, I pulled items out as if I was going to do some work."

"Trying to get it to move?" Adam asked.

"Yes." Amber nodded. "When it did not, I decided to try something different so I turned on my computer. That's when it moved from the top of my computer to the keyboard as if it wanted to capture what was on my screen. That's when I covered it with a petri dish."

"What was on your screen?"

Amber blinked at Ned's question. "Excuse me?"

"What were you looking at on the computer?" Royce asked.

She was not about to tell them she was looking up information on Adam.

"J.M.A.L.T.S. I typed it in a word document. Then an email came through from you," she said to Adam.

"I sent everyone the basic info on J.M.A.L.T.S."

"Is it possible it's been following you since yesterday?" Royce asked.

"Did it infiltrate the Sit Room during our meeting?"

"It's possible." Adam nodded as he stood.

"Well, we have it now," Phillip stated as he walked over to glance at the dismantled device.

"But are there more?" Adam sighed. "Look, whoever is behind this may have manufactured more than one. I know I would have."

"What other steps would you have taken?" Ned asked.

"This was a test. I would have others. At least one other that I would not have put in jeopardy."

"I would manufacture more," Ned stated. "Especially now that I know it works."

"You are off this investigation," Phillip stated.

"You just put me on it." Amber stood in protest.

"Against your will," he replied. "Now I'm taking you off."

"'I'hat's not going to eliminate the threat," Adam advised. "She needs to be out of range."

"Two hundred mile radius if I remember correctly," Royce stated.

"That's why he needs the manual," Adam added. "He needs to identify limitations."

"To adjust at will," Ned added in agreement.

"I'm going to have Pierce take you away from the city," Phillip stated as he pulled his cell phone from his pocket.

"What?" Amber asked.

"What?" Adam frowned.

"You need to be at least two hundred miles away from here," Phillip stated. "Just until the man is found."

"She is not going anywhere with Pierce," Adam told her father.

Phillip froze at the tone of Adam's statement.

Amber gave Adam a stern look. "Everyone calm down." The men in the room all looked at her. "Now, Dr. Sullivan, thank you, but Brent would only be able to shoot the thing and before he can do that he has to be able to see it. He can't with the naked eye. So far, in our circle only you, Adam and I are able to detect it in a room. So Pierce would not do me any good. It would be better for him to track down the people behind this. That leaves you, and Adam, Dr. Sullivan...."

"I'll do it," Adam cut her off.

"You just started your training, son. You leave now and it's back to the starting point," Phillip stated.

"Yes, Adam," Amber echoed her father's objection. "We would not want to interrupt your training. Dr. Sullivan, I don't believe any of this is necessary."

"On the contrary, I believe it is. As a precaution, I suggest you not return to your apartment or your car. That goes for you as well, Adam."

Adam looked stunned. "Me?" He smirked. "I am quite capable of taking care of myself. Amber is a different story."

"You are just as much of a target, if not more," Ned advised. "They took the manual for clarification. If that doesn't work, they will take you next."

Adam smirked. "It would take them getting onto the grounds at Quantico to get to me. In fact, I believe Amber would be safer there than anywhere."

"I don't know." Royce shook his head.

Phillip paused for a moment. "We could arrange that." He nodded to Royce who turned and walked out of the room.

"Wait, Daddy, do something here," Amber pleaded.

"I wish Pierce had not involved you, but the fact remains that he did. Now I have to ensure your safety as well as Lassiter's."

"I'll take personal responsibility for her safety, sir," Adam stated.

"Son, you haven't been trained to ensure your own safety. I'm certain you mean well, but you simply aren't prepared." He looked at his daughter. "The best way to ensure her safety is to locate the person who has that manual and eliminate the threat."

CHAPTER TWELVE

"Why there?" Brent asked.

The headache had been coming since the moment Brent called with his concerns. "The alternative was not acceptable to me. This will allow me to work and satisfy my father's need to protect me."

"By putting you literally doors away from Lassiter," he yelled into the phone.

Amber had reached her limit with men wanting to control her life for the day. "Is your concern with my safety or your jealousy of adolescents?" She began to massage her temples where a migraine was certainly threatening to appear. "Look Brent, you are my friend, that is all. Now, I value your friendship but in no way does that give you the authority to dictate what is going to take place in my life." She sat on the side of the bunk bed that in no way felt like her pillow top mattress at home and sighed. "If you want to see my current living situation come to an end, solve the case so that I can go back home." She disconnected the call, then sat mesmerized by the change of events in the last twenty-four hours. All she did was answer a call from a friend and now she found herself in the middle of a top-secret murder investigation, wedged between two men. One who was about to drive her crazy with jealousy and the other with desire.

Amber fell back on the bed. Looking up at the blank white walls the memory of the day she met Adam Lassiter came to mind. It was during the time when she was doing her residency in Richmond and was called in to assist with the case of a burn victim. She had given her diagnosis to the family when this young man spoke up, questioning her at every turn. While she did not like her bedside manner being tested, his questions were not only intelligent, they were precise and should have been asked. But it was the intensity in his eyes that she was not able to clear out of her mind. That same intensity was there today as they talked and examined the device. Adam Lassiter was a quandary to her. While the left side of her brain was telling her to stay as far away from this man as she possibly could, the right side of her brain was demanding she pull him close and never let go. A knock at the door caused her to sit straight up.

"Who is it?"

"It's Adam. I just wanted to check on you."

She stood and ran her fingers through her hair, fluffing out the curls. She took a quick look in the mirror. The dull black slacks and white blouse stared back at her. It was what she wore to work this morning so it would have to do until her clothes arrived. She took a deep breath and then opened the door.

"I thought you had weapons training."

"I did," he replied as he leaned against the doorjamb. "Lunch break so I thought I'd bring you some since you can't really go anywhere."

Amber smiled. "That was thoughtful of you." She stepped aside and let him into the room. "I don't understand why you get to go on with your life and I'm going to be stuck in this room for who knows how long."

"It will probably be just for two or three days, then you will be back home." He placed two bags on the desk in her room. "In the meantime, we might as well make the best of it. And believe me my life isn't that great right now. My instructors aren't too thrilled with the situation."

"I'm sorry." Amber empathized with him. "I'm certain you were excited about your first day here at the academy. Bonding with new friends who may turn out to be partners. Learning to do all the things FBI agents are expected to do. Although I have to say I'm a bit curious on why you decided to be an FBI agent. I don't mean to belittle your decision and all, and of course being an agent is honorable; however, you're a very intelligent scientist therefore I cannot help but wonder why the FBI."

Adam pulled out the chair at the desk then motioned for her to have a seat. "I brought hot pastrami with coleslaw and fries." He pulled the sandwich from the bag. "Or you may have a salad with all the fixings. Which will it be?"

She took a seat then smiled up at him. "You want hot pastrami, don't you?"

He shrugged his shoulders. "It just happens to be one of my favorite sandwiches."

"Why don't we split the sandwich, fries and salad?"

"Oh, a woman who can compromise. I like that." Adam opened the containers and started to separate the items when Amber stopped him.

"You don't have to go through that. We can eat from the same container." She stood, then walked into the bathroom to wash her hands. When she returned, he was sitting on the floor leaning against the bed biting into half of the sandwich. She picked up the other containers, placed them on the floor between them then leaned back against the bed. She handed him a fork, he in turn handed her a bottle of water.

"How much time do you have?"

"Forty-five minutes." He glanced at his watch. "Make that thirty minutes."

"That is enough time for you to tell me why you joined the FBI instead of working with the CDC or NASA or about 100 other agencies I'm certain tried to recruit you."

Adam smirked. "My mother asked me the very same question." He shrugged his shoulders. "I have this family of patriots." He bit into his sandwich. He thought before answering. "I have five brothers," he shrugged, "and six sisters."

"Wow, that's a big family," Amber stated as she took a bite out of her sandwich. "Must've been a lot of fights over the bathroom."

"Ha ha," Adam laughed. "That's an understatement if I ever heard one. Not only for the bathrooms, a seat at the breakfast, lunch and dinner table, front seat in the vehicles whenever we were going on a trip, first to get to the bowl when my mother baked some cakes. It was a fight over everything." He smiled.

Amber picked up a fry and bit into it. "But you love them. I can see it all over your face."

Nodding, Adam agreed. "I'd give my life for any one of them."

"The FBI?"

"My brother Joshua-" Adam took a drink of his water "has always been larger than life to me. I always envied him. All my life I've wanted to be just like him. When he started working for the agency I knew that was what I wanted to do, too. I saw how difficult it was for my mother to have him gone for months, years at a time, not knowing if he was dead or alive. She relied heavily on her faith, but it was a struggle." He picked up a few fries and threw them into his mouth. "I didn't like seeing her going through that so I decided when I went to school I would go into medicine. You know, do what I could to save a few lives here and there. At some point the natural curiosity that leads to creating things from my mind took over, especially during chemistry."

"Blew up a few things, did you?" Amber asked, grinning.

Adam laughed, nodding his head as he drank his water. "One or two labs, that's all." He stopped smiling and became thoughtful. "It started when the school asked a group of us to speak with a local high school. There was this one kid that the other students teased because of his weight. The kid was at least fifty pounds overweight."

Amber nodded. "I remember being teased because I was the smart kid."

"Same here. I think that's why I reached out to the kid. I met his mother. She was a single parent working a minimum wage job. Too much for public assistance, but not enough to live off of. He spent all day sitting in front of the television playing a video game and eating junk. It bothered me to a point where I did some research on the number of children in his same situation. In my mind, it was an epidemic. So I contacted the CDC with a few ideas. Thus the project on obesity in children came to fruition. It was amazing pulling the project together, selecting the children to be a part of the pilot then seeing what a major impact it had on their lives. That really inspired me to look at other ideas that played around in my head."

"And J.M.A.L.T.S., how did that come about?"

"A few years back, the President's daughter and niece were abducted. Once they located the children, the problem was getting eyes inside to see how dangerous the situation was. My brother Joshua entered the building only to discover it was loaded with explosives. When I heard the story I decided to develop a device that would prevent him or law enforcement from endangering their lives in that way. It took me forever to get that transmitter to work. Once I increased the size the problem resolved itself."

"What did your brother say when you told him why you invented J.M.A.L.T.S.?"

"I never told him."

"Why not?"

Adam shrugged. "There was no need for him to know. I'm sure he knows now."

"Wow." She blinked. "I would have never guessed it."

"What?" Adam asked as he emptied his bottle of water.

"Behind all that bluster, you are a pretty modest man."

His cell phone buzzed. He looked at it. "Oh, hell. I have to go." He jumped up and began moving the empty containers. She reached for them at the same time.

The touch caused them both to stop.

"Tactical stimuli," Amber whispered.

"The sense of touch." Adam nodded, making no attempt to move or pull his hand away. "My friend Xavier created a word when he met his wife to describe the feeling they experienced."

Amber licked her lips. She whispered as her heart rate steadily increased. "What?"

"Sinergy."

"The interaction of elements that when combined produce a total effect that is greater than that of the individual elements."

Adam smiled as he shook his head. "No. Sinful energy."

Amber looked up at him as she pulled her hands away. "That is not the meaning of synergy."

"It's the perfect meaning of sinergy between a man and a woman."

"You can't make up words to fit what you want them to fit. There is a standard dictionary that is used by the general public as a guide for the English language."

"There are times when you have to step outside of the standard and away from the mundane. Why do we have to limit ourselves to what we already have or know? Open your mind to creating other possibilities."

"You cannot create words," she argued. "There is a standard dictionary filled with words."

Adam shoved the discarded containers into the trash can. "People create words every day. That is how we expand our horizons."

"There are perfectly good words in the dictionary that could be used."

"Ironically, none of those fit what he felt for his wife. Thank God he was sensible enough to pick a woman who did not argue with him because he felt she was unique and welcomed the way he expressed the special feelings he was having for her."

Amber blinked. "You have some feelings for me?" she asked, almost dumbfounded.

The questions stopped the anger that was building inside of Adam, causing him to think. The two stood in the middle of the room staring at each other. Amber's tongue slowly slid across her lips.

That caught Adam's attention. He answered her question by pulling her into his arms, touching his lips to hers, gently forcing her lips to part. His tongue took advantage of her parted lips by plunging inside.

"Hmmm," was her only response to the sensations surging through her body. The roughness of his tongue contrasted with the smoothness of his lips as the pressure caused her to widen her lips to give him room to explore deeper into the recesses of her mouth. Her arms circled his neck as his tightened around her waist. Their bodies merged into one fluid being.

His phone buzzed between them, but neither was ready to pull away from the pure pleasure they were experiencing. His phone buzzed again.

Adam's hands roamed the curve of her waist, her hips, her behind. He could feel the natural reaction of him straining against his zipper. Her heat was rising, causing his nostrils to become inflamed with her scent. The sweet taste of her mouth mixing with his was driving him to a point of no return. Then her arms moved against him and he knew he had to stop. He pulled away slightly, allowing his nose to inhale the scent of her hair. His lips kissed the soft skin of her neck. "Neural and pressure receptors in the skin, hair, tongue and throat." He kissed her throat as she held her head back.

"Touch," she whispered against his ear, then sucked it.

Slowly, he stepped out of her embrace, placing her arms to her side. He nodded. "Your touch is hypnotic." He reached for the doorknob. "It will make me forget everything I came here to do."

Her eyes were still narrowed, her lips now swollen, her body reeling from his touch. "Mesmerizing. I don't know what to think."

He stood at the door straining not to go back into her embrace. "Narcotic," he said, allowing a small smile on his lips.

"Seductive."

Adam's smile widened. "Me." He walked out closing the door behind him.

Amber stood in the middle of the floor for a long moment after the door closed. She had been kissed before. Hell, she'd had sex before. But neither ever made her feel unsure of what to do next. She looked around the room, wondering for a moment where she was. Then it came back to her. She was in one of the FBI trainee's dorm rooms. Adam brought her lunch. They ate, touched then kissed.

She exhaled. "The touch." Her body reacted as if it had just happened. She frowned. They argued about words. Then he kissed her. "Stupid, stupid, stupid."

There was a knock at the door. It startled her for a second. "Who is it?"

"Brent."

Brent, she thought, then opened the door. She pulled him inside kissed him, then pulled away. He looked more astonished than she did. She kissed him again, this time harder, more demanding. Then she pulled away.

"What....?" Brent mumbled.

"Nothing," she said more to herself than to him.

"That was a little more than nothing." He reached for her and she stepped back.

"No, Brent."

"No?" He looked at the door then back at her. "You just pulled me into a room with a bed. Kissed me crazy. Not once, but twice and you are now saying no?"

Amber shook her head. "I'm sorry, Brent. I had to be sure. There is nothing there. I did not feel anything when I kissed you."

"I damn sure did."

"No, you really didn't. You are horny. You need to get some. But not with me."

There was a knock on the door. Brent took a moment, just staring at her. "I don't know what just happened. But you can't go around grabbing men and kissing them then declaring 'No'."

He opened the door. "Sorry about that, Kalli." He closed the door as Kalli walked inside with two overnight bags. "You two know each other?"

"Of course." Amber extended her hand. "Hello, Kalli."

Kalli nodded. "Dr. Nicolas."

"I spoke with the Director and he agreed you needed someone with you. Kalli has volunteered to shadow you until we catch this guy."

"I'll be bunking with you for a few days." Kalli put her bag on the bed closest to the door. She handed the other bag to Amber. "Your mother sent this for you and her love."

"Thank you. Can I at least speak to her? Just to let her know I'm okay."

"Not with your phone," Kalli replied.

Amber turned to Brent. "May I use yours?"

Brent was still thrown by the way she'd greeted him. "Sure." He pulled it from his pocket with a surly attitude. "I hope it won't be for nothing." He walked out of the room.

Amber sighed.

"You hurt his feelings." Kalli raised an eyebrow. "He really likes you."

"I know," Amber sadly replied. "But I don't feel the same way about him."

"I know," Kalli replied. "I'll talk to him while you speak to your mother."

"Thanks."

CHAPTER THIRTEEN

The instructor had called Adam's name twice when Flex nudged him with his elbow. "Hey, Lassiter, what's wrong with you? Answer the woman."

Adam glanced at Flex, then Clive to his right before sitting up straight. "I'm sorry, ma'am. What was your question?"

"When you do an investigation your attention must be on every word your suspect may say. It could be a simple slip of the tongue that will crack your case wide open, Mr. Lassiter."

"I follow your tongue....words."

"Ahhh." The instructor, who was quite attractive in her own right, smiled. "It's a woman." She walked back to her desk. "Now is not the time to be distracted by the whims of a female. You have six months of training to go. Look to your left, class." The class did what was instructed. "Now look to your right. One of you will not be here at the end." She glared at Adam. "Don't let it be you."

Adam sat up, cleared his mind, then concentrated on the question on the table. Thirty minutes into the class Adam looked up to see Deputy Secretary Nicolas and two men walk into the room. He watched as they spoke to the instructor and knew something was wrong. For a moment his stomach clinched thinking something must have happened to Amber. That would explain Nicolas' appearance, but not his brothers.

"Class, we have been honored with the presence of two of our most successful trainees. Samuel and Joshua Lassiter. Also present is Deputy Secretary Nicolas. They are here on other business, but I would be remiss if I did not seize the opportunity for you to meet these gentlemen." She stepped aside.

Deputy Secretary Nicolas stepped to the podium. "Good afternoon. Welcome to the Bureau. We have a legacy of the best and the brightest law enforcement personnel in the world. These two gentlemen trained here, but chose different paths. We are pleased to see their younger brother was smarter."

Karen leaned back behind Flex. "Hey, Lassiter," she whispered. "Are all of your brothers tall, dark, and finger licking good?"

"I can't say," Adam replied, annoyed. "I'm too busy trying to figure out why they are here."

"The big one could put the fear of God in a man just by looking at him," Flex stated.

"Sammy?" Adam shook his head. "He's as mild mannered as they come. Joshua, well, he will kill you and have you buried before you know you are dead."

"That fine brother right there?" Karen raised an eyebrow as she looked from Adam to Joshua. "That man is dressed from head to toe. There is no way he would mess up that suit or that pretty chocolate face."

"You sound like you are ready to sop the man up with a soup spoon," Clive laughed aloud.

The people in the front of the room speaking to the class looked his way.

"Mr. Lassiter." Samuel spoke.

"Oh my GOD." Karen turned to one of the other women in the class and nodded. "Yep, she felt it too." Adam glared at her. "Hey, I thought you were fine, but your brothers..." She grinned. "I'm getting off just looking at them."

"Would you mind joining us outside?" Samuel finished his statement.

"I prefer to stay where I am," Adam replied.

"It wasn't a request, Adam." Samuel narrowed his eyes. "Don't make me ask again."

"Don't make me call Sally," Adam threatened.

Joshua glanced at Sammy, then cleared his throat to cover his laughter. Samuel looked at Joshua, then took a step towards Adam's seat which was four rows up.

Karen, Clive and Adam stood. Flex's eyes were still on the tree trunk of a man walking up the aisle. Other classmates stood, blocking Samuel's way to Adam.

"I like them," Joshua said to the instructor.

She smiled at the man she once knew intimately. "They got his six."

"So I see."

"Mr. Lassiter." Deputy Secretary Nicolas spoke. "Front and center, sir. The remainder of the class, be seated."

Most sat at the order, but Karen, Clive and Flex remained standing until Adam grabbed his things and began walking towards his brother.

Adam stopped in front of Samuel when he reached the aisle. "You just couldn't resist, could you? I'm going to tell Momma."

Samuel rolled his eyes upwards. "Spare me," he asked the higher power as he followed Adam to the front. At some point in time he had been through this tug of war with each of his younger brothers when they wanted to establish their manhood. "The last one." He shook his head then followed Adam to the front of the room.

The Director spoke. "Young Lassiter will be back. I expect his team to keep him abreast of classroom information upon his return. Thank you." With that the four men walked out of the room.

"You couldn't help it. You had to single me out before my classmates."

"Adam, you were already singled out," Samuel stated. "They know who you are and what you have accomplished. Stop trying to play it down."

"Haven't you ever wanted to be part of a team? A normal person. That's all I want for the next six months."

"You're not normal and never will be, Adam," Joshua stated in a calm reassuring tone. He stepped in front of him. "You are a man with a huge brain. It's a gift from God and you have no reason to be ashamed of it."

"That was deep." Samuel smiled. "I see you've been working on your delivery."

Joshua grinned wide displaying his double dimples. "Thank you, Samuel. Roc has been working with me. She said she wants a calmer Joshua once the baby arrives."

"Excuse me." Adam interrupted them. "What are the clothes for?" he asked Joshua.

Joshua shoved the suit into his younger brother's arms. "You've been summoned."

"By who and why?"

"The President of the United States," the Deputy Secretary stated. "You don't ask why, son. You simply appear."

Adam looked at the Director. "Is someone with Amber?"

"Yes, Pierce is with her."

The look on Adam's face was clear. "Joshua...."

"No. I'm on you."

"I'm on my way to check on her now," Phillip stated as he extended his hand to Samuel. "Bring him back in one piece."

"Will do, sir," Samuel responded then walked down the hallway with Adam sandwiched between him and Joshua.

"Pierce is a good man," Samuel stated. "He'll protect her."

"Of course he's going to try to take her from you," Joshua added. "I mean the kiss in the room was good technique wise, but you could use a few more lessons."

"I taught him that move," Samuel said as he looked around Adam at Joshua.

"That's why he didn't get any further than first base. My moves, he would have had that."

Adam stopped walking and stared at the backs of his brothers. "You've been watching me?"

Joshua and Samuel stopped at the door. "Yes," Samuel answered.

"Sally is not going to kill us because something happened to you," Joshua informed him as he opened the door.

"I'm a grown man. How many times do I have to prove to you that I can handle myself?"

"Hey," Joshua said in a soothing voice. "It's not us you have to prove it to. I have faith in your abilities."

"That was a gentle delivery. You are getting better."

"Thank you." Joshua smiled at Sammy.

"Do you two mind?" Adam yelled.

Samuel exhaled, then closed the door. He spoke sincerely to his brother. "Adam, it's hard to be in your position. You are the baby boy in the family. Like it or not, your parents are going to worry about you. And so are we. You are in a dangerous situation. We are trained in protecting people like you. Why wouldn't we want to have your back? And that's all we are doing.

You are going to have to do the FBI thing on your own. But this threat is a little different. It's not because you are a Lassiter. This threat is because someone wants to control your mind. That is something we as a country cannot allow. At this point, your last name could be Smith and the President would order exactly the same type of coverage."

Joshua took a step closer to Adam. "We happen to be the best this country has to offer. We are proud of that and you should be too. You have a big brain. Use it right now. You know your best chance of survival is with us."

Adam knew everything they were saying was right. They meant well, but he had to wonder if he would ever be able to lead the life he wanted. Or would he always be in the shadow of his brothers.

Adam nodded. "I'm going to change here. Would you give me a minute?"

"Sure," Samuel said as he watched Adam walk into the restroom. "Are we crowding him?"

"No," Joshua sighed. "Little brother has a lot on his shoulders. Always has."

"Who's after him, Joshua?"

Joshua shook his head. "I don't know, Sammy. I've checked with my intel in a number of countries and there is no chatter."

"You think it's internal?"

"It's been known to happen."

"All of this is about this J.M.A.L.T.S.?"

"No. I mean whoever is behind this wants the mind that created J.M.A.L.T.S."

Samuel leaned against the wall. "It's pretty cool he named it after us."

"What are you talking about?" Joshua frowned.

"Joshua, Mathew, Adam, Luke, Timothy and Samuel. J.M.A.L.T.S."

Joshua stared at Samuel. "I was wondering where he got that dumb name from." He laughed. "That's pretty ingenious."

Adam stepped back into the lobby dressed in a suit and tie. He joined his brothers as Joshua grinned from ear to ear. "You named the device after me."

"No, I named it after all of us."

"Yes, but my name is first," Joshua bragged as they walked out of the building.

"My name is last," Samuel retorted. "End with the best."

"It actually comes from the Book of Revelation. I am the Alpha and the Omega," Adam advised.

"Chapter 1 verse 8," Joshua acknowledged.

"You two are the Alpha and the Omega of the Lassiter family. Joshua is the beginning. Samuel is the end. The other brothers are in the middle to support the power the two of you possess. Together we are an unbreakable force called family. We are all inclusive of each other. You watch over us to ensure we are safe and secure. Nothing can penetrate that bond unless we allow it. J.M.A.L.T.S. is capable of doing the same thing. It watches over us. Yet, just like family, if we allow it to be penetrated by evil forces it can destroy."

His brothers stared at him in wonder. Samuel opened the back door of his SUV. "Then let's find the person who is threatening to penetrate our bond."

Joshua nodded as he climbed into the driver's seat. "Let's destroy them before they can destroy us."

A telephone on a home office desk rang. "He's leaving the grounds with two of his brothers."

"Any idea where they are going?"

"No. But the Deputy Secretary pulled him from class. Indicating he will be returning."

"Were there only two with him?"

"Yes, however, if you plan on taking him from those two, you better have a magnitude of firepower."

"I'll handle my end. You resume your duties." The call was disconnected.

The man pulled a cell from his pocket. "He is on the move. He will be outside the grounds for a while. Kill anyone who gets in your way. Remember, I want him unharmed." The man disconnected the call, then sat back in his chair grinning. Soon he would control one of the best minds in the world.

CHAPTER FOURTEEN

The Lassiter brothers made a statement when it was just Samuel and Joshua. With Adam added to the mix the female staff at the White House was helpless to the magnitude of raw swagger that was just a way of life for the men. They walked through the entrance oblivious to the racing hearts they were causing with their easy smiles and charming personalities.

"Good afternoon," Samuel spoke as they reached the gate.

"Hello, Samuel," the guard spoke. "The President is in the residence. He is expecting you." The man looked up. "Joshua." His tone changed from pleasant to cautious. "I trust all rooms in the building will remain intact during your visit."

Joshua reached for his visitor's badge. "I don't recall disturbing anything on my last visit."

"Your parents were with you. It was refreshing to see someone keep you under control." The man smirked. "Young Lassiter." The man nodded to Adam. "It is good to see you again."

Adam nodded. "Thank you, sir."

The guard smiled. "Impeccable manners." Then raised an eyebrow at Joshua.

As the men walked away, Samuel shook his head. "I wonder why you receive unhappy reactions from people everywhere we go?"

At that moment a woman walked out of the side entrance.

"Hello, Joshua." The perky blonde smiled shamelessly. "Gentlemen," she greeted as a second thought. "Mr. Thompson will be with you shortly."

"Hello, Susan," Joshua replied. "You are ravishing in that dress."

"This old thing." She blushed.

Joshua held the door open as he looked back at Samuel. "Not everyone is unhappy to see me."

"I wonder how Roc would greet the ravishing Susan if she was here," Adam whispered as he walked through the door.

"The same way she greets all the women from my past. With a very satisfied grin, indicating he is all mine now."

"More like an ass whipping indicating that." Samuel smirked.

"Hello." Another staffer appeared from around the corner. "I'll take them from here, Susan," she stated.

"Thank you for offering, Tammy, but I think we're good."

"Ladies, what are you doing?" Mrs. Langston asked from the doorway.

Nervously, Susan replied, "Showing the Lassiters to the residence."

"I'm certain they know the way," Mrs. Langston replied. "Please return to your duties."

"Yes, ma'am," the ladies responded, sending an embarrassed look over their shoulders at the men.

"Why do you have to cause confusion every time you walk into this building?" The men turned to see

Brian Thompson, the President's personal bodyguard and Samuel's boss.

"It's that animal magnetism. What can I say?" Joshua grinned.

Samuel shook his head. "Don't get him started. Where is the President?"

"In the residence," Brian replied as he began walking. "The President has been made aware of your situation. I'm afraid we are about to add a little more to your plate."

"Do you have some new intel?" Samuel asked.

Brian nodded as he opened the door to the residence.

"You want to take a moment to fill us in on what you have?" Joshua asked as he stepped inside.

Brian nodded. "Adam, why don't you have a seat in the sitting room. We'll join you in a moment."

Adam watched as the men walked off. "It's just my life. No need to include me," he said sarcastically to himself.

Adam walked into the pleasantly decorated room and was surprised it had a homey feel to it. By it being the personal sitting room for the President and the First Lady, he expected it to have that look, but a 'don't sit on the furniture' feel to it. But it didn't. Maybe because of the toys neatly placed in one corner of the room, or the book bag hanging on the arm of a chair. Or it could have been the little girl sitting in the corner swinging her legs back and forth that made the room welcoming.

He studied the little girl before approaching her. She was dressed in a sweater, jeans, with ankle length socks and sneakers. Her hair was in a single braided ponytail with a yellow ribbon to match her outfit.

"Hey, Gabby, " Adam greeted as he walked towards her.

"Hi." The little girl looked up at him. "You're Uncle Sammy's little brother."

"I am." Adam sat down in front of her. "My name is Adam."

"I'm a little sister but I'm not as big as you."

Adam smiled. "You will be one day."

She shrugged her shoulder as she picked up her tablet. "I can't get my game to work."

"Really?" He reached for it. "Let me take a look at it."

"Okay." She slid from her seat then walked over to him. She gave him the tablet.

Adam turned the tablet on then began to push some buttons.

"What you doing?"

"Adjusting the settings?"

"What are settings?"

"Settings are where you can tell the computer what you want it to do and how."

"Why?" the little girl asked as she crawled in the seat beside him.

Not thinking twice, Adam put his arm around her pulling her closer. "So the computer will work the way you want it to when you turn it on."

"How come it stopped working before?" She looked up with bright brown eyes.

"Sometimes it gets tired and needs to be recharged."

"Like my daddy."

Adam looked down at the little girl. "What's going on with your dad?"

She shrugged her shoulders. "He can't go to sleep."

"Your dad is a really smart man. He will figure things out. Don't you worry about that." He pulled her braid.

She giggled then sighed. "He yelled at my mommy."

That caused Adam to raise an eyebrow. "Parents yell at each other all the time."

"Not my daddy and mommy. Do that mean they're going to get a divorce?"

"No." Adam hugged her. "That just means that they had a disagreement, that's all."

"What's that?"

"A disagreement? Well, have one of your brothers ever taken something that belongs to you and you got mad?"

"Yes," the child replied sternly. "William takes my toys all the time and I yell at him."

Adam smiled. "Well, it's the same thing with your mom and dad. It doesn't mean that you don't love William anymore. You were just mad for a little while."

Gabby shook her head. "I don't know. My mommy told my dad that he better go take a nap before she loses her temper."

Adam smiled. "So you think if your dad takes a nap he would feel better?"

"Yep. I will feel better too and so will Mommy."

"Okay, I tell you what. I'll go in and talk with your dad and make sure he takes a nap."

The child's head jerked up. "Can you do that?" The big brown eyes of a child looked up at him and he could not say no.

"For you I can do anything. Which room is your dad in?"

"The library." Gabby pointed towards the room to her left.

Adam stood. "Okay." He gave the child her tablet. "You play with this. I'll be right back and when I come out your dad's going to take a nap."

"Okay." Gabby took the tablet and was thrilled when she saw it was working again.

Adam nodded to the agent standing next to the door. He knocked twice then walked through the door.

A few minutes later Samuel and Joshua walked back into the foyer area with Brian.

Samuel looked around then turned to Gabby. He bent down. "Hi, Gabby, did you see my brother?"

Gabby bobbed her head up and down. "Yes, he's right there." She pointed to Joshua.

Samuel smiled. "I meant Adam. Did you see where Adam went?"

"Un huh. He went to make Daddy take a nap."

Samuel stood and smiled down at the child. "He went to make your daddy take a nap?"

"Yep." She nodded as she looked up with the most sincere eyes. "Mommy told Daddy to take a nap. Daddy didn't do it. So Adam said he can make Daddy take a nap."

Joshua, who had been talking to Brian, suddenly stopped. He looked at the child first then slowly looked up at Samuel. They both shook their heads no.

"Gabby, what room is your daddy in?" Samuel asked.

"Did you bring Samantha to play with me?" she asked about Samuel's daughter.

"Gabby, where is your dad?" Brian asked, as he looked from Samuel to Joshua, not certain why he felt it was suddenly important to know.

"In the library."

Before the child could get the words out Joshua and Samuel took off running to the room. Brian followed.

The brothers burst into the room with Brian in tow. "Mr. President...Mr. President."

"What is it?" JD asked as he stood from the urgency in their voice. "What is it?"

Adam stood, ready to protect the President from whatever the threat may be. "What's going on?" he asked, responding to the urgency as well.

"Are you all right, sir?" Samuel asked as he stared intently at the man.

"I'm fine. What's going on?" JD looked at Brian.

Brian shrugged his shoulders. "I'm not certain." He glared at Joshua.

Joshua had grabbed Adam by the arm and was walking towards the door. The agent who was standing outside the room was now in the opening with his weapon drawn.

"Nothing important, sir," Samuel stated as he began to follow his brothers out the door. "We need Adam for a minute."

JD nodded, still uncertain about what was happening. "Adam," JD called out. "You have the full support of the White House in this situation. We regret placing you in this position. Rest assured we will protect you at all costs. As for the personal conversation, I appreciate your insight."

"Adam barely had time to say, "Anytime, Mr. President," Adam barely had time to say before he was pushed out of the room by Joshua.

Samuel closed the door just as Joshua pushed Adam in his chest causing him to land half way across the room. "Have you lost your damn mind?"

Adam looked up at his two older brothers, startled. "What are you talking about?"

With arms crossed over their chests, Samuel and Joshua glared at him.

"Did you just try to hypnotize the President?" Joshua snarled in a whisper so he could not be overheard.

"No, he didn't do that for that would be treason," Samuel all but yelled.

They looked around cautiously.

Adam stood, straightening his suit jacket. Without looking into his brothers' eyes, he stated, "Of course I didn't. I'm not stupid."

The brothers' stance relaxed.

"I simply administered a powerful suggestion to his subconscious."

The two were about to pounce on him when JD and Brian walked out of the library.

"Gentlemen, Brian stated he informed you of the latest intel we received."

"Yes, sir, he did," Samuel replied, clearly not focused on what the President was saying.

"I trust you know what is expected."

"We do, sir. We have him covered."

"Three, two, one," Adam said, then snapped his fingers.

"Get back with me in about an hour with your plan of action," JD stated as he rubbed the back of his neck. "I'm beat, man. I think I'll take a nap."

Gabby came back into the room holding her mother's hand. "That's them, Mommy. Uncle Sammy, Joshua and Adam were fighting."

Tracy looked up at the brothers then to JD and lastly to Brian. "What's going on?"

Brian frowned. "Why are you looking at me?"

"Because you are usually the one causing problems."

"Brian is fine, Babe," JD stated. "I don't know about those Lassiters, they have been acting strange. Whatever the problem." He yawned. "I'm too tired to deal with it at the moment." He yawned again. "I'm going to bed."

JD walked out of the room with the agent following.

"Thank goodness," Tracy said as she walked out of the room with Gabby in tow.

Brian stared at Samuel, then Joshua and lastly at Adam. "Either of you want to tell me what's happening here?"

"No." Joshua and Samuel both shook their heads.

Adam looked at the two and frowned. "The President indicated he had been having trouble sleeping. I gave him one or two suggestions to ease his subconscious into a relaxed state. It seems to be working." Adam smiled.

Samuel and Joshua held their breath praying Brian would not read too much into Adam's explanation.

"I don't know what in the hell you just said." Brian then turned to Samuel. "Control your brothers."

Samuel nodded. "I got them." He relaxed as they began following Brian out of the room.

CHAPTER FIFTEEN

When they reached the car, Joshua turned to Adam, who was sitting in the back seat. "You cannot go around hypnotizing people at will," he said through clenched teeth. "Especially the President of the United States. It is our duty to protect him from people like you." He adjusted the seat as he started the vehicle. "Do you realize what a predicament you just put us in?"

Adam looked out the window into the night. "I don't understand the problem. The man needs to sleep to be able to make the best decisions for this country. All I did was relax the man's mind."

The fact that Adam spoke so matter of factly told Samuel he had no idea that what he had just done would be considered a threat to the country. Joshua began to speak again, but Samuel put a hand on his arm to stop him.

"Adam." He spoke calmly. "Imagine someone with your power of persuasion, approaching the President in the same manner you did but instead of him suggesting he take a nap, they suggest he launch a nuclear weapon. What would you do?"

"Kill the perpetrator before he reached my President. But that was not my intent and I'm certain you both know that."

Joshua hit his hands against the steering wheel in frustration. "But you have the power to persuade him to do things. You cannot...cannot use those powers with The President."

"It's a moot point now," Adam voiced as he moved the clothes he had changed from to the side, then positioned himself in the middle of the seat. "The man is going to sleep for two hours, then start fresh. Now, you want to tell me what the new threat is or are we going to continue with the insults to my loyalty to this country and our President?"

Joshua glared at his younger brother through the mirror, as Samuel watched the passing traffic out the window. Inside, he was itching to laugh. For the frustration Joshua was feeling trying to deal with Adam's new position was the exact frustration he had had to go through with him. The word karma kept repeating through his mind.

"It seems we're not sure but it seems, some of our own people may be targeting you."

"Why and who?" Adam asked.

"The who we are not sure of," Samuel replied. "However, we aren't trusting anyone in our government at this point."

"The President indicated he believes some may want to attempt to corrupt my mind," Adam stated. "Is that what you think, Joshua?"

"I'm not going to lie to you, Adam." He glanced behind him. "Since J.M.A.L.T.S. has the ability to be weaponized, people are going to want to see what other things your brain can conjure."

"Big brains go for a premium in certain countries," Samuel added.

"Adam." Joshua's voice demanded his brother's attention. "We will give our lives before we allow anything to happen to you." He held Adam's glare through the mirror. "You know that."

Adam nodded for he knew, even if it wasn't for his big brain, his brothers would kill anyone who attempted to harm him or any other of their family members. "I know and I would do the same for you."

"Using your toy gun provided by the Bureau?" Joshua grinned trying to ease the tension.

"If need be." Adam returned the smile. "So how do we go about this? I'm assigned to the investigation on Dr. McCoy's death and I have my training."

"I agree with DD Nicolas, Quantico is the safest place for now," Samuel stated. "While Joshua searches for who is behind the second threat, I'll be on base with you as an instructor."

"Sammy." Adam slumped back in frustration. "You saw the impact your appearance created in class today. I need to do this on my own."

Samuel turned sharply. "I need to ensure you are capable of protecting yourself. Your pride is not my concern at the moment, your ass is."

They were all quiet for a moment. "Look," Joshua added, "I understand. I went through the same thing you are dealing with trying to be my own man with Samuel Lassiter as a big brother. It's not easy."

Joshua didn't notice when Samuel and Adam glanced at each other in disbelief. "You think that living up to Sammy is the problem? Do you even realize how many antics you have pulled working with the CIA?"

"Who? Me?" Joshua looked surprised. "Sammy is the one."

"Requesting activation," came the sexy female voice Joshua had programmed into his vehicle.

"Request granted. Hello, Genevieve?"

"Hello, Joshua. My sensors are picking up hostiles in the area. Shall I initiate defensive tactics?"

Joshua glanced out the side view mirror as Samuel did the same on his side. "Number of hostiles?"

"Two above, two vehicles four occupants each, trailing."

"Establish base line of blood pressure on each occupant of the vehicle," Adam instructed as he looked to the sky.

"Do you mind?" Joshua glanced at him.

"I'm just trying to ascertain the moment they intend to attack."

"Can you get a visual?" Samuel asked.

"Affirmative." A picture appeared on the console of the vehicle.

"Black SUV at three o'clock," Sammy advised as he checked the ammunition in his weapon.

"Show me the sky, Genevieve." The picture on the monitor changed. "I don't see it," Joshua said.

"Stealth mode," Adam said and Genevieve announced. "What are they doing, sending an army after me?"

That was exactly what was concerning Joshua. "I'm afraid so."

"This is my country that I just took an oath to protect. Oh hell no. Lock in, give visual," Adam ordered.

"Do you mind if I instruct my vehicle," Joshua hissed. "And this is not your country. Whoever it is has gone rogue. It's our duty to stop them."

"Radar locked," the vehicle complied.

"Genevieve, that order did not come from me."

"Confirmed, Joshua. My sensor indicates it came from the superior mind of Adam Lassiter."

"Ha ha," Joshua responded as he carefully watched the approaching vehicle.

"Things are not always black and white, Adam. You know there are good people and bad. We just happen to be going up against some of our own bad guys," Samuel said. "How do you want to play this?"

"Open field, try to outrun them like before. Get Adam back to the base."

"Not a good idea." Adam shook his head.

"Coming from the man with the limited field experience."

"You may be able to outrun the vehicle in an open field, but as you know a Black Hawk has the ability to lock in. In an open field, you are toast."

"I concur," Genevieve added.

"Okay, brainiac, what do you suggest?"

Adam thought for a moment. "Genevieve, find the closest abandoned building with a two or three level parking deck."

Joshua and Samuel glanced at each other.

"Confirmed. Setting coordinates for the location." Genevieve put the directions on the display.

"The cover of the parking deck will limit the visibility of the Hawk. The occupants will have to land it to participate in any combat. This will also eliminate the use of the Hawk's weaponry system. The concrete will block its radar's ability to lock in on us."

"We can battle one menace at a time." Sammy smirked.

"Good call, Adam." Joshua gave an appreciative nod.

"It's the superior mind at work."

Samuel laughed as Joshua groaned.

"It still puts three against eight."

As they took the exit leading into the city, Adam asked, "Either of you have an extra weapon?"

"Two against eight. You haven't taken firearm training," Samuel argued. "You stay in the car and keep your head down."

"What?" Adam yelled.

Joshua pulled into the parking deck of an abandoned office building. He made several turns before stopping on the third level. He and Samuel rushed out of the vehicle. Joshua pulled out a semi automatic, as Samuel pulled out an Uzi from the back of the SUV.

"Down!" Samuel ordered Adam.

"I'm going to tell Mom you left me in the car by myself."

Samuel slammed the backdoor of the SUV. They heard the vehicle when it entered the deck. Joshua pushed a button, the back panel in the SUV came up. "If they come towards the vehicle, slide in here. Genevieve, stealth mode protection."

"Affirmative."

"I can't believe you are locking me in the damn car," Adam complained.

"We'll talk about it after we save your life." Joshua closed the driver's door and in a flash he and Samuel were out of view.

Adam heard as the vehicle approached. They parked not a hundred feet from where Genevieve was parked in stealth mode. He heard as they called in reinforcements and knew Samuel and Joshua were in trouble. They had another vehicle of men on the other side of the building. His brothers would be sandwiched between them.

"Genevieve, can you activate your stealth mode functions?"

"With limited capabilities."

Adam huffed, "I'll have to change that. Give me a view of the surroundings."

"Activate."

Genevieve's monitor came to life. Adam observed as two men fell to the ground. The other two took shelter. He watched as one pulled a rope from his belt, swung it to the next level then climbed up, giving him a better view of his brothers, below.

"Shit," Adam exclaimed.

"My sentiments exactly," Genevieve announced.

"I have to go."

"Negative."

"Genevieve." He watched as the other man advanced beyond the column. "Deactivate stealth mode."

"Stealth mode deactivated."

"Check the vitals on the downed men."

"No vital signs."

"Good. Thank you, Genevieve. Give me specs on the weapons the men are carrying."

Genevieve began reading the base specs on the Glocks. "Skip, go to firing techniques."

"Got it. I'm going to get out."

"Watch your back," Genevieve replied.

Adam looked before exiting the vehicle from the back driver's side. He eased around the vehicle, checked for a pulse on the first soldier then grabbed his Glock from his holster. He did the same with the other soldier. And yes, they were US soldiers. He shook his head. He checked them for extra mags and placed them in his pocket. He ran back to Genevieve.

"Stealth mode."

He started the vehicle, glancing at the monitor as he drove in the direction of his brothers. He stopped when he saw they were pinned down behind a dumpster.

"Expand visual."

Genevieve complied. "Shall I arm?"

"No," Adam replied as he looked around. "What are those tanks behind my brothers?"

"Gas tanks to the Residential area on the left," Genevieve explained.

He thought for a moment. "Sometimes you just have to go raw. Cover my back, Genevieve."

"Affirmative."

He didn't stop to think or consider the danger to himself as he stepped out of the vehicle. He held the Glocks high, one in each hand. Walking quickly between his brothers and the soldiers he continuously fired, hitting two on his left and one on his right. Two men on the top of the parking deck took cover behind a column, then fired on him. Adam ducked, rolled onto his back then fired upwards taking them both out.

Suddenly the gunfire ended. The area was quiet. Adam rose slowly, looking in the direction of his brothers. "You good?" he asked Joshua who was staring at him in disbelief.

"Who in the hell do you think you are, walking in the line of fire like it's the OK corral with guns loaded?"

Ignoring his brother's rant, Adam kept his eyes searching around. "There's two more somewhere."

Samuel and Joshua both pulled up, shielding Adam between them. "Do you see them?"

"Negative," Samuel stated.

"Upper deck to your right," Adam answered.

"I got this." Joshua reached into his pocket, pulled out a small grenade and threw it to the upper level of the parking deck. He quickly turned, knocking Adam to the ground covering him with his body. Samuel covered Joshua's back.

Boom!

Samuel grabbed Joshua pulling him up by his coat as Joshua pulled Adam. The three ran towards Genevieve.

Genevieve pulled up with doors open. As soon as the men were inside, she closed the doors then accelerated out of the deck.

No one said a word until they were back on Quantico grounds. Joshua was the first to speak. "You are not superman," he yelled as he banged on top of the vehicle. "Bullets don't bounce off, they go through your body. And those white pipes behind us were gas tanks. That's why we were not firing back. If you had hit that it would have wiped out the entire block. What in the hell were you thinking?"

"I don't know about then, but right now I'm thinking that it's a damn good thing I didn't miss."

"What the hell do you mean? You don't even know how to fire a weapon."

"I beg to differ, Joshua. I just took out six men. It really wasn't that difficult," Adam said in an amazed voice. "I took in the position of the men, the travel distance of the bullet when propelled from the Glock and the wind velocity. Then I pulled the trigger. I was surprised there was a little kickback from the weapon. I'm going to have to note that. I'm sure there's got to be a way to eliminate that."

"Adam!" Joshua was furious. "Stop thinking with your brain for a minute. Men were firing real bullets. They did not have to do all the bull you just mentioned, they simply fired."

"Why are you so upset? Genevieve had my back."

Samuel was laughing so hard by the time Joshua looked at him he could not control himself. The look of disbelief on Joshua's face was priceless. "I can't wait to tell Roc about this."

Joshua kicked Genevieve to keep from hitting Adam. "Get inside the building," Joshua yelled at him, then he looked at Samuel. "What in the hell do you find so hilarious?"

Samuel stood, wiping his eyes. "I knew one day God would pay you back for all the hell you put me through when you joined the agency." He hit Joshua on the shoulder and began laughing again. "Damn I miss this. I haven't had that much fun in years."

Adam looked at Samuel throwing his hands in the air. "Boo yah!" He grinned. "I aim to please." He walked toward the dorm building with Samuel next to him.

Joshua stared at their backs as he took Adam's clothes from the back seat. "Boo yah my ass," he said, trying hard to hide his smile. "Damn, he's going to be good."

CHAPTER SIXTEEN

Amber looked up from the computer where she had been making notes on the device. There was something off with the serial numbers. She wasn't sure what. Amber shrugged it off. She thought the finding was significant enough to share with Adam, so she would wait and mention it to him when he returned.

The thought of him caused her to look up. It was close to midnight. Was he going to return? Why should he? she thought. He may have gone to his room after class. There was no reason for him to stop by here. She stood, stretched and then began pacing.

"Getting restless, Doc?" Kalli asked from the adjoining room.

"No...Yes," Amber replied. "Have you heard anything from Dr. Lassiter or Brent?"

"Brent checked in about an hour ago. He's doing some research so he's in for the night."

Amber waited. When Kalli said nothing further, she asked, "And Dr. Lassiter?"

"Funny you should ask." Kalli got up from the bed then walked around the corner, leaned against the wall that separated them, to see Amber glance up with a questioning gaze. "There's some chatter regarding gunfire not far from the White House."

"The White House? Adam wasn't at the White House, he went to PT training here on the grounds."

"It seems he was summoned to the White House a few hours ago."

"But my father's orders were explicit," she spoke in a voice laced with concern. "He indicated it would not be safe for either of us to leave the grounds."

"I'm afraid your father's orders do not supersede those of the President."

"I did not mean to insinuate they did," Amber replied. "I wasn't aware the President had summoned Adam." She spoke hesitantly. "Did something break in the case?"

"Not that we are aware of," Kalli replied as she watched Amber. "Did you find something in your notes?"

"More questions than answers I'm afraid." Amber changed the subject. "You stated there was gunfire. Is Adam okay?"

Kalli noted how the name changed from Dr. Lassiter to Adam. "There were a number of bodies found at the site, however, there has been no identification at this time."

"People are dead?"

"Yes." There was a knock on the door. Kalli drew her weapon, pointing to Amber. "Step back," she whispered as she stood to the side of the door.

"Amber, it's Adam," the voice called out.

The relief Amber felt hearing his voice was evident to Kalli as she opened the door.

The man who appeared in the doorway was a complete contrast to the man who left there earlier in the day. This man was dressed in a dark suit, shirt and tie that looked like he'd stepped out of a "Men's Style" magazine. He leaned against the door staring at Amber.

"You clean up well, Mr. Lassiter," Kalli commented. The man never glanced her way. Her head turned from him to Amber. The look between Adam and Amber was so intense, Kalli had to fan herself. "You two need to get a room." Kalli grabbed her phone. "You have one hour," she said as she walked out.

Adam stepped inside then closed the door behind him. He leaned wearily back against it. "I killed several men tonight."

Amber gasped as he spoke.

"I never took an oath, but my life has always been about saving lives, not taking them."

There was a force pulling her towards him. This wasn't sexual as it was earlier in the day. This was something different, something deeper. Her heart was crying from the hurt she could sense he was feeling. She walked slowly towards him. "Were they trying to kill you?"

"No." He looked up at her. "They were trying to kill my brothers."

She wrapped her arms around his neck pulling him away from the door. Adam's arms circled her waist as his head fell in the crook of her neck. His weariness from the day was easing in the comfort of her arms, but it wasn't enough to take away the vision of the men who fell to the ground from his actions. Nor did it erase the memory of how simple it was for him to pull the trigger. Instinctively he knew exactly what to do in the situation and that puzzled him.

"It sounds like you saved your brothers' lives," she whispered in his ear. "That takes precedence over anything else." She took his hand. "Come sit with me for a while."

Adam unbuttoned his suit jacket then joined her on the floor where they sat earlier.

Amber entwined her fingers with his. "If those men were pointing weapons at your brothers it was your duty to protect them. That's what family does, protect each other." She hesitated then began to tell him a story. "I killed a man once. It wasn't deliberate. But somehow it doesn't matter how or the reason why it happened. It certainly doesn't change the fact that I took someone's life."

Adam sat up at her words. Her head was down and looking away from him as she spoke.

"During a certain point in his career my father was gone a lot. My mother would only say he was working for the government, but I never knew in what capacity until I was much older. It seemed like my father was a voice on the other end of the telephone for years because he was away from home for so long. I graduated from high school when I was sixteen so during my freshman year of college, I couldn't go to places like my roommate or other freshmen could. Normally I would just stay in the dorm and study, but this particular weekend this sophomore guy had hurt my feelings by going out with my roommate even though he knew I liked him. So that Friday after class, I drove home which was about forty-five minutes away at that time. In hindsight, it was clear something was wrong in the house when I pulled up, but..." She shrugged then continued. "I paid no attention to it. But the moment I walked into the house a feeling of unease came over me. For some reason, I didn't call out to my mother like I would normally do. I stood in the mudroom and just listened. When I heard the first sound of my mother being hit, I froze. I knew my father would never harm my mother so that meant an intruder was in the house. The more I listened, I could tell the man was trying to get information about my father from my mother. I knew where my father's gun was in the study, so as quietly as I could I made my way there. I pushed the silent alarm next to the safe, then pulled the gun from the top bookshelf, loaded it then walked up the back staircase. When I reached my parents' bedroom, my mother was tied to a chair. Her face was bruised. Blood was running from her nose, and..."

Tears began to run down her cheeks. Adam wiped them away with his finger then squeezed her hand. "What happened?"

Amber inhaled as she wiped her other cheek with her free hand. She swallowed then continued. "I raised the gun, pushed the release then told the man to step away from my mother. He turned, surprised to see me standing there, then he looked at the gun and grinned. He told me 'You should never point a gun unless you are ready to kill. Are you ready to kill, little girl?' I told him to step away from my mother again. My mother cried out but the sound was muffled from the tape covering her mouth. I took my eye off the man for a split second to look at my mother and he lunged at me. The gun fired as we fell to the floor. It seemed like minutes passed away as the man laid there on top of me. Finally, I pushed him away. I stared at him lying there for the longest time until my mother's muffled cries penetrated my mind. I ran over and untied her, then wrapped my arms around her, crying. She pulled me up, put one of her coats on me and told me to leave the house. She gave me a number to call then told me to go back to school and tell no one what happened here. She said if anyone asked tell them you went to a free movie off campus. But I was to tell no one I came home."

"What did you do?"

"Exactly what my mother told me. I went back to my dorm room, crying hysterically every mile. When I arrived, Uncle Royce was there waiting for me. He put me in his vehicle while another man drove my car. I never saw that car or that house again."

She took a moment, then exhaled. "I have no idea why I told you that story." She shook her head. "It's the first time I've allowed myself to go back to that night."

Adam pushed a curl from her face. Then used his finger to turn her face to his. "You saved your mother's life."

She nodded her head. "I know. That doesn't change the fact that I took a man's life in the same way you saved your brothers' lives tonight." She tilted her head. "The hurt from taking a life never goes away. We learn to live with the fact, but we also triumph every time we save a life. It's a give and take, Adam. We can't be the good guys without taking the lives of the bad guys."

Adam held her eyes. "Are you deliberately trying to make me fall in love with you?"

Amber pulled back. "What? No," she said with an indignant wipe of another tear that had fallen. "Why would you say such a thing?"

"Are we about to argue again?" Adam asked with a grin.

"Yes, if you are going to say indecent things."

"Good." He smiled.

"What do you mean good?"

He shrugged. "Your actions today have proven each time we argue there is a more tantalizing kiss that will follow."

Amber glared at him, appalled. "I share something with you I have never shared with another human being and your reaction is to see the physical benefit for you?" She reared back on her heels.

"No..."

She cut him off. "Did it occur to you that I was sharing that story to ease your burden?" Her eyes narrowed.

"Yes, but I...." She cut him short again.

"Do you have any idea how devastating taking a life could be for someone like you if it is not addressed properly?" She stood as she crossed her arms over her chest.

This time Adam did not attempt to respond. He sat there and watched as she paced above him. His father once told him when it came to women it was imperative to know when to shut the hell up and let them have their say. Adam's gut was telling him this was one of those times.

"Answer me, Adam Fitzgerald Lassiter."

"The whole name, huh? I must have hit a nerve." He reached up, grabbed her arm, then yanked her down onto his lap.

A small scream escaped her as she fell to the floor.

"May I now have a moment to speak?"

There was that look in his eyes again. The one she had come to recognize as his, 'I've reached my limit' look. "Are you going to kiss me again?"

"Yes." It was a simple, blunt reply.

Amber thought about that as she stared at him. "Very well. Speak."

Adam smiled. "I'm not upset about taking the men's lives tonight. I'm concerned with how easy it was for me to do it. I've held guns in my hand before, but I have never fired one. Never took target practice or any type of weapons training. Yet, I handled those guns as if it was an every day occurrence."

"That doesn't surprise me. You are a highly intelligent being. You knew to calculate the time and distance of your targets."

"It takes constant practice to become proficient with firearms. I haven't had that and I'm telling you, I hit those men with pinpoint accuracy. I took the kill shot. It scares me that I could do it so easily." He frowned.

Amber could feel his confusion and wasn't sure how to help him. "I'm sensing you feel compromised in some way."

Adam nodded. "I always wanted to create in order to save lives. In the last twenty-four hours my invention killed one man whom I admired and at least two other men have died at my hands." He closed his eyes. "That's not my life. At least, it's not what I want it to be."

"What is it that you want?" She licked her bottom lip.

Adam wondered if she knew her involuntary reaction to wanting to be kissed was the licking of her lips. He could feel her heart rate increase from his stare. He swallowed as his eyes held hers. "What's happening with you and Pierce?"

She hesitated then decided to be honest. "We've had a teasing relationship. Nothing more."

"Are you sure?"

Amber nodded. "Yes."

Adam exhaled. "Then what I want to do more than anything is kiss you until you wonder if you're going to die in the next moment if I don't stop...and feel you will die the moment that I do."

Her breath caught in her chest. "I want that too," she whispered, gazing into his eyes.

His lips had just touched hers when the door opened.

"That's an interesting way of sharing information."

Amber scrambled to get up from Adam's lap as Kalli walked back into the room. She was frazzled and couldn't understand why standing was so difficult. Then she realized Adam was holding her in place.

"Will you let me go?"

"No," he replied. "I like you here."

"It's not proper," she declared.

"It was a second ago."

"Well, it's not now."

"Why not?"

Amber's skin flushed as she attempted to get Adam to release her. "Someone else is in the room," she whispered.

"And?"

She stared wide-eyed at him.

He looked up at Kalli. "What information?"

"Something about the serial number."

Adam glanced at Amber who was still trying to break free of him. "You found a code?"

She huffed. "I don't know if it's a code-code but I don't think the numbers Brent took from the device are a serial number." She glared at him. "Will you release me?"

"Why?"

She sighed. "Because I want to get up."

"I don't want you to," Adam replied as Kalli smiled at the two. "Why don't you think it's a serial number?"

Amber stopped fighting, then began scowling at him. "There's something about the numbers."

"What about them?"

"Will you let me up?"

"I will. What about the numbers?"

"Most serial numbers have a mixture of numbers and letters. The letters usually indicate a state or manufacturing location."

"Brent stated he had no luck so far with that number," Kalli added.

"You built the original, right?" Amber asked Adam.

"Yes."

"When you sold it, whom did you deal with on the sale?" Kalli asked.

"McGarry. From the DOD."

"Then he should know who they hired to build the transmitters," Amber suggested. "Simply contact him and ask."

"I'll contact Brent to let him know to try that angle." Kalli stepped into the other room.

"Adam, let me go," Amber whispered quietly.

"Okay." Before granting her request, Adam's lips covered hers completely by surprise, consuming every inch of her lips, her tongue, her mouth. The kiss was so juicy, he licked her lips until he had taken every drop. He released her then watched as her eyes opened. The smoldering look caused him to kiss her again, this time it was as soft as silk, yet as satisfying as a full round of love making. "You're like a narcotic, Amber Nicolas. One taste and I'm hooked."

"I'm not myself when you are around." Amber said in a breathless tone. "You put me under a spell."

He kissed her temple. "I believe it is the only time you are you."

She frowned. "What do you mean by that?"

"Are we about to argue again?" Adam smiled.

"You are incorrigible." Amber stood with his assistance. "Out."

"Now you are throwing me out." He dropped his head. "After the day I've had."

Amber glanced at Kalli, who smiled, shaking her head. "Go to your room. We'll talk tomorrow."

"Good night, gorgeous." He closed the door behind him.

Kalli watched the blush come over Amber's face. "Doc, I believe you have been hypnotized by Dr.

Lassiter," Kalli commented. "My only question is where does that leave Brent?"

CHAPTER SEVENTEEN

It was four in the morning when a message popped up on his FBI issued computer. Adam, half asleep, turned toward the sound, pulled his pillow out then covered his head to block it out. The weird music from the message became increasingly louder every ten seconds. Adam sat up, wiped his face. He moved to the desk then opened his laptop.

"What's going on?" Flex asked from the opening between the two rooms.

"Not sure," Adam replied as he pulled up the email. Adam knew better than to click on unsolicited emails so he shut the computer down. He stood to return to bed, but the laptop turned itself back on. Adam stared at it, then lifted the top again. The message appeared across his desktop.

'Responsible rebellion unifies a perfect government of redeeming faith.'

"What does that mean?" Flex asked.

Adam looked over his shoulder to see Flex standing there. He turned back to the computer. "I have no idea."

"Who did it come from?"

"I don't know that either," Adam replied as he hit a few keystrokes on the keyboard. "That's what concerns me."

"Why?"

"It's a secured computer issued by the Bureau. No one should be able to get into it."

"Looks like someone did." Flex yawned. "Check the IP address."

"In the process of doing it now," Adam answered as he watched a series of numbers populate the screen.

"Longitude and latitude for Alexandria, VA."

Adam glanced at Flex and grinned. "That's right."

"You look surprised, Lassiter. I didn't get here on my good looks, you know."

"You would have never made it if that was the case."

"Ha, ha," Flex groaned.

Adam sighed. He was tired, but he also knew the depth a person had to go to in order to hack into an FBI computer to leave a cryptic message. He clicked a few keys and entered the program of the computer.

"Whoa, I don't think you should be doing that."

"Whoever hacked in shouldn't be doing that either. How do you think we will find out who it is if we don't follow his trail?"

"Turn it over to Vanderbilt. He'll know what to do."

"That will take hours." Adam shrugged. "Why do that when we can figure it out right here." He sat forward when the location he needed popped up. "There you go," he said as he continued to click keys. "Now who are you?"

Flex raised an eyebrow, then leaned further over Adam's shoulder. "You have an address. How in the hell did you do that?"

"Just about any true computer geek can do this."

"You are a science geek, not a computer geek."

"I'm a geek, period."

"Damn," Flex said as he watched Adam pull up surveillance video of the location he found. He pulled up the chair from his desk then sat backwards leaning over the top, watching as Adam worked. "Hey, that's the Cyber Cafe right outside of headquarters."

"I know." Adam continued to push keys.

"The Cafe has been closed since midnight. The message had to have been keyed then scheduled to go out at four in the morning." He yawned. "What are you looking for?"

"I have no idea. But if I keep watching the feed something might pop out at me."

"Like what?" Flex asked as he pulled his tablet and stylus from his desk.

"What are you doing?"

"If you can do that, I'm certain you have access to face recognition software. As you match the names, I'll do a search on them to see what we can find." He shrugged. "Who knows, we might be able to crack this 'secret' case you're working on and get on with our training."

"You're willing to help me?"

"I discovered two things about you today. One, you are not trying to skate by on your brothers' reputation. Two, more important than one, you are not trying to horn in on my woman."

"Who?"

"Karen."

Adam laughed as he turned back to his computer. "You can't handle that."

"Watch me."

"Yeah, I'll watch her hurt you."

"Hurt me, hurt me," Flex sang out. The two laughed. "So, does this message have something to do with what you are working on?"

Adam shrugged, somewhat perplexed by the message himself. "That I don't know. What I do know is the message came from a computer at this location. It was keyed in and stored at 4:50 pm on yesterday."

"Each computer in that location has an independent IP address. Lock in on that computer and we should see the person leaving the message."

Adam opened his personal computer. He pulled up a program, locked into the IP address they were working from then hit enter. "Done," Adam stated, then went back to the FBI issued computer. "Check the surveillance camera for that 4;50 timeframe."

While Flex checked Adam's personal computer to search for the person, Adam was tracking the FBI computer to determine who hacked in.

Twenty minutes later Flex turned the computer to Adam. "This is your man."

Adam studied the picture.

"Do you know him?" Flex asked.

"No," he sighed. "We're not going to find him in the facial recognition system."

"Why not?"

"That's a disguise."

Flex looked at the picture then back to Adam. "How do you know?"

"I know." Adam glanced at the clock. It was close to 5:00 am. "Let's start removing the layers." Adam clicked a few keys to adjust the picture of the man on the computer. "Let this run. I have a date."

Flex glanced at the clock on his desk. "At 5:30 in the morning?"

"Yep," Adam replied as he jumped in the shower.

Ten minutes later Adam was knocking on Amber's door. Kalli answered dressed in the traditional black pant suit and white blouse, sensible heels.

"You're a little late. I'm afraid Brent beat you to the punch." She checked her watch. "They are probably on the second round by now." She sipped from her coffee cup.

"How many laps does she normally take?"

"I have no idea. This is my first full day on her." Kalli left the door open as she walked back to the desk. "I'm sure Brent can tell you."

Adam caught her look. "How long have you two been partners?"

"About three years."

"Hmm, you two remained partners after you told him. That's pretty good."

Kalli sat up a little straighter. "What do you mean?"

Adam closed the door then stood next to the desk. "He continued to partner with you after you told him you are in love with him."

Kalli froze as she glanced at him over her cup. She looked away as she sipped then set it down. "Is that wishful thinking so you will have a clear path to the Doc?"

"My path isn't blocked, not by Brent. They are too much alike." He shook his head. "No. My analysis is based on observation. Each time you mention his name, your eyes soften a bit, your heart rate runs a little higher. I can also tell by the vein in your neck. You show signs that you like Amber, but she is the woman who has Brent's attention. So from time to time the inflections in your voice changes when speaking to or about her. But don't worry. Once he clears his mind of Amber, he'll recognize it too."

"I don't recall asking for your thoughts on my love life."

"Or lack of." He stepped away. "But hey, I have my own matters of the heart to deal with."

"A person would have to be deaf, dumb and blind not to see the Doc is hot for you."

Adam shook his head. "I don't like her being in the middle of this investigation."

"I think she can handle her own."

Adam thought for a moment then leaned against her desk. "You mentioned a code last night."

"Oh I get it. You can get all up in my personal life, but when it comes to you the topic is off limits."

"I was all in there, wasn't I?"

"Yes, you were." Kalli took another sip of her coffee. "As for the numbers, I'm sure the Doc will fill you in when she returns."

He glanced at his watch. "Which should be in five, four, three, two..." The door opened.

Kalli shook her head laughing as Amber and Brent walked through the door.

Adam grinned. "Predictable."

"Good morning, Adam." Amber smiled. "Did you get some rest?"

"Good morning, gorgeous. You look like a redbird with your cheeks all flushed, and your red nose."

Amber laughed. "That's funny. That's exactly what my parents call me." She looked towards Brent only to see he was frowning at Adam. "I'll..um..go take my shower."

"Yes." Adam checked his watch. "You'll be late if you continue to stand here talking." He nodded to Brent. "Morning, Special Agent Pierce. You're out of uniform."

Amber gave him a knowing look. "Adam, behave yourself," she warned as she walked out of the room. "You too, Brent," she called out behind her.

"What are you doing here, Lassiter?"

"Working on the case. And you?"

"The same. Amber tells me the numbers may not be a serial number. Not that you would have noticed since your mind is only on Amber's attributes."

"They are rather tempting." He grinned.

Brent hissed, "I received a response to my request on the number, but The DOD wasn't very helpful."

"It was ambiguous at best."

Brent raised an eyebrow. "Yes it was. You read it?"

"You sent it. I read it. Did you notice who the response came from."

Brent nodded. "McGarry. Did that seem off to you?"

"Why would McGarry respond to an inquiry regarding a serial number?" Kalli asked. "Didn't he retire?"

"That is the question curious minds need answered." Adam winked at her.

"How well do you know him?" Brent asked Adam.

"He handled the J.M.A.L.T.S. negotiations for the government while he was still in office."

"He knows all the capabilities of J.M.A.L.T.S.?"

"No." Adam shook his head.

"Why not?"

"I didn't like him."

Brent gave Adam an incredulous look. "You can't deny the government information."

"Sure you can if you have something they want," Adam replied as his cell phone buzzed. "Lassiter." He listened. "I'll be right there." Adam disconnected the call then opened the door to walk out.

"Lassiter, do you think McGarry is involved in this?"

"I don't know, but we'll get to him. This is more important. We got a hit."

"A hit on what?" Brent asked Adam's back as he followed him to the next room. "You're next door to Amber?"

Adam walked into his room. Flex was sitting at his computer. "Who do we have?"

"Jack Dalton," Brent said from over his shoulder.

"Right," Flex replied as he looked over his shoulder. "Special Agent Pierce." He looked the man up and down. "You're out of uniform."

"Your point?"

"Nothing." Flex glanced briefly at Adam. "Who's Jack Dalton?"

"Pretend you never heard that name," Brent said. "Lassiter, outside." Brent motioned towards the door. "What have you told Lander?"

Adam stepped out. "Nothing. He knows nothing about the investigation."

"Keep it that way. I'm going to change clothes and check out Dalton. Meet me in Amber's lab at seven."

"Flex?" Adam walked back into the room, sat in his chair and waited.

"Jack Dalton, age forty-seven, married, wife Corinne thirty-eight, three children, Jack Jr, fourteen, Stephanie, ten, and Peter, seven. Worked with Allied Computer Systems, Western Pharmaceuticals and Jordan Chemicals before joining the DOD six years ago. Annual reviews with each company listed similar traits. Lack of drive, on one, needs consistent motivation to perform on another, the last from the DOD, Dr. McCoy, No initiative. Does not think outside of the box. Self-contained'."

Adam nodded. "Where is he now?"

"Last signal for his GPS indicates he was at his residence in Fairfax."

"What else do you have?" Adam leaned against the desk.

"How did you know I had anything?"

"For one, you are nosey. A good trait for an investigator, but lousy for friendships. Two, each time you keyed into my computer it sent me a message."

"I prefer curious." Flex grinned. "I couldn't help but notice you did not tell Special Agent Pierce you suspected I had more information."

"Pierce is good. He'll find out everything you tell me before he gets to Dalton's house."

"Okay, there is one more thing." Flex could barely contain the excitement as he pulled his chair closer to Adam.

Sensing Flex was on to something, Adam leaned in closer.

"I kept looking at the message. To me it reads as if someone has something against the government and wants them to redeem the faith that has been lost. The more I looked into Dalton, the more he fit the pattern. The word redemption made me think in biblical terms."

Adam nodded as he followed Flex's train of thinking. "There are several passages in the Bible that refer to redemption. To my recollection that message isn't one."

"No, but what if it's a combination of several."

Adam let that play around in his mind for a minute. "There are many versions of the Bible."

"Yes and guess who's an expert on all things biblical?"

Adam raised an eyebrow.

"Your boy Clive."

Adam sat back. "We can't bring anyone else in on this. As it is you know too much."

"He doesn't have to know why the information is needed. Which would be easy since I have no idea what in the hell is going on. We could give him the passage and ask his opinion on its meaning."

Adam stood. "I'll think on it. In the meantime, do not mention this to anyone. We will both be put out of the academy for conducting an unauthorized investigation if anyone finds out about it." He then wiped the information from the Bureau's computer, but saved it on his. "I have to change for this meeting. I'll meet you in class at nine." He walked toward his bed, then stopped. "Flex, thank you."

"I got your six." Flex grinned.

Precisely at seven am, Adam knocked on the door of Amber's lab with his computer in hand. Brent and Ned looked up as Amber pushed the button. He shook his head when she was about to speak. He waited for the door to close then held up his computer to survey the room. He nodded when all was clear.

"I created a tracker on my way over." He walked over to her computer. "I'm installing it on your computer." He pulled out a small disk.

"You created something while walking over here?" Brent threw Adam an incredulous look.

"Is it a sensory program?" Ned asked.

Adam nodded. "Yes. It will detect any foreign item that enters this room." He pointed to the computer. "See that light?" He glanced at Amber. "It will blink if something is detected. It will also emit a piercing sound like this." He pushed a button. "Did you hear it?"

Amber nodded. "Yes."

"I didn't hear it."

Adam turned to Brent. "Close your eyes."

"What's with the eyes thing?"

"Close your eyes."

Brent huffed, then complied. "Clear your mind. Then listen."

Brent stopped frowning then did as Adam requested. Slowly he began to hear the sound. Surprised, his eyes flew open. "I heard it."

"Good. I'm sending this to you in a message. Download it to your phone. And Brent, right now you don't have the ability to pick up on the device so I put an extra sensor in the message I sent to you. If the device comes within fifty feet of you the sensor will pick it up and send an alarm."

Brent stared at Adam a bit confused. "You looking out for me?"

"I got your six just as I'm certain you have mine."

Amber smiled. "That was nice, Adam. Thank you."

Ned nodded. "Good move, Lassiter. Pierce was just telling us about Jack Dalton. What are your thoughts?"

"He's a good suspect with something to prove. On his last performance evaluation Dr. McCoy stated some damaging concerns for a scientist. Dalton's motive could be to prove Dr. McCoy and the government were wrong about him."

"You hacked into the DOD's computer system?" Brent glanced up from his phone.

Adam started to answer then thought twice. He did not want to implicate Flex in any way. That would jeopardize his standing with the agency. "A man's got to do what a man's got to do."

"Lassiter, that's a federal offense," Brent warned.

"We're trying to locate a traitor to our country," Ned cautioned. "We take any means necessary to accomplish our mission."

Brent's sense of loyalty to the Bureau caused him to take pause for a moment. "There are laws in place for a reason. We can't just step over them."

"To protect the country we can do just about anything," Adam countered.

Amber added, "I have to agree with Brent on this one. Laws are in place for a reason. We have to abide by them."

Ned and Adam glanced at each other, both thinking how naive some people can be. "It won't happen again." Adam turned to Brent. "But you have to admit, the information will help to get you a probable cause warrant to search his house."

"As an agent I can't use the information if I know it was obtained illegally." Brent shrugged his shoulder. "I'll figure out a way around it."

"I'd like to join you." Adam stood.

"You have class at nine." Brent turned to Amber. "Kalli was called into the office. Are you going to be okay until she gets back?"

"I'll be here." Adam grinned.

"That's not very comforting."

"We'll both be here, waiting on word from you regarding an arrest," Ned replied.

"Be careful, Pierce, he may not go down without a fight," Adam cautioned. "And scientists do not fight with guns. You get my meaning?"

Brent nodded. "I'll keep that in mind, Lassiter."

The two held eye contact until Brent turned and walked out. "He's not a bad guy," Adam said as he turned to Amber. "Just not the man for you."

"I realize that," Amber replied.

"Do you?" Adam questioned. "If Dalton is our guy this case could be over. You will be returning home to your routine life with Captain America."

"Captain America, as you call him, is not a part of my routine. As for me returning to my life, I'm okay with that."

"Ah, but your eyes just gave you away. I don't think you like your life as it is. In any event, you will miss the excitement I bring each day."

"I believe the last two days have given me enough of a supply to last for a while."

"I think the lady doth protest a bit too much. What say you, Ned?"

"I think you are as incorrigible as your brother when it comes to women," Ned replied, not taking his eyes from the note on the desk. "Did either of you come up with any thoughts on this series of numbers?"

CHAPTER EIGHTEEN

Adam and Amber turned to Ned.
"The combination keeps calling out to me." Ned looked up as if in thought. "What caused you to question them," he asked Amber.

"Usually serial numbers indicate something regarding the state it was manufactured in or the facility, something to give credit to the designer. There was nothing but numbers."

"Numerology could be at play here." Ned shrugged.

"What about biblical numerology?" Adam added.

"What about it?"

"A message was sent to my bureau issued computer this morning. We all know the security on the bureau computers is as tight as they come, yet someone was able to hack into it and send that message. We traced the IP address to a café outside of the grounds and found a picture of the person who sent it. That's what led us to Dalton."

"What kind of message was it?" Amber asked.

Adam pushed a button on his computer. Then turned it towards them.

'Responsible rebellion unifies a perfect government of redeeming faith.'

"Sounds as if someone is planning a rebellion," Amber stated.

Ned looked at the message. "If that's the case we will see that message again and again. When someone has a cause they want people, in this instance the government, to know about it. Have we seen the phrase anywhere before now?"

Amber thought. "Not that I can recall."

"What if it's in another format?" Adam snapped his fingers then pulled up the numbers on his computer. He stared at the numbers for a long time. Then he grinned. "What's the 10th letter in the alphabet?"

Amber looked up as if thinking. "J," she replied.

Adam looked from her to Ned and smiled. "What's the 13th letter?"

"M," Ned responded as he pulled something up on his tablet. "No, it can't be that simple." He shook his head.

Adam nodded. "The first letter of the alphabet is A. How much do you want to bet L is the 12th, T is the 20th and S is the 19th?"

"The son of a bitch is playing with us." Ned grinned.

"He spelled out J.M.A.L.T.S. with numbers." Amber frowned. "Who is this guy?"

"I don't know." Adam's eyebrow rose. "I'll double that those numbers correspond to this message in some way."

"If you still think it's biblical I'll take a run at decoding it."

Adam smiled at Amber just as his alarm on his watch sounded. "I do believe you are after my heart." He stood, taking her face into his cupped hands, then kissed her as if he was going off to war. The kiss affected him more than he wanted to admit. He took a step back staring at her lips then up at her. "I have class," he said as he licked his lips. Never taking his eyes from hers, he released a small rush of breath. "Keep working on those numbers." He walked to the door, glancing back at Amber. "You are going to miss my spontaneity, Redbird." With that he was gone.

"He may have something to this number theory. Look at this, Dr. Nicolas."

Still reeling from the kiss, Amber sighed. "Are you this unfazed by the things people do around you all the time?"

Ned looked up at her. "When you have worked with Joshua Lassiter, nothing, I do mean nothing, surprises you anymore."

Amber raised an eyebrow. "His brother would just up and kiss women with no warning around you?"

"Kiss?" Ned looked at her dumfounded. "I've witnessed him making love to them on the desk, floor, a wing of a plane, wherever the urge strikes him."

"And they let him?" Amber asked, appalled.

"It's as if they enter into a different world when Joshua is around." Ned turned back to the numbers. "I suspect Adam Lassiter's adventures will go far further than his brother's in many ways. However, I believe you have captured his heart."

"Really?"

Ned looked up from the computer. "You seem to doubt that."

"I...well." She hesitated. "We are so different."

"On the contrary, Doc Nicolas, you and Adam Lassiter are one kindred spirit. The only question I have is which of you is going to screw it up before you get it right?"

"We may not screw anything up, if we both approach it logically."

Ned smiled. "For two days Adam has been trying to tell you that life is not about being logical. It is about living. Logic limits possibilities. Adam is a free spirit who has been enamored for the first time in his life. I admire his gusto to go for it." He sighed at Amber. "I believe you will soon discover Adam's openness is not that of an immature man, as you have accused him. But simply a man who hasn't learned the art of bullshit."

He turned back to the computer as Amber first gaped at his words, but then let them sink in. She sat in the chair in front of her computer with Ned beside her. "He's been telling me from day one about his feelings and I've been criticizing his honesty."

"You have."

Amber took a deep breath. She had been so used to men approaching her in the conventional way with a bunch of crap that never fazed her. Here Adam was very blunt in his delivery and she criticized. "I'll fix it."

"I'm certain you will," Ned replied as he smiled inside. "Now, let's concentrate on these numbers."

Joshua opened the door and slid in beside Monique before she could punch him. Catching her fist with his hand, he smiled. "Doing a little surveillance work on the side?"

"You almost lost your life a moment ago," Monique huffed as she looked around. "Where did you come from?"

"McGarry. And you?"

"Ashton."

"You want to tell me why?"

"Is this an 'I'll show you mine if you show me yours' moment?"

Joshua shrugged. "More like I know you are not on an assignment concerning my brother and did not tell me."

Monique sighed. "Don't blame me. I told Ned to bring you in."

Joshua held his temper. "What do you know?"

"Ashton is gay."

"General Ashton." Joshua whistled.

"Shocked the hell out of me too," Monique grinned. "I also know he is unaware of McGarry's plans."

"Which is?"

Monique hesitated. She knew she was about to open a can of worms that needed to remain sealed. But he asked a direct question. She had never lied to him and wasn't about to start now. "To take over Asmere."

The name of the small country in Africa brought back memories of Akande. She was the woman he had once asked to marry him. However the President at the time believed that a union between Asmere and Emure would settle the region and provide the needed protection for the country that had just discovered several diamond mines in the area. It was also determined that the true Queen and ruler of Asmere was his Akande. She was given the unenviable task of choosing between her country and him. She chose her country, as he would have done. Unfortunately it all occurred after he had fallen in love with her. The incident sent him into a whirlwind of self-destruction and her back to Asmere carrying his child. As expected she married Prince Raheem, the son of the King of Emure and had the child. While the parents knew the truth, to protect the child, no one else was ever told. Even when asked, Joshua was told Theodora, who they called Teddi, was not his child. He walked away knowing it was the best thing for the child. That did not stop him from checking on Teddi multiple times throughout the year to ensure her well being. Now that he was married with another child on the way he found himself thinking about Teddi more and more. To find out now she may be in danger had his blood pressure rising.

"Is she in danger?"

"Not that I'm aware of. I'm pretty sure her husband will be."

"How?"

He had waited so long to response Monique thought for a moment she would have to expand on her answer. She sighed. "I don't have all the answers yet. But I am certain one of your brother Adam's inventions is at the forefront of this plan."

"What proof do you have?"

"Calls between Ashton and McGarry have all been aimed at pressing Adam to come work for the CIA."

"And Ned is aware of this?"

Monique nodded. "Yes, but Ned is not connected with them. He seems to be taking orders directly from Davenport when it comes to Adam."

"McGarry's gone rogue." Joshua stated. "But why Asmere and who is helping from the inside?"

"The name Conteh keeps coming up."

"Naftali Conteh?"

"Yes, you know him?"

Joshua nodded and grinned. "Yes, I know him."

"You want to clue a sista in?"

"No." Joshua stepped out of the vehicle. He looked back through the window. "Monique, there is business and there is family. Family always takes precedence. Remember that."

Before she could respond, Joshua was gone.

Monique glanced at her watch. She would give him a few hours before calling Ned.

Brent arrived at the Dalton residence to find the man dead from an apparent suicide. While searching his office, which was in an unattached building in his back yard, they found evidence of the device being assembled and the manual.

"The package is too neatly wrapped," Brent said to Kalli.

She nodded. "It's as if someone wanted you to come to the conclusion that he was the only person involved. Do you believe that?" She looked up at him.

"Do you?" he asked.

"No. The place is too clean. Too exact."

"Like it was staged," Brent agreed.

"Exactly. So now what?"

"I get the feeling there is something bigger here. Dalton would not have the connections to get these parts. Lassiter said he negotiated with the DOD. Dalton worked for the DOD, but not at that level."

"He may have been the patsy to build the device, but there is no way he was the mastermind behind the stealing of that manual or the death of Dr. McCoy." Kalli looked around, pushing papers on the desk around with her gloved hand. "Take a look at this." She gave Brent a piece of paper.

"That's the same phrase Lassiter had on his computer." Brent frowned. "Someone has a grudge against the government. They probably knew Dalton had one too and used him." Brent pulled out his cell to call Ned to advise him of his findings. "Any progress on the code Amber found?"

"Hey, Brent," Kalli called out.

"Hold on, Ned. "He covered his phone. "Yeah?"

"You better take a look at this."

Brent walked over to where Kalli stood at Dalton's computer.

"It's a photo of Lassiter and his roommate in their room at the academy."

"Ned, where is Lassiter at this moment?" Brent spoke into the phone as he and Kalli began to walk briskly towards their vehicles. "We may have a problem."

CHAPTER NINETEEN

Samuel was distributing weapons as Adam walked into the target area. "You're late."

"I was at a meeting. Sorry."

"Doesn't work here, Lassiter. Where is your partner?"

Adam looked around. "Flex? He should be here."

"Well he's not. Take your position."

"I think I should check on Flex." Adam started to walk away but Samuel stopped him.

"I'll have him checked on. You take your slot."

Adam nodded, picked up his assigned weapons, then took his position.

Samuel called security. "Check on Lander."

The class was ten minutes in, when two security guards along with Special Agent Vanderbilt approached him. Samuel listened as they spoke. He nodded his head then walked over to his brother. "Adam, we have a situation. I need you to come with me."

Adam gathered his rifle and ammunition then followed Samuel back to the dorm. As they entered the hallway leading to his room, Adam could feel the tension. Ned was standing outside the door of his room. He glanced at Amber's door then looked up at Ned. "Where is Amber?"

"Inside," Ned replied. "She's fine."

Adam nodded then stopped outside the door. He took a deep breath then walked inside. There was a certain smell of death that could not be mistaken. He knew what he would find, but that did not ease the pain. Flex was sitting in the chair backwards with his head lying across the top. His eyes were wide open. Foam was oozing out of his mouth.

Amber stood in her lab coat with her hands gloved. Adam focused on her. "Are you okay?"

"Yes," she replied. Her instinct was to stay where she stood behind Flex, but her heart was feeling his hurt and all she wanted to do was comfort him. "He was poisoned," Amber informed him.

Adam nodded as he walked closer to Flex's body.

"There's a message," Ned said as he opened Flex's computer.

"I know what it says." Adam turned, closing his eyes.

"Responsible   rebellion   unifies   a   perfect government of redeeming faith."

He shook his head. "I should have seen it coming."

"Adam." Amber reached out. "There was no way you could have known Flex was in danger."

He stepped out of her reach. "I knew you were, and Brent." His voice was smooth but the anger could be detected in the tone.

"Adam." Ned closed the computer. "This is not on you."

"It is, Ned. I should have never allowed him to look at those files. I should have..." He looked up at Amber remembering the reason he left the task to Flex was to get to her room. He closed his eyes.

Deputy Secretary Nicolas appeared at the door with Director Vance of the FBI.

"Gentlemen, we contained this area." Director Vance spoke to the men in the hallway then stepped inside. "Deputy Secretary Nicolas has filled me in on the details. They believe the target was you." He looked at Adam.

"I don't," Adam stated. "They need me. Whoever is behind this killed Flex as a message to me."

"That may be true, son," Director Vance spoke. "Since you understand the facts, the next step I have to take should come as no surprise."

Adam hung his head as he sat back on his bed. "May I be present when his parents are notified?"

"No," Samuel replied. "After the meeting with Davenport you will be placed under protection."

"Protection?"

"Adam, it is clear the people we are dealing with will kill for their mission," Samuel exclaimed. "You are leaving here."

"Adam, he's right." Amber looked at the man she was certain had to be one of Adam's brothers. "If you had been in this room..."

He took her hand and squeezed it. "I wasn't," he reassured her then released her hand. "You could have been here." He held her eyes for a long moment. "I would never forgive myself if anything happened to you."

"That will be remedied." her father stated.

"Dad..." Amber was cut off.

"No." He shook his head. "The decision has been made."

"May I have the room for a moment?" Adam suddenly stood.

The Director nodded. "My office in thirty minutes." He walked out the room followed by Nicolas who held his hand out for his daughter.

Amber hesitated.

"Go." Adam said. "You too, Samuel. Just give me a minute."

Adam waited until the door was closed behind them then walked over to Flex. He stared at the man who was becoming a friend. Adam covered Flex's eyes with his hands, then closed them. He knew not to move the body, for the investigators would want the scene preserved. He leaned against Flex's desk.

"I know you are here...watching. Whoever you are, you have no idea what I am capable of. I will find and destroy you, your family and any remnants of your existence. You wanted to send me a message. Consider your message received." He bent down to the far corner of Flex's desk to be directly in the line of sight of the device. "Take heed of mine."

When they entered the Director's office, Royce stood, extending his hand. "I am sorry about your friend."

"Please have a seat," Director Vance stated as he pointed to a chair in front of his desk. "I'm certain you know everyone in the room."

Adam looked around to see Brent and Kalli in the room along with Director Nicolas, Ned, and Amber. He held Amber's eyes for a long moment for he knew it may be the last time he would see her. Two days, that was all the time that he had spent with her. 48 hours and it seemed as though his heart was being ripped from his chest to know he would have to leave her. He looked around and noticed Samuel did not walk in behind him.

"Your brother does not agree with the actions we are about to take." The Director spoke first. "For your safety and that of others around you we are releasing you from your commitment to the Federal Bureau of Investigation."

Nicolas spoke next. "We understand none of this is your doing, son. However we have an obligation to the safety of the men and women of the Bureau. Your presence here, as unfair as it may be, is a hazard for those around you." He glanced at his daughter.

Adam sat listening as the people around him determined his future. He understood what they had to do. He also knew exactly what he had to now do. It was almost as if fate had led him to this moment. He looked up at Ned, who stood quietly in the back of the room leaning against the wall. His stance was so casual Adam almost laughed. But he couldn't. His life was being determined for him and he did not like it. Not one damn bit.

"Your record will not be negatively impacted by this incident," the Director stated.

Adam held up his hand. "Am I still on the case to determine who killed Dr. McCoy and now Flex?"

Vance and Nicolas glanced at each other. Royce glanced up at Ned.

"I believe you have earned the right to lead this investigation," Ned spoke. "Other than your friend Flex, you are the only one being sacrificed here."

"I agree," Brent spoke up.

Adam turned in his seat to the back of the room, surprised at the statement.

"Surprised, right?" Brent stood. "Yeah, me too. I see a man who did something for his country. He only asked for one thing in return. That was to become an Agent with the FBI. Now, because some mad person has taken his device, that I remind you, was in the government's control, he is being stripped of the one thing he wanted. Instead of us rallying to protect him, we're throwing him out. What a gracious way of rewarding him for his service."

"You have made your position quite clear, Agent Pierce," Vance roared.

Brent stared at Vance, then at Nicolas. He shook his head then he walked out of the room.

Kalli stood there for a moment, then followed her partner out the door.

"It doesn't seem as if justice is being served here," Amber argued.

"Amber," her father cautioned.

"Are you speaking as my father or Deputy Director right now?"

"There are other issues at play here, Amber."

"I'm sure there are. But the very agency that heads the Department of Justice has failed miserably in their mission. Dr. Lassiter did not cause the death of Flex Lander, or Dr. McCoy. As Special Agent Pierce mentioned, the device he invented was under your control, not his. Yet, he is the one being held responsible." She turned to Adam, then looked at her father. "In my opinion, it is the Department of Defense who should bear the responsibility for the events of the last few days. If Dr. Lassiter is dismissed from the Bureau, consider this my resignation as well."

"Okay, everyone, let's take a breather, a moment to reflect on what we are doing." Adam stood. "Let the emotions settle before we make rash decisions. Director, thank you for the opportunity. My things are packed. I will not be returning to Quantico."

"Adam..." Amber started to speak.

"It's okay. I don't want anyone else to lose their life because of me." He turned back to the Director and extended his hand. "Thank you, sir."

"Any other circumstance, Lassiter."

"I understand, sir." He turned to Nicolas. "Sir, it was a pleasure." He glanced at Amber. "Please keep your daughter safe."

Nicolas extended his hand. "I will, son. You take care as well."

"Secretary Davenport, I'm certain we will speak soon." Adam walked towards the door and turned when Ned followed. "Where are you going?"

"With you," Ned replied. "I can't allow anything to happen to that mind of yours."

"Don't you have a job here?"

"You, are now my job." He grinned.

"Isn't that special," Adam joked.

"Adam?" Amber called out.

He could see the tears threatening to fall. This was the hardest part, walking away from her. But he knew for her safety, he had to...for now. "You take care, Redbird." He smiled then walked out of the room.

Samuel was standing outside the door. "Let's go, Adam." The tone of his voice indicated how pissed he was. The walk demonstrated how determined he was and the look on his face let everyone know to get the hell out of his way.

"I'll follow you," Ned said to Adam.

"Don't want to jeopardize your life in the car with us?" Adam grinned.

"Not at this moment." Ned walked to his car.

Adam stopped when he walked outside of headquarters to see Karen and Clive standing outside. Karen walked over and gave him a hug. "Take care, Lassiter."

Adam returned the hug. "I will. You do the same."

"Adam." Clive shook his hand. "If you ever need anything, call."

"I appreciate that, Clive." He opened the door and slid into the passenger seat. "Do Flex proud," he said then turned to his brother. "Let's go, Sammy."

Samuel pulled off as he glanced over at his little brother. "I'm sorry about this, Adam."

"It's okay, Sammy. It was only a dream," Adam said as he unfolded the piece of paper Karen placed in his pocket.

"What's that?"

"A number." He smiled.

"You were unjustly dismissed from the Academy and you are smiling about a phone number from a woman." He shook his head. "You are as bad as Joshua."

"This number is different. It has an 'I know who did this' message attached.

"What?"

Adam held the piece of paper up, showing it to Samuel.

"How?"

"I don't know, but now that I am out of a job, I have time to devote to nothing else but solving this case." His cell phone buzzed. Adam looked at the caller ID. "What can I do for you, Special Agent Pierce?"

"Where are you headed, Lassiter?" Brent asked.

"My brother's place. Why?"

"Give me the address. I'll meet you there."

"You don't have to do that, Brent. I understand the position of the Bureau."

"I don't understand it at all. Other than they want to cover their ass."

"Hold up. What's happened to 'follow the rules' Captain America?"

"Look, the rules are in place to protect us. I respect that. But there is something more in play here. They know it and you know it too."

"Listen, the last thing I want or need is any more casualties."

"We have a case to solve. Don't you want to know who this son of a bitch is that killed, not one, but two of your friends? And what about Amber? Do you think because you are no longer with the Bureau she is no longer a target? I think she is more of a target away from you than with you."

"I think she has a better chance of survival without me around her. I'm certain her father is putting security around her as we speak."

"How do you think she feels about you walking out? Leaving her before you two even have a chance at something special." He hesitated. "Look, she is not into me. To tell the truth she never was, but with you...hell, I see it. There is something there."

Adam had to admit, leaving Amber behind was not what his heart was telling him to do. He knew it was best, but that was his brain talking.

"I thought you cared about her, Lassiter. Or was I wrong?"

Adam glanced out of the window. "I do care."

"Then give me the address."

Adam gave him the address then disconnected the call. "Sometimes your best ally is the person you once looked at as your enemy."

"Pierce?" Adam nodded. "He's a damn good agent. It's good to know he has your back. What do you think Johnson knows?"

"I have no idea. As soon as we get settled at the house I'll reach out to her."

"How much do you know about her?"

"I know she, Clive and Flex had my six."

The drive became quiet again. "Flex could have been you." Samuel finally spoke. "We should have protected you better. Joshua and I wanted to give you some space because we understood what you needed to discover for yourself. The Bureau was not for you."

"I agree," Adam replied as they pulled onto the private road that led to Joshua's home. "But I think we have a much larger problem than that."

Samuel glanced at Adam. "What's that?"

Adam pointed. "That's Sally's car in front of us."

"She can't know already."

"No, I think the Bureau is going to contain this. They do not want the public to know Quantico was infiltrated in any way. I should have placed the detector in their security system. It just didn't dawn on me to do that. As soon as we get inside, I'll call the Deputy Director. He could have it installed."

Samuel parked the vehicle in the underground garage then turned to Adam. "The Bureau just kicked you out and you are thinking of ways to improve their security system?"

Adam held his brother's glare. "You would do the same thing, Sammy. Look," Adam sighed. "Am I happy with the turn of events? No. But the facts are clear. I'm a threat to anyone around me right now. That includes Nicolas' daughter. I would have made the same move to protect her."

Sammy watched as Adam glanced out the side window. "You like her."

Adam smirked as he continued looking at the back of the house. "I feel like I left a part of me behind." He turned to Samuel. "The last thing I want is for her to become a target because I'm one."

"That's just it, I don't get why?" Samuel stated, then stopped Adam when he was about to speak. "Hear me out. It would be insane to try to kill you. They want your brain. Whoever they are they want you to cooperate with them of your own free will. That's the best way to get you to produce. What I don't get is why do they want you isolated?"

"It's the divide and conquer theory," Adam suggested. "They want me vulnerable to the point that they can win me over."

"You're a patriot, Adam, you would never side with another country against the United States."

"True, but suppose this isn't another country. What if the person, or persons behind this is us as the President suggested?"

Sammy stared at his brother as he contemplated his statement. "It's been known to happen. We have rogue agents within our midst."

"Joshua has brought down one or two right under our nose," Adam stated. They both sat thinking. "I had several agencies recruiting me for different reasons. At the top were Department of Defense, Central Intelligence Agency, and the Department of Justice."

"We can rule out the Department of Justice, they just put you out."

"That leaves DOD, CIA and...Homeland Security."

"You can rule out Davenport." Samuel shook his head. "He is loyal to this President."

"Then that leaves DOD and CIA."

"We're leaving out independent contractors who work with outside entities. We sometimes contract out services to them."

"There are too many possibilities. We need to narrow it down." Adam turned to Samuel. "There is one name that popped up during the investigation. In fact, it was Flex who found it."

"Who?"

"General McGarry."

"The ex-Secretary of Defense?"

"Getting to him is not going to be easy." Adam nodded. "I say we put all the scenarios into the computer and see who comes to the top of the list."

Samuel looked out of the window to the door that just opened. "I say we will deal with the larger problem first."

Adam turned to see his mother Sally Lassiter standing near the door with her arms folded across her chest. "She doesn't look too happy," he said as he stepped out of the vehicle. "I'll clear things up with her." He frowned as he walked towards her. "Mom, Sammy and Joshua got me put out of the Bureau," he cried.

Samuel froze when he heard Adam's words. "I'm going to kill him," he mumbled as he followed his brother inside.

CHAPTER TWENTY

"What do you mean you were put out of the Bureau?" Sally stood in the kitchen of Joshua's house with his wife Rochelle, better known as Roc behind her, pregnant and all. "You've only been there for two days. Did you blow up something?"

"You were released by the Bureau?" Roc asked, surprised. "Why?"

Adam turned to Sammy. "You want to explain to Mom what happened?"

"Yes, I want to hear this, too." Monique grinned as she walked into the kitchen.

The front doorbell chimed.

"That would be Ned," Monique offered. "You continue with your explanation." She nodded to Adam. "This should be good."

"Who is Ned?" Sally asked.

"You don't want to know who Ned is." Roc smirked as she took a seat at the table.

"Where is Joshua?" Samuel asked.

"That's the reason I'm here," Sally said as she took a seat next to Roc. "He's missing in action again."

"We were with him last night. He's not on an assignment or working a case." Samuel placed Adam's suitcase near the door.

"That is partially correct," Ned advised as he rounded the corner from the living room.

"I told you, you didn't want to know." Roc smirked as she popped a grape into her mouth.

"You must be the lovely Sally Lassiter. Mother of Joshua, the most difficult, but efficient employee I've had to date." He sat his computer and briefcase down on the table. "The reason the beautiful Rochelle is not happy to see me is because when I call she must pack her bags. Now that she is married to Joshua, she fears I will call him off to an assignment at a time when she will need him the most." He pulled out a chair and sat across from Sally and Roc. "The mere fact that I am here should ease your worries, for I am stepping down from that role. So as you see, you have nothing to fear from me."

The room was quiet until Monique spoke. "I swear that is the most I've ever heard you talk."

"You're stepping down, Ned?" Roc took his hand. "Why?"

"Right before your last mission when you rescued Joshua, it seems I was discovered."

"How could that be?" Samuel pulled out a chair and sat, surprised at the announcement.

"Yes." Ned nodded. "That was part of the reason we knew it was an inside job."

"So what exactly do you do?" Sally asked.

"I-" Roc kicked Ned under the table before he could answer. He took the subtle hint. "...manage people."

"For the Government," Monique quickly added.

"You are Joshua's boss?"

"Exactly." Ned smiled at Sally.

"Well it is nice to meet you. Then you are able to tell us where he is."

Monique glared at Ned, as did Roc. Both curious to see how Ned would respond.

Before he could the front doorbell sounded again. "I got it," Lucy, Joshua's housekeeper, called from another room. "This sure is a busy front door today. What ever happened to using the Bat-cave?" They all heard her then grimaced when Commando, the dog let out a series of warning barks.

"Commando, down," Roc called out. The dog immediately stopped barking.

"Well, I see you have gained control of the house in a short period of time." Ned smiled at Roc.

"Hey, I'm responsible for taming the biggest dog of them all." She laughed.

Lucy walked in frowning as Brent and Kalli followed her. "Adam." She looked over her shoulder. "These two say you are expecting them."

"I am."

"They're FBI." Lucy rolled her eyes heavenwards.

"So was I until an hour ago."

"I knew you would come to your senses." She looked the two up and down as she turned to walk out. "Commando, heel." The dog sat. "Watch those two," she said, then walked out of the kitchen.

"My apologies for Lucy. She's not too fond of agencies with initials." Sally stood. "Would you like to have a seat?"

"No, ma'am, thank you. We're here to speak with Adam and Ned."

"And you are?"

"Special Agent Brent Pierce, ma'am." He shook her hand.

"Special Agent Kalli Hayes." She smiled at Sally.

"Are you two a couple?" Sally asked.

"Mom," Adam warned.

"Well, they should be." Sally smiled. "You don't feel the chemistry between them?" She turned back to Brent. "You two are good partners, aren't you?"

"Yes, ma'am, we are," Kalli responded.

"See," Sally exclaimed. "I'm not so far off."

"Why don't we carry this down to the situation room?" Samuel stood.

"Someone better answer my question about Joshua before anyone goes anywhere," Sally demanded.

It took a minute with her very round stomach, but Roc stood. "Joshua had to fly out of the country. He should return by tomorrow night." She grabbed a bunch of grapes. "If everyone will follow me to the Cave, we can get this meeting started."

"What meeting?" Sally asked.

"We'll fill you in later, Mom." Adam kissed her on the cheek, then motioned to Brent. "Follow me."

Ned picked up his items then followed Monique out of the kitchen. Only Samuel remained.

"Joshua is fine, Mom. It's Adam I'm concerned with. But I'm sure we'll get everything ironed out." He kissed her cheek. "How's Pop?"

"Your father is fine." Her eyes lit up as she spoke.

"I knew that would put a smile on your face." He kissed her cheek again then left the room.

Samuel walked into the Cave where Lucy was declaring certain areas off limits to Brent and Kalli. "I've told her they are good people," Adam whispered to Samuel, "but she's not feeling them. How is Mom?" Adam looked at his brother.

"Worried."

"I'll handle her. You handle this."

Adam walked upstairs to the kitchen. His mother was standing at the sink staring out the window. He walked up behind her and hugged her. "Stop worrying. I'm going to be okay."

Sally patted her baby boy's hand then turned to lean against the sink. He stepped to the side and did the same. "You want to tell me what happened?"

"I can't tell you much due to security constraints, but I can say one of my inventions got into the hands of some bad people. Now we have to figure out how to get it back and contain the fallout."

"Did the Bureau really dismiss you?"

"Yes, ma'am. For safety reasons. Two people have lost their lives because they were connected to this investigation. I don't want anyone else to die for that reason."

"Baby, I'm sure they don't blame you."

"I blame me, Mom. Not for the lost lives. I know that responsibility doesn't fall on my shoulders. I should have listened to Joshua. I tried to fit into a world that wasn't right for me. The truth of the matter is I'm a geek. If I had accepted that from the beginning I would have never been at the Bureau and Dr. McCoy and Flex would still be alive. Now I have to find a way to balance it all out."

Sally hugged her son. "You will, Adam. You will find your place in this world. Joshua recognized who he was early. For you, it may take a while. But that's okay. You can come back home until you do."

"Thanks, Mom, but I think I'm going to stay here with Joshua and Roc until I find my own place. If it's okay with them."

"I'm sure they would love to have you."

"We'll see." He hugged her again. "I'm going back downstairs." He walked towards the opening then stopped. "I met her, Mom."

"You met who?" Sally asked as she turned back to her son.

"My Sally."

"You did?" Sally beamed. "Well at least you are not taking after Joshua on that note. I swear that boy went through twenty girls before settling on Roc."

"Ha, ha," Adam laughed out loud, thinking, you better try hundreds. But there was no way he would say that to his mother. "Yes, it's a good thing."

"Are you going to do something about it or let her slip away?"

Adam shrugged. "I can't do anything until this mess is all cleared up."

"Don't let her slip through your fingers."

"I did that once before. I don't plan on doing it again."

Sally watched as her baby boy walked from the room. A small frown creased her brow, but she let it go then said a prayer instead. Lucy walked in the room just as she said amen.

"I hope you added me to that prayer." Lucy chuckled. "If one more person walks through the door we'll have an official baseball team in that room."

"What are they working on?"

"Something about malt balls." Lucy waved the question off. The doorbell rang out again.

Sally and Lucy looked at each other and laughed. "It's official." Sally wiped her hands on the towel. "I'll get this one."

Sally opened the door to a beautiful woman with curly reddish brown hair. "Hello. May I help you?"

"Hi, I'm looking for Adam Lassiter. Is this the right address?"

"That depends," Sally replied as she continued to gaze at the woman. There was something familiar about her. "Do I know you?"

"My apologies for not introducing myself. My name is Amber Nicolas. Dr. Amber Nicolas. I was trying to find Dr. Adam Lassiter."

Sally could see the woman had been crying, but that wasn't what kept her staring. "Have we met before?"

"I'm not certain," a nervous Amber replied.

"Dr. Nicolas...Dr. Nicolas, yes." Sally's smile brightened. "Please come in. You helped my friend Anne Davenport when she was injured in a fire." Sally stepped aside then closed the door once Amber entered. "I'm Sally Lassiter, Adam's mother."

Amber smiled. "Then I would say yes, we probably met when I spoke with the family that night."

"We did. What an impression you left on my so...family." Sally caught herself before saying son. She remembered the impact the young doctor had on Adam the night of the fire.

"Why don't you come into the kitchen? We're about to have a cup of tea." She spoke a little louder hoping Lucy caught her drift.

"Thank you. I would love a cup of tea."

"Of course." Sally led her to the kitchen. "I know when I'm nervous a cup of tea settles me right down. Lucy," Sally called out. "This is Dr. Amber Nicolas. She is here to see Adam. But I think she needs a cup of tea to settle her nerves."

"Hello," Amber spoke.

Lucy stood with the teakettle in her hand. "We can't have that. Have a seat. We have a variety of teas to choose from."

"Get her a cup of chamomile. That should do the trick." Sally pulled out a chair and sat next to Amber. "Now what are you nervous about?"

Amber sat her purse on the floor and sighed. "My first problem is I just quit my job."

Sally nodded. "There seems to be a lot of that going around."

"Hmm huh, sure is," Lucy echoed. "But you're a doctor which means you are smart. You'll bounce back."

Sally nodded in agreement. "You will. Don't worry about that." Sally patted her hand. Lucy sat a cup in front of her then poured hot water. Sally pushed the tray with the different teas to Amber. "What else is bothering you, dear?"

Amber picked up the tea bag and began preparing her tea. "Well, as I said at the door I'm here to see Adam. I wasn't exactly invited by him, but I really need to see him."

"Oh, I'm certain he will be happy to see you. Why, any man in his right mind would be crazy to refuse to see you." Sally nodded her head up and down. "Isn't that right, Lucy?"

Lucy jumped right in. "Crazy as a bed bug, he would be."

Sally gave Lucy a side eye. "Why would you think he wouldn't be happy to see you?"

Amber sipped her tea. "It was my father who fired him today."

"Adam isn't like that," Lucy said. "If he doesn't want to see you it's because of something you did. Not your father."

Sally kicked Lucy under the table. "What she means is Adam wouldn't hold you responsible for something another person did."

"I hope you're right." Amber looked around. "So, is Adam here?"

"Oh, yes." Sally stood. "I was enjoying your company so much I forgot why you were here. Follow me, I'll take you to him."

Sally took Amber through the greenroom then down a back hallway to an elevator. "You have a nice home," Amber complimented.

"Oh, this isn't my home. I live in Richmond. This is my son Joshua and his wife, Rochelle's home. It's my understanding Adam will be staying here until he gets his own place."

They took the elevator down one level, then walked by the theater room and gym on the left and a guest bedroom on the right before reaching the double doors at the end of the hallway. Commando immediately came to attention. Sally heard Amber's gasp as the dog came into view.

"Are you afraid of dogs?"

"Only really large ones." Amber's voice shook.

"Commando weighs about as much as you do, but he's as gentle as they come," Sally said as she patted the black and tan German shepherd. "Hold your hand out."

Amber looked at Sally as if she had lost her mind as she clutched her purse.

"Seriously." Sally smiled. "I promise he will not bite you." Sally held her hand out to Amber.

Amber slowly placed her hand in Sally's.

"In dealing with animals it is best to let them get to know you first, then they will love you for life. Men are the same way."

Sally held Amber's hand to Commando's nose. He sniffed, then licked her hand. Amber released a breath then smiled. Sally removed her hand allowing Amber to rub Commando's head.

"He's so soft." Amber smiled. Commando put his paw on Amber's arm as if holding it in place, then he proceeded to lick her hand continuously.

"He likes you." The voice came from behind them.

"Adam." Sally gave a knowing nod as the two stared at each other. "You have a visitor."

Amber stared at Adam in the doorway of the guest room they had just walked by. He had changed into jeans and a grey sweater. She had seen the work dressed Adam, and the suited down Adam, but this was the everyday Adam. He was more dangerous to her senses this way than any of the others.

"What are you doing here?"

She put her chin up in defense. "I don't leave anything unfinished. We still have a case to solve."

"If I remember correctly, you quit."

"I quit the Bureau, not you...I mean the case."

"Does your father know you're here?"

Amber tilted her head. "I did not bother to mention it to him."

"How did you get here?"

"I drove."

"Well it seems you two have a lot to talk about so I'm going to go back upstairs." Sally made her way past Adam back to the elevator. "Come, Commando." Commando walked slowly down the hallway looking from Amber to Adam. When he reached Adam he stood for a long moment, rolled his eyes upwards then continued on his way to Sally. "I'm with you, boy." Sally patted him. "I don't want no parts of that either." The two stepped onto the elevator when it arrived.

Adam never took his eyes from Amber. "You should not be here."

"Did you think I was just going to walk away from this case the way you walked away from me?"

Adam pushed off of the doorframe and quickly walked towards her. "I did not walk away. I was dismissed. What, did you forget so quickly? That's usually referred to as selective memory."

Amber sighed. "Look, Adam, I'm as much a part of this investigation as you."

"No, Amber, you are not. No one is killing people because they're getting too close to the truth or too close to you. That's the reason your father made the decision to keep you away from me. It was the right decision. You should not be here. Being close to me puts your life in danger."

"So you were just going to walk away, Adam? This isn't just about the case. Are you walking away from what was happening between you and me, too? What did you call it - hypnotic?"

"No, if I remember correctly that's how you referred to me which is an accurate assessment."

They both smiled.

"I believe you said that I was like a narcotic. One taste and you're hooked for life. Is a lifetime span only 48 hours for you?"

Adam sighed, then removed a curl from her face with his finger. "It's not as simple as that." He dropped his hand.

"Then I suggest you resolve this case and make it simple." Hesitantly, Amber stepped to him, softly kissed his lips then stepped back. The silence was awkward. She smiled nervously. "How is that for spontaneity?"

He stepped closer to her. "It's a start." His lips fused with hers in a way that was demanding. She leaned back against the wall for support from the sudden embrace. A sense of weakness consumed her as his tongue plunged deeper into her mouth, circling the roof, touching the sides, sucking her tongue. He pulled away, capturing her bottom lip between his then released it. He gazed at her, willing her eyes to open. When they did, he smiled. "Spontaneity should never be a tease. It should be demanding, all consuming, unrelenting." Adam titled his head to one side. "You want to try again?"

Amber sighed. "You are a juvenile in a man's body, Adam Lassiter."

"Is that a yes?"

"Yes." Amber captured his lips, slipping her tongue between them, then proceeded to ravish his mouth.

Neither heard the door open or knew they were being watched until Ned grabbed Adam's arm pulling him away.

"You don't have time for that. We have a lead."

Adam wiped his mouth as Ned pulled him backwards into the room. He held his hand out.

Amber grabbed it and in that moment she knew she would fight to the death before she would ever let it go.

CHAPTER TWENTY-ONE

The Cave, as Joshua called it, was a state of the art command center in the basement of his home that in certain aspects did rival the Pentagon. From there, Lucy, who was an ex-CIA operative, had the capability to monitor his missions from all over the world. The room consisted of wall monitors, world maps and satellite systems. There was a computer conference table in the center of the room.

For now the monitors were off with people gathered around the table piecing together different angles of the investigation.

"Now that all parties are here, let's start with what we know as fact," Ned started.

"Fact, Dr. Cyrus McCoy and Flex Lander were killed by an imitation J.M.A.L.T.S.," Adam began. "Fact, the manual to the device was stolen."

"Fact," Amber chimed in, "both were killed from a lethal injection."

"Fact, I received a cryptic message," Adam added.

"Fact, that same message was found on Jack Dalton's desk," Brent stated.

"Fact, that same message was on Flex's computer."

"Put the message up on the monitor," Roc requested.

Adam keyed the message into the computer then clicked on the monitor.

'Responsible   rebellion   unifies   a   perfect government of redeeming faith.'

Roc read the message. She shook her head. "It reads like a grudge, but I don't know."

"It could be a decoy," Brent suggested.

"Something put in place to keep you from the actual target." Kalli threw in.

"Kalli may have a point," Adam said. "We've been spending time on the message, the numbers, and J.M.A.L.T.S. When we should be asking what is the goal? What is the desired outcome?"

"If we go on the premise that the death of Dr. McCoy was a test..." Ned looked around the room at the participants of the meeting. "A test for what?" He looked at Monique. "What did you find with McGarry?"

"That name has come up a few times." Adam sat forward.

The attractive, wavy haired operative stood dressed in dark jeans, boots, a dark tee and leather jacket. Monique clicked on a separate monitor leaving the message up. A picture of the General appeared on the screen. "McGarry was the top man at the DOD during the mission when Joshua was shot down. He retired soon after to quote un-quote spend more time with his family," Monique offered.

"That's government's code for you're fired, but we'll allow you to save face," Adam explained.

"Exactly," Monique continued. "Once he retired he became involved with this man, Naftali Conteh." The man's picture appeared. "Conteh headed up the rebels who kidnapped Princess ZsaZsa Ashro, daughter to once King Ahmed Ashro of Emere. Since then his oldest son has taken over. The kidnapping of Princess ZsaZsa was the beginning of an elaborate plot to take control of this region of Asmere." A picture appeared of the mountainous countryside. "This was the region of Asmere three years ago." Another picture appeared. "This is Asmere now. Approximately three years ago, untouched diamond mines were discovered in the small country making it one of the wealthiest areas in that region. In the last three years, it has surpassed all the diamonds harvested in the last year in all of South Africa. This small country is ruled by King Raheem Ashro and Queen Akande." A picture of Akande appeared. "The two married a few years ago to secure the region. King Ashro began building an army to protect the country's newfound wealth. His progress has been admirable but it is not strong enough to withstand the rebels in the area. Namely, Naftali Conteh. Even more so with the assistance of the ex-head of the DOD for the United States of America." A picture of both men appeared on the screen side by side. "We are not sure how, but we believe McGarry is assisting Conteh rebel forces with a takeover of the region. In return, he will receive millions from a continuous flow of uncut diamonds."

"Are you saying that one of the top leaders responsible for protecting the United States is working with this man," Brent asked. "I can't believe that. Why?"

"Wealth." Adam sat back with his arms folded across his chest.

"The root of all evil." Amber added sitting next to him. "What I don't understand is how does J.M.A.L.T.S. come into play?"

"Yes, bring it back to something reasonable." Brent shook his head. "This is all a bit far-fetched for me."

Ned and Monique exchanged glances. "Weapons of mass destruction that will not cause an all out war are needed to complete the mission," Ned explained. "You see, if they were to attack with armies, Emere would become involved with the conflict. Since Emere is an ally of the United States, we would undoubtedly send forces to assist."

"If people begin to die from unknown sources, there will be no conflict. It would be a region in Africa consumed by another incurable disease," Adam explained. "Using J.M.A.L.T.S. to dispense the drug would leave no evidence of foul play."

Monique smiled. "Drop the mic, I think he got it." She sat.

"This is really out there, guys." Kalli smirked. "I mean how does any of this connect with the deaths here in the United States?"

"The death of Dr. McCoy was to get their hands on the manual," Brent surmised. "The attack on you and your brothers was an attempt to kidnap Adam. Which means something is not working properly and they need you to correct the problem."

"But they know you would not work for them willingly." Samuel had stood quietly in the back of the room until now. "So they have to coerce you in some way to do what they want."

"Or now that Dalton is dead, they may need you to assemble the device," Amber offered.

Adam suddenly sat up. "Where is Reyes Sugden?"

"Who?" Samuel asked.

"There were three people on Dr. McCoy's team. Dalton, Sugden and McCoy. Where is Sugden?" He began searching on his computer. "He has to be the next target."

"Put it up on the monitor, Adam," Monique suggested.

The DMV photo of Sugden appeared on the screen. Adam then searched for a cell phone in the man's name.

"According to the receptionist, he did not report to work today." Brent looked up from his phone. "No one reported in."

"That could mean one of two things." Ned stated. "He's been taken or he could be working with them."

"There is a third option." Adam continued to key into the computer.

"He could be dead," Amber added.

Adam stared up at her. The room was silent for a moment. "He has two cell phones." Adam continued on his computer. "I've locked onto both."

Brent stood. "Send me his location." He walked towards the door with Kalli in tow. "We'll find him."

"Be careful, Brent, he could also be working with them," Amber cautioned.

"Wait, I'll come with you." Adam picked up his laptop and was immediately blocked by Samuel.

"Not happening."

"Sammy, the man's life may be in danger," Adam rebelled.

Sammy nodded. "Pierce and Hayes will handle it. You are staying put."

"I don't want another life taken because of me."

"We'll get to him." Brent and Kalli ran out of the room.

"Sammy, I have to do something. I can't let this happen again."

"Adam." Amber stood, placing a hand on his shoulder. "I think we could use this time to take a break. You've been going non-stop for over forty-eight hours. Your body needs to rest."

Adam's phone buzzed. He reluctantly glanced at it. One of the monitors on the wall beeped. They all turned to the screen to see Joshua.

"You're a sight for sore eyes." Roc smiled. "How goes it?"

"Quiet...too quiet. How is Macgyver?"

Roc rubbed her stomach. "Bauer is in silent mode."

"Are you two still having the Jack Bauer vs Macgyver argument?" Monique laughed.

Joshua smiled. "There is no argument, Macgyver makes his own gadgets to blow up things."

"Jack Bauer had more lives," Roc countered.

"She has you there, Joshua." Adam smiled.

"You stay out of this, brainiac. I sent you the location of Conteh's last transmission between him and McGarry. I need you to lock into the satellite from that location and give me a starting point," Joshua said from the chopper. "The man has gone underground."

Adam sat back down and began inserting the information provided by Joshua into his computer.

"Has the thought of succession dawned on anyone?" Amber asked.

"What do you mean?" Monique asked.

"Well, if what you all suspect is true, this Conteh person cannot take over the region unless there is no one to succeed the current hierarchy. Other than the King and Queen are there any other family members? If so, they would have to eliminate them as well. Right? If not wouldn't any children in the royal family be the succession to the throne?"

Adam was so ingrained in the search he did not notice the silence that came over the room. Amber did.

"I apologize. I'm trying to understand all of this."

"Your questions are valid." Monique stood. She looked at Joshua with a questioning glance. "With your permission?" He nodded. She put another picture on the screen. "The line to the throne goes through Queen Akande. This is Princess Theodora Lasheera Ashro." Monique smiled. "All of three, about to be four, and she rules her household." Monique became serious. "She is the only child to the royal couple. All of Akande's family is dead. If she and her daughter are eliminated the region will be up for grabs."

Amber smiled. "She is beautiful and full of mischief. Look at her eyes, they remind me of..."

"Got it, Joshua," Adam called out. "His last location was Emure, one hundred miles outside of Asmere." Adam looked up.

"For them to be that close, it could only mean that things are escalating," Ned cautioned.

"Advise the President and King Ashro of the situation," Joshua stated as he started the chopper.

Ned pulled out his computer and began keying. "On it."

"Roc."

"I got your six."

"Monique, LaVere' needs to be in Emure."

Monique was putting on her jacket. "On it," she said before rushing out the door.

"Adam, I need the tracker activated."

Adam rolled his chair over to the main computer console then pushed a few keys. He looked up at the monitor. "Activated."

"One more thing. Is that the Doc behind you?"

Adam's eyes narrowed as he slowly replied, "Yes."

"She's almost as pretty as my Doc." Joshua smiled. "Not bad for a virgin."

Amber's smile faded after the last statement. "I'm not a virgin," she responded with a huff.

"He wasn't referring to you." Sammy smiled.

Adam had closed his eyes and sighed as his head fell to his chest.

"Payback," Sammy laughed. His phone buzzed and he stepped outside the room.

The only people left in the room were now Adam, Ned, Roc and Amber. Things had moved so fast when she first arrived she never had a chance to meet the other woman in the room. She walked over.

"Hi, I'm Amber. Is there anything I can do or get for you?"

Roc smiled as she attempted to stand. "That's what I should be asking you," she said as Amber reached out to help her.

"I'm Rochelle, wife to the daredevil on the screen. Ex-professor to Dennis the Menace over there on the computer."

"I heard that," Adam responded without looking up.

Amber smiled. "Why do you call him that?"

"Please don't..."

"It's the name the President of the university gave him after he blew up the first lab."

"The President of the university?"

"Yes, and that was the name he called him in public. In staff meetings, he was referred to as that smart ass mother....." The two women laughed as they walked out of the room.

"Man," Adam sighed. "My family is going to ruin any chance I have with that woman."

Ned shook his head as he continued to work on the computer making connections for Joshua once he lands in Ashmere. "Oh, I don't know. She's already fallen half in love with you, not much anyone can do about that."

Adam looked up, somewhat surprised. "Do you think so, Ned, I mean really. Do you...do you think she feels that way about me?"

Ned looked up. It was the first time since he met Adam Lassiter that he'd heard a little insecurity. Of course they had been working on the case from the moment they met. Their conversations had been in a comfort zone for him. After working with Joshua, it never occurred to him that any Lassiter man would be insecure when it came to women. The way Adam spoke to Amber the few times they were in the room together, Ned just assumed the young man was as well versed with women as his brother.

"I can only go by my observation of the two of you when you are in the same room. It would appear to a blind man that you generate an insurmountable amount of heat when one is around the other." Ned shrugged. "In my limited knowledge of the sexual experience, that is the definition of sexual tension. Sexual tension is drawn from a mutual attraction between two people. It has been known, on occasion, for that attraction to manifest itself in the area of feelings." He frowned. "Feelings, as we know, tend to lead to the heart becoming overwhelmed making one feel as if they are becoming vulnerable. Hence the term falling, which is risky. It all stems from the lower brain, which can lead one to become irrational, acting a bit bizarre, almost cult like. Not being willing to be outside the presence of the other. But one cannot rely solely on the brain. The heart must play a role in the selection of a true mate."

The expression on Adam's face gave Ned pause.

"Shall I go on?" He raised an eyebrow.

"No," Adam replied quickly. "I believe you have said enough." Adam shook off the response from Ned and made a note never to ask him about love again.

"Love is a relative word, you know. The thought of sharing one's heart with another can be frightening. If that love is unrequited, it could be devastating. I don't believe you or Dr. Nicolas have that concern."

Adam smiled as he continued to work. That was as close to a yes as he was going to get.

CHAPTER TWENTY-TWO

Once Joshua landed in Asmere, Adam stepped out of the room leaving the monitoring to Ned. It was clear the man was in a zone. Adam understood. They hadn't spoken since he asked the question about Amber. Adam smiled at the ridiculous mumbled reply he received. But had to marvel at the simplicity of it as well. The bottom line was he and Amber had a connection that would not be an easy one to break.

Adam leaned against the wall and dropped his head. Lord he was tired. It had been days since he had a good night's sleep. He stepped away from the wall then walked to the guest room. The October night breeze assailed his nostrils as he entered. He inhaled the fresh cool air loving the way it cleared the toxins taken in throughout the day. Glancing around, he saw his suitcase sitting next to the chair near the closet. In the chair was Amber's purse. What was that doing there? He thought. He looked up and noticed the sliding door to the balcony was open. He rushed outside searching from left to right until he saw her walking along the trail near the pond in the back of the house.

"Amber?" He ran to her grabbing her arm. "You can't be out here."

She pulled her arm away. "Roc indicated there's a force field around the entire compound. The device will be detected if it comes anywhere near here."

"You think the device is the only thing we have to defend against? Well it's not. People are trying to take me. And believe me the firepower they come with does not have names attached. Whoever is around me is fair game to these people." He spoke as he literally dragged her back inside.

"Adam, stop it. You are behaving like a juvenile."

"A juvenile? Look at me, Amber. I'm a grown man, who is trying to protect you."

"I'm a grown woman who does not need your protection. I have a father who is well versed in military combat. A father who has shared those things with me throughout my life. What I need from you is to see me...the woman, Adam. Stop trying to send me away. I'm not going. The truth is I don't think you really want me to go."

This territory of feelings was new to him. But he'd been around love all his life. He recognized exactly what was happening between them. He stepped back and shook his head. "No, I don't want you to go."

Amber stepped closer to him. "Then stop trying to send me away."

He pulled her into his arms. "Do you want to know what I see?" He ran a finger down her cheek and watched as her body trembled from his touch. "I see desire for this juvenile of a man when you look at me. I see the anticipation of my touch when I'm near." He stepped away from her. "You know the reason I'm sending you away. Flex is dead, Amber, dead because he was helping me. What do you think my reaction would have been if I had walked into that room and it was you there? I would not have been able to live with myself. It is killing me to have to do this. But it would mentally destroy me if one strand of hair on your head was harmed."

What could she say to counter his words? Nothing came to mind. Tears began to form in her eyes as she struggled internally to find the right thing to say to get him to let her stay.

"I can't go." She shrugged. "Today I quit my job. I walked out on my father when he demanded I stay away from you. I hung up on my mother because she was backing my father. I understand their concern. I do. But there is something larger here than this one case, this one investigation." She stepped closer and took his large hand into hers. "There's this thing called love." She closed her eyes. "And as incredible as it seems, there is something about you that makes me think you are the yang to my yin, the Clyde to my Bonnie."

"Sally to my Joe." Adam smiled softly.

"I don't know who they are, but...yeah." She smiled. He took her other hand in his. "It's taken me twenty-eight years to find you. I'm not ready to just let you walk out of my life without exploring the possibility of tomorrow with you." She wrapped her arm around his waist then placed her head on his chest. His heart was beating strong. She liked that. "My parents fought to be together. Even in the military, with my father being Black and my mother Caucasian, they had to deal with racism from their parents, co-workers and strangers." She looked up at him. "They taught me to recognize, accept and fight like hell for love. I don't know what we have. I only know what I feel and my heart is telling me not to walk away from this. To fight even you to keep this."

Adam's heart knew the truth. You can lie to the world, but you can never lie to yourself, he thought. That was a quote from the big man Joe Lassiter himself. When it's facing you, all you can do is accept the truth then fight your way through the bull crap. Adam smiled within. There was no need in fighting the inevitable. He and Amber were going to be together.

He sighed. "I'm not a virgin, Amber," Adam blurted out as he ran his hands down her back. "I will admit, I've never made love before. But I have had sex. In fact, I'm very good at the mechanics. At least that's what I was told."

Amber stopped caressing his back at his admission. It surprised her. She nodded. "I guess we are even on that. Why are you telling me this?"

He shrugged as he took her hand and began walking towards the bed. "Open communication is the best way to eliminate disappointment or nervousness. Knowing what to expect from one another is paramount to sexual satisfaction."

"You think so?" Amber suppressed the laughter building inside.

"I do," he earnestly replied. "And though I detect the suppressed humor in your voice, I believe you will appreciate this conversation when we make love for the first time."

Amber laughed softly. "First, I'll say in the name of full disclosure, I do find this conversation humorous. We've talked about devices, murder, takeover plots and God knows what else. So yes, this conversation is funny, but I was not laughing at you. I am tickled that a man as intelligent as you has this incredibly sweet, almost vulnerable side to him." She stopped talking and looked up at him. "Yet, there is an arrogance on how certain you are that we will make love."

"Oh." Adam's deep, sexy voice rang out. "There is no doubt on that note." He smiled, then stepped closer to her. "We are going to make love, Amber Nicolas. There is an inferno building inside of us. I feel it and I know you do." The palm of his hand cupped the side of her face as he stepped closer. The gaze into her eyes commanded her full attention. "I've had sex with one very, very talented woman in many different positions, but with you..." His thumb smoothly rubbed the area under her eye. "I'm going missionary all the way. I know some consider that boring, but for me..." His lips came closer to hers. "I want to gaze into your eyes from the excitement of the first kiss," his tongue snaked out then trailed across her bottom lip as he released her hand then circled her waist pulling her closer, "to the first intimate touch of my tongue on your nipples." His arousal brushed against her thigh. "To the moment when I place a pillow or two under you to raise the sweet juices I know you will produce to my lips as you begin to surge towards the urgency plateau." He rubbed the tip of his nose against hers. "Once I've had my thirst quenched," he grinned, "I'll come over you so our faces can touch and I'm close enough to see your eyes when I enter you. Close enough to hear that soft moan each time I move deeper inside of you. Touching your skin with the perspiration dew drops from the internal heat generated as you soar towards that orgasm." He ran his fingers through her hair. "Nothing...nothing is more erotic than seeing you lift your body to meet mine in midair. To feel your breath catch in your throat when I hit that spot. Or the way your eyes will glaze over when you come." He guided her backwards. "No, the experts can say what they want. But give me the intimacy of good old fashioned, one-on-one missionary style to make love to you."

He waited. He knew it was coming. The moment her tongue parted her lips he captured it. Sucking, exploring, tasting every particle on it. While ravishing her open mouth, his hands roamed her back until he reached her behind. He pulled her snug against him.

He could feel her pulsating through her clothes. The heat so intense it was causing him to swell more, expanding his erection down her thigh.

Her body tensed, her heart rate increased, her nipples hardened; she could feel the moisture between her legs. This was a first. No one had ever made love to her with words.

"I've never discussed the mechanics of making love before." Her voice was low, as if in wonder of it all. "So...what are you waiting for?"

Adam pulled her into his arms. "For you to ask."

Amber put her hands under his sweater then pulled it over his head. He was right. This was not the body of a juvenile. His broad shoulders, the contour of his arms, the ripples of his abdomen clearly were that of a man. "Make love to me, Adam..."

Their lips fused before she could complete the request. The moment his tongue touched hers it was as if she was lost in the sensual hands of a master. They roamed over her to the rhythm of his kisses as the nice white sensible blouse was pulled over her head. His touch was almost angelic yet devilish as he held her hands above her head then used his thumbs to caress the ulnar vein in her wrist causing the blood flow through her entire body to increase. He brought her wrist to his lips and kissed it as if he was making love to it. His eyes held hers captive as his fingers gently traveled from the elbow of her arm, down the side of her breast, outlining the curve of her waist. Removing her pants, he slowly massaged her inner thighs, across the back of them to the backside of her knees, applying pressure with those long fingers around the calves of her legs, down to her ankles at the acupressure point known to increase your sexual energy. Her pants and panties fell to the floor. This man was dangerous to her senses. He knew the female body well. He knew what to do with his hands and where to do it. At this point, he had not touched one sexual area of her body yet she was swimming with desire. Her heart was racing, her inner muscles contracting, her nipples became erect and sensitive to everything and he knew it. The moment he stripped out of his pants, and slipped on a condom, his lips circled one nipple as his hands, oh, those hands, covered the other. Amber was so engrossed in his touch she never noticed when he unsnapped her bra. All she knew was his mouth covered her nipple and his sucking had her squirming off the bed. As if the assault on one wasn't enough, he switched hands. Replaced his mouth on one and his hand on the other. The torture was the same. She couldn't keep her nails from digging into his shoulder as his thumb touched the kiss swollen nipple.

Every nerve ending in her body, from the tip of her fingers to the bottom of her feet, was crying out for release.

"Adam," she pleaded with him to stop the torment, but knew she would die the moment he did. It was not to be. She realized what he was about to do the moment he positioned the pillow under her. His hands followed his tongue down to her navel, resting under her hips. His fingers massaged the sensitive area right above her buttocks as his tongue licked her clitoris causing her hips to rise from the pillow. His mouth covered her so intimately, that she had to scream. The soft sound sent his tongue downwards, dodging, licking then dodging in and out until she had no recourse but to release. She bucked uncontrollably as her juices flowed. His hands now on her behind squeezing, releasing, then squeezing again in a calming motion, easing her climax to a little less than a roar. The pillow was removed and there he was, over her, gazing into her eyes. His smile displaying dimples she never noticed before.

"It's my turn." He kissed her lips gently, entwined his fingers with hers then slid easily into her warmth. He held her eyes until his had to close from the sensations assailing his body. She was sucking him in so tight he shuddered. She moved, he groaned, as waves of ecstasy flowed through his veins. He pulled out, only to slowly re-enter her until the tip of him hit her inner walls. The feeling enticed him to do it again, and again, and again, until his body moved involuntarily, capturing every angle of her scorching lips that closed around him. Building to the point where friction ignited and her explosion ricocheted his.

They laid there, unable to move as perspiration mingled with the scent of their love making. His hands now in her hair, massaging her scalp, still sending sensations throughout her body.

"You are still inside me."

He inhaled. "I know." He inhaled again. "Do you know there is a unique scent that penetrates the air after making love? When inhaled it arouses the senses more, making it impossible not to succumb to another round."

She smiled against his shoulder. "I did not know that, Dr. Lassiter."

She kissed the side of his neck. "Did you know that one of the best exercises for women is also the most intriguing feeling for a man?"

He smiled, as he pushed her curls from her neck and kissed her right below her earlobe. "I did know that."

She could feel him growing inside her in anticipation. "I'm ready for a workout." She contracted her inner lips. His intake of breath at the motion made her smile. "Do you like that, Dr. Lassiter?"

He nodded. "I do." He pulled her thigh over his, then squeezed her behind. She followed the rhythm of his hand with her inner lips and soon they were moving to a song of their making. Kissing, caressing, loving the newness of his yang to her yin, his king to her queen, their Adam and Amber.

Hours later they fell asleep spooned together with smiles on their faces. The world could be coming to an end for all they knew or cared. For them, this was heaven.

The fragrance from Amber's hair swimming through Adam's nostril's awakened him, stirring his need to have her just one more time before he completely surrendered to the depth of no return from sleep.

Amber felt the moment his arousal touched her backside. His arms tightened around her pulling her closer. The movement incited her inner lips to the point of no return. Now, she had to have him again.

He could feel her smile on his arm where her head lay. "You are asking for trouble." His groggy voice was low and stimulating.

She pushed her behind intimately against him, while taking his forefinger into her mouth. She sucked on it, tracing the length of it with her tongue. "I need you inside of me now, Adam."

Each time she sucked on his finger, he grew thicker, longer, more eager. Placing her thigh on top of his, he slid the tip of him easily inside the warm moist lips that were waiting for him. The vibration from the inner contractions stimulated him more. She bent her body forward more as he moved deeper in. The deeper he ventured, the harder she sucked. The harder she sucked, the more urgent his movements became.

Her breathing became labored as he snaked in and out until both of their faces turned into the pillow to silence the sounds of an all-encompassing orgasm.

Neither moved as their eyes closed welcoming the needed rest for their bodies, their souls, their minds.

CHAPTER TWENTY-THREE

This could not be happening again, rolled through Adam's subconscious, as he held Amber in his arms. Refusing to accept the interference, he pulled the warm body next to him closer.

The knocking persisted.

"Sleep," Adam called out to the rude person knocking on the door.

"Adam." The demanding voice of Sammy reached the recesses of his mind.

"Yeah," he replied groggily as he attempted to gather his senses. Amber stretched beside him causing a smile. "Hmm."

"Adam!"

"Yeah, I'm coming...I'm coming," he said as he pushed the sheet aside.

"He's coming," Amber giggled under the sheet.

Adam turned back over covering her body with his. "We have jokes early in the morning?" He kissed her face, then scrambled from the bed.

Amber watched as his naked backside walked into the bathroom. "Nice buns," she said as she laid back on the pillow. "Thick thighs."

The next statement stopped both of them mid sentence. "If the Dr. is in there with you, bring her to the Cave when you come."

It took a moment for him to reply. "Okay."

"How did he know I was in here?" A shocked Amber jumped from the bed to gather her clothes. Then she looked at her clothes in horror. "I don't have anything to change into."

Adam watched as she ran from one piece of clothing to another, buck-naked with her hair bouncing with every step. "Why are you so frazzled?"

Amber froze to stare up at him. "Your family is going to think I'm a harlot or something for sleeping in here with you."

He walked over, knocked everything from her hands then held her still by the shoulders. "They will not think that. They will know that you are the person I have chosen to be in my life." He kissed her gently on the lips. Then looked down at her. "You are short without heels on." He turned and walked back into the bathroom.

"You kissed me with toothpaste in your mouth." She frowned at the thought.

"Nice, fresh, minty." He smiled. "It really will be more efficient if you jump in the shower with me."

"Together? Like share the water...together?"

"Yes, together." He turned the shower on as he replied.

Amber stood there for a moment. She had never taken a shower with anyone before. The more she thought about it, the more ridiculous she knew she sounded. "What the hell, we shared more body fluids than that last night."

Adam held the shower door open. "My sentiments exactly." He grinned as she stepped in.

Twenty minutes later, they were both in the cave with Ned, Roc and Samuel.

"It seems we are a little late to the party," Ned informed them. "According to Queen Akande, young

Theodora has taken ill. Their medical facilities are nowhere near the level of ours."

"What are the child's symptoms?" Amber asked as all thoughts of her wanton behavior dissipated.

"This is all happening within the last hour," Monique, who was now in Asmere, picked up. The transmission was shaky at best.

"Are there any signs of the device there?" Adam asked.

"Inconclusive," Monique replied. "The child was fine when we arrived. King Raheem, Joshua, LaVere and a contingent of Emere soldiers left to secure the mines. Queen Akande is with Teddi in the infirmary. The doctor there has no idea what to do."

"Are they protected?" Ned asked.

"The guard, Sampson and a few men are with us. I'm outside the door."

"Is it possible for us to see the child," Roc, who had an extensive military medical background, asked.

"I'll do what I can." They watched as Monique walked inside a room. The child was lying in a hospital bed with an oxygen mask over her face. The woman standing next to the bed was her mother Queen Akande and a guard stood next to the door.

"Akande, our people want to see Teddi."

Akande turned to Monique. "She is so still. I have no idea what happened." Her voice was thick with accent and worry. "She was playing in the garden as she always has. The next thing I saw was her on the ground."

"I know. We're going to try to help her." She touched the woman on the arm. "Let me get closer." Monique was now standing over the child.

"Let me see her eyes." Monique held up the child's eyelid. The doctor reached over to shine a light. "Fluids," Amber immediately said upon seeing the coloring of the child's skin. She turned quickly to Adam. "How long will it take us to get there?"

"The Supersonic jet will get you there in four hours." Ned began pushing information into the computer.

"She's been drugged," Amber stated. "I don't know with what, but I know that look."

"I concur," Roc agreed.

"But in the other cases people died immediately," Samuel said.

"A child's system is different," Adam replied. "Their metabolism is much faster and able to eliminate a foreign substance sometimes before it can manifest. They probably did not account for that."

"If the poison was administered by J.M.A.L.T.S. the effect of the drug could have been altered by the incorrect assembly of the device." Ned offered. "That strengthens the need for the people involved to capture you, Adam."

"We can't think about that right now." Adam turned back to the screen and spoke to Monique. "Can you draw her blood and send it to me for analysis?"

"That would take too long. Get me to her. We can take the equipment there." Amber took Adam's computer and began keying. "These are the items I will need."

"No." Adam caught her as she was rushing out the door. "You can't."

"Adam, I have to. There are things I can do there that I can't do from here. I will never be able to live with myself if that child dies."

"Neither would I." Roc tried several times to stand, accomplishing it with Samuel's assistance.

"You definitely are not going." Samuel held Roc back.

"Gentlemen," Ned interrupted them. "If that child dies, you will all have a price on your head. Adam, this is what Dr. Nicolas does. Let her go."

"She's not going without me."

"No, Adam. It's clear these people want you. I can't protect you over there."

"I can," Monique chimed in. "What I know is Joshua is not aware of this situation. Believe me when I tell you, we want this situation under control before he finds out."

"I concur with Monique." Roc glared at Samuel.

"Samuel, one of my best operatives will be flying that plane. Adam and Amber will be covered by Monique from the moment they land. This is no longer only about Adam. It's about a small country and a little girl." Ned removed Samuel's hand from the door. "Let them go."

"Sammy, I'll be with Joshua," Adam pleaded. "Every minute we debate this puts that child closer to death."

Samuel looked at Ned. "Is Sly on that plane?" Sly Dawson was the operative who trained Joshua. He did not like the man but knew his skill level.

"Yes," Ned acknowledged.

Samuel pointed to Roc. "You stay put." Then rushed Adam and Amber out the door. "There's certain equipment you need to take with you." They literally walked through a wall when Samuel commanded it to open. The wall slid to the side to reveal a stairwell. They walked down one level underground. Samuel placed his palm on the panel next to the door. Adam looked around amazed. He had never seen the staircase or the room they were about to enter. Samuel opened the door and a light automatically came on.

Adam could not contain his awe. He walked through the closet of weapons on the wall, touching each as if he was a child in a candy store. "I want one of these," he exclaimed, his excitement visible to all.

Samuel pulled two cases off the shelf in the back. He placed them on the table and opened one. "You know what is in this kit, Adam."

"So do I," Amber stated from behind their backs. Both men turned to look at her questioningly. Realizing they did not believe her, Amber began describing the items in the case. "Beretta ARX-160 automatic rifle. Night goggles, and GPS body armor."

They still looked as if she was a ghost. She shook her head. "Men." She took the rifle, assembled and loaded it in less than a minute. "I'm a little out of practice." She shrugged at Adam. "It's been a while."

Samuel stared at her for a minute then took the weapon from her. He broke the gun down, placed it back inside the case, then closed it. He gave them each one then closed the door. They heard the lock go into place as they rushed up the stairs.

Roc met them in the hallway with duffle bags. "Adam, here's a travel bag for you. I put your computer inside. Amber, I have a change of clothes I believe will fit you, along with a few necessities. A medical bag will be on the plane." She stopped at the door as Samuel rushed them out to the garage past vehicles and up another flight of stairs.

Lucy, who was piloting the chopper turned the switch. The blades began to move the moment they set foot on the landing pad. "Let's move it," she ordered.

Within a matter of minutes of the decision being made, they were on their way to Africa. Lucy spoke through the headset. "Once on the sonic jet you will only have four hours to sleep. I suggest you use it. When you land there is no way of knowing when you will be able to close your eyes again. Adam, your mission is to detect if the devices have been released in

Asmere. If they have, it is your duty to your country to destroy them. Amber, you have one mission...save the girl. That child must not die."

Ten minutes later they were boarding the jet. A tall slim man dressed in a pinstripe suit, alligator shoes and a fedora stood in the middle of the roomy passenger area of the jet. To the left was a long sofa, to the right four seats with a table in the middle. Towards the back there was a conference table with eight seats, a monitor and several computer stations.

"This is what sleek luxury looks like." Adam raised an eyebrow.

"I guess so," Amber replied, surprised by the travel accommodations.

"There are times when this is the only place you can rest when on a mission." The man removed his hat, brought Amber's hand to his lips. "Sly," he introduced himself as he kissed her knuckles. Adam took her hand from the man. "Adam...Lassiter," he replied in a rather poignant tone.

"Ah, the young genius." He straightened to his full height, then replaced his hat. "Little brother to Joshua."

"Younger brother," Adam replied as he placed his duffle on the seat.

"Sensitive, isn't he." Sly smirked at Amber as he took the duffels and placed them in the cabinet that divided the two sections of the plane. "Alright, younger sensitive brother to Joshua, we have a four hour flight scheduled. Little time for you and I to connect. For now we'll keep it civil." He walked back to where they stood. "I'll keep my hands off the lady if you keep the attitude in check."

"The lips, too," Adam warned.

Sly raised an eyebrow. "Right. I will keep my lips off her." He looked Amber up and down then stopped at her face. "May I gaze into her eyes?"

Adam took a step in front of Amber who was smiling at the charming man. "No, definitely not the eyes."

Sly's gaze moved to Adam. "The shoes?"

"Okay, enough," Amber interrupted the teasing. "Who are you?"

"Sly is all you need to know. I'll be protecting you in Asmere. You may want to buckle up." He walked over to the monitor then pushed a button. "They are on board, Sir."

Adam and Amber took a seat, surprised to see the President on the monitor.

"Adam, it's good to see you again. I don't like the circumstances."

"Hello, Mr. President. I have to agree with you on that point."

"Ned tells me we have a conspiracy between forces in Asmere and a high ranking official here." He sat forward. "Secretary Davenport tells me we have a lead on this end. I've deployed my best team to assist you and Dr. Nicolas. Joshua and Monique are on land. Sly is flying you over. Whatever the government has is at your disposal. The devices must be found and destroyed."

"Yes, Sir."

"Dr. Nicolas it is not a coincidence that you are on that plane. I cannot impress upon you the importance of Princess Theodora's survival. The region is a boiling pot that we need contained. She is the key."

"Yes, Sir."

"You two have been through a rough few days from what I understand. Putting a mission of this magnitude in the hands of...well, amateurs is not the norm.

However, with the aid of our established team, I believe your mission will be successful."

"Thank you Sir," they both replied.

"Sly."

The man turned off the monitor, but continued to listen. "I will, Sir." Sly disconnected the call then turned to them. "Buckle up. I'm going to see how fast this baby can fly."

The man walked to the front of the plane a little too eager in Adam's estimation. "You're flying this plane?"

"Relax, younger brother to Joshua. You won't even know you're in the air." With that the door to the cockpit closed and the engine roared to life.

Adam opened his laptop then connected to Joshua's GPS location. Once he established the connection, he sent a secure message. He waited.

"Adam." He looked up to see Amber sitting directly across from him. "You haven't said much since leaving the house."

His computer beeped. "Hold that thought, sweetheart."

It wasn't what he said but the way he said it. With the emphasis on the word sweetheart.

"Adam, make it quick."

"I'm en route to Asmere."

Joshua paused then brought his watch up to look into it. "What?" The question wasn't asked in a surprised way...well maybe he was surprised, but it wasn't a happy surprise.

"Our investigation on J.M.A.L.T.S. has led us to the same person. I promised Sammy I would contact you as soon as we took off."

"Sammy let you do this?"

"Let me?" Adam shook his head. "It's my investigation, Joshua."

"There is more involved than you know, Adam."

"We've been brought up to date."

"We? We who?"

"That's not important. What you should know is I'll be landing in about four hours."

"You're on the jet? Who is piloting?"

"Someone going by the name of Sly."

"Ned made the arrangements?"

"Yes."

He slowed his progress a bit more, clearly thinking through the information. "We are nearing the mines."

"Hold on before you go in. I'm sending you a link. Download it now." He pushed a button on the computer.

"Got it. What is it?"

"A tracker. If the device is in the area it will sound an alert."

"Any idea how to stop this thing?"

"If we can find a way to interfere with the neurotransmitter that will incapacitate its ability to transmit or receive electromagnetic waves." He shrugged.

"What in the hell is that?"

"Never mind, I'll have something in place by the time we land."

"You do that. In the meantime watch your back."

"You do the same." With that the connection was dropped.

CHAPTER TWENTY-FOUR

Adam closed the computer then looked into the eyes of Amber. She was not too happy. Neither was he. A few hours ago she was dressed in a nice white blouse, navy trousers and heels with soft curls framing her face. Now she was dressed in a dark tee shirt, dark jeans and Timberland boots with her hair up in a band. He liked the idea of her being every woman, but he also had a strong desire to know the person he was falling in love with. He put his feet up in the seat across from him, rested his head in his hand with one finger extended. "You have my undivided attention."

The memory of what that hand did last night filled her mind. She closed her eyes and exhaled. She needed to concentrate. Clearing her throat, she opened her eyes then tilted her head. "Your vitals indicate you are a little miffed with me."

"Don't try to entice me with the sexy doctor talk."

Amber laughed. "Okay, you caught me. Why are you upset?"

"It's unclear who Amber Nicolas is at the moment. I have the boring by the book Dr. Amber and now I find GI Jane Amber, who not only knows her weapons, but clearly knows how to use them." He sighed. "Who are you?"

"Adam, my father was a military man before sitting behind a desk. He taught me about guns when I was ten years old. I've been going to the firing range since I was twelve. Why does that bother you?"

"I've been walking around boasting about protecting you for two days. Now to find out you probably know more about weapons than I do."

Amber moved to the seat next to him. "Not all weapons, just guns." She kissed his cheek then looked up at him. He had the prettiest eyes and long lashes any woman would kill for. Then it was the vulnerability she saw. She put her arm through his and laid her head on his shoulder. "Tell me about little Adam."

He kissed the top of her head. "You don't want to know about him."

"Yes, I do. I want to know how you became you." Adam smirked. She could sense his hesitance to talk about himself. This only made her want to know more, to find a way to ease his yearning to keep proving his worth. "Please." She blinked those light brown eyes up at him.

Adam looked down at her. Was he ready to share his inner thoughts with her? "You're an only child. I'm not sure you would understand the dynamics of a large family."

"I may not, but it would help if you told me about each one."

"Where should I start?" He thought for a moment. "The Lassiters according to Adam." He put his arms around her and they settled in. "There are two sets of children. The older set, Samuel, Joshua, Ruby, Pearl, Diamond and Mathew. They were all in high school or middle school when I was born. It was like having several sets of parents. Samuel and Ruby had just as much say when it came to the children as my parents did. If they told you to do something, you did it, the same as if my parents gave the order. Then there is the second set of children, Luke, Opal and Timothy, they are twins, so are Jade and I, and my baby sister Sapphire. Everyone calls her a brat, but she really isn't." He shook his head. "She is at the bottom of the totem pole trying to find her way."

"Like you?"

Adam nodded. "Like me."

"That's a lot of people to look up to."

"You're telling me. And every one of them is incredibly successful in their professional lives. It's hard to determine which role model to follow. I mean, look at Samuel. He was a star football player in high school. He joined the service and what does he do...become a freakin' Navy Seal of all things. There isn't a more elite team than that. Unless you go clandestine like my brother Joshua did. His security level rivals that of the President. Half the time we have no idea where he is or what he's doing. I remember watching television with my family when this news report came on about the capture of the leader of some drug cartel in Mexico. My father looked at my mother and said, Joshua should be home soon. For a while many of the major missions involving the United States, I was certain Joshua was on the scene. Then there's my sister Ruby. She is the closest thing to an angel you will ever know. She not only spent her life making sure her younger brothers and sisters had everything they could possibly want or need, she does it for other people too. After her nine to five she goes to this homeless shelter. There she cooks and cleans, helps the women learn new skills, finds them jobs, and takes time to tutor the children. I don't think she has ever missed a day from that shelter. And Pearl." He shook his head. "She is on a completely different playing field. As the press secretary for the President of the United States, she is one of the most recognizable women in the world. And she didn't get there by her looks. She joined the President's very first campaign and never looked back. She literally worked her way up. Now Diamond." He smiled. "She is the essence of her name. If you want a person who could take the most cantankerous person and turn them into a gentle kitten within minutes, she's the one. She works in customer relations for her husband's construction business. Diamond takes the time to learn what people really need, not just what they think they want and it pays for her. Of course in every family there is that one you have no idea how they are going to turn out. For us, it's Mathew. He's a basketball coach at one of the high schools. He's good and great with the boys. I mean he looks out for them on the court and off. Matt may not have the spotlight when it comes to jobs, but I think his is the most rewarding. Those of us in the lower half, all got to attend college. Each of the older children took on the responsibility of helping with college tuition for us. As each one of us was accepted, they would all pool together to ensure nothing interfered with our education. Because of that, Luke got to play football and was drafted as the second round pick in the NFL draft when he graduated. He is now one of the top running backs in the league. Opal and Timothy each received a Master's in accounting, they sat for the CPA exam, passed it and opened their own accounting firm. Jade has her Master's in journalism and is working as an investigative reporter, but she really wants to write crime novels. She has a few manuscripts but hasn't submitted them." He turned to her grinning. "I've read them and they are good. She doesn't believe me when I tell her that and I can't seem to convince her to go for it." He shrugged his shoulders. "I don't know when it comes to the two of us. It's like we are struggling to live up to the others."

"What about your little sister, Sapphire?"

"Phire." He grinned. "My mom sure knew how to name her children," he laughed. "We call her Phire, my mom calls her a spitfire. Whatever she is called by she is hell on wheels."

Amber laughed at the expression on Adam's face. "Nothing stops her from saying what she thinks or going after what she wants. Ironically, she is the one that is more like my mother than any of us. My mom was a ballerina on the semi professional level and I'm pretty sure Phire is going to be a dancer. She loves performing and she's good." He thought for a moment. "Phire knows who she is and makes no excuses for it. She's in college now, but when she was in high school she announced she was going to abstain from sex until she is married. She caught hell from the kids at school. Some teased her, while others tried their best to get her to break her vow. But, they did not break her," he said with pride. "She found the person she wanted to be early and has lived her life that way." He exhaled. "I'm still looking."

Amber snuggled closer in the seat. "It's amazing the way your family loves each other. You have a connection...a bond. Are any of them married?"

"Yes, Samuel, Joshua, Diamond and Pearl are all married."

"How do their spouses fit in?"

"Like they belong. It's like Cynthia, Roc, Zack and Theodore, were just waiting to be adopted."

"Wow." She thought before speaking. "You have placed each of them on a pedestal so high you don't feel you can reach them."

"No I haven't," he protested.

"Yes, you have. As wonderful as they all sound, I am so certain if you speak to any one of them they would have you on a pedestal as well. I will also wager they have issues in their lives just like every other human being in existence. They have insecurities just like all of us. You may not hear about them, but they exist."

"We would know about them," Adam protested.

"You may hear about personal or financial problems, but you don't hear about the insecurities, Adam, because people tend not to share those." She sat up. "I listened to you speak about each of your siblings' accomplishments. What do you think they say about you?"

"That I've caused them more headaches from bad publicity and financial burdens than one family should have to experience. I've blown up several labs, caused people's skin to turn colors, been on the brink of being suspended from school so many times I can't even count and now I've been dismissed from the Bureau. I wouldn't blame them if they were on the verge of disowning me. When I think about the shame I've brought to my family, I find it hard to face them all."

"Are you serious right now?" Amber could not believe what she was hearing. She popped him on the back of his head as she stood. "You have a brain the size of Texas yet you can't see what you have brought to this world. You've created things that most people can't even fathom. Everything you touch has turned into a new toy for the government. I am in awe of the way your mind works. Yet, you are sitting here whining about not living up to your siblings."

"I don't whine."

"What the heck do you call it?" With a hand on her hip she began pointing at him with her finger. "I am moments away from falling in love with you. And let me tell you, I don't pick duds. I'm a woman with a very high level of intelligence and the last thing I want or need is a man who does not recognize his own abilities. You are on a freakin' plane on your way to Africa on a mission for the President of the United States. Do you think he would send someone to handle this who is not up to the task? I don't. Samuel equipped you to make this trip. Do you think he would have sent you if he did not believe you would come back alive? And Joshua, he just got off the phone with you knowing that by the time you land you will have an answer on how to stop the damn device you created. The bigger than life Joshua is looking to little brother Adam to come in and save the day. Hmmm, I wonder why? Let's forget your family for a minute. Do you think for one moment I would put my life in the hands of a man who was not capable? Who does not know how to make my body sing? How to keep me laughing? Or in the hands of someone who could not protect me?" She searched around the cabin as she fussed then stopped when she found a blanket. "Yes, you may have done all of the things you mentioned before. But to what end? What was the outcome? How many lives have you saved because of those things? I don't know who you think you are, Adam Fitzgerald Lassiter, but you damn well better have it figured out by the time I wake up." She stretched out on the sofa then covered herself with the blanket. "And don't even think about coming over here to touch me with those hands until you do."

Adam listened, stunned, as she continued to mumble under the blanket. It took him a moment to realize she was angry over his admissions. They were all legitimate things he had done. When he walked out of Vance's office his major concern was how could he face his father with yet another failure, another rejection? How dare she belittle his concerns? Amber sounded worse than Jade when she used to berate him for being so hard on himself. Yes, he had done some good. But he had made a lot of mistakes along the way and it had cost his family. He would never forget the medical bills his family had to pay to the frat boy's families when he turned their skin another color. He knew his father had been looking to buy a new house in a nicer neighborhood, but had to take his savings to cover the debt. Proceeds from different inventions he had sold had more than replaced the funds, but the opportunity for his parents never returned. That is something he would never forgive himself for.

Adam picked up his computer. He tried to concentrate on the transmitter in J.M.A.L.T.S. but he kept looking over at Amber. He thought about her words, Samuel and Joshua were depending on him. Even the President of the United States was looking to him to solve this situation. Most importantly, she was depending on him. He smiled. The beautiful Amber was depending on him to protect her.

"You like the way my hands roam over your body, don't you?"

"It depends." She never lifted her head from under the cover. "Are you going to allow little brother to Joshua to block you from becoming the man I know you can be?"

He thought about that then sprang up. "That's it."

Amber turned the cover down and looked at him.

His fingers were flying across the keyboard. "What?"

"I can build a force field that will block the waves from the transmitter, which it needs to work."

Amber threw the blanket aside then walked over to him. "It would prevent them from receiving the signal from its base."

He glanced up. "That's right. You are so sexy at this moment. Can Adam make love to you?"

"Little brother to Joshua sure as hell can't."

CHAPTER TWENTY-FIVE

Sleep never came for the two as they spent time designing the force field. Once on the ground a chopper was waiting to transport them to the compound where the palace was located.

Sly had just landed the chopper on the grounds near the palace when they were immediately surrounded by armed soldiers. Sly pushed a button on the console of the chopper. It fired, sending all the soldiers to the ground in a matter of seconds.

"Oh my God, you killed them," Amber screamed. "You killed them with no warning."

"They had guns drawn on us," Sly said in a matter of fact tone as he walked by them to the hangar.

"They were blanks," Adam explained. "Just something to stun them for a moment."

Amber looked out of the window. "They are not moving, Adam."

"Trust me, they were blanks."

"How do you know?"

"The impact from firing that many bullets from the size of the weapon on this Hawk would have thrown us from our seats if they were real."

She thought about that as Sly opened the back door to the hangar. He tilted his hat. "Shall we go?" He grinned.

Amber saw the men on the ground begin to stir then angrily turned on Sly. "There is something seriously wrong with you."

"Is that any way to talk to the man who is supposed to protect you at all costs?"

Adam took Amber's hand and helped her down to the ground. He looked at Sly and smiled. "I like the hat."

Sly grinned. "My man."

A soldier approached them from the rear of the palace. "Dr. Lassiter?"

"Yes." Adam extended his hand.

"Sampson is my name. They are waiting for you in the infirmary. Hurry."

Adam and Amber grabbed their duffels and followed the man. Inside, they were taken to the basement, where the hallway led to several rooms. There were waiting room chairs lined up against the wall. Two guards stood outside a room.

Adam stopped at the door as the guards stepped aside. He looked through the single windowpane at the child hooked up to an IV lying on the bed. A woman sat beside her. "Princess Theodora?" he asked Sampson.

"Yes," he replied in a deeply accented voice.

"How long has she been here at the infirmary?" Amber asked.

"Just around six hours." He was clearly shaken. "I have come to care deeply for the child. At first, I could not understand how her parents would allow her to cause such mayhem each day. Now, I find myself looking forward to her mishaps."

It was apparent to Adam and Amber, that the child was loved, not only by her parents, but also by those protecting her.

"Whatever evil has caused this, I will kill."

Adam and Amber shared a strained look. "I'm going to see what I can do." Amber nodded to Adam.

Adam turned to Sampson. "Will you show me where this happened?"

Sampson nodded, then walked away as Adam followed.

Amber walked into the room.

Monique stood. "Akande, this is the doctor I told you about."

Queen Akande stood, taking both of Amber's hands in hers.

"We call her Teddi." The voice of Queen Akande was riddled with sadness. "She is so spirited and full of laughter every day. To see her like this, so still....." Her cry caught in her throat, then she shook her head and looked up at Amber. "I will give my life for her. Please, whatever I have is yours. Just bring my child back."

Amber touched the Queen's arm. "I will do everything in my power." She motioned to Monique. "I'm going to examine her. When I'm done, I will come out to speak with you."

"Take a walk with me, Akande." Monique guided her towards the door. "Let her work." She glanced at Amber. "We won't go far."

Amber nodded as she covered her hands with latex gloves then turned her attention to the little girl. She was beautiful, with smooth dark skin, natural soft curly hair, rose lips and the imprint of dimples on each cheek. The oxygen mask was out of place and too big for the child. Amber removed it.

"Let's see what they have done to you." She talked to the child as she began her examination. After checking her heart rate and blood pressure, she examined the child's eyes to confirm what she saw earlier. It was as she thought. The child was heavily sedated. "So what caused you to go to sleep, sweetie?"

she asked as she continued. She checked the child's neck since that was the location of attack on the other victims. There was nothing on either side, nor her back and nothing on her throat. She then slowly moved her fingers through her hair. Using a comb and a light, she examined every inch of the girl's scalp. She still found nothing. Next she checked her extremities. First her arms, hands, and fingers. It was on the forefinger of her left hand that she found the little prick.

Amber took her light and held it to the child's finger. She could tell that it did break the skin, however it didn't penetrate too deep. Amber looked around for her chart. There wasn't one. She ran to the door.

"Where is the physician that attended this child?"

Akande sprang up from the place she had insisted they wait. "Calah," she called out urgently.

The doctor stepped out from another room. "Yes, Your Highness."

"The doctor wishes to speak with you." She pushed him forward and followed. "Did you find something?"

"Not yet." Amber motioned to Monique to handle Akande as she turned to Calah. "Was the child's finger bleeding when she came to you?"

"Not much, but a little." He nodded.

"You wiped her finger," Amber asked eagerly. "Did you take a sample of her blood as we requested."

"Yes, yes, right over here." He took her to the room he had just come from. It was no larger than a closet, with shelves. On one shelf there was a refrigerator type object. He opened it then gave her the vial. Amber looked at the device she took to be their microscope and knew it would not give her the power needed to examine the blood. She ran out to the chopper.

"I need help setting up the machine," she said to Sly who had piloted the Black Hawk. She hoped he knew how to operate the equipment on it.

"Done," he replied helping her into the hangar area.

Surprised, she looked around checking to ensure everything was hooked up correctly. "Good." Amber glanced over her shoulder at him as she opened the laptop attached to the machine. "Looks like you know your medical equipment. What else do you do?" she asked as she keyed in pertinent information about the patient.

"A little of this, a little of that."

"That's a vague reply."

"I'm a vague person." He grinned as he watched her keying in a request. "What are you looking for, Dr.?"

"A drug that will sedate, could also kill if received in a large dosage."

"Arsenic, Nicotine and Morphine. The general stuff." Sly smirked. "The question I think you need answered is was the drug used home grown or was it brought in? You see, people tend to use what is convenient."

Amber looked at the man who was dressed like Youngblood Priest, a character from the 80's Blaxploitation movie, Super Fly. She was certain if anyone knew about drugs he would. Even the way he was leaning against the cargo lining of the Hawk, with his legs stretched out and the hat almost covering his eyes. To her it was as if he was sitting in a big black Cadillac with a sunroof top and a gangsta lean. She thought about his statement. "That's a good point. I mean if you wanted to poison a magnitude of people you would use what's at your fingertips. Not something you would have to transport here. What is plentiful here?" she asked almost as an afterthought.

"Opium." He grinned.

Amber turned back to the computer and made an adjustment. "You may have something there."

"I have a good thought from time to time."

Amber turned back and smiled. "I'm sure you do."

"I have another I'd like to share with you." He stood as he adjusted his hat. "A man needs to feel like he can protect his woman, even if she is capable. My daughter-in-law had to learn that same lesson." He shook his head. "Believe me, it wasn't pretty."

Amber held his glare then turned away. "Will you let me know when that report comes back?"

"Will do."

She hesitated for a moment. "I'm very capable of taking care of myself." She shrugged. "I've been living on my own for a while." She exhaled. "It would be nice to have a man who could take over that task just a little." She nodded her head, looked around then huffed. "Well, thank you," she turned "for the advice too." And with that she was headed back into the one story infirmary. Why did things with men have to be so complicated? One minute they want you helpless and needy, and the next they want you to stand on your own two feet. How was she supposed to be both? The question that was really bugging her was who in their right mind would have children by Sly? It was clear to her the man was missing one or two brain cells. Come to think of it, Adam wasn't far behind.

When she returned to the room Adam was standing outside. "Did you find anything?"

"No." Adam shook his head. "Not in the garden." He rubbed the back of his neck. "They are here. I know it. I don't understand why we can't find them."

"You'll find them. I know you will." Amber touched his face. "I'm running tests on her blood. It should only take about an hour to get a preliminary read."

"You still believe she was poisoned?"

"Yes." She walked into the room. "Look at this."

She held up the child's hand to show Adam the puncture mark.

"That was done less than twenty-four hours ago."

"Right." Amber gave him her light. "Take a look at her eyes."

Adam did as she asked. "Hmmm. She's sedated." His computer buzzed. He sat it on the bed next to the child then opened it. "Joshua, I know how to stop the device."

"Good, because we're surrounded by rebels. We need you and Sly to knock a few of them off our backs."

"Send me the location."

"Done."

Adam closed his laptop, then kissed Amber. "I have to go. We'll get back to you as soon as we free Joshua."

Adam stepped outside the room. "Monique, do you know the area where the mines are?"

"Yes." She looked at his computer screen then pointed. "This is open space. They can see you coming a mile away."

"Is there a back way in?"

"There wasn't the last time I was there."

"There is." Akande stood. "Raheem would come in from the area behind the woods to check on the workers. They cannot see you until you are right on top of them."

"How do we get in?" Akande pointed to his computer screen as she explained each entrance.

Amber ran out to the chopper to grab a few things before they took off. "I will need you to send me the toxicology report as soon as it comes out."

"You're looking for this," Sly offered.

Amber looked at the small container. "Naloxone hydrochloride." She looked up at him. "Yes, if she was poisoned by any opiates, this is the antidote."

"Take this with you, too." He gave her the weapon package Samuel had supplied them with. He then put a band around her wrist. "Do not remove." He pointed to every word imprinted on the band.

Amber looked at the band then at him. "Should I ask?"

"No." Sly closed the door to the hangar just as Adam jumped in.

"Be careful," Amber mouthed to him.

"Hey, you're talking to Adam."

She smiled. "See you soon."

"See you soon, Redbird."

Amber stood back and watched as the chopper took off.

Monique stood behind her. "Inside, Doc. He's in good hands."

Amber turned and walked into the building. "Are you sure about that?"

Monique laughed. "Sly is the best. The team isn't going to be the same without him."

"He's leaving?"

"This is his last mission."

"And exactly what is it you do on these missions," Amber asked as they reached Teddi's room.

Monique shrugged. "A little of this, and a little of that."

Amber paused at the door. "That's exactly what he said."

"It should be, he trained Joshua and Joshua trained me."

"So if I ask Joshua, he would have the same response?"

Monique nodded. "Yes."

Akande turned as the women walked in. "Any word yet?"

"No, I'm sorry." Amber set down the items she'd gathered from the Hawk. "But I have several things here. Depending on that report, I will be able to

administer whichever of these antidotes we will need."
She checked Teddi's vitals. "She is still the same. Which
is good." She touched the worried woman's hand. "Her
condition has not deteriorated in any way. For now she
is stable." Amber brushed her hand across the child's
hair. "She's a beautiful little girl." Amber shook her
head. "She reminds me of someone, but I can't put my
hands on who."

"Joshua," Akande whispered, causing Monique's
head to snap up.

"No." I've never met him."

The breath Monique was holding was released with
the thought that Amber did not pick up on what she
was certain was Akande's blunder.

"You've never met Joshua?" Akande smiled. "He is
a very brave man." Her head fell to her chest. "Funny
too. A little misguided on the MacGyver vs Bauer
judgment, but other than that he's quite intelligent."

Monique laughed. "Bauer all the way."

"I beg to differ." Amber sat on the bed next to the
child. "MacGyver hands down."

"What?" Akande and Monique exclaimed.

"No way," Monique laughed. "Give me a gun and
good explosives and it's BOOM! Done deal."

For the first time all day Akande smiled.

"Ah but you see, MacGyver can make something
from whatever is around and save the day."

"You and Joshua would be a match made in
heaven." Akande smiled then turned to her daughter.

Amber shared a knowing glance with Monique. "I
know it's hard, but we will find out what happened."
Her phone buzzed. She looked at the message from
Adam.

Traces of chemically altered morphine.

Amber nodded then jumped into action.

"What is it?" Akande asked.

"We are going to wake this child up." Amber prepared an injection.

"What can I do?" Monique stood next to the bed.

Amber shook her head and She raised an eyebrow. "Just be ready." She inserted the needle, choosing to administer the drug intravenously for a quicker reaction. She dropped the needle into the dispensary, checked her watch and did a count down.

"Nothing's happening," Akande cried out.

"Oh, it will," Amber assured her.

Teddi sat straight up in the bed. She looked around the room then let out a wail that rivaled a bullhorn. Akande stood shocked at the child's reaction. Then she clapped her hands in joy. Grabbing the child into her arms she cried right along with her.

Amber was surprised when she saw tears streaming down the tough Monique's cheeks. "A child can break through anyone's barriers." She smiled. She allowed the Queen to hold her daughter a moment longer as she sent a message to Adam.

Child awake.

"I need to examine her just to ensure there are no lingering effects of the drug."

Akande reluctantly released the crying child into Amber's hands. Within a minute, she had the child settled down. Akande watched as Amber checked her daughter over, even eliciting a smile or two.

"We are going to keep her awake for a while. Isn't that right, Teddi?"

The girl nodded, still a little hesitant towards the stranger. Amber touched the girl's hair. "Pretty."

Teddi nodded her head yes. She then touched Amber's curls. "Pretty."

Amber smiled. "Thank you."

That was when a sound caught Monique's attention. She walked to the open door and looked out. Sampson was walking towards them.

"Several helicopters are in our airspace. I want to secure the Queen and Princess."

"How many?" Monique asked as she began checking her weapons.

"Two large ones like what you arrived in." He nodded to Amber.

"How many men do you have on hand?" she asked as she sent a message to Ned.

"Less than twenty. We're cut low. Half of the men were at the mines. King Raheem and Absolute took most of those remaining with them."

"Amber, are you strapped?"

Amber stopped playing with the child. "I have a duffle. What's wrong?" she asked as she opened her duffle.

"I'm not sure." Monique looked around. "My gut is telling me to make a move." Taking one of the weapons out, Amber put it in her waistband then pulled her blouse over it.

Monique checked the bag. "I see you came prepared."

"Samuel."

"Good. I have a feeling we are going to need it." She threw the bag over her shoulder.

"Sampson, let's move out." Monique checked her phone. "ETA, twenty."

"The two should not be in the same place."

Monique nodded. "I agree. Akande, take me up the back way to your suites."

"I'm not leaving my daughter." Akande reached for Teddi.

"I promise to protect her with my life." Amber took the woman's hand from around the child. "You must go with Monique." Amber looked at Teddi. "Put your arms around my neck." The child did as she was told.

"Mother," Teddi cried out.

Akande contemplated what she should do. "Very well." She kissed Teddi. "You must do what the pretty doctor tells you to, okay." She hugged her. "It's okay, Teddi." Akande stood behind Monique. "Amber will take good care of you."

They stepped into the hallway. "Calah, go to the bunker and stay there until I return." Sampson said to the young man. They continued until they heard gunshots coming from the direction where they were heading.

"Is there another way out?" Monique knew a Hawk could carry up to twelve men in full armor. That mean at least twenty-four if not more were on the grounds. She had to keep everyone alive until help arrived.

Sampson turned before she finished the statement. "The exit to the courtyard."

"The courtyard is too open," Monique replied as they quickly walked the corridor. When they reached the exit, they heard more gunfire.

"Sounds like they are downstairs now." Amber looked around anxiously.

Sampson stepped out just enough to look around. Monique joined him. She surveyed the area looking for anything that could shelter them. "What's that door right there?" She pointed to an area under the palace.

Sampson glanced around. "Storage area for the gardener."

"How big is it?"

"Big enough," he replied as he led them out.

They eased out of the exit, stayed flush to the building and slid inside the storage area just as gunfire erupted in the basement.

"Calah!" Akande began to pray.

"Mother, are the bad people here?"

"Yes, I'm afraid so." She reached out to touch her child's face in the dark. "But it will be okay."

"Shhh." Monique cautioned as she heard the side door open.

Sampson had walked to the back of the storage area to ensure they were secure. He took up the rear. Monique guarded the front.

Amber pulled out her cell. There were no bars. "I can't call Adam."

"I sent a message earlier. Help is on the way."

"How long?"

Monique did not answer. She held up her finger to her mouth. Sampson came up next to her as she pushed the door slightly ajar. There was a soldier walking backwards towards them with his weapon up ready to fire. It was one of the palace guards. Sampson motioned for them to move back from the door. He gave Monique his gun, reached out and grabbed the soldier from behind. Monique had her gun to his head before he hit the ground.

Sampson stopped her. "He is one of mine." He helped the soldier up. "What did you see?"

"They have taken the top floors of the palace."

"Who?" Monique asked.

"American soldiers."

"How many?" Sampson asked.

"We took out three. They are looking for the Queen."

Monique looked at Akande. "Where are they in the palace?" Monique surveyed the area outside.

"Some upstairs in the King's quarters, others on the main level and some in the basement."

"Damn," Monique exclaimed.

"We can't stay here." Amber glanced at the frightened child in her arms.

Akande stepped forward. "There is a way out of here. When I was a prisoner here, I would crawl out of that very window. If I could crawl out, we can crawl in."

"Where does it lead?" Monique asked.

"Into the dungeon of the palace."

"Okay." Monique thought for a moment. "We are going to split up. Amber, you are going to stay here. The guards will remain with you. Akande, you and I are going into the dungeon."

"No," Sampson protested. "They will capture the Queen. I cannot allow that. It is my duty to protect her."

"It is my duty to do the same," Monique explained. "It is more important that you protect Teddi. When the chopper arrives you get them to it in one piece. I will protect your Queen."

Sampson wasn't buying it.

"Sampson." Akande stepped forward. "I am ordering you to protect Teddi with your life. Get her on that chopper." She turned to Amber. "Take care of my daughter."

"With my life," Amber replied.

The voices from outside grew louder. "We have to go, now." Monique ordered.

Akande ran over to the window. She waited until there was another round of gunfire, then pulled the window open. Monique slipped inside first, then Akande followed.

The dungeon, as Akande called it, was partially lit. The room they landed in was a small ten by ten cell. They stayed to the corner, careful not to be seen.

Monique sighed. "Akande, we've been through a lot together. I need you to trust me on what I'm going to ask you to do."

"I know you will only ask that I do what is necessary."

Monique suppressed a smile. "We have to pull the soldiers' attention from Teddi. To do that, we will have to expose ourselves."

Akande thought about what she was asking, then slowly nodded. "Promise me, if anything happens to me you will ensure Teddi gets to Joshua."

"Nothing is going to happen to you."

"Promise me."

"All right, all right, I promise. But nothing is going to happen. They will have to kill me to get to you. I have a man in the States I have to get back to."

Akande smiled. "There was a time when we did not care for one another. Now, we are good friends, yet you have not mentioned this man."

"That's what you want to talk about right now?" Monique smirked. "Let's concentrate on getting out of here so I can have me a Teddi or two."

They heard men coming into the area.

"We have to get away from this window," Monique said as she looked around.

"Come." Akande pulled Monique to the door of the cell. She looked over her shoulder at Monique. "It will alert them once we open this door."

Monique checked her watch. "Let's wait until we hear the chopper."

"You will not hear it from here."

"Shit," Monique exclaimed. "Okay." She shook it off. "We are going to have to wing it."

A confused Akande stared at her.

Monique chuckled. "I forgot how literal you are. We are going to do our own count down and pray that the cavalry arrives in time."

CHAPTER TWENTY-SIX

The chopper was just about to break the tree line when the message came in from Ned. Sly glanced at Adam.

"It would be prudent for us to dispense of this situation and return to the palace forthwith."

"Forthwith?" Adam raised an eyebrow at the man who he would have bet his last dollar did not know what the word meant. "Teddi okay?"

"At the moment," Sly stated as he motioned to Adam. "It seems they may be under attack."

"What?" Adam pulled out his cell and dialed Amber. "No response. Shit." Adam opened his laptop to an infrared program, and then activated it. "Open the guns."

"We don't have a target."

"Open the damn guns," Adam demanded as he scanned his computer. He pointed to the screen. "That should be Joshua and his team."

"So if that's Absolute and that's the King and his men. Who are they?" Sly pointed to an area on the backside of the mines as they emerged from the forest. There were at least twenty men fully armed.

Adam unbuckled then stepped into the belly of the Hawk. He pulled out the M16 assault rifle. He checked the mag to ensure it was fully loaded, then put another mag in his pants pocket.

Adam looked back. "Keep it steady."

"How many rounds you got?"

"30 mag," Adam replied as he swung the door open.

Sly smiled as he said to himself, "I like that youngen." He swung the Hawk up and over the trees.

Adam stood in the opening of the door and fired until every man on the ground was down. Sly continued flying over the mines until they reached the other side.

"Take me down a little lower."

Joshua looked up to see the Hawk fly over them with Adam in the open cargo door, looking like Rambo with his gun taking out anything that moved.

He came back to his seat as Sly circled the area to ensure the danger had been eliminated.

"Joshua," Adam spoke into his cell.

"What in the hell is wrong with you?" Joshua yelled into the phone. "You could have fallen out of the damn chopper."

"The Palace is under attack. Get out of there as soon as you can. We're heading back."

"Teddi?" Joshua's scared voice questioned.

It took Adam a minute to respond. He had never heard fear in his brother's voice before. "I don't know."

"Get to her, Adam. I'll meet you there."

Before Adam had finished the call, Sly had the chopper going full speed back to the palace.

Sly came in from the rear of the palace. Adam was lying on his belly firing at the men in the rear of the palace.

Monique knew the time had come. It wasn't a loud sound, but it was distinctive. "Time to go." She looked at Akande. "Which direction to the courtyard?"

"To the left, then up the stairs."

Monique stood. "Stay behind me." Taking a deep breath she pushed the cell door open and ran to the left and up the stairs with Akande on her heels.

They froze the moment they reached the top. Walking in the door to the palace from the courtyard was none other than General Gerald Ashton, Vice-Chairmen of the Joint Chiefs of Staff.

Monique was stunned at first, but when his men pointed their weapons her way, she knew they had been very wrong and raised her weapon pointing it directly at the General.

"Ah." He stood with his legs braced and had the nerve to be grinning. "Just the person I have been looking for. Come out, Queen Akande. Let's not draw this out."

Monique held her arm out blocking Akande from moving forward. "You will eat the first bullet."

"How noble. I can simply have my men shoot both of you, you know. But I have no quarrels with you. Whoever you are."

"I have one with you, General Ashton," Monique replied as she scanned the room making a mental note of how many men she would have to kill and in what order.

He raised an eyebrow. "You know who I am?"

"I do. I'm certain the President will be disappointed, but not surprised."

"The President. How could someone like you know the President?" He shrugged. "But then we must remember he came from the slums of Virginia. You may very well know him, but it does not matter. You will not live long enough to tell him."

"I beg to differ." The voice came from behind the General.

Monique wanted to curse. What in the hell was Amber doing there? But it did not matter. She watched as Amber opened fire with her weapon taking out four of the eight men she counted. She knocked Akande to the ground covering her. Monique sat up and fired taking out three more, but Ashton had disappeared.

Monique looked around to see Ashton had Amber in a choke hold with a gun to her head. Monique held her weapon steady on him.

"It was the perfect plan. No one would have ever known the difference if it hadn't been for you." He smirked at Amber as he kept his eye on Monique. "The plan would have been over and done by the time the toxicology reports came back on McCoy. You almost ruined it." He jerked her. "But we adjusted."

"Shoot him, Monique," Amber yelled out. "Shoot him."

"You don't want to do that, little lady. My finger might twitch and your friend here will be dead. All you have to do is turn over the Queen and her bastard child. We can share the wealth."

At that moment Teddi broke away from Sampson who was behind the pillar.

Everything seemed to go in slow motion. Ashton laughed. He moved the gun from Amber's head to point at the child. Amber pushed him to the side and grabbed Teddi. Gunfire erupted as she ran out the way she came.

Amber covered the child's head. She ran and fell to the ground on her knees. Two soldiers shielded them. Warning yells to take cover were heard. Amber looked over Sampson's shoulder to see several men in uniforms running towards them. More gunfire was heard and several of the men fell to the ground.

Sampson then picked her and the child up and ran towards the helicopter that was landing. Sampson pushed them inside.

Adam jumped off the Hawk with weapons drawn taking out anyone firing in their direction. "Get them out of here, Sly," he yelled.

Sly lifted the Hawk just as Joshua landed. The chopper turned left and then circled around. Amber looked out to see a multitude of soldiers descend from the other Hawk. The one leading the pack she knew was Adam's brother. The two stood literally side by side firing at the remaining men. Then she saw the General come out with the Queen. Amber looked around frantically. There was no sign of Monique. The Queen looked to be bleeding. Adam's brother held his gun up and put a bullet right in the middle of the General's forehead. The Queen dropped to the ground. A man ran to her and knelt beside her.

"Who is that?" Amber asked as she shielded the child's eyes from the scene below.

"King Raheem."

She held the screaming child tight. "Shh, sweetheart. It's going to be okay. "Was the Queen or Monique injured?" Amber asked Sly who was still surveying the area below.

He held up his hand and listened as the transmitter squeaked with chatter. The information was coming quickly as she stared, waiting for a response.

"Is the Queen injured? What about Monique?" she asked again.

Sly spoke into his headpiece as he nodded his head. "Protect the Queen at all costs. I will remain with the Princess." He listened for a minute then took a quick up and down look at Amber. "One piece. No holes." He listened again. "Will do."

"Was that Adam?" an anxious Amber asked. "They are going to need me at the hospital," Amber stated. "I have to check on Adam and Monique and the Queen."

"Where's Mother?" Teddi asked as tears streamed down her cheeks.

Amber hugged the child then wiped the tears from her cheeks. "Your mother is in good hands." She smiled. Teddi nodded, with big tear filled eyes. "Will Mother be here soon?"

Amber held the child to her chest, as the figures below became blurs from her tears. The last thing she wanted to do was lie to the child. She had no idea what was happening on the grounds. She looked at Sly. The expression on his face indicated something was wrong. Something was very wrong. "Not right now, darling." Amber began to rock the child as she replied. "Not right now."

Sly landed the Hawk. He glanced down as he walked past Joshua and the King who were both kneeling next to the Queen.

"How is she?" he asked.

"Shoulder wound," King Raheem replied as he continued to bandage his wife.

Sly nodded, then stepped over Ashton's dead body. He walked into the entrance to the palace. There were several bodies on the floor, but he was only interested in one. Adam was over Monique trying frantically to stop the blood that was flowing from her abdomen.

"How bad?" Sly asked as he removed his suit jacket and placed it under Monique's head.

Adam gave him a look but did not stop what he was doing.

Joshua joined them. "How bad?"

"Stop asking," Adam curtly replied. "Give me your shirt."

Joshua threw off his trench coat and it hit the floor with a thump. Adam glanced at him.

"Don't ask," Joshua replied as he dropped his suit jacket on the floor, then stripped off his shirt.

Adam used the material to put direct pressure on the wound. "Joshua, take Teddi and send Amber to the infirmary. Sly, pull whatever we have on the Hawk to treat gunshot wounds. We will have to work fast." He picked Monique up and briskly walked towards the infirmary. "How is the Queen?" he asked.

"Alive," Sly replied then was out the door.

Two hours later Akande and Monique were still unconscious.

Amber stepped outside the room where she had worked to remove the bullet from Monique's abdomen.

"How is she?"

Amber looked up. Sly was leaning against the wall with the fedora hiding his facial features. "Have you ever lost that hat in battle?"

Sly's head slowly came up. "Never. It's an extension of me."

Amber shook her head as she began to remove her gloves. "Where is everyone?"

"Absolute is with the little one and Hypnotic is in the room with the Queen."

"Hypnotic?" Amber raised an eyebrow.

"Adam to you."

Amber's lips curled into a half smile. "Why Hypnotic?"

Sly shrugged. "He has a way of making people come around to his way of thinking. Its driving Absolute crazy but I'm enjoying the show." Sly smiled. "How is Spicy?"

"Spicy?"

"Monique."

"What is with these names?" Amber shook her head as she sat on the bench. She looked up. "Once I stopped the bleeding I was able to locate the bullet and remove it. I'm concerned about infection. We need to move her to the nearest military base or back to the States."

"I'll make the arrangements." Sly nodded then walked off as he pulled out his cell phone.

Amber stood then walked down to the next door. She opened it to see Adam checking Akande's vital signs and the King sitting next to the bed holding his wife's small hand in his. It was clear to her that he cared deeply for his wife.

"How is she doing?" she whispered to Adam.

Adam inhaled then released it. "Gunshot wound to the shoulder. Minimal blood loss. Once she regains consciousness we can do a more extensive evaluation."

Amber listened then nodded. "Blood pressure?"

"Normal."

"Good." She nodded. "As with Monique I think it would be wise to move them to a more sterile environment."

"I'm concerned with them going into shock," Adam stated. "I think we should wait until they both are stabilized before moving them."

"That could take weeks. Especially in Monique's case."

Adam motioned her to step outside the room. When the door closed behind them Adam pulled her into his arms. His lips touched hers with a determination to ensure she was indeed all right. The excitement of the day seemed to increase his desire to taste her lips. He needed to feel her pulse roaring beneath his touch. He needed to hear the silkiness of her voice just to be sure he was alive. Once the kiss ended he simply held her.

She relished being in his arms. Amber had no idea how he knew she needed to be held and to hold him, so that she could assure herself that they were both okay. She would never know nor did she care. The only thing that mattered at the moment was the power his kiss radiated through her veins.

"What was that for?" Amber asked as she melted in his arms.

Adam looked down into her eyes. "I figure if we are going to argue again I would get the reward out of the way first."

Amber glared at him. "Why are we going to argue?"

Adam stood back. "I think we should let the ladies stay put."

"I think they need to be in a sterile environment. An infection can take them out faster than a bullet."

"I don't think that's true. A bullet in the head can be instant death. But I get your analogy." Amber started to speak, but he stopped her. "Moving them could cause shock. With gunshot wounds, a high percentage of people die from secondary shock to their systems."

"The last time I looked you did not have an MD behind your name. I do," Amber huffed.

"That is true."

"Therefore my ruling takes precedence and I rule that both patients should be moved as soon as possible, Dr. Lassiter, and that's that."

They turned to the sound of a man clearing his throat. "Excuse me." King Raheem stood in the doorway of the room. "My wife will remain here in her country. We must reassure the citizens as a united front that all is well."

"Your Highness, it is imperative that the Queen is free of germs that could cause further damage."

King Raheem looked over Amber's shoulders and nodded. "That is why my brother has come."

Prince LaVere walked up the hallway with Joshua and a contingent of men from Emure.

"Where is Teddi?" King Raheem asked.

"Mother has her," LaVere replied. "How is Akande?"

"Well, but still unconscious," King Raheem replied as he hugged his brother.

"Akande should be moved to a more secure area," Joshua stated.

"My wife will remain here," King Raheem spoke. "My brother has brought medical supplies and personnel to care for Akande."

"What happens when the second wave of this attack comes through?" Joshua argued.

"We will be prepared," the King replied in a tone that left no room for argument as he looked directly at Joshua. "I would suggest you take care of yours and allow me to take care of mine."

Everyone within the hearing distance understood there was an underlying message in that statement, but no one spoke.

"I would be grateful if you would ensure the safety of Teddi until the area stabilizes. If you would be so kind as to take her to your home until the time her mother is recovered, I would be forever in your debt."

"Teddi is the future of this area, Joshua," LaVere spoke. "My brother is putting his country in your hands. I know you will protect her with your life."

Joshua was seconds away from ending King Raheem's life until he mentioned Teddi. Men had died at his hands for much less. He understood that Akande was Raheem's wife and he also knew he, himself had a wife at home. His intent was to take both mother and daughter back to the United States.

"You failed at your task to secure this region. If you had not, there would have been no reason for me to return."

"To be fair, Joshua." Adam stepped between the two men. "The force King Raheem has built is sufficient for an attack by forces in this region. This attack was made possible with the assistance of the United States. He was fighting us." Adam captured Joshua's eyes by blocking his line of sight to the King. He could sense something more was at play between the two men. "We know there are few if any countries capable of defending themselves from us." He looked over his shoulder. "King Raheem did not fail to protect his country or his...wife."

Joshua's glare at his brother would have made most men move, but Adam remained steadfast. "Teddi will be with me until her mother requests her return."

King Raheem started to speak but LaVere stopped him. He knew his friend Joshua and his brother Raheem very well. Neither would ever back down. "I believe that is a wise decision, Raheem. Thank you, Joshua."

Joshua turned. "I'm checking on Spicy."

"I will join you." LaVere patted his brother on the shoulder. "Have the supplies brought in," he said to his men then joined Joshua.

Amber watched King Raheem walk back into the room then watched as Joshua entered Monique's room. "Man, talk about intense. Am I missing something here?"

Adam shook his head and exhaled. "I thought Joshua was about to kill the King."

"You are going to make a good diplomat," Sly said from his casual stance behind them. "It isn't easy to get a man like Absolute to stand down. You got balls." He smiled then looked at Amber. "The President agrees. He wants Spicy back in the United States."

Amber turned to Adam and grinned. "The President agrees with me."

"This time." He kissed her then walked down to Monique's room.

When Amber turned she was smiling.

"See what I mean." Sly smiled. "He turned your head with just one kiss. Hypnotic." He tilted his hat, turned and walked out of the exit.

CHAPTER TWENTY-SEVEN

Adam, Amber, Joshua, Teddi and Monique were flown into the capital by Sly. A medical team met them at the private landing strip then escorted Monique to the hospital with Amber in tow. Sly turned to Adam.

"I did not think another man could impress me. But you're okay, youngin. It was a blast."

"A blast?" Adam laughed. "You made a memorable mark with your fedora."

"You like that? It's called doing your job in style."

Joshua walked up with Teddi on his shoulder asleep. "He taught me everything I know about dressing to impress."

"You were an arrogant learner, but you did all right." Sly nodded to the child. "You look good with a baby on your shoulder."

Joshua grinned from ear to ear. "It's kind of nice."

"You'll have one soon enough," Adam laughed.

Sly and Joshua shared a knowing glance. "I'm off."

"Where to now?" Joshua asked.

Sly looked around then held Joshua's eyes. "I'm off to get a life."

Joshua returned a sad smile. "Hat's off to you. Take care."

Sly tilted his hat then climbed into the Hawk. Joshua stood to the side holding a coat over Teddi's head as the Hawk took off. "Another great man lived through the chaos of protecting this country."

Adam patted Joshua on the back. "I think Sly is going to be just fine." He began walking. "You, on the other hand, I'm not too sure about."

"Me?" Joshua joined him as they walked towards the waiting vehicle. "Why would you be worried about me?"

"Well." Adam stopped at the door of the vehicle. "You are about to go home to your wife with another woman's child. Which if my notion is correct, is yours." He shrugged. "If you survive that with Roc, you then have to tell Joe and Sally they have a grandchild that you have kept from them for four years. I would say Sly's future looks a whole lot more promising than yours."

Joshua stood there staring at Adam as he got into the backseat of the waiting sedan. He glanced at the sleeping Teddi. "Please don't be like Brainiac."

Hours later Amber walked into her condo for the first time in a week. Her mail was stacked up at the door, where she assumed her mother had stored it.

"It's been sitting this long, it can wait." Amber said then headed straight for her double head shower and set the pressure to massage her sore muscles. She was in good shape. Hanging out with Adam had proven to be an adventure and she loved it and him. She froze under the shower at the realization. The man had snowballed into her life and had been picking up speed ever since. The danger and excitement had been non-stop since she walked into that 5 a.m. meeting. She rinsed off then stepped out of the shower. She wrapped a towel around herself and began blow-drying her hair. Now that the case was solved would their connection be lost? The thought slowed her motions. Would Adam have a reason to call? They found the manual when Federal Agents searched Ashton's home. The device that poisoned Teddi was found in a chest that Akande would allow her daughter to play with. The device was placed there by one of the servants who was working with the rebels. Akande was the target, not her daughter. There were no questions left open, leaving no reason for Adam to reach out to her.

"But I can call him," she spoke the realization aloud. "There is no reason why I can't be the one to pursue..."

"Pursue what?"

Amber jumped, dropping the blow dryer onto the floor. "Adam?" She bent over to turn off the dryer that was now dancing across the floor. "What are you doing here?"

Leaning against the door dressed in a grey sweater, jeans and snow boots, he looked delicious. "I think I'm here to pursue."

"Pursue what?"

"You." He smiled. "Nice towel."

She looked down. Realizing she was half naked, she reached for the robe hanging neatly on the hook by the shower. "How did you get in here?" she asked as she put the robe on.

"I came through the front door."

Amber gave him a funny look. "The door was locked, Dr. Lassiter."

"It was," he agreed. "I unlocked it."

"With what?"

"I put a plastic solution in your key hole. Dried it with the heat sensor from my tablet to make a plastic key. Only took about five minutes. Then I turned the key."

Amber gave him an incredulous look. "You broke into my house?" She rushed by him to check her front door.

"You wouldn't open the door." Adam chuckled as he followed her into the great room. "I knocked twice."

"I was in the shower," she explained.

"How was I supposed to know you were in the shower?" He shrugged.

She looked at the white carpet and followed the trail of his footsteps to where he now stood by the bedroom door. "It's snowing?"

"Yes," he replied as he watched the play of emotions on her face.

"And you tracked snow on my carpet?"

That voice sounded like his sister Pearl whenever they did something to a pair of her shoes. "They were on my feet when I walked in," he replied slowly.

Amber stormed over to him. "Adam Lassiter, take those boots off this moment and put them in the mudroom."

He started to take a step then stopped. "Where is the mudroom?"

Amber's arm snapped up pointing in the opposite direction of the front door. "By the garage entrance."

As Adam walked in that direction he noticed everything in her great room was white. The only color present were the picture frames, which were black. It was beautiful, but there was no life. It looked like something out of a magazine. He removed his boots thinking it was his duty to bring some life into her world.

He walked back into the great-room to find Amber vacuuming the area where he had walked. He walked over and jumped on the white sofa, put his hands behind his head and crossed his feet at his ankles. "Are you a germaphobe?"

Amber turned and almost gasped out loud. She turned off the vacuum and stomped over to where he lay then stammered out, "Are you on my white sofa with blue jeans on?"

It took every ounce of will power to keep Adam from laughing in her face. The look she gave him was that of a mother about to kill her child for tracking mud in the house. He wiggled around. "Yeah, but it's kind of crowded with all these pillows." He began throwing them in different directions. Amber looked as though she was about to have a hissy fit. Her mouth was open in horror. No words were coming out. Her hands were swinging in the air as she tried to keep the pillows from hitting the white carpet. He was enjoying the view every time her robe gaped open as she ran around. Finally, when he thought he had made his point, Adam stopped throwing the pillows then laid back with his hands behind his head. "Now that's better."

Amber looked around her once pristine room and was fuming. He had been there less than fifteen minutes and her house looked like a hurricane had hit it. "Adam Lassiter, look at what you did to my house."

Adam looked around. "You're welcome," he said with a smile.

"What?" She walked over to him. "Take your feet off of my sofa." She pulled his feet down.

Adam grabbed her and pulled her down to him. She was still fussing when his lips captured hers. Still mumbling when his tongue entwined with hers. It then became a low groan as he reached under her robe, yanked the towel away then traced her bare thigh with his fingers. Making small circles over her skin, easing the intensity as her body's resistance lessened. Then her arms surrounded his neck, kissing him as vigorously as he was her. His fingers slipped between her thighs. His thumb found her nub, circling with the motion of his tongue until she voluntarily began to raise her body to him. His forefinger eased inside. She gasped. His lips kissed her neck, right below her ear, then traveled between her breasts, burning a trail of heat along the way. His mouth captured a caramel nipple and sucked as if he was taking in air to breathe. Soon the contractions between her legs began to match the suction of his lips on her breast. His thumb moving faster against her. The juices within her began to flow over his fingers as she gasped once, twice and then she screamed out his name.

"Adam."

Adam stood, stripped out of everything then rejoined her just as the eruption began to subside. Positioning himself at her entrance he pushed her beautiful, unruly curls out of her eyes. "I'm coming inside of you bare, Amber. If you have a problem with that tell me now."

In response, Amber raised her body to him. His head reared back as her inner lips surrounded him in her warmth. Her legs circled him giving him deeper access. Bracing his hands on both sides of her, he drove in with a vengeance and she met him stroke for stroke. Rising to his demand over and over until her contractions were so fast and furious there was no stopping the eruption. The reaction of her release was so tight around him it squeezed every ounce of his semen out of him with a roar. He collapsed on top of her.

Moments later, he moved to her side, holding her close to his heart. He put his leg over the one she put between his. He then kissed the top of her head.

"We slid down your white sofa to make love on your white carpet and the world did not end."

She sighed.

"In fact, the world as I see it is a much better place."

"You would see it that way."

He caressed her back. "In the last week a number of people lost their lives. We saved a young child and a small country. In the grand scheme of things I would say that a little snow on white carpet is small stuff."

"You have turned my world upside down, Adam."

He smiled. "Good. I aim to please."

She playfully punched him in the side. "Why did I ever ask God for the yang to my yin? I liked my life the way it was."

"No, you did not. That's why you asked God for me."

"The man must have a sense of humor for thinking you would be a good match for me."

Adam switched to his side and smiled down at her. He touched her cheek. "God don't make mistakes. He sent me to you because you needed me to lighten your heavy load. And I need you to keep me focused. You are my yin and I am your yang." He kissed her gently on the lips. "Now that all the craziness is over we can enjoy our newfound love and explore the possibility of a life as one."

CHAPTER TWENTY-EIGHT

Amber walked into the two story colonial brushing the snow from her coat and called out. "Dad. Are you home?"

It was her mother who appeared in the doorway of the kitchen.

"Amber." She ran and gathered her daughter in her embrace, as tears ran down her cheeks. "Are you all right?" She looked her over.

"Yes, I'm fine." Amber beamed.

"Redbird," Phillip called from the top of the staircase. "I see you made it home in one piece."

He hugged his daughter as he reached the bottom of the stairs.

"Yes, we arrived home last night."

Adam held his hand out. "Mrs. Nicolas, I'm Adam Lassiter." His hand remained in the air unclaimed.

"I know who you are," the slim, fair-skin, auburn haired angry woman stated. "You are the man who put my baby's life in danger. You are not welcome here."

"Hold on, Jill." Phillip stood in front of Adam. "That is unfair."

Before more could be said, Brent walked through the front door stomping the snow off his feet. He grabbed Amber in a bear hug and swung her around.

"You're a sight for sore eyes, Doc." He then turned to Adam. "Lassiter." He shrugged, "I couldn't believe it when I heard. Ashton?"

"He was working with the rebels in Africa," Adam responded as he put his unclaimed hand down.

Brent shook his head. "Well, I'm sure the President is going to have a medal waiting for you for this one. You too, Amber."

"Why don't we all have a seat in the family room," Phillip suggested as he gave a curious glance at his wife. "Jill, would you get some refreshments?"

Jill held her husband's eyes for a long moment.

"I'll help, Mom." Amber took off her coat and dropped it to the floor. She followed her reluctant mother looking over her shoulder at a confused Adam. She winked to let him know all would be well.

"So, Lassiter, the director tells me you found a way to stop J.M.A.L.T.S.?"

"We blocked the satellite transmission to it."

"Simple as that."

"I heard you were shot, son." Phillip nodded. "Are you okay?"

"It was one of our operatives that was shot. She's at Walter Reed making her way back."

"And the Queen?" Brent asked. "How is she?"

Adam flinched. "She was up and moving around at last word from the region. How is Sudgen?"

"He is safe. Kalli is with him."

"Speaking of Kalli, how is she?" Adam raised an eyebrow.

Brent grinned. "Kalli's good."

"Here we are, everyone," Amber called out as she walked into the room with a tray of drinks in her hand. Adam stood to help her with the tray.

Jill sat on the arm of the chair her husband occupied. He took her hand in his the moment she sat there.

Amber sat beside Adam. "Mother, I did not have the opportunity to introduce you to Adam Lassiter." She glanced at him. "Adam, this is my mother Jill Nicolas."

"Mrs. Nicolas." Adam nodded

"I understand you are a doctor," her question asked coolly.

"Not exactly. I have a Ph.D. in Chemical Engineering."

"And what type of living do you propose to make from that?"

"A hell of a lot more than working for the FBI," Brent joked as he took a drink.

"Lassiter will be well compensated for the work he does." Phillip squeezed his wife's hand. "As well as a number of inventions he has created."

"Yes, well what does your family do?"

Adam smiled. "It depends on which family member you are asking about. I have eleven brothers and sisters. Each have different careers, with the exception of my baby sister who is in her first year of college."

"Your parents have twelve of you," Brent joked, trying to ease the tension he was feeling in the room.

"Twelve wonderful children," Amber added, glancing at her mother.

"Brent, how many children do your parents have," Jill asked with fondness in her voice.

"Two. I have a sister and we fight constantly over who my mother loves the most."

"Redbird is our one and only." Phillip smiled. "I wouldn't trade her for anything."

"Neither would I." Adam smiled at Amber.

"Look at you blushing," Brent laughed. "Dr. Nicolas, I think you have been bitten."

Adam kissed her cheek. "So have I."

"What are your plans now that you are no longer employed by the Bureau?" Jill broke in with a note of distaste in her tone.

"I have a few options," Adam replied. "Mrs. Nicolas, I sense you have some reservations where I am concerned. Please know, I have only the best intentions for Amber."

Jill stood before he could say anything more. "You can have all the intentions you like, Mr. Lassiter, but you cannot have my daughter. You were responsible for the death of three people from what I've been told. Do you think for one moment I want my daughter around constant danger? I'll have you know I do not." She huffed. "Your mother has twelve babies, she can afford to lose one. I only have Amber. And I will not have her around the likes of you."

The room fell quiet.

Phillip stood. "That is not my sentiment, Adam. Jill, you are wrong about this young man."

"Really, Mrs. Nicolas." Brent sat forward placing his drink on the table. "I have to back Adam here. I know what happened at the Bureau. And I can tell you that Adam was a victim as much as anyone, hell if not more. This man just saved a small country from a takeover."

"Mother..." Amber stood.

"Amber," Adam spoke in a dangerously calm tone.

"No, Adam, I have to say this."

"No, Amber, you don't."

Adam stood and began buttoning his suit jacket. "Mrs. Nicolas, I understand your fear for your daughter and I respect your position. But in the future please refrain from referring to my mother's lack of love for all of her children."

"That's not what I meant," Jill sighed.

"I know what you meant. I've heard it all my life. People raising an eyebrow at the number of children my mother has. She had all of us because she wanted to. And if she lost any child...it would kill her inside. No parent can afford to lose a child under any circumstances. I'm here because that mother you criticized a moment ago raised all of her sons to be chivalrous. Therefore, I came to ask your permission to marry your daughter. But please know...I don't need it."

He extended his hand to Phillip. "Director Nicolas, it was good to see you. You have a lovely home."

Phillip shook his hand. "Adam, don't leave like this."

"I never stay where I am not wanted." He turned to Brent and shook his hand. "I'll see you around, Special Agent Pierce." He saluted with a smile.

He turned to Amber and kissed her lightly on the lips. "I'm going to Richmond. That invitation is open if you care to join me. Brent, would you see to it that Amber makes it home safe?" With that he turned and walked out of the door.

Amber never took her eyes off her mother.

Brent stared at Phillip then at Amber. He sighed. "I have to speak on this. Jill, Amber and I have known each other for a long time. But I never really saw her come to life until the day she met Adam." He shrugged. "The man doesn't need me to sing his praises. He has an entire country singing them right now. But this isn't about all his accomplishments or your views on the number of children his parents have. This is about your daughter's happiness. And he just walked out the door."

"Brent, Dad, may we have a moment alone?"

Phillip squeezed Jill's hand. Then kissed his daughter's temple. "Brent, let's have a drink."

Amber waited until both men had walked out of the room. She smiled at her mother. "Why?"

Jill closed her eyes and exhaled. "Do you think for one moment I don't know what you are feeling?" She opened her eyes and glared at her daughter. "I know because I have been in your shoes. You know why your father wasn't in your life until you were twelve? He was in that world. The same one your Adam is heading to. Do you have any idea what it's like to be waiting day in and day out for the man you love to call, to walk through the door or be delivered in a pine box? I do. I don't care about his achievements or his family. Those things don't matter to me. You do. Any idea what it feels like to be beaten near to death for information you know nothing about only to have your daughter have to kill a man to save your life? That's what I'm trying to protect you from." She swallowed back a cry.

"Would you have changed anything, Mother? You told me once that you had to go through hell to be with Dad, but you did it because you knew your life would be useless without him. I feel that way about Adam. I don't suspect our life will be filled with roses and laughter all the time. There will be frightening times. But you know what?" She took her mother's hands in hers. "I'd rather go through them with Adam than go through life without him." She kissed her mother's cheek, picked up her coat and walked to the door. She looked back. "All you ever have to do is pick up a phone. I love you, Mom." Amber turned and walked out the door.

CHAPTER TWENTY-NINE

Adam climbed into the back of Genevieve. His mood had been sullen since arriving back to the house. Joshua and Roc shared a glance.

"I thought Amber was joining us for dinner?" Roc stated as she glanced at Teddi who was sitting opposite Adam in the car seat.

"She has family issues to deal with," he replied while looking out the window as Joshua pulled out of the tunnel onto the road that led to I-95 south to Richmond from Quantico. This would be the first year his brother would make dinner with the entire family in years. This time he would be coming with a family of his own. Adam thought about the years Joshua spent away protecting the country and the freedom most people took for granted. He did it alone, with no support system waiting for him when he returned home. Yes, the family was always there, but what about that one person who could make the world right? With all the craziness that was happening around the world, a man on a mission needs a woman who understands and supports the career he chooses. He needs a yin to his yang. Did he have that in Amber? He thought about Mrs. Nicolas' question. What was he going to do with his life now that the FBI was a wash? Looking back, he now knew that was too limited for him. He could teach, but that meant a classroom every day and he knew that wasn't for him either. For a man who some deemed a genius, Adam was at a loss on what he would do next. How would he support a wife and family, which he dearly wanted? Financially he was well compensated for his past inventions. He could live for years very comfortably with the bank account he had. But he needed something to occupy his mind, something that would challenge him. Maybe a lab. Yes, he thought. He would set up a lab. It would need financing, but that shouldn't be hard to get. By the time they reached Fredericksburg he had made a decision. He would build a laboratory and work on creating more devices that would save the world. It was a huge, egotistical thing to believe, but his name was Adam Lassiter. He was capable of doing anything he set his mind to. With the right person at his side. By the time they reached Richmond, Adam's mind and disposition were back in the same place they were when they left Joshua's place...wishing Amber was with him.

Joshua and Roc walked into the kitchen of the family house. The room was bustling with so much activity no one noticed the little girl hanging onto Roc's hand.

"Good, you're early," Mathew said as he passed the football to Joshua. "You can be one of the captains. Zack over here is trying to take over."

"Will you guys take that in the family room," Cynthia huffed. "Do you see all this food we are preparing? We are going to need that table."

"We?" Pearl glared at Cynthia then glanced down at her hands. "I don't see the first spoon in your hand. Here." She put a bowl of cooked potatoes in Cynthia's hand along with the spoon. "Stir the potato salad."

"Oh, no, no, no." Diamond grabbed the bowl and all the fixings to go with it. "You are not messing up my potato salad," she said then pushed Zack away from the table. "Honey, will you let me have your seat and call Xavier to see how his day is going with Nicole and the Brooks?"

Zack kissed her before replying, "Anything for you, sweetheart."

"You two need to get a room," Cynthia huffed.

"Not here," Sally laughed as she walked into the kitchen. "The inn is full. Timothy, Luke, out. Mathew, you too." She swung her dishtowel until the guys were out of the kitchen.

Seeing all the confusion happening, Roc looked around at all the people. "Where is Ruby?"

Sally sighed. "She got caught up with something at the shelter. She'll be along soon. Opal, take the cakes into the dining room." Sally walked over to the sink to wash her hands. "Jade, you get the pies. Joshua, grab that pan of rolls and Roc, you take the baby and go sit down somewhere."

Everyone moved at Sally's command. Pearl and Diamond looked at each other as Roc walked by them.

"Baby?"

Sally stopped washing her hands, turned and watched Roc remove the coat from the little girl dressed in the cutest black, red and white plaid dress with black leggings and shoes. A headband matching her dress held her afro puffed hair back from her face.

"Stop." Sally dried her hands on the dishtowel, then laid it across Roc's protruding stomach. She bent down to the little girl. "Who are you, sweetheart?" She smiled.

"Princess Theodora LaSheera Ashro of Asmere," she replied in the sweetest accent Sally had ever heard. "Who may you be?"

Sally raised an eyebrow as she glanced up at all the shocked faces staring at the little girl. "Well, I'm Sally Lassiter. You are as cute as a button."

The child smiled and Sally almost fell backwards. The dimples appeared and the resemblance of another young child came to her mind. Pearl braced her mother as she slowly stood.

Sally held out her shaking hand. "It's a pleasure to meet you, Princess Theodora..." As the child shook her hand Sally's eyes traveled up to Joshua's.

"You may call me Princess Teddi."

Pearl and Diamond looked from one to the other then up at Joshua.

"Roc." Diamond took the dishtowel off her stomach. "Why don't we take Princess Teddi to meet the other children?"

"Yes," Cynthia added as she glanced at Sally's face. "I will join you."

"I think I will join you." Pearl nodded.

Sally held her son's eyes as everyone cleared the room. Before saying anything she turned the stove off where the greens had been cooking. She turned and leaned against the sink just as Joe came in.

"Pearl said you need me," Joe announced as he entered the kitchen.

Sally nodded. Seeing there was something brewing in her eyes, Joe simply stood next to her then stared at Joshua.

"Something you need to tell us, son?"

Joshua pulled out a chair. "This may take a minute."

"The question is a simple one, Joshua." Sally sat in the chair Joe pulled out for her as he stood behind her. "Are you her father?"

The question wasn't simple. There were so many political ramifications connected to the answer. The one thing Joshua had never done in his life or career was lie to his mother. He may have omitted things but he had never lied to her when asked a question. He looked up at his father for help.

Joe nodded, understanding his situation. "We understand there are things you cannot share with us." Taking his wife's hand in his, Joe sat down next to her.

"I'm your mother, Joshua, and I asked you a question. I expect an answer."

There it was and there was no getting out of it. Joshua told the truth. "I asked Teddi's mother. Her reply was no."

Sally gave her son an incredulous look. Joshua had to grin. When he did his dimples appeared.

"Joshua," she began. "Now I know you are not blind nor stupid. That child is the spitting image of you when she smiles."

He took his mother's hand from his father. Joe sat back and sighed. "Mom, Teddi's mother, Akande, is the queen of a small country in Africa. She has a population of people she is responsible for. When the President asked her to choose, she chose her country. So did I. At the time neither of us knew a child was involved. When that became apparent, Akande had to make another decision. If nothing else she is consistent. She chose to protect her country. As have I. She is the bloodline to the throne. That makes Teddi the next queen of Asmere. Her biological father isn't important."

"It is to me." Sally frowned.

"I would hate the thought of having a grandchild in this world in trouble and I not know about it, son." Joe spoke. "Is she in trouble?"

"Not now. Adam was able to foil the attempted coup."

"Adam." Sally pulled her hand away. "What does Adam have to do with this?"

That's when it dawned on him that his parents had no idea what Adam had done in the last week. "The President requested his help with a situation that arose in Asmere. For the last week Adam has been working with the US government."

Sally glanced at Joe. "But I thought they let him go from the Bureau?"

"They did." Joshua nodded. "Everything that happened at Quantico with Adam was connected to the situation in Asmere. He was an integral part of resolving that situation."

Joe held his son's eyes and knew there was more. "Well, whatever he does from this point on we'll be proud of him."

Adam walked through the back door, pulling off his gloves, and coat.

"Hey, we were just talking about you." Sally smiled at her baby boy, then frowned.

"People have to make decisions for themselves, right?"

No one replied as they sent a puzzled look his way.

"Well, there are times......." Sally began then was cut off.

"I mean everyone has different paths to choose. But when you find the yin to your yang, you know it and should act accordingly, right?"

"If you can give us some idea of...." Joe tried but got the same.

"It doesn't matter, right, Joshua?" Adam shook his head at his thoughts. "Life is what it is. The direction I chose did not work out." He shrugged. "Then you go to the next thing. So what if I'm not certain what direction I'm going in now. That's my cross to bear. It's up to her to accept me as I am. And that's not so bad. I'm a pretty decent person, right?"

Joshua stretched out his legs then crossed them at the ankle, grateful to his brother for taking the attention away from him. "Damn right you are."

Adam faced them as he leaned against the sink, folded his arms across his chest and shrugged. "She knows I love her. I told her. I showed her. Not much more I can do than that." He stood there looking into space. "She's going to make the right decision...right?"

This time everyone remained silent. It was clear Adam was having this conversation with himself and did not need their participation. So they all simply stared up at him.

"Why are you all staring at me? Did you hear my question?"

Sally stared at him for a long moment. "Oh...you want us to answer that one?" she laughed.

"Mom." A frustrated Adam frowned.

"Okay, son." Sally tried her best to stop laughing, but a small chuckle escaped. "I have raised five boys before you. In my estimation, next to Samuel you are the most serious. However, in the last year you seem to have begun enjoying life, as you should." She took his long strong hands inside hers to offer the most comfort a mother could in a situation like this. "I can't answer for Amber. I assume that's who you are talking about. But it seems to me, she is very much in love with you."

"What happened?" Joshua glared at Adam.

"Why did something have to happen?"

Joshua gave him an incredulous look. "Are you serious? For the last week you have pulled stunts that even I would question." He raised an eyebrow. "You don't think before you act."

Joe and Sally, whose attention was on Adam, both turned to look at the son who always acted first and asked questions later.

"What?" Joshua shrugged when he noticed they were staring at him, again.

Sally shook her head then turned back to Adam. "What happened?"

Adam sighed. "I went to ask Amber's parents for her hand in marriage."

"Oh Adam!" Sally jumped up. "How wonderful." She kissed him.

Joe remained seated, glanced over at Joshua and waited for the next shoe to drop.

"I thought so too until I was completely shut down by her mother."

"What?" Sally raised an eyebrow, now going into defense mode. "What reason would she have to shut you down?"

Adam was about to speak then stopped. There was no way he would tell her about the conversation.

Joe saw the play of emotions on Adam's face. He needed help with his mother too. This was his job. Helping the girls when they needed it and the boys when they did not want to hurt their mother's feelings. "Her mother's reasons are not important. How does Amber feel?"

"You are not marrying the mother." Joshua shrugged. "Did Amber say yes?"

"I haven't asked her yet. I wanted to get her parent's permission first."

Sally touched his cheek with the palm of her hand. "You are a good man, Adam." She smiled.

"You are going to ask her...right?" Joe raised his eyebrow letting his son know it wasn't a question.

The kitchen door opened and Ruby walked in.

"I am so happy to see you." Sally beamed as she reached for her oldest daughter.

Ruby hugged her mother, then looked at her two brothers. "What have you done?"

Adam took a step closer to the exit and Joshua sat up straight. The tone in Ruby's voice was one they rarely heard, but when you did you better have the right response. "Nothing," the two men replied in child-like voices.

"That sounds like an untruth if I ever heard one," Ruby said as she pulled off her gloves and coat and put them on the hook by the door. She saw Adam's thrown across a chair at the kitchen table. She rolled her eyes at him as she picked it up. "Did the hook move?"

"No," Adam replied as he watched her hang it up. "I wasn't thinking when..."

"That's just it." She walked over to the sink to wash her hands. "Men don't think," she huffed as the people glanced at each other. "No, they do think, but they think with their dicks instead of their head."

Sally's eyes grew in size as Adam spoke. "Aren't they one and the same?"

Ruby slowly turned from the sink glaring at him as did Sally.

Joshua stood. "That's my cue to leave." He walked out of the room.

Adam stood there a moment longer. "I...I think, I'll join the guys."

"You do that." Sally sighed.

Adam walked into the family room to see the kids playing in the corner with Teddi. It was good to see she fit right in with the other grandchildren. Samuel and Cynthia looked up.

"Good job in Asmere," Samuel offered as he looked around. "Amber in the kitchen with Sally?"

"No," Adam exhaled as Joshua walked up.

"You got some 'splaining to do, son," Samuel joked. "How is Sally?"

"Nobody's fool, that's for sure," Joshua replied.

"Mom's only concern will be not being able to see her Teddi grow up along with her other grandchildren," Adam stated as he looked around the room.

"She's upstairs," Diamond stated.

Adam nodded then walked towards the stairs.

"Tell Jade it's her turn to set the dinner table," Opal called out as he left the room.

"I will," Adam said then turned as his father walked out of the kitchen. "Is Ruby okay?"

"Man trouble." Joe smiled then raised an eyebrow. "How are you?"

Adam sat on the stair as he looked up at his father. "Did you ever wonder about Mom? If she loved you enough to turn her back on everything she knew?"

"Oh yeah." Joe leaned against the banister. "Your mother was a dancer, a pretty good one at that. The minute we met I knew she was going to be my wife. For her, it took a little longer. Your grandmother had plans for her little ballerina and it did not include Joe Lassiter, a postal worker from the North side of Richmond." He smiled. "But I knew what I wanted in life. It wasn't the lights of fame. I wanted love and that was all I had to offer Sally. She on the other hand had to make a choice and I wasn't sure for a while if that choice would be me. As it turned out, I was her decision. Shocked the hell out of me. But once made, I promised to never let a day go by without letting her know how much I love her."

"You loved her twelve children's worth. That's a lot of love."

Joe laughed. "And I still have a lot to give. So do you."

"I don't know, Dad. I'm asking this woman to be with me and I'm not sure who I am or what I'm going to be. I mean I have all this book sense and don't know what to do with my life."

"Think about what you just said...your life. Not Joshua's, Sammy's or Luke's...yours. As the youngest male you always felt like you had to beat your older brothers at something. What you haven't realized yet is you have the key to your future within your reach. Don't look to others to define who you are. You have the mind to do wonders for this world. Don't short change yourself by trying to be anyone else. Be you. No one can beat you at that. As for your young lady, well, give her a chance to make the right choice. It may lead to a lifetime of love and twelve children."

Adam laughed. "I think four will be my limit."

Joe stood and nodded in a knowing way. "We planned for two." He laughed and walked away.

Adam shook his head then continued up the steps in search of Jade.

"What's wrong?" Jade asked without looking up from the television broadcast of her favorite ballet, The Nutcracker.

He swore she could perform every move for every character. "I'm in love with Amber and I believe she is in love with me."

Jade sighed, then moved the pillow she was lying across to make room on the bed beside her.

Adam took off his suit jacket, then kicked off his shoes and laid down next to her.

She muted the television and turned to him. "So what's the problem?"

Adam put his hands behind his head and looked up at the ceiling. "Waiting," he sighed. "Not knowing for sure which way she will go."

"I'm missing something, so start from the beginning." She turned over with her hands behind her head and stared at the ceiling with him.

Just like they had when they were young, the entire time they were in college and now here as adults, he told her everything. He started with Dr. McCoy's death, to Flex, to Asmere including Teddi and his unsuccessful visit to Amber's parents. After he finished, Jade asked him one question.

"Do you feel complete with her?"

Adam smiled then looked at his sister with a smile. "Yes, I do." He sighed. "Does that bother you?"

She looked at her twin. "I love you, Adam. But I'm your sister." She sat up on her side, balancing her head on her hand. "This was bound to happen at some point. We can't stay joined at the hip for the rest of our lives."

He turned on his side mirroring her position. "I feel a sadness inside you."

"Yeah, well, it seems like everyone is moving on. They are fulfilling their goals. It feels like I'm the under achiever here."

"What are you talking about? You've just been accepted into one of the top dance troupes in the country....hell, the world."

"I'm on the third travel team. That means I may never actually get on stage."

"Well, you sure as hell can't get on stage if you're not on the team. Small steps, Jade. Don't knock what you've already achieved. There are at least four hundred and seventy people who did not make the thirty roster count. You did."

"Yeah, number twenty-nine."

"Better than thirty-one." He raised an eyebrow. "Look, it is your dream to be a dancer. Follow it. Sally did."

"She ended up with twelve children." Jade smiled.

"Then you go for twenty-four," Adam laughed.

Jade pulled the pillow and hit him with it. "Bite your tongue, Adam Lassiter."

Adam pulled the other pillow and began fighting back. Opal walked by the door. "What are you two doing?"

Adam and Jade looked at each other then threw the pillows at Opal.

"No, you didn't," she yelled as she grabbed a pillow and began beating Adam with it.

Timothy ran up the steps to see Jade and Adam pounding pillows on top of Opal who was now on the floor. "That's not happening." He pulled Jade up first and threw her on the bed. He then grabbed Adam, wrestling him to the floor. Jade and Opal grabbed the pillows and began swinging.

Phire ran into the room with Mathew, Luke and Diamond behind them. "Pillow fight," she yelled and jumped into the battle. Pearl ran into the room with Samuel and Joshua behind her.

Pillows were being swung from every direction when Sally appeared in the doorway. There were bodies on both beds, between the beds, in front of the closet and even under the bed. She went into her room then came back with her bullhorn.

"Every last one of you stop...right this minute."

All eyes turned to her. Feathers from the pillows were all over the room, in people's hair, mouths and all over the floor.

"Do you have any idea how much those pillows cost? You are going to replace every last one of them. Grown people," she huffed. "Grown people," she emphasized. "Who started this?"

"Adam," a voice from the hallway replied."

Adam, who was under the bed with Joshua and Samuel, peeked out.

"Amber, you came."

"It's good to see you treat your parents' home the same way you treat mine."

"See, what had happened was..."

"Don't bother, Sapphire," Sally stopped her. "Start cleaning. Jade and Opal, go downstairs and set my dinner table. Luke, Mathew and Timothy, get the extra chairs from storage." As the layers of children began peeling off, Sally could not believe Diamond was in the middle of the pile.

"Oh, this is a nice example, Daddy." Samantha had her hands on her hips tapping her foot.

Samuel stood as he helped Diamond to her feet. "We parents get to have fun just like you kids," he said as he picked up his son Franklin who was standing next to his daughter.

"The grandmother of all grandmothers is going to spank you good," little Zoey, who was holding Teddi's hand, said from the hallway. Teddi then pointed her finger at all the grownups in the room and smiled at Zoey. The siblings in the room laughed.

Joshua crawled from under the bed, blew the feathers from his face then took his daughter. "Who is the grandmother of all grandmothers?"

Teddi pointed to Sally.

Sally raised her eyebrow to dare him to contradict her. "You are fitting in too easily." Joshua kissed his mother on the cheek. "Good to see you, Amber," he said then walked downstairs.

The room emptied out leaving Adam as the last one crawling from under the bed. Sally looked from her son to Amber. "Why don't you two come downstairs and talk." She smiled, then gently touched Amber's arm.

"Leaving me here to clean up this mess by myself?"

"Why don't you let Adam and me clean up here?" Amber said. "It will give us time to talk."

Phire rushed out the room calling over her shoulder, "Make sure that conversation is held vertically and not horizontally."

Sally watched her sassy daughter walk by with one hand on her hip and the other holding the bullhorn. She looked back at Adam. "What she said." She turned and walked down the stairs.

Amber stood in the doorway. "Do you have an invention to gather all those feathers?"

Adam looked around. "Not yet." He turned back to her. "Give me a year, I'll have something in place."

Amber walked over and sat on the floor next to him and laid her head on his shoulder. "I love you, Adam. I don't know how I know after only a week of meeting you. But I know that I do. Nothing my mother says, or thinks, will change that."

"She doesn't like me."

"I don't like you very much when you track snow in my house or throw my pillows around the room." She smiled.

"The thing is..." Adam rested his head on top of hers. "Your mother asked a very valid question about my future."

"The last thing I'm worried about is your future. If I haven't learned anything else in the last few days, I've learned you know how to take care of yourself." She lifted her head and looked into his eyes. "You have a brilliant future ahead of you, that I am certain of."

Her touch, her gaze, her smile erased all doubts from his mind. "We're going to need a house with a big basement. I want to build a laboratory."

She held his gaze. "I think I want to go back to trauma."

"Rough hours," he replied.

"I'll have you to ease out the kinks."

He kissed her lips. "Yes, you will."

"Time to give thanks, you two," Joe said from the doorway.

At the dinner table, Joe sat at the head opposite Sally. Looking from one end to the next, he smiled at the woman who blessed him with twelve beautiful children. Then he looked at the table, which held the next generation of Lassiters and laughed out loud. Samantha, the oldest grandchild, was instructing Teddi, the newfound grandchild, on how to put food on her plate.

"But there is no food on the plate."

"You have to put it on there," eight-year-old Samantha huffed.

"No." Teddi shook her head. "Ashanti prepares my food."

"Well, she's not here. So if you want to eat you better learn how to put food on your own plate."

"No." Teddi frowned at Samantha.

"Then you will be hungry."

"You are yelling, Sammy," four-year-old Frankie said to his older sister as he put his hand to his forehead. "Ugh," he sighed. "I feel a headache coming on."

Zoey, who was all of two, sat on the other side of Teddi. She put the roll she had been picking off of on Teddi's plate and smiled.

Joe turned back to his family. "We have a multitude of things to be thankful for. Samuel, begin."

Sammy nodded. "I am thankful for my wife, my children and God's grace for allowing me to be here for another year."

Cynthia smiled. "I'm thankful for my husband, my spoiled daughter and my very handsome son."

Ruby was next. "I'm thankful for parents who accept our flaws and love us anyway."

Joshua hesitated. "God granted me life. He gave me a wife, the special gift of Teddi and a newborn on the way." He nodded his head. "I'm a blessed man."

Roc smiled. "Whew, I'm not used to having so many people in my family. I'm an orphan with one best friend. It seems God has granted me a ready-made family and one to spare. I'm thankful for this day."

Pearl held her husband Theo's hand and smiled. "I am so thankful my siblings had the foresight to expand this dining room because this time next year we will need more chairs at the table."

Everyone stared at her for a long moment.

"You're pregnant?" Phire asked.

"I am that," Pearl replied.

Theo stood so fast he knocked his chair over. "You're pregnant?!?" He looked at his wife with his mouth wide open. "Thank God!" he exclaimed as he cupped her face with his hands and kissed her.

Congratulations rang out around the room. "Well we know what you are thankful for," Phire laughed. "That'll slow her down." Pearl flashed her baby sister a frown. "I'm just saying."

"Another grandchild." Sally clapped her hands.

"Keep the clapping going," Zack said as he smiled at his wife, Diamond.

"As always, Pearl stole my thunder, but yes, we are expecting again."

"I'm thankful God is granting me a boy this go round," Zack added.

"We don't know that yet," Diamond chastised her husband. "But we are hoping to give Zoey a baby brother."

Cheers went around the room again. "Y'all are breeding like rabbits around here."

Joe looked at his baby and shook his head. He turned back to the happy faces at the table. "Matt."

"I'm thankful we are half way through being thankful so I can eat."

Luke patted Mathew on the shoulder. "I'm with you, brother." He laughed. "But more than that, I'm thankful the NFL saw fit to approve my trade so I can do what I love closer to family and friends."

"Yes." Sally said a silent prayer.

"Well, I'm thankful for my family, of course," Opal began. "The new business with my brother and look forward to the holiday season."

"You should be thankful for that fine Grant Hutchinson."

"We are just friends."

Phire raised an eyebrow. "Friends with benefits."

"Phire." Sally frowned, then turned to Timothy.

"I too am grateful for Grant because my sister is a work-a-holic and I need a break." The family laughed. "Seriously, it's been a good year for us at Lassiter and Lassiter. I look forward to what the next year will bring."

Jade hesitated, then glanced at Adam. "I'm thankful for my brothers and sisters, but especially for Adam, who reminded me to take small steps. With that said." She smiled. "I got a spot with the Ted Bailey traveling dance troupe."

"Oh my goodness," Sally screamed. "Are you serious?" She ran around the table to hug her daughter.

"Congratulations." Cynthia laughed. "They are phenomenal."

"When did you hear?" Sally asked as she sat back down.

"Last week." Jade beamed, shocked by the reaction around the table. Adam winked at her and smiled.

Sally was smiling so bright Joe had to smile.

"All right, Adam." Joe nodded.

"The last few weeks started out so promising. I saw a dream realized, then it was taken away. I lost some people I looked up to. But I gained something more precious than gold." He took Amber's hand in his then looked into her eyes. "I met my Sally and her name is Amber. I'm thankful God placed her in my life. And pray that she remains by my side."

"Ask me." Amber held his eyes. She didn't care that she did not really know the people around the table. All she needed to know was that Adam loved her the way she loved him.

Adam pushed the chair back from the table.

His siblings began cheering and clapping. "Get on those knees," Mathew yelled out. The girls gasped with excitement.

Luke held up his phone to record the moment.

"I am a poor man with nothing to offer, but with you I am a king. Will you be my queen and rule a kingdom filled with love?" He kissed her hand. "Will you be the yin to my yang?"

Sally gasped as she realized they were the exact words Joe said to her when he proposed. Well, with the exception of the yin and yang stuff. She looked up to see him smiling at her.

Amber laughed through the tears that were rolling down her face. With all eyes on her, she nodded. "Yes, Adam Lassiter, I will..." She stopped. "Wait, are you asking me to marry you? It's important that I know so I can answer the correct way."

"Amber..."

"You did not ask if I will you marry you, which is traditional."

"It's boring," Adam replied. "This is more romantic, more meaningful than..."

"There is nothing boring about a traditional proposal," Amber huffed. "I've had an emotional day, Adam Lassiter, and this argument goes to me."

"Who won the last one?" Samuel asked

"I did," Adam replied.

"Then yes, it is her turn to win, Adam." Diamond nodded.

"Why?" Mathew asked. "If his logic is better why does he have to concede to her?"

"Because, it's her turn," Theo replied.

"Now we all understand why you don't have a woman in your life," Zack noted.

"Well damn it, is it yes or no?" Phire banged on the table.

All eyes turned to her. She looked around then settled back down into her seat. "I'm just saying."

Adam's head dropped in Amber's lap. He was laughing, as was Amber.

"Yes," Amber laughed with him. "It's a yes."

Adam cupped her face with his hands and kissed her. "Thank you." He sat back in his seat as those around the table congratulated them.

"Good," Phire exclaimed. "Is it my turn yet?"

Joe looked at his daughter and sighed. "Yes, Phire. It is your turn."

She stood and smiled at everyone around the table. "I am thankful for my family and God's guidance with a decision regarding my education. I've decided to enter the School of Divinity at Howard."

Every mouth at the table gaped open at the table as Phire looked around. Minutes ticked by as no one spoke. They were taught never to make light of anyone's dreams.

"Well," Sally finally replied as she looked around the table at the stunned faces. "Divinity school. That will be a discussion for another day." She glanced at Joe.

"What is Divinity?" Samantha asked.

"The school of Divinity prepares you to become a minister," Phire replied.

"They are letting the devil into heaven." Samantha hit her forehead.

Phire laughed. "I was just joking to see how you would react." There were sighs of relief around the room. "On a serious note, I've decided I want to be an investigative reporter. I don't want to just tell the stories. I want to uncover them and report the wrong doings around the world."

"So you want to get paid for what you do every day, tell other people's business?" Mathew laughed.

"I thought you wanted to be a professional cheerleader," Luke asked.

"I want to do that too." Phire sat back down. "Who's to say a girl can't multi-task."

"No one," Pearl tapped in. "You can be anything you want."

"Until a man comes along and changes your outlook on things," Opal chimed in.

"You mean like Grant has done with you?" Phire smirked. "I'm just saying...." everyone at the table finished her line.

Joe glanced around the table and smiled at his family. "I am grateful for moments like these. When I have all my children at the table sharing their lives with us. I'm thankful for my wife, good health and good food." He picked up his glass. "Let's raise our glasses." The others followed. "May we continue to love, support and encourage each other in our endeavors as we have been taught to do by the love of my life, Sally. Here's to you for this wonderful meal and this unpredictable family."

"Here, here," went around the table as glasses clinked together.

Joe turned to Amber. "Welcome to the world of the Lassiters. Now let's eat."

CHAPTER THIRTY

The day after Thanksgiving, Adam and Amber's first stop was the hospital to see Monique. They knew she was in good hands, but Amber wanted to see for herself. As the two women talked, Adam received a text message from Clive. They had not spoken since he left Quantico. It seemed like forever, but in reality it was only a week ago.

'Where are you?'

'In Bethesda,' he messaged back. *'What's going on?'*

'Meet me at Coffee Stop at 2.'

Adam was about to call Clive when his cell phone rang. "Lassiter."

"Dr. Lassiter?"

"Speaking," Adam replied as he stepped out of the room.

"Secretary Simon McGarry would like to meet with you at 9 am. on Monday morning. Where shall I send the car to pick you up?"

"Secretary of what?"

There was hesitancy to the woman's voice. "The Secretary of Defense."

"You mean the ex-Secretary of Defense McGarry?"

"Yes. He would like to see you on Monday morning."

"Monday." Adam thought. "I'll be busy."

There was another delay in the response. "Dr. Lassiter, this is the Secretary of Defense. You do not refuse a meeting with him."

"The President I cannot refuse. McGarry I can. Have a good day." Adam disconnected the call then pushed a button. "I just received an invitation to meet with McGarry. Actually it bordered on a demand."

"McGarry." Joshua stepped away from Teddi who was building a snowman. "What does he want?"

"Good question."

"It surprised me he wasn't involved in the Asmere incident. He was a part of the inner circle to marry Akande to Raheem during the old administration."

"He knew about the diamond mines?"

"Yes."

Adam heard a spree of laughter in the background. "It sounds as if you are under attack."

"Roc has taught Teddi how to make snowballs."

Adam smiled. "You being hit by snowballs. Sorry I'm not there to see it." He heard his brother laugh. He liked the fact that Joshua was taking a moment to enjoy the simple things in life.

"Got her right in the center of her back."

"Teddi?"

"No, Roc." Joshua began running. "Take the meeting with McGarry when he calls back. I'll have your six. Got to go."

Adam was smiling when he returned to the room.

"Who was that?" Amber asked.

"Joshua, Roc and Teddi are throwing snowballs."

Amber smiled. "I'm sure the Queen would love to see that."

Monique laughed. "Akande seeing another woman with her daughter and Joshua?" She shook her head. "Not likely."

"You want to enlighten us on that situation?"

Monique sat up. "I'm not touching that one." She frowned from the pain as she moved. "You will have to reach out to your brother on that one."

"It's not important." Amber helped Monique with the pillows. "What are your doctors saying about your recovery?"

"Yeah," Adam asked. "When can you bust out of this joint?"

"Thanks to you, I can walk out in a few more days."

"Then what?" Amber asked.

"A few weeks to recuperate and then I'll be back to work."

"Not if I have anything to do with it."

They turned to see none other than Al "Turk" Day standing in the doorway.

Monique rolled her eyes. "Daddy, don't start."

Al stepped into the room. "Good afternoon." He extended his hand to Adam.

"Hello, Mr. Day." Adam shook his hand. "Adam Lassiter, and this is Amber Nicolas."

"It's a pleasure to meet both of you. Thank you for saving my daughter's life."

"We could do no less after she saved so many," Adam replied as he picked up Amber's coat and helped her into it. "Since you have another visitor, we'll leave you now."

"We'll check back soon," Amber stated. "And stop giving the doctors a hard time. You'll be out when your body is ready."

"You two take care and congratulations." Monique called out as they walked away.

"Whew, that was Al Day."

Amber smiled up at him as they walked down the corridor. "Something I should know about him?"

"He's a legend." Adam pushed the elevator button. "Back in the day he was a Kingpin. Ran the streets like a corporation. He turned himself into President Harrison who was the Assistant District Attorney for Richmond at the time." He pushed the button inside and the elevator began its descent. "As the story goes, he asked JD to protect his sister while he did his time. The President ended up falling in love and marrying Tracy. He was sentenced to forty years but his time was reduced in conjunction with a case and his involvement in a gang reduction program. He heads it to this day."

"Wow, what a love story." She smiled up at him.

Adam stepped in front of her and braced his hands on the wall beside her head. "You would pick up on the love story. What about the rehabilitation of a Kingpin?"

"I like the love story better." She kissed his lips just as the elevator jerked and changed direction. Rather than going down it was now moving upward at an unusual speed. They held onto each other.

"Adam?" Amber screamed.

He pulled out his phone, pushed a few buttons, then pointed it towards the control panel. The elevator slowed, but still did not stop. He knew immediately that someone outside was controlling the elevator. He pushed Amber to the front left corner of the small moving box, clicked a few buttons on his phone, then stood in the middle where the doors would eventually open and waited.

The elevator stopped.

"Adam." Amber spoke from the corner.

"Stay put."

The doors opened to Adam standing front and center with his legs braced apart, his caramel coat swinging out and his hands cradled down in front of him. A man stepped in front of him. Adam did not ask any questions. He pointed his phone at the man and sent a laser beam right to the center of his forehead.

"The next person to step out, I aim straight for the heart."

There was no movement, only a voice. "Dr. Lassiter, I see you keep interesting gadgets on hand."

"The better to protect me and mine. Who are you and what do you want?"

"May I step forward?"

"I insist you do."

An older man with a stocky build, mixed gray hair, and dressed in, at the very least, a three thousand dollar suit stepped forward and stopped.

"Mr. McGarry." Adam held the man's glare.

"Most refer to me as Secretary McGarry out of respect."

"I'm not most people and so far you have not earned my respect."

Adam could see the squint in the man's eye. He did not like his response. But it was clear he wanted something. So Adam waited.

McGarry shrugged. "I would have thought the way I controlled the elevator would have garnered a little respect."

"Anyone can go to Radio Shack to get the items needed to create a remote control. You will have to do more to impress me."

McGarry smirked as he nodded. "I requested a meeting with you, yet you refused."

"Did I? I thought I indicated I was busy on Monday. That's not a refusal...I'm busy."

McGarry shook his head. "I'm not one who responds well to refusals."

"You appear to be a grown man. I'm certain you will find a way to survive. My patience is running thin. What do you want, McGarry?"

"A little information about your latest invention."

"Which invention would that be?"

McGarry was not used to people questioning him. When he asked for something he expected to receive it, no questions asked.

"Tell me about all of them," he replied in a tone that would intimidate most.

Adam held McGarry's stare. "I don't think I will. Now if you will excuse me." Adam pointed his phone at the control panel and the doors began to close.

"Wait!" McGarry stepped forward and yelled.

Adam pointed his phone and the doors reopened. He kept his same stance as McGarry glared at him.

"I have a syndicate of men who would like to speak with you regarding your future."

Adam nodded. "Not interested." He pointed the phone at the control panel and the doors closed. He pushed another button and the elevator began to descend.

"Stop the elevator," Amber said from the corner.

"Not yet." Adam held out his hand stopping her from moving.

"I want to get off this elevator, Adam."

"And we will." He glanced at her to reassure her then his attention stayed on the control panel. The elevator did not stop until it reached the parking garage on the third level, where they had parked. Adam stepped out, looked both ways then held his hand out for her to take.

Amber slowly took his hand. "What in heck was that all about?" she asked him as she looked around.

"I have no idea," Adam replied as they weaved their way through the parked cars. "The real question is how did they know where we were?"

"GPS?" Amber offered as she held his hand tight and followed his lead.

"I blocked the GPS on my phone...." He hesitated then turned to her. "They locked in on yours."

"How did they know I was with you?"

That was the question that concerned Adam. Was McGarry watching them? If so, why?"

"Something's off," he stated. "While we were visiting Monique, Clive sent me a text to meet him."

"From the FBI class?"

"Yes."

"Why?"

"I don't know."

"Let's go find him," Amber said as she walked towards the car.

"Let's?"

"Yes." Amber looked over her shoulder. "We're in this together, right?"

Adam shook his head. "What happened to the traditional, by the clock woman I met?"

"She changed into this adventurous woman, who wants to help you save the world."

Adam closed the car door he held open for her. "I've created a monster."

Clive met them at a restaurant outside the base. They were sitting at a table talking.

"It's good to see you," Clive said as he sat back. "I intercepted this message." He pushed a piece of paper to Adam.

Adam read the message. "Who was it intended for?"

"Karen."

"Karen Johnson? What's her connection to McGarry?"

Clive shrugged. "No idea. Thought you might know."

"No." Adam shook his head. "But we just had an impromptu meeting with him."

"McGarry?" Clive asked. "About what?"

Adam held up the note as he shared it with Amber. "Something about a syndicate."

Amber read the note then looked at Adam. "She's involved with McGarry?"

"I think we better find out." Adam glared at Clive. "Thank you for the information."

Clive stood. "It's back to class for me." He stared at Adam and nodded. "Watch your back." With that he was gone.

Amber sat in the back, her mind reeling from the elevator adventure and now the conversation between the guys. Her mother's words came back to her. This is going to be a part of her everyday life. Just as the wives of police officers and FBI agents. But Adam wasn't either. He is a scientist. It's not supposed to be a dangerous life. In her mind, he would go to the lab to work and she would go to the hospital. Her occupation should be more dangerous than his.

Amber sighed. "What do you think we should do?"

A number of things were running through Adam's mind. The first was Amber's safety.

"Amber..."

She turned to Adam. "I don't care," she cut him off. "Joshua and Roc found a way. Samuel and Cynthia found a way. And so did my mother and father."

"This is a little different." Adam took her hand. "It will never stop. As long as people out there feel I can somehow create something that would make them a heap of money they will come after me. Once we get married that will make you a target."

"Then you better invent a way to protect me, because I'm not going anywhere."

Staring at her, Adam had to smile. As crazy as his situation was, he had Amber by his side and that made everything all right. A traditional boring life was never meant for her or him. She was beginning to see life his way. Adam looked out at the snow-covered ground. His problem was finding an occupation that would keep her safe and give him the ability to serve his country in a unique way. Inventions would always be a part of his life, but what was missing was the adventure. His brother Joshua's life of intrigue and espionage appealed to him. But it did not afford him a life with a family. Adam needed to find a way to incorporate both.

He stood then reached out to her. "We'll worry about McGarry and the rest of the world another day. You know, it's the week after Thanksgiving. We need to do some Christmas shopping. Find a tree, then decorate the house."

"I have a tree," Amber said as she stood.

"You have a fake tree, don't you? And I lay odds it's white."

"And it is beautiful."

"It's sterile," Adam said as he opened the door and followed her out. "We need lights and lots of them."

"You mean like the thousand lights you and your siblings put on your parent's house. I don't think so."

"You enjoyed putting those lights on the house. Your face was all aglow."

"It was fun," Amber laughed as they walked hand in hand through the snow.

"I guess we better shop for tree decorations and a ring."

Amber stopped. "We're picking out a ring?"

Adam pulled her to him. "I can't have my fiancée walking around without a symbol of our love." He kissed her, then continued walking. "I have to let all those doctors you will be working with know you are taken. Off the market. No longer available."

Amber laughed.

"Then we'll go home, put up the tree then begin searching the Internet for our new home."

Amber smiled. "Really?"

"Yes, everything else can wait."

Adam ignored the vehicle that followed them from the coffee shop. He made a mental note of the license plate number, certain when he did the search later it would turn out to be McGarry or one of his people following them. He did not want to alert Amber to their presence. He liked the carefree Amber and wanted to do the normal things a couple in love would do during the holiday season. If McGarry or anyone tried to interfere with that, he would find a way to make them pay.

CHAPTER THIRTY-ONE

The text message was on his phone when he awakened the next morning. It was a picture of Amber in the ladies room at the restaurant where they stopped to eat after picking out her ring. Every time she looked at the 2-carat emerald-cut solitaire engagement ring, her eyes would tear up. Finally she gave up trying to hold them back and let the tears flow. She excused herself to go to the ladies room. That's when they must have taken the picture. He read the message.

'This is how close we can get. Don't ignore us.'

It was a threat pure and simple. Adam thought for a minute, then sent the message to Ned on his secure line asking him to trace the message. He then pulled up and reviewed all the information he could find on McGarry. Two can play this game. His phone buzzed while he was reading up on McGarry.

"Lassiter."

"Royce Davenport here. I understand McGarry has contacted you."

Adam stopped reading. "Yes, he did. Any idea why he wants to know about my inventions?"

"No. Did he give you any specifics?"

"I got the impression he had one in mind, however, I did not open the door. What do you know that is not written anywhere on McGarry?"

"There have been mumblings of a syndicate."

"He mentioned that."

"Do you plan to meet with him?" Royce asked.

"Oh, yes," Adam replied. "I have a message to deliver to him."

"Adam, contrary to what you may think, you are a scientist, nothing more." Royce cautioned. "McGarry is not the type of man you play with."

"He started this. I am simply a man trying to live my life. He crossed the line into my personal life. I'm going to establish some boundaries."

Royce was silent on the other end for a moment then he spoke. "It may be an opportunity to infiltrate the syndicate."

Adam sat back. "I'm listening."

"There are entities within our country who feel they know better than the President what is best for the United Sates. They have the power, the money, and the worldwide connections to make things happen. There are times when we agree with their actions. However, there are times when their actions are dangerous. I can only assume they wish to add you to their established arsenal of options to carry out whatever diabolical scheme they cook up."

"Why haven't they been stopped?"

"Until now, we could never identify the members. If McGarry is representing them in this matter, he may be our way in. The question is what do they want from you?"

"Is everything with J.M.A.L.T.S. secured?"

"Yes, the lab has been moved to an undisclosed location."

"Who is heading up the team?"

"This impressive young man named Adam Lassiter. Since you are no longer with the FBI, why not have the inventor spearhead the production?"

"Is that a job offer?"

"Unofficial." Royce cleared his throat. "The President has yet to sign off on it. There seems to be another offer with your name attached."

"Offer from whom?"

"I'm not at liberty to say. Just know your name is on a very short list for several positions."

Adam smiled. "A man needs to know these things when planning for the future, Davenport."

"I heard congratulations are in order. Phillip tells me Amber is ecstatic. Her mother...not so much."

"She doesn't like me too much."

"Make Amber happy and Jill will come around." Royce sighed. "Now, back to McGarry. What are you going to do?"

"Meet with him," Adam replied as Amber walked in the door from her run. "I have to go now. We'll talk soon."

"Adam, be careful with McGarry. He can be a dangerous man."

"So can I," Adam advised then disconnected the call.

"Who was that?" Amber asked as she walked by him in the direction of the shower.

"Secretary Davenport," Adam replied as he watched her begin removing her clothes.

"Was he looking for me?" she asked as she pulled her robe out.

"No, talking about a job."

Amber turned to him. "A job? Where?"

"Heading up the production team for J.M.A.L.T.S."

"That makes perfect sense." She smiled. "You created it."

"Why are you putting that robe on?"

"I'm about to take a shower."

"You plan on taking your shower with the robe on?"

"No, silly. I'm going to take it off when I get in."

"So why are you putting it on at all?"

"Because I'm taking my clothes off with you in the room."

"I've seen every inch of you. You do not need to hide your body from me." He laid across the bed on his stomach. "In fact, I prefer to see you without the robe."

Amber frowned at him. "I'm not going to walk around the room naked."

"Why not? No one is here but you and me."

"Because." She blushed as she shrugged her shoulders. "It's not normal."

Adam rolled off the bed, pulled off his sweat pants and allowed them to drop to the floor. Naked as a jaybird, he walked over to her, closed her gaping mouth with a finger, then stripped the robe from her body. He turned her towards the mirror in the corner. "Look at us." He wrapped his arms around her waist. "We are God's creation. Why would you cover anything so beautiful?"

Amber looked at their reflection. He was right. His dark skin tone was a perfect compliment to her fair skin. "This carefree way of living is going to take some getting used to."

He kissed her neck as his hands roamed her body. "No worries. I'll shed you of all your inhibitions, including this insane notion of getting up to run at six in the morning."

"I need my exercise," she replied seductively as her eyes closed to the touch of his fingers traveling between her thighs.

She gasped the moment he touched her clit.

"Adam," she moaned.

"Yes," he chuckled. "I can help with that. Touch your toes." He bent her at the waist, then slowly entered her from behind.

"Adam...." His hands caressed her thighs as he slowly moved inside her. He stretched out over her back, her arms holding on to his. They moved in slow, unhurried, loving motion until they both moaned from the sweet mellow explosion that took their breath away. They both collapsed to the floor, allowing their breathing to ease. "I bet your heart rate is faster than after that run you took."

Amber lay against him laughing. "How am I supposed to speak with the administrator at the hospital about a position with this on my mind?"

"With a smile on your face."

Amber laughed as she pushed up from the floor. "You are incorrigible, Adam Lassiter."

"That I am." He watched her walk into the bathroom. "And you love it."

"That I do," she replied as she walked into the shower.

An hour later, Amber was on her way to the hospital and Adam was hard at work.

"It's time to teach people not to mess with the smart boy." He pulled up the address he found for McGarry. Checking court deed records he found the builder of the house and pulled the blueprints to the house. Reviewing the specs he found some things he did not understand. He picked up his cell and made a call.

"X-man. It's Adam. How are you?"

"Happy, man. How are you?"

"Engaged."

"What?"

Adam laughed at his friend's response. "I met this incredible woman and asked her to marry me two weeks later."

"Hey, man, when you meet the right one there is no reason to wait."

"It comes with challenges. One that I need your help with."

"You got it. I'm in Tyson's visiting with Nicole's parents. Are you in Atlanta?"

"No. I am in Georgetown. In fact, what I need you for is closer to you."

"Give me an address. I'll meet you."

"Before you do, I have to warn you. This is ten times more dangerous than our adventure in Atlanta."

"Adam, after all you did for my family. You need me. I'm there. Give me the address."

Adam disconnected the call and thought through his plans. When they were in Atlanta neither he nor Xavier Davenport were married. They were young and naive. What they did could have easily landed them in jail or six feet under. But everything worked out. X-man won the girl in the end. That was all that mattered.

That night Adam and X-man sat outside the gated home of ex-Secretary of Defense McGarry, dressed in dark slacks, turtleneck shirts, black leather jackets and boots.

"This is not going to be as easy as Atlanta," Adam said to X-man as they watched the infrared images on his computer screen. "This man is politically connected like you would not believe. If we get caught, we're talking Guantanamo...not prison."

"I trust your gadgets to get us in and out," X-man replied. "I still say that underground tunnel looks like it would be the best way to get in."

"I don't think so." Adam shook his head. "If I had a tunnel like that, I would have sensors set to let me know when someone is coming through. I'm going through the front door."

The two men stepped out of the vehicle. They surveyed the area then began to walk across the street when a hand grabbed them by their collars, pulling them behind the tree they had parked next to and throwing them into the snow.

"Good evening, younger brother to Joshua. Interesting finding you here."

Adam looked up. As the man bent over them, Sly's face came into focus.

"Sly, what in the hell are you doing here?"

"Stopping you and your friend from taking your last breath." He held his hand down to help Adam up. "Your excuse?"

"McGarry threatened my woman."

"The Doc?"

"That's right," Adam replied as he held a hand down to X-man.

"That can't go unanswered," X-man stated.

Sly's eyebrow rose at X-man then he turned to Adam. "So you brought Davenport's nephew on a mission?"

"This is not my first time around," X-man replied as he stared at the strange man dressed in a 1960's pimp suit, hat and all. "We have a plan."

"Do you?" Sly glared at the two men. Adam had skills that he knew. This would be a good way to test them. "I'll stand down. I take it you are going to approach McGarry since it was your woman he threatened?"

"Oh yeah, he's mine."

Sly nodded. "One bit of advice." He took his fedora off and placed it on Adam's head. He adjusted it over one eye. "Facial recognition equipment works on the triangle identification. Always cover one eye to delay the process." He leaned back against the tree. "You going in through the tunnel?"

"Nope, I'm going through his front door," Adam replied. "Let's go, X-man."

"I'll be here when you need me."

Before crossing the street, Adam pushed a few buttons on his handheld device then waited a few minutes. "Camera's deactivated."

"You're sure?" X-man asked.

Adam gave the man an incredulous look. "Of course I'm sure."

"Just checking," X-man replied as the two men walked to the gate, and bent down.

Adam held his device to the keypad then pushed a few buttons, seconds later the gate clicked open. The two quickly entered the yard, staying low and using the trees as cover while they made their way up the half-mile driveway to the front porch. The floor plans indicated the security panel was just inside the front door to the left. The trick was to open the front door without triggering the chime. Adam keyed into the security company's records and had the chime disabled. He then pulled a small tube from his jacket pocket. He squeezed the contents inside the lock on the door with a dribble running down the handle.

"Hit it with the laser."

X-man pulled the laser from his pocket and pushed a small button. The substance began to harden making a makeshift plastic key.

Adam waited a moment, then used the dribble to twist the key. The door clicked signaling it was now unlocked. The two eased inside the house, closing the door behind them.

They stood in the foyer while Adam checked his tablet. He pointed out the infrared images in one room upstairs that appeared to be someone lying in a bed. Adam assumed that was McGarry's wife. There was one person downstairs in the back of the house, also lying down. Must be the maid, Adam thought. The one they were interested in was in a room to the left.

"That's the office," X-man whispered as he pointed at the screen. "There is a stairwell behind that bookcase that leads down to the tunnel."

Adam nodded then walked in the direction of the office. X-man followed holding the tablet, watching every move of the figure in the office. Adam opened the door and walked in.

McGarry looked up from his desk. He masked the surprise from his eyes quickly as he recognized the intruder. He sat back in his chair.

"Well, it seems you decided to meet with me after all."

"Responding to your message."

"A daring response coming into my home in this manner. Don't you think?" McGarry narrowed his eyes on the menacing figure.

"An appropriate response to deliver the message I have for you."

"The message came from the Syndicate, not me. I am merely the messenger."

Adam watched McGarry's hands closely. He saw the instant the man's thumb touched the button on the desk. He knew his time was limited. He hoped X-man was watching for movement of figures on the tablet.

"Not one for a lot of words, McGarry. My message is simple: come after mine and I will come after you."

McGarry chuckled. "You have no idea who you are dealing with, Lassiter. Don't let your arrogance be the cause of unpleasantness. The Syndicate only wishes to explore your mind. To give you unlimited freedom and resources to bring your creations to life."

"My mind isn't for sale. However, I'm happy to share at least one of my devices with you." He flicked his fingers, tossing a small button to the bookcase directly behind where McGarry sat. The bookcase exploded.

McGarry dropped to the floor as debris from the shelves flew outward exposing the opening and setting off alarms. When the dust and flying debris settled, McGarry crawled from under his desk, staring at the hole in his wall. Nothing else in the room was disturbed by the explosion. He looked himself over, nothing had touched him. The gun in his hand had not discharged. The device with pinpoint precision only exposed the entry to the tunnel. He turned to where Adam had been standing to find the man gone. In his place was a holographic message.

'BOOM!'

Adam and X-man walked across the street to the tree where they left Sly. Adam's walk slowed at the sight of his brother as he approached. "Why am I not surprised?"

"Did you think I would let you two have all the fun?" Joshua stated from his casual lean against the tree next to Sly. "Next time wear a long coat. People will take you more seriously if you dress the part."

"And it gives you more room for gadgets," Sly added as if he was teaching a class.

"That's true." Joshua turned to Sly and nodded. "What do you give him on execution?"

Sly looked at the house. "Hmm, no exterior damage. Any casualties?"

"None," X-man replied with a grin.

"I'll give him an eight."

"An eight?" Adam raised an eyebrow.

"Your presentation was off, man," Sly explained. "There was no style to it."

"It was his first time," Joshua offered. "The true measure comes with knowing if you pissed him off."

"That's the purpose behind a stunt like this." Sly nodded. "To piss off your enemy to the point that they will think twice before coming at you again."

"I think McGarry is pretty pissed," Adam stated. "If not by the explosion, the message."

"We'll see." Sly stood and began walking down the road. Joshua did the same.

X-man looked around. "Where's my car?"

"I moved it," Sly replied.

"Why?"

He answered as Adam and X-man followed them down the road.

"Lesson number 2..."

"Number 2," Adam questioned as they walked down the snow-covered road.

"Yes, the hat was lesson number 1. Speaking of which..." Sly reached back, taking the hat from Adam's head and placing it back on his. "As I was saying, lesson number 2. Never bring anything personal on a mission."

"Too easy to track," Joshua added as police cars raced by them. "Are you listening, Adam? If you are going to do this type of work you need to learn from the King."

"If he is the King, who are you?"

"The King Maker." He grinned.

Sly smiled. "Lesson number 3- never let them know you are coming."

X-man tapped Adam on the shoulder. "Is old school supposed to be teaching new school here?"

"Old school has been around and going strong for years," Sly said without turning around. "Listen and you just might learn how to survive."

CHAPTER THIRTY-TWO

Not this room, Adam thought, as he was ushered to the door. It was one thing to be ordered to the White House, quite another to be brought to the Oval Office.

"You may enter." Mrs. Langston held the door open as Adam hesitantly walked in.

"Do you know why you are here today, Adam?" Chief of Staff Brooks asked.

"I don't suppose I'm receiving another medal or something."

"No," James chuckled. "Have a seat, Adam." James pointed to the chair at the top of the oval shaped carpet.

Adam hesitated, then sat.

James walked around the sofa on the right to stand opposite from where Adam sat. With the Secretary of Homeland Security, Royce Davenport on one sofa and his soon to be father-in-law, Deputy Director of FBI, Phillip Nicolas on the other he felt somewhat intimidated, but he would never show it.

Adam crossed his legs and listened.

"It seems you..." James let the word hold for a moment "broke into the home of ex-Secretary of Defense McGarry, cutting through several layers of security the United States government installed in his home. You destroyed a perfectly good entrance to a secure tunnel. In addition you blocked our satellite so no one would be able to detect your actions. What do you have to say for yourself?"

Adam looked around the room at Royce, Phillip, and James. It was not in his DNA to lie when asked a direct question. However, since the question was general he believed he could play around with the truth a bit.

"Technically, I did not break in. I had a key. As to the tunnel, well, I simply exposed a flaw in the design of the camouflaged bookcase." He sat forward and folded his hands on the table. "As to the satellite, well, I was experimenting with a new invention. The great news here is that it worked." He cleared his throat and waited. Looking around the room there were no smiling faces.

A door in the back of the room opened. Secret Service Agents walked in followed by President Harrison. Everyone in the room stood.

"Please take a seat, gentlemen." JD looked at Adam. "You seem to be in a bit of trouble here, Adam."

"It seems so, Sir."

JD stood next to James. A glance passed between them ending with a nod from James.

"It was all a ruse. Secretary of Defense McGarry, Karen Johnson, and Clive Mason were all pawns in the test. You see, while members of your family have proven to be loyal patriots to this country, I needed to determine where Adam, the man's, loyalties lie. You have not only proven your loyalty to this country, you have also demonstrated a skill level well above our expectation. What we are about to ask of you should not be taken lightly. I strongly urge you to speak with your fiancée before you make a final decision. Know that you have the full faith of this President in your ability to carry out the task that will be set before you."

JD stood. The men around the table did the same. "Your President is asking you to serve."

JD nodded to James, then walked out of the room, followed by the Secret Service Agents.

A confused Adam looked at James. "Serve as what?"

"Gentlemen," James said. Everyone in the room stood. Adam decided to join suit. "Follow me, Adam."

"Okay," Adam replied and followed the men out of the room, down the hallway, down a few flights of stairs to a set of double doors.

James placed his hand on a pad. The doors opened. The men stood back allowing Adam to enter first. Adam stepped inside the room, then turned when the doors closed quietly behind him. He glanced around the room and slowly grinned from ear to ear. He had heard of it, read about it and dreamed about it, but he had never thought he would ever be in this room. He was in heaven. From the monitors on the wall, to the computers around the room, he had just entered his realm - The Situation Room inside the White House.

"Adam."

He turned to the voice and was surprised to see Ned standing at the far entrance door. "Ned?"

"You recognize me?" The neat suited person standing in the room would have never been recognized by a normal person as the same long haired, rough looking scientist he had first met.

"Yes, of course. You can change the outer layer but you can never change the core of a person. Your aura is all around you."

Ned laughed. "So much for starting a new life." He pointed around the room. "So, what do you think?"

Adam's face lit up as if it was Christmas morning for a child as he looked around the room. "A lot of toys to play with."

Ned smiled. "Yes, it is." He nodded as he looked around. "Please, have a seat."

The table was long enough to seat at least twenty people if not more. Ned was standing at the far end, so for fun, Adam took the seat closest to him.

"Adam, I've been given the green light to make you an offer on a position that is about to be vacated."

"Okay." He shrugged. "What position?"

"You may want to prepare yourself for it's going to be a shock." Ned laughed. "The Secretary of Defense and the President of the United States are asking you to serve your country as a Handler for the Central Intelligence Agency Clandestine Service."

Adam looked blank for a long moment. Ned allowed the statement to settle before continuing.

"Your job?"

Ned nodded. "Yes."

"What are you going to do? Retire?" Adam shook his head. "You have too much left in you to do that. I watched you during the Asmere operation. You are still wired for this. You can't walk away."

"I don't plan to." Ned reached across the table and pushed a button. One of the monitors on the back wall came to life. "This is the team we have assembled."

Adam sat up to see a chart with The President at the top, Secretary Davenport beneath him, Ned under him and Adam Lassiter listed just below him but above four blank spaces.

"As you can see, there are blank spaces under your name. The names of those agents will not be revealed until you accept the position. It seems in your circle everyone knows who is who, but trust that is only within your small circle. No one knows who our operatives are and we plan to keep it that way." Ned pulled out the seat next to Adam out and sat. "What is being offered to you is an opportunity to serve your country in a way that very few others before you have done. The primary lives of four agents will be placed in your hands. Their mission will be to strengthen national security and the collection of human intelligence by using covert actions. It takes a unique human being to handle such a responsibility. You have demonstrated as well as constantly informed us all that you are such a person." Ned leaned towards Adam. "I have worked in this capacity for fifteen years and I have never come up against a combination such as you and your brother. You are a natural for this honored position. No agency in which you would have to ask permission to do what your gut tells you would ever satisfy you as an employer." He sat back. "As it stands I wonder how I'm going to contain you." He smiled. "But I welcome the opportunity with open arms."

The thrill of having this conversation touched Adam to the core. Every instinct in his body knew this is what he was meant to do. There would be no limitations, no red tape, no going by the so-called moral compass. He would be free to protect the United States of America by any means necessary. He would be able to save lives. Then Amber came to his mind. The thought of having to be away from her for days, weeks, maybe even months at a time cut him deep. Adam stood then paced across the front of the room. The memory of his mother's worries the many times Joshua disappeared came to mind. He would do anything within his power to take that worry away from her just as he would do anything in his power to keep that worry from Amber's eyes. This quandary was something that he'd always feared, having to choose between his profession and the woman he loved. He stopped pacing and looked at Ned.

"Amber."

The quiet way he spoke her name brought a smile to Ned's face. "The wonderful progress of our profession gives us the opportunity to work from home. You can work from anywhere in the United States with the right equipment. It's no coincidence that we chose this room to hold this conversation. Take a look around. Everything that's in this room, in addition to the many things I'm certain you will create, will be available to you wherever you choose to set up your base. I would be remiss in my duties if I did not divulge the fact that I blew up my last base. That of course was after ten years of being there." Ned stood. "Allow me to make this easy for you. Your President is asking you to serve."

Adam stood there in his suit, his trench coat open, with his hands in his pants pockets. This decision should be discussed with Amber, he knew it the moment he spoke the next words. "Introduce me to my team."

Ned smiled, reached across the table then pushed a button on the console. The double doors opened.

Joshua was the first to walk in. Adam smiled as he shook his hand. "I knew you would do the right thing." He punched Adam on the shoulder then took a seat at the table.

Monique gingerly walked in next. She kissed him on the cheek. "Welcome to the dark side, baby brother." She sat next to Joshua.

The next person to walk in was Clive Mason. Adam was pleasantly surprised. "I knew there was more to you, than meets the eye, Mississippi."

"I had you covered the entire time you were at the Bureau. I'm honored to be a part of your team." He shook Adam's hand then sat in the seat across from Monique.

The last person to walk through the door knocked Adam back a step or two. The young man extended his hand. "It's my pleasure to serve you, The President and our country."

"How old are you?" Adam asked.

"Just turned eighteen, Sir."

Adam looked to Ned then back to the young man. "Is there an age requirement for this agency?" He looked back to Ned.

"There is." Ned nodded in his nonchalant way.

"We thought you would have some reservations, Sir." The young man spoke. "Therefore, I have one observation to hand to you. Countries around us disperse children a lot younger than I to be educated in our country then later rally against us. We need to have forces in place to identify and bring down all enemies, foreign and domestic, regardless of their age, creed or nationality. You all," he looked around the room, "do not have the ability to infiltrate some areas. I mean no disrespect, but none of you will be in a position to do covert action at a high school, or college. I have the ability and the intelligence to do so."

Ned raised an eyebrow as he glanced at Adam. "Sound familiar?"

"That may be." Adam moved from Ned's smirky grin back to the young man in front of him. "How do you anticipate handling the physical demands of this career path?"

"The plan is for me to work as an intern with you. One of the weaknesses we've come to realize is not planning for the future. I am a solution to that area of concern. It has proven to be a good tactical stance for the young to learn from the best we have in the field. I believe you will prove to be the best."

Adam grinned. "Oh you are smooth."

"Thank you, Sir." The young man smiled for the first time. "It's the one trait I inherited from my father."

"Speaking of which, what is his position on this career path of yours?"

CHAPTER THIRTY-THREE

Adam walked in the condo with presents in his hand. He knew what he had to do. He was confident Amber would support his decision. But he also knew he should have discussed it with her before making it. He received a short reprieve. The Christmas tree was lit and music was playing. Amber walked around the corner dressed in the sexiest red skirt, top and heels he had ever seen. She handed him a drink.

"We have company." She smiled.

Adam raised an eyebrow. "We do?"

"Yes, my parents are here."

The concern must have shown on his face. Did Phillip tell her about the President's' offer? Or was Jill here to make her daughter feel guilty about her decision to marry him. Either way, it wasn't good for him.

"Smile." Amber took his arm and walked with him into the living room. "Adam's home."

"Good evening." Adam smiled taking a quick glance at Phillip.

"Hello, Adam." Phillip stood and shook his hand. "I thought it was time for us to talk."

Adam nodded. "Mrs. Nicolas."

"Hello Adam."

Short and sweet, Adam thought, as he sat on the sofa near the fireplace.

"Mother," Amber coaxed.

Jill cleared her throat and stood. "Yes, well." She turned to Adam. "First, I apologize for anything I may have said to offend you or your family. There is no excuse so I won't try to make one. What I will do is welcome you to our family and wish you and Amber all the happiness Phillip and I have shared over the years."

Adam stood. "Thank you, Mrs. Nicolas. I realize you love Amber as much as I do. I don't want her to be caught in the middle of us. Please know her happiness is my goal in life." He kissed her on the cheek.

"I'm happy to hear that." A moment of awkward silence followed. "I must say." Jill looked around the room. "There have been a number of changes around here." She smiled. "Um...the tree...well, it's colorful."

Amber laughed as Adam joined in. "You have Adam to thank for that. I don't think my life will ever be black or white again."

Phillip and Jill looked at each other and laughed out loud. That simple statement seemed to have cut the ice in the room.

"How about I fix us some real drinks?" Phillip offered as he stood and walked over to the bar.

"I'll give you a hand." Adam joined him. "Did you tell your wife?"

"No," Phillip replied. "Have you told Amber?"

"No," Adam replied. "I plan to tell her tonight."

Phillip nodded. "The truth, the whole truth and nothing but the truth."

"So help me God," Adam added.

Phillip nodded then walked back over to the women. The gathering ended with dinner, drinks and laughter.

Later that night Adam enjoyed making love to Amber as they laughed through the night.

"I can't remember having more fun during the holidays than I have with you."

Adam smiled as he held Amber on pillows in front of the fire. The lights from the tree glowing on her skin, wood crackling in the fireplace and smooth R&B coming through the speakers put him in a comfort zone to talk.

"Life should be this way every day. It's important to have moments to remember. My family always seems to have more than most." He smiled. "People often wonder how my parents were able to feed, clothe and educate twelve children on one income. My father will be the first to tell you, it takes a damn good woman to manage that. I have to agree. My dad is larger than life to all of us. We love him beyond reason. We fear Sally."

Amber laughed. "It seems she runs the Lassiter household."

"Believe me, she does. Now she will be the first to tell you it's the love of a good man that gave her the strength and endurance to deal with all of us. I believe it's a combination of both that made it work." He hesitated then began.

"President Harrison offered me a position today. I accepted. In hindsight I should have waited and talked with you first. I'm new at this fiancé thing, so give me time to get it right."

"Congratulations, Dr. Lassiter. I knew you would ascend to new heights."

"Don't you want to know what the position is?"

She kissed his neck. "It doesn't matter. You are going to excel at it."

Adam smiled, then told her. "He has asked me to join the CIA as a handler. I will take over Ned's position. They have a team assembled just waiting for me to accept." He held her closer. "The government will fund a laboratory at a location of my choosing as my cover. My first project will be the production of J.M.A.L.T.S." He stopped then added, "I want you to know my heart skips a beat when you smile. It doesn't matter if you're smiling at me, or a little girl lying in a bed or even Special Agent Brent. Your happiness is my priority. If you have any doubts about this job, tell me and I will walk away. What I can't do is walk away from you."

Amber listened as he continued to tell her about the job. Not for one minute did she think he would be happy doing anything else. This life gave him the infinite possibilities of inventions and adventure. What a wonderful way to use that big brain of his. Didn't he know she would never interfere with that? Didn't he know she would walk through the fires of hell for him to be happy?

Amber turned and lay on top of him. She looked into his eyes. "You know these insecurities of yours are really getting old. I am here to stay. I don't care if you are a boring old scientist with big-rimmed glasses or the tall, debonair secret agent. I will be here, beside you all the way. I only ask two things. One, you will not hypnotize me, and two, you will give me more than one child. I want my children to have the crazy life I saw at your parents' home."

"Hmmm....more than one child." He lifted her body and eased her down onto his swollen shaft. "I think I can accommodate you there."

They made love until they fell asleep in front of the fire in each other's arms.

The telephone ringing in the middle of the night is never good. Two ringing at the same time is devastating.

Adam held Amber in one arm as his other felt around the floor with the other.

"Yeah," his sleepy voice answered. "What?" He slowly sat up. "Hold on, Phire, calm down." He listened a little more as he awakened Amber. "Where is Sammy? Did you call Sammy?"

Amber turned, alert to the fear in his voice. "What is it?"

"Let me talk to Mom." He listened. "What do you mean you she can't talk?" He stood looking around then grabbed his pants as he continued to listen. "We'll be right there." He hung up the phone then pulled a sweater over his head.

"Adam?" Amber asked as she quickly dressed.

He looked over at her. She froze, waiting.

"My father was just shot."

Amber went right into doctor mode. "What hospital?" He answered. She picked up her phone and dialed while grabbing a brush from the bathroom vanity. "Dr. Nicolas, code trauma2258. I need a status on Joseph Lassiter, stat." She was putting on her shoes as they walked out into the hallway.

Adam's phone buzzed with a text from Joshua. "We're meeting Joshua in the breezeway."

"How many bullets?" Amber listened as she climbed into the chopper. "Location?" She listened again as Joshua took off. "Prep him now. Who is on call?" Amber shook her head as she spoke into the telephone. "Call in Dr. Patel. Have Dr. Amos prep the patient and stop the bleeding. Dr. Patel will handle the surgery. I'm...." She looked at Adam.

"Forty-five." He answered her question. "Which surgical room?"

"Forty-five minutes out. Which room are you using?" She listened.

Adam keyed into his laptop. He locked onto the police computer system to listen in on the chatter. When that did not appease his curiosity, he locked into the security cameras at Upton Investment Warehouse where his father worked.

"I expect an update every ten minutes until I arrive." Amber disconnected the phone as they watched.

Two men were at the first bay loading boxes into a truck when his father walked in from the back. A few words were exchanged then his father walked over to the desk. Adam watched as his father's hand went under the desk. "Good thinking Dad," Adam said. As he continued to watch, his dad's hands went up in the air. Something caught his attention because his father's head turned to the back. He ran and jumped right in front of a man coming from the back, knocking him to the ground. "He took a bullet for that man."

Adam looked up at Joshua. He didn't bother to say anything for he knew Joshua was deep in prayer. Amber touched his shoulder from behind. Adam reached back and held her hand. A few moments of comfort were all he could afford. He continued watching and saw where the police immediately surrounded the two men as they tried to pull out of the warehouse parking lot. Adam zoomed in on the faces. The one who shot his father was the one he wanted to see. He took a screen print of the man's face and ran it through his facial recognition program. Armed with that information, all he needed to know was where the man was being held. He then connected into the Richmond Police Department computer system. He found the precinct he was being taken to. That was all he needed.

"Are we set?" Joshua asked as he landed the chopper.

"Ready," Adam replied.

"I'll check on Dad," Joshua said as he disappeared down the corridor of the hospital.

"Adam." Amber held his hand as they quickly walked towards the trauma rooms. "What are you planning?"

"An eye for an eye," he said with a calmness that chilled her blood.

Amber stopped, pulling away from him. "I am not bailing you or Joshua out of jail tonight," she said as he kept walking.

Adam joined his family taking Jade into his arms, as Amber walked over to the nurses' station. "It's going to be all right, Jade. It's going to be all right." He sighed.

A few minutes later Joshua appeared with a doctor. They all gathered around Sally as the doctor spoke.

"Mrs. Lassiter, I'm Dr. Patel. Your husband is out of surgery. There is some neurological damage. The extent cannot be determined at this time. For now he remains in critical condition."

Sally stood. "Thank you, Dr. Patel." The doctor was hesitant to move. Sally tilted her head at her son. "Joshua."

Joshua raised an eyebrow at her. "He's free to go."

Dr. Patel did not hesitate, he quickly moved from the middle of the family.

Adam stood back and smiled as Sally asked about her grandbabies. All wasn't well yet, but at least there were signs of things getting there.

"You get their location," Joshua asked.

"Got it." The two walked briskly down the corridor and out the door to warnings from their loved ones.

"You know what we have to do?" Joshua asked Adam as they climbed into the chopper.

"I know what I'm going to do," Adam replied as he opened the laptop and began keying. "Hey, hold up for a minute." He got out of the chopper and walked back into the hospital. He looked around until he found Devin.

"Devin, did you know that Claiborne is the half-brother to one of your employees? A Tania Reid."

Devin nodded.

"According to the records from several social service agencies Claiborne has had a pretty good side line going on with kickbacks on supplies ordered for different facilities."

"I'm going to kick her ass." Ruby walked briskly past Adam.

"Ruby," Devin called out.

Adam shook his head. "Jade."

"I've got her back."

Adam ran back to the chopper. "We might have to hang around once we finish our business."

Joshua glanced at his brother as he took off. "What's up?"

"The name that popped up on my computer was one of Devin's employees. She is related to the robber named Claiborne. Ruby is on her way to her house now."

Joshua nodded. "Ruby won't kill her. She'll only make her wish she was dead."

When they reached the precinct, Joshua disappeared. Adam walked up to the desk and flashed his FBI ID, holding his finger over the "trainee" part printed on the top. "I understand you brought in a Jeremy Claiborne tonight. Good work. We've been after that guy for a while for money laundering. Any way I could interview him for a minute?"

The officer checked the computer, then nodded. "I need you to sign in." He turned the pad around to

Adam. He signed in as Special Agent Brent Pierce. The man looked at the name. "Thank you, Special Agent Pierce. He's in holding room four. I'll have an officer meet you." He pushed a button unlocking the electronic door. "Down the hall, make a right, second door on the left."

"I appreciate that," Adam replied without blinking and walked through the door. He really didn't need a key to open the door, but he waited for the officer as a courtesy. After all, the desk commander was so accommodating, it was the least he could do.

Jeremy Claiborne was a pretty boy, Adam decided, when he walked into the interrogation room and sat across from the man.

"Man, just like I told the other officer, I'm not talking to anyone until I see my attorney."

Adam did not say a thing to the man. He simply sat there staring at Claiborne. The man was nervous, his mind was fidgety and it was hard to get him pinned down, but Adam persisted.

"Did you hear me? I said I want a lawyer." Claiborne slammed his hand on the table, leaned across it then stared into Adam's eyes. That was his mistake. Adam pushed a button on his phone. It sent a signal scrambling the signal from the camera to the computer he was certain men were observing from another room.

Adam spoke calmly. "Have a seat, Jeremy." The man slowly complied. "Did you shoot the man at the warehouse?"

"No."

"Did you know the man has a wife, children, a family that loves him?"

"No."

"Do you have a wife and children at home?"

"Yes."

"What would you do if I harmed your wife?"

"I would kill you."

Adam smiled. "Stand, Jeremy, and lean over the table."

Jeremy complied.

"When I count to three try to kill me." Adam pushed the button on his phone again, unscrambling the camera. To the men observing the two of them were in the same position as they were when the cameras blinked.

"One, two, three."

Jeremy came across the table with his hands going for Adam's throat. Adam punched the man once, knocking him to the ground. He put his foot on the man's throat and applied pressure. By the time the officers made it to the interrogation room, Jeremy was on the floor with blood running from his nose about to pass out.

Adam stepped away from the man as the officers turned Jeremy onto his stomach and handcuffed him.

"Did you see that?" Adam shook his head.

"We did, man. We were watching from the observation room," the officer with the cuffs spoke first.

"Yeah, then he just lost it," the other officer finished. "You good, man?"

"Yes," Adam replied. "I'm good." He turned and walked out of the room.

When he reached the chopper, Joshua was waiting for him. "Feel better?" he asked.

Adam nodded. "I'll feel better when Daddy opens his eyes." He climbed into the passenger seat. "How is your guy?"

"He didn't make it," Joshua replied then took the chopper up.

By the time Joshua and Adam returned to the hospital, Roc had arrived. They all made arrangements to stay at Samuel's house until their father came home.

The week that followed, they were inundated with visitors. Everyone from the President, the Governor, Senators, the Brooks', the Davenports, Al Day and his family, Brian Thompson, even Sofia Thornton, Cynthia's mother and the woman Sally took Joe from, came to see if they could do anything to help the family. Everyone was expressing their dismay and sending prayers for Joe. Hospital administration had to move Joe to a private area of the hospital to better control the number of high profile visitors. The most impressive was the visit from the royal family - King Ahmed Ashro, Queen Nasheema, King Aswan Ashro, Princess ZsaZsa, and of course Prince LaVere.

Everyone tensed when King Raheem and Queen Akande arrived. Looking regal as ever, Akande walked into the hospital room and sat with Sally for hours. No one knew what they talked about except Joe and he was still unconscious so he wasn't telling. Later that day, Queen Akande arrived at Samuel's house to collect Teddi.

Roc had gathered all of Teddi's things and packed them neatly into her suitcase. Her back was bothering her something fierce, but it was the sadness of seeing Teddi leave that caused a tear to drop.

Joshua held his daughter in one arm and his wife in the other as the King and Queen entered the family room. Samuel, Cynthia, Adam and Amber stayed in the kitchen as moral support for Joshua. They had no idea how the meeting would go.

Akande smiled bright at the sight of her daughter.

"Mother." Teddi wiggled from her father's arms and ran to her mother.

"Teddi." Akande picked her up in one scoop. "I missed you so much."

"Me too, Mother."

Raheem was pleased to see the child as well. "Are you ready to go home, Teddi?" He smiled at her.

"Oh yes, Father."

Roc rubbed Joshua's back as the child spoke to Raheem. "Uncle Joshua and Auntie Roc made snowballs and a snowman. You want to see?"

"I think I would like that." Raheem took Teddi's hand and followed her to the bay window in the kitchen.

Akande walked over to Joshua and Roc. "Thank you for taking care of Teddi."

"She can come to stay with us anytime," Roc replied, attempting to coax Joshua to say something by pinching his back.

"I will see to it that she visits her Uncle Joshua and Auntie Roc each year."

That seemed to ease the tension in Joshua a bit. "She calls him father?"

"Yes," Akande replied and held his glare. "As it should be, Joshua." She turned and smiled at Roc. "It will be soon now, I see."

"Next week." Roc rubbed her stomach.

"Oh, no," Akande laughed. "You have a few hours at the most." She then called out to Teddi. "We must go now, Teddi. Uncle Joshua and Auntie Roc will be busy real soon."

Akande kissed Roc on the cheek. Then hugged Joshua. "We will talk soon."

He nodded then carried the bag out to the car. When he returned the room was quiet as everyone waited, trying to gauge his mood. "I did not kill him."

"Whew," Samuel exhaled. "No bomb in the car?"

Adam laughed. "No, Samuel, we don't do bombs anymore. We put a J.M.A.L.T.S. in his pocket."

Joshua and Samuel turned and glared at Adam.

"Joking, people, come on."

The family decided to spend Christmas Eve at the hospital. As people wrapped up their plans they gathered in the corridor outside Joe's room. They prayed, played games, talked and did just about everything they would have done if they were at home.

Joshua was sitting with his father as Sally read a scripture from the Bible. Roc was sitting in a chair when she motioned Amber to come over.

Amber sat next to her and whispered, "How far apart?"

It took a moment for Roc to respond for the contractions were hitting fast and hard. "Whew, whew, whew," she inconspicuously blew out. "About two now."

Amber laughed, causing several of her soon to be sisters-in-law to turn her way.

Diamond was the first to realize what was happening. She walked over. "I'll get a wheelchair."

"I don't know if we have time." Amber held Roc's hand as she squeezed, not showing any other signs of outward distress. "This is going to be a natural birth. I think someone should get Joshua."

Adam, who was talking with Jade, looked over. "What's wrong?"

"Roc is in labor," Amber said. Before anyone could say another word Phire ran into the room.

Adam helped Roc from the chair as the family began gathering around.

"Roc." She was pointing.

Sally looked at Joshua, then back to Phire. "What are you doing?"

Phire ran over and grabbed Joshua's hand, pulling him from the chair just as Roc appeared in the doorway.

"This is coming out of me tonight."

Joshua jumped up. "The baby?"

"No, the damn Easter bunny. Yes, the baby."

"Mom, I got to go." He kissed her cheek. "Dad, the baby is coming." He stopped to see his father's eyes on him. "Dad."

Sally looked over and gasped. "Joe," she cried. And asked someone to get the nurse. "Joe." She touched his face as a teardrop fell to his cheek. "Joe." She smiled, then gently kissed his lips.

"Daddy." Phire stood behind her mother.

The nurse came in checking his vitals. "Mr. Lassiter." She held a light to his eyes. "Welcome back. Can you blink for me?"

Joe blinked his eyes and Sally cried more. "That's good, Joe."

"Do you know who this pretty lady is?"

Joe smiled. He licked his lips. "My sweet Sally," he whispered.

"How did you luck up and get such a pretty one," Dr. Patel asked as he rushed into the room.

Joe looked up at Joshua. "Josh."

"Joshua, your father wants you." Sally moved aside.

Joshua put his ear down to his father's lips and listened. He nodded his head. "You got it."

"What?" Phire asked as Joshua left the room.

"I'm going to have a baby."

Dr. Patel nodded to the nurse. "Will you get them down to obstetrics? We are going to have two miracles on this day. What do you say about that, Joe?"

"Sounds good," a mere whisper of a voice came out.

Sally broke down and cried as Joshua ran from the room.

Adam helped Roc into the wheelchair as a nurse walked behind them. "I'll take this one," Amber said to the nurse. "Prep the birthing room."

Adam, Timothy, Mathew, Luke and Samuel all patted Joshua on his back. Diamond, Pearl, Opal, Jade and Phire kissed Roc as they strolled way.

"Jade, Opal, Timothy and I will take Joshua," Adam declared. "The rest of you stay with Dad. Text us with updates."

"You do the same," Pearl replied.

Joshua paced outside the room until Adam finally pulled him aside.

"Sly sent me a message to meet him near Quantico. Any idea what that is about?"

"What did the message say?" Adam showed Joshua the text. "I know the area. Check it out."

Adam nodded. "Looks like we are going to have a Lassiter Christmas after all." He looked at Joshua. "It would take you to have a baby at Christmas."

"What better way is there to honor our savior?" Joshua grinned.

"Joshua," Amber called from the door. "You can come in now." She smiled at Adam. "It's a boy."

They all laughed and cheered at the news.

Epilogue

The next few days were spent assessing Joe's condition. The best news was there was no paralysis. His speech and short-term memory were clearly impacted. But all of those things could be helped with the right rehabilitation. They assembled the best medical team they could and ran every test known to man, including some Amber and Adam created, to determine the extent of damage to Joe's brain. Amber and Adam researched every aspect of information they could pull from his charts until they were able to devise a recovery plan for his father. The words his father told him came back.

'You have the mind to do wonders for this world.'

All Adam wanted was to do wonders for his dad. For the first week of his rehab, Adam spent every day reading basic books with Joe. He would encourage his father to read more himself every night when he left the hospital. Amber worked with Dr. Patel on the physical aspects of the rehab. It was a six-day marathon, but when Joe was moved from the hospital to home, where the boys had cleared out the dining room and set up a rehabilitation area, they both felt good about the progress Joe was making.

It was New Year's Eve before they made it back to Amber's condo in Georgetown. The tree and all the things they had left in a rush to get to Richmond had been cleared out by her mother. The gifts were all neatly placed on the dining room table. There was one addressed to Adam that was on top of them all.

"Who is it from?" Amber asked as she walked into the bedroom.

"I'm not sure." Adam opened the small box to find a card inside with a skeleton key underneath. He read the card. "It's an address."

"To where?" Amber called from the bedroom.

"I don't know." Adam was still examining the box when Amber walked over.

She looked at it and shrugged. "You want to check it out?"

"We just got home and I'm exhausted. You have to report to the hospital in the morning. We should try to rest."

"It's still early. Where is the adventurous Adam Lassiter I fell in love with?" She looked at the address. "It isn't that far away."

"It's actually pretty close to Joshua's place."

"I double-dare you." Amber smiled remembering the Lassiters sitting in Joe's room on Christmas Day watching the holiday favorite.

He pulled her close. "I got your double-dare, right here." He kissed her.

Amber laughed. "Let's go."

They put the address in the GPS and twenty minutes later they pulled onto a secluded road.

"This looks interesting." Adam smiled.

"It's beautiful with the snow falling from the trees. It's majestic."

Adam looked around as he drove up the curving road where large trees lined the road making the area secluded. As the trees cleared, a wrought iron fence came into view. The double gates were open so they pulled in, then drove about a half a mile when a massive Mediterranean style house with tan stones, a double red door and a beautiful fountain came into view. They parked in the curved driveway in front of the house.

"Wow," Amber exclaimed as she stepped out of the car. "Tell me the key you have is the key to this house."

"You like it?" Adam scanned the area.

"My goodness, yes. Don't you?"

Adam came to stand next to her. "I have to admit, it has a bit of charm to it."

"I wonder who lives here?"

"Somebody does. The snow is plowed, the walkway is clear and there is mail." Adam walked to the door. There was an envelope with his name on it.

Amber glanced over his shoulder as he read, "A house isn't a home until the right family crosses the threshold. Phillip and Jill.

Amber gasped. "Do you think..."

Adam pulled the key from his pocket then held it up for her. "Only one way to find out."

Amber smiled. "Okay." She put the key in the lock. "It fits." Her eyes grew wide as she turned the key. The door swung open. "Wow, this house doesn't look this big on the outside."

Adam looked around at the tall ceilings, to the open foyer and straight to the back of the house that had windows for walls.

"Look." He pointed to Amber who had walked into what looked to be the formal dining room on the left. To the right was a formal living room with windows showcasing the driveway they'd just used.

She walked back to him. "I'm looking, I'm looking."

He took her hand and walked from the foyer to the great room with a huge fireplace in the center of the room. To the left was a gourmet size kitchen, on the right a huge family room. On the other side of the fireplace was a sunroom that seemed to extend through the entire first floor.

"Look at the grounds on this place." Adam was beaming.

"Is that a lake?" Amber walked over to the windows in the sunroom.

Adam looked where Amber was pointing. "I think it's the Rappahannock River."

"Wow, wow and wow again." Amber walked to the right following the sunroom. At the end, she entered French doors, which lead to a bedroom. "Adam Lassiter, you better come see this."

Adam quickly made his way to where she stood. The bedroom covered the entire right side of the house. There was another double-sided fireplace in the center of the room. One side had a sofa, chaise lounge and a chair, all placed in front of a window with a view of the gardens. The other side had a huge bed in the center of the room facing the window with a view of the river. To the left was a door. Amber opened it to find a walk-in closet the size of her bedroom at home. She walked through to a marble encased bathroom with a walk through shower, a private toilet room, a huge claw foot tub and more. She walked to the other side to see there was a closet the same size as the other.

Amber walked out to see Adam standing at the bed. "Adam, what is it?"

"A card from Queen Akande." Adam read out loud.

"When I heard you were in need of a home in the area, I remembered this property I visited once. I fell in love with the views of the river. I asked Joshua to see if it would work for you. The house I am certain

Dr. Nicolas will love. The lab in the basement will rock your world, as Joshua would say. If you want it, please accept this as my token of thanks for saving my country."

"Can we do that?"

"Accept the house?" Adam asked looking around. He shrugged. "I don't know. But she said there is a laboratory in the basement." He grabbed her hand and began walking in and out of rooms until he found the door that led to the basement.

Amber ran with him, laughing with excitement in her voice.

On the opposite side of the house there were four bedrooms, each with a bath attached, a game room and a theater room. Adam kept opening doors until he came to one behind the kitchen. He opened the door to a stairway leading down.

"Finally." He grinned and was about to walk through when Amber pulled back.

"Is that an elevator?"

Adam stepped back and looked.

"Man, I'm loving this." He pushed the button and the doors swished open. They stepped in grinning like children as the elevator descended.

The doors opened to a white hallway with doors and office space that expanded for what seemed like miles. They stepped off the elevator and just gawked at the space.

"I'm going that way," Amber squealed.

Adam walked into the first door. The room was bright and open. Monitors lined the walls. He turned and walked from room to room to room.

Inside one room there was counter space, shelves, sinks, cabinets - just about everything an exploring mind would need. "I could work forever in here."

"I see another MacGyver in the making," Amber said as she walked from another room. "Is the government funding your liability insurance?" Amber continued exploring the basement.

Adam stopped talking to register the question she asked. "I don't know." He frowned as he met her in the center of the space. "Do you believe this?"

"I'm still trying to figure all of this out." Amber continued looking around. "What is the mortgage on this place?"

He looked around and noticed the computer monitor was on. "I'm not sure there is one," he said. "Whatever it is, we are never leaving this house."

"There's another room over there." Amber ran in one direction as Adam went in another.

Adam walked over to the monitor and pushed the spacebar on the computer sitting on the counter. The smiling face of Sly appeared on the screen. The first thing Adam noticed was he was not wearing a hat or a suit.

Hey, younger brother to Joshua. As you know by now, I've retired from the Agency. We have a tradition in this life. When one agent leaves a team, he gets to name his replacement. The skills you have are impressive. But it's your heart that drives you. Since meeting the Doc you've come full circle. Unlike the old heads in this business, you have the key within your grasp. Hold on to her with all that you have. You have the opportunity to be in this life with a partner. We did not have that in the past. More important than anything else I've taught you so far; realize you are no longer the younger brother trying to live up to anyone. You are a man with the ability to hold the world's attention. For that reason, I deem you Hypnotic.

Sly.

PS: I left you a present in the Doc's office space.

Adam smiled. He hoped Sly would find happiness in his new life. He looked around. "We need a map for this house."

Amber walked into the room where he was standing. She had stripped out of her clothes and was dressed in a white lab coat with a fedora on her head.

"Hey." She posed at the door. "I found this in a room over there that would make a perfect office for me."

Adam turned to see her standing in yet another doorway. "How did you get in here?"

"I came through there."

Adam looked in the direction she pointed. Inside that room was a desk with a book placed on the side of it. "The manual."

Adam picked up the book. A row of bookshelves parted. Adam turned, then walked over.

"It's a safe," Amber gasped.

"A place to keep the notes on my inventions." Adam suddenly exploded. "I am loving this place!"

Amber turned. "This would be a great office for you and it's connected to the one I like as mine."

Adam laughed. "We are talking like this is our new home."

"I think it is." She twirled around. "What a great way to start a new year." She kissed him. "A new job for me."

"A new adventure for us." Adam pulled her close. "I think we are home." He leaned against the desk and the wall to the right of them slid open.

They both stood, stunned at the new discovery. "It's a tunnel." He grabbed her hand and walked through. The hallway was lined with pictures. On the left was Joe, Samuel, Joshua, Mathew, Luke, Timothy, and him. On the right was Sally, Ruby, Pearl, Diamond, Opal, Jade and Phire.

"There are pictures of my parents in the hallway off the office I like."

"They have been here." Adam shook his head. "When did they find time?"

The two laughed as they continued to a door at the end of the hallway. There was a card posted on it. Adam took it down and read it.

Family is your backbone...Samuel.

Adam smiled, shook his head then pushed the door open. It led to a four bay garage. Inside was a black SUV wrapped in a big red bow with a sign in the window.

You found your way... Joshua.

They ran down the steps to the vehicle and opened the box on the hood. Inside was a small device with Genevieve II printed on it. Adam picked it up, looked at Amber then pushed the button. The side of the garage slid open leading into an outside tunnel.

"Let's go for a ride," Amber squealed.

His by the book doc had transformed into an adventure-seeking junkie. Not bad for a brainiac, he thought, as he reached over, took the hat off her head and placed it on his.

"Are you ready for an adventure?"

"With you, Adam Fitzgerald Lassiter, I'm ready for anything."

"Anything?" Adam opened the back door of the SUV. "Have you ever made love to a man wearing a fedora?"

Sneak Preview
Of
The Barrington's

Chapter 1

Winnieford Barrington mourns the loss of her husband of thirty-eight years, Hepburn Ellington Barrington, the President and CEO of one of the most prestigious banks in the country. Today, at the first meeting of the board of directors, a predecessor will be named. The question is who will take over the leadership role of the nation's largest African-American owned bank.

Today's meeting of the board of directors for Barrington Bank and Trust was certainly out of the ordinary. This one was special in every way imaginable. Seated around the oval shaped cherry-wood table, in the conference room on the twelfth floor of the downtown Richmond headquarters office, were directors with very solemn faces. None thought this day would come this soon. After twenty years as president and CEO of Barrington Bank and Trust, Hepburn Ellington Barrington had passed away suddenly of a heart attack during a family dispute with his youngest daughter Annemarie.

The tension, caused by the effect of Hep's death, was felt throughout the room by the members of the board seated at the conference table. William Mitchell, vice-president of the bank, sat in his usual seat on the left at the head of the table silently scrutinizing the other three non-family members who had voting rights. The members were diverse in nationality and age. Hep always prided himself with the knowledge that he was open to all who worked hard and proved their worth. Mitchell shivered at the thought. It was always his belief to stack the board to ensure his directions were carried out as he saw fit. Now that Hep was dead and gone, that was no longer a concern as long as the vote went his way. In his estimation, Elaine Jacobson, who had been his sounding board for the last ten years whenever he was displeased with Hep's decisions, would surely support him as president. His gaze moved on to Preston Long, a young thirty-something Italian or Mexican, Mitchell wasn't sure which and didn't care. As long as Preston voted with him, he would give him the promotion he promised. The only one Mitchell was not sure about was Cainan Walker, the newest member. Cainan was a bit of a mystery. Hep had brought him onboard about a year ago from Wall Street to head up the Investment Department. On paper, he was a very accomplished young man in his late twenties, but investigations were not complete on his personal background and that bothered Mitchell. He liked knowing all he could about the people around him, good and bad; that way he could always manipulate at will. The double doors to the conference room opened, interrupting his assessment of his chances and in walked the Barrington family board members.

Winnieford Barrington walked in on the arm of her second son Michael Anthony. If anyone had seen them on the street, they could have easily been mistaken as a couple. Looking at least fifteen years younger than her fifty-five years, she was fashionably dressed in a black shell dress with a thick red belt around her slim waist, black pumps, the usual pearl necklace with matching earrings—accessories complimenting her short haircut and radiant, but sad face. Michael, dressed impeccably in Armani gray with a pink shirt, that only a very secure man could pull off, and matching tie, escorted his mother to the head of the table. Gary Hepburn, the youngest and most outspoken of the sons, wore Sean John, navy blue silk, no tie and that confident swagger that seemed to run in the family. Then there was Grace Heather. The woman that dressed as the ultimate professional wore her usual navy blue blazer and skirt set with a white blouse and matching pumps. Last, but certainly not least of all—Myles Monroe, the oldest son who was the spitting image of Hep, strolled in dressed in Gucci gray, as if it was made just for his body. This was the man. This was the only person William saw as a threat to him taking over as president and ceo of Barrington Bank and Trust.

Winnieford took her seat at the right of her now deceased husband's chair, directly across from Mitchell. Doing the one thing she did not feel, she stood, smiled and brought the meeting to order. "Thank you all for coming to this emergency meeting. As chairman of the board of directors, I officially call this meeting to order. Our first order of business is the selection of the new president and ceo of Barrington Bank and Trust. To clear up rumors, I would like to say as much as I love this great institution and as much as I respect its rich history, I have no desire to take over where Hep left off. I will remain as chairman of the board of directors, but will not take over as president and ceo." She stopped, exhaled, "With that said, the floor is now open for nominations for the position."

Preston Long stood, "May I be heard?"

"You have the floor," Winnieford replied, then took her seat.

"Thank you Mrs. Barrington. First I would like to

offer my condolences to the Barrington family. Hep was a great mentor and employer, but a lousy golfer." The group smiled, for they all knew that was true. "Knowing he was at the end of the hall was always a comfort to me. There was never a time in my professional or personal life that Hep wasn't there encouraging me. He will be missed. Now, to the matter at hand, it is important that we show our clientele the tradition of encouraging entrepreneurship, self-dependency and financial stability at Barrington will continue the way that it has over the last twenty years. I believe the person to do that would be the same person that has been by Hep's side during that time, William Mitchell."

The expected nominations did not take anyone by surprise. Winnieford reached over and placed her hand on the arm of the chair where Hep would have been seated. Never showing any emotions, she silently vowed, *"Don't worry darling, I will not let it happen. Your wishes will be carried out."*

Elaine Jacobson stood, "I second the nomination," she stated, as Preston took his seat, and then quickly retook her seat.

Winnieford waited patiently, sending a silent prayer for someone to step in. A subtle glance down the table showed her eldest son Myles begin to stand and her heart knew he was going to give his backing to Mitchell. But before Myles could speak, Michael called out, "Before we go further, may I address the board?"

A sigh of relief crossed Winnieford's face, "Yes of course," she replied, as a stern look was sent down the table to her oldest son.

"Since its inception in 1840, Barrington Bank and Trust has been led by a Barrington. Mitch, I mean no disrespect and commend the job you have done for the institution, however, we have two very capable

Barrington's on the board; Grace and Myles. I respectfully submit both names for consideration."

Before Winnieford could place the names into nominations, Grace stood and chimed in, "I just as respectfully decline the nomination, but second the nomination of Myles Monroe Barrington." Grinning at her oldest brother, Grace retook her seat.

Silence ensued as all eyes went to Myles. Winnieford closed her eyes for a moment to give her son at least the opportunity to decline, but secretly prayed that he would not. When the moment passed, her heart burst with joy. It took all her will not to let it show. "The nomination of Myles Barrington will be added to that of William Mitchell. Are there any others?" She waited. There were none. "William Mitchell and Myles Barrington, as you know the voting of positions are done in private to ensure no retaliation. Will you please step out while we deliberate?

William stood, adjusted his suit jacket around his protruding abdomen, walked over to the door and opened it as he waited for Myles to stand. Myles sat there with pen in hand and looked to his brother Michael. The smirk on his face was something he'd had to deal with all his life. He then looked at Grace, who he thought would have his back on this, but instead she sat up straight and had the nerve to smile at him. He turned from her and looked at Gary who was grinning like a cat that ate the canary. Last, he looked at his mother. The sadness of the loss of her soul mate was still evident in her eyes, but so was the hope that he would do the right thing. That was his undoing.

Myles placed the pen on top of his portfolio and walked out the door wondering if everyone in his family was out to destroy his life.

In the reception area outside the conference door, Myles nodded and smiled at Marie Vazquez, his father's private secretary for the past twelve years.

Mrs. Vazquez returned the smiled with a chuckle. "They roped you in?"

"Something like that," Myles replied with a tilt of his head.

"Well, son, you know I'm here for you no matter how the vote goes," William stated with the right amount of assurance to convince a less observant person.

Mrs. Vazquez walked towards the men, patting Myles on the back. "We will all be here, for you Myles." She smiled then walked out of the area completely ignoring William.

Looking down at the five nine, two hundred-fifty pound pudgy man for a long minute, he always wondered why his father kept him around. Once when he and his father had a disagreement about Mitch, his father said, '*it's better to keep your enemies close.*' With that in mind, Myles extended his hand, "Same here, Mitch."

As they shook hands, William was seething inside. He'd hated when Hep called him Mitch. Now, if this vote did not go his way he would have to deal with his sons calling him that. His name was William, not Mitch. It seemed a norm for these people to shorten each other's name at will. Well, not him. It appeared the only person who respected that was Winnieford. Of course he had to explain it to her in the early days, but she had not forgotten. She always, always, referred to him as William. That was one of the things he loved about her. Well, as much as a white man could love a black woman, that is. Back in the day Winnieford was a beauty. *Hell she's not far from it now.* But there was no way he could have her once he'd made the mistake of introducing Hep to her. They all went to college together. Hep played on the football team with him and

Winnieford was his history tutor. Imagine that—a black girl tutoring him. But she was smart, pretty and he was hot for her. Then he'd made the mistake of introducing her to Hep and that was all she wrote for him. Once Hep graduated, he married Winnieford and out of gratitude offered William a job at his family owned bank. As it turned out, it was the best offer to come his way, so he settled knowing that one day he would take the business over. Today was that day.

Ten minutes later, Winnieford opened the door to the conference room and asked them to step in. Closing it behind the men as they entered, she walked back to the head of the table to make the announcement. "The new president and ceo of Barrington Bank and Trust is Myles Monroe Barrington." Smiling, Winnieford put her hand on the back of Hep's chair. "Please take your seat at the head of the table."

Twenty years of practice had granted William with the acting ability to appear to be genuinely happy with the results, but inside he was seething. Standing back at his place at the table, William joined the members of the board in applauding the selection. As the members retook their seats, Myles Monroe Barrington remained where he stood. He would accept the position, but he was not ready to take his father's chair. Unbuttoning the single button on his suit blazer, the handsome, reserved thirty-five-year old—six-two, two hundred twenty-five pound—first born of Hepburn and Winnieford Barrington inserted his hands into his pockets and hung his head. When he looked up, his heart may have been hesitant to take his father's position, but his eyes showed he had accepted the responsibility and was ready to be at the helm. "My father once told me that a man's place is determined by his worth. While I am willing to accept the position of president and CEO, I will not take his seat at this table until you, the members of this board, declare me worthy." He retook the seat at the far end of the table to continue the meeting.

When Myles took his seat, Winnieford spoke, "It is with honor and pride that I now turn over the control of Barrington Bank and Trust to Myles Barrington." She pushed her chair under the table as Myles began to speak.

"The first line of business will be to assure our employees that all is secure and we are ready to move forward. The second will be to assure customers of the same."

Although she knew it was not proper, Winnieford stopped at Myles' seat, kissed her son on the cheek and then left the room.

Unable to resist, a smile tugged at Myles' lips as he continued with his statement. Gary, the prankster of the family, rolled up a sheet of paper and threw it at his oldest brother, hitting him right in the middle of his forehead. "Mommy's boy," he laughed.

Myles stopped mid-sentence and stared at his little brother as members around the table joined in laughing. The action eased the tension remaining from the vote. In his mind Myles knew there were some feathers ruffled and they would need to be addressed before Barrington Bank and Trust could flow smoothly again. He looked at William Mitchell, nodded as his way of acknowledging the man's feelings, and for a split second he saw the hatred in the man's eyes, before he returned the nod with a smile. *Keep your enemies close.* The statement from his father ran through his mind. Moving the paper to the side, Myles continued with the meeting.

About the Author

Iris Bolling's published her first novel, Once You've Touched the Heart in 2008. This self-published work was the first of the five additional books to complete the Heart Series. The popular Heart Series has captivated the hearts of readers and awarded Iris the Emma Award as Debut Author of the Year in 2010

In May of 2011, Iris introduced a new cast of characters in her in Night of Seduction Series. The second book in the series, The Pendleton Rule was reviewed in USA Today and received, the 2014 Emma Award for Suspense of The Year.

In 2012, she began the Gems & Gents series with her novel Teach Me, which generated an importune shoe contest on Facebook that spanned the international waters. It continued with the release of the very popular Book of Joshua I and Book of Joshua II. The series has earned Iris several awards including 2014 Hero of The Year and 2015 Heroine of The Year.

The beginning of her third series, The Brooks' Family Values, was introduced in her novel Sinergy in 2014, followed by book 2 Fatal Mistake and Propensity For Love, both released in 2015. Propensity For Love was awarded the Villain of The Year honor and has been nominated for several 2016 Emma awards.

Iris received the honor of being named Author of The Year twice since the inception of her career, 2012 and 2014.

In 2014, Iris stepped into a new venture geared towards bringing books to film. She produced The Heart, a television series based on her popular novels. Season two will air in the spring of 2016.

Adding more to her resume' Iris is now doing quest-speaking engagements to share her experience and to encourage others to follow their dreams.
Iris currently lives in Richmond, Virginia where she is working on her next series.

Join <u>Iris mailing list</u> for news about new books and upcoming appearances in your area.
Follow her on <u>Facebook</u>, <u>Twitter</u>, and on <u>Instagram</u>. Join <u>Iris Book Palace</u>. You can reach Iris at <u>irisb@siriaustin.com</u>

Made in the USA
Middletown, DE
04 November 2022

13991157R00194